MITWA

KATE MACLEOD

 Created with Vellum

CHAPTER ONE

OMESH

HE WAS A HUNDRED THOUSAND KILOMETERS FROM home when he decided what his name would be. He had managed to put off thinking about it in the last few weeks, but now that all the bureaucracy was done and he had left Earth, never to see home again, there didn't seem to be anything else to occupy his mind. Omesh had always been the special name only his mother and her family used; the rest of the world called him Rashid. But now he would be living with his uncle and aunt, two of the few who had always called him Omesh. They would call him Rashid if he asked, but he suddenly wanted the change.

His old life was dead and gone; perhaps a new life needed a new name.

The loud boom that echoed through the shuttle felt like it was punctuating his decision, and Omesh almost smiled at the coincidence. But then he noticed that unlike all the other loud bangs and roars that had occurred randomly but continuously throughout the trip, this one seemed to agitate the other passengers.

"Is that not normal?" he asked the woman sitting next to him. She had pulled a small computer tablet out of her pocket and her thumbs were flying over the keys.

"Normal? Definitely not. Sounds like something blew."

"Blew?" Omesh repeated.

"First time in space?" she asked, her fingers never slowing as she threw a curious glance his way.

"Yes. Does this happen a lot?"

"Too much lately. But no one is going to retire these shuttles until one catastrophically fails, all hands lost. Probably not even then, unless someone really important is on board."

"So, what's happening to us?"

"They'll limp to the nearest station if possible. Call for a pickup if not."

"But how can they? The fuel and life support were calculated for this specific trip, weren't they?"

"Well, kid, we either use less or we die."

Omesh sensed that he was gaping at her and deliberately closed his mouth. She didn't sound panicked in the least, as if this sort of thing were a nuisance and nothing more. Strangely, that attitude gave him hope.

The woman glared at her pocket computer, shook it forcefully, then put it away with a sigh of disgust. "Too far from the comm satellites, dammit. I don't know what this pilot is up to, but we're way off course."

"My uncle is waiting for me on the *Dauntless*," Omesh said.

"They'll make an announcement there, I'm sure," she said. She looked him over very carefully, taking in his old but sturdy shoes, stiffly new jeans, and the brightly colored kurta his mother had made for him especially for this trip. He doubted he looked his best. It had been baking hot inside when he'd boarded the Avatar RLV at the Mumbai spaceport and he had sweated profusely waiting for takeoff. When they'd reached orbit, the sticky heat had become a moist cold, and he could feel the itchy fabric sticking to him, curls of his hair plastered to his forehead. But her eyes gave all of that a cursory once-over before settling on his hands, of all things. She grabbed one, turned it over, and began to examine it closely. "Farmer?" she guessed.

"Student," Omesh answered, but he knew that was a shade dishonest, so he added, "but my father is a farmer."

"You're too young to be heading out because of lack of marital prospects," she said, releasing his hand.

"I'm seventeen," Omesh said.

"Just bailing on the Collective, then? I can't find fault with that impulse."

Omesh caught the tip of his tongue between his teeth. That wasn't why he was leaving, but he was scarcely going to discuss the real reason with a total stranger.

"It's a shame this is your first introduction to humanity in space. Most of the time, it's not this bad."

If that had sounded ominous, the "good luck" she gave him after they'd docked was even more unsettling. He had never been on a train when it broke down, but everyone knew that if it happened, you just waited until the next train came down the tracks. How could this be any different?

All the other passengers were gathering their belongings and floating out of the compartment. Omesh waited for them all to leave before unbuckling his own restraints. He had never been in free fall before, not even in simulation, since this trip into space had been sprung on him so quickly. It seemed easy enough at first, like swimming in a pool: you could push off a wall and just let momentum take you.

He caught the handle of his trunk easily enough and quickly found how different from swimming free fall could be. He had watched all the others pull their briefcases and backpacks out of the bins with ridiculous ease, but when he tugged on his own handle, rather than pulling the trunk out of the bin, he nearly pulled himself into it. Once he got his motion under control, he braced himself to pull again, but still the trunk wouldn't budge. It should be weightless, the same as he was. So why did it feel like he was trying to pull a ten-ton weight?

"It's caught."

Omesh stopped what he belatedly realized was some pretty spastic wrestling with his luggage and looked around for the source of that sleepy voice. He had thought he was alone in the compartment, but now he saw a glint of silver. Not real silver, just a very whitish-blond fan of hair that was spreading itself out like a peacock's tail but quickly pulled back into one long stream as the boy to whom it was attached pushed himself out of his seat to reach the back of Omesh's trunk.

"You've got a loose corner plate," he said, fingers moving around the wire mesh to snap something back in place. "Pull it now."

Omesh tugged—too hard, he realized, as the trunk met his face with a dull smack. He rubbed at his forehead, blinking hard.

"At least you missed your nose," the boy said, sounding half asleep.

"Thanks," Omesh said. "For the help."

The boy was nodding when something seemed to distract him. He looked at it again more intently, and Omesh turned but couldn't figure out what he was staring at. "It's not nearly time for us to be at the *Dauntless*."

"No, apparently there was some trouble. I don't know where we are."

"That's unacceptable."

For a moment Omesh thought the boy was annoyed with him and his lack of knowledge, but then the boy propelled himself out of the container and down the aisle and Omesh, still struggling with the awkward mass of his trunk, followed.

The turn at the end of the last pair of shipping containers was tricky, the narrower opening of the airlock even more so. Omesh had been imaging some sort of hangar beyond, a large open space filled with ships and cargo, but he was startled to find himself in a very ordinary hallway. A few cargo nets full of boxes and sacks floated on short tethers near the airlock doorway, bottlenecking the traffic. Omesh clung to them gratefully, pulling himself and his trunk along at a crawl, trying to stay out of the way of the people zooming past, all completely at ease being weightless. By the time Omesh caught up with the silver-haired boy, he was frowning as a man in a pilot's uniform floated away from him.

"What's going on?" Omesh asked.

"We're in Haven, of all places."

"What's Haven?" Omesh asked.

The boy shot him a surprised look. Then his eyes swept over Omesh in an appraisal much like the woman had previously given him, minus the hand grab. "Where were you heading?" he asked at last. Somehow, Omesh could just tell that the boy considered "First time in space?" a question with too obvious an answer to even ask.

"Chandi V. My uncle works there."

"Really."

"Yes. Do you know it?"

"I've never been, but as your luck would have it, that was my destination as well."

"That is lucky," Omesh said. "My name's Omesh."

"Hjalmar. And to answer your original query, Haven is a squatter community. No, perhaps *community* is too small a word. Haven is a corporate city in space that's been entirely taken over by riffraff. Although *riffraff* might be too small a word."

"You've been here before?"

"Hell no. No one in their right mind goes to Haven. The good news is my grandfather has a contact here who owes him a very hefty favor. The bad news is he's on the other side of the station. So you and I are going to have to slum it for a while, so to speak. But at least you're dressed for it."

Omesh's mind was reeling. There was a lot of information packed into those few short sentences, and he was pretty sure an insult as well.

"How do you know that? Two minutes ago, you didn't even know where we were."

"Trust me."

Then Omesh remembered the way Hjalmar's eyes had rolled up and to the left, just at the moment he realized what time it was. He looked the boy before him over, doing an appraisal of his own. Hjalmar's clothing had seemed nondescript at first glance, but on more careful examination

Omesh could see that the shoes were real leather, the jeans new but supple—not stiff like Omesh's A&MC ration jeans—and the shirt that had appeared solid black was covered with a fine embroidered tracery: black on black, but he could discern the outlines of dragons and Chinese characters.

A rich boy. Probably a corporate prince, although he wasn't one Omesh recognized. And with that silver-blond tail that would hang past his waist if it wasn't floating free in a swirl around his head, he would be hard to forget.

So Hjalmar had a chip in his head. Every second, he was sending and receiving information. By now, his grandfather's contact probably already knew they were on their way.

"Lead on," Omesh said, pulling his trunk into his arms.

"Allow me." Hjalmar caught one of the straps and pushed off from one of the larger boxes caught up in the cargo net Omesh had been clinging to.

As they moved down the hall, Omesh realized it was shaped like a corkscrew, always turning. There was no up or down, no floor or ceiling. Smudges from countless hands covered every surface; whatever color the paint had originally been was anybody's guess. Omesh clung to his trunk, reluctant to touch anything. Hjalmar propelled them forward in long bounds that became shorter as the pull of the station's centripetal force increased.

Omesh hopped off the trunk, but moving was nowhere near as easy as Hjalmar made it look. He was constantly bumping into the curving walls, putting out a hand to avoid ramming his head on the ceiling, stumbling rather than bounding off the floor.

"You'll get used to it," Hjalmar said. "Quicker than you think."

"Chandi V has spin, though, right?"

"Sure, but free fall is fun."

Omesh couldn't see beyond the next curving turn of the hallway, but he heard a low roar of sound that was growing steadily louder.

"How big is this place?" he asked Hjalmar.

"Compared to what?" Hjalmar asked. "For a corporate city satellite, it's smallish. There's no simulated weather here; you'll feel indoors everywhere."

That wasn't the most reassuring of answers. Anxiety weighed heavily in Omesh's stomach as the hallway came to an end, turning out into the station proper. The noise had been a warning, but it hadn't prepared him for the sight of it all. The hallway ended at a balcony, wide staircases to either side leading down, to where he could not see. Omesh stepped up to the railing. The space station was a wheel type. He had just traveled down one of the spokes and now looked down into the wheel itself: one long open space, filled with people. Millions of people all talking at once, to companions near at hand or more loudly to those getting swept away by the crowd. Little booths were set up everywhere, some sensibly against the walls but others right in the middle of traffic, and vendors were crying their wares to every passerby.

And the smell. Greasy food and overripe garbage receptacles were bad enough, but over that was the smell of millions of people, anxious people, people in a hurry.

Millions of people. Omesh forgot his earlier repulsion and reached out a hand to steady himself against the nearest wall. There were more people on this space station right now than in all of India these days, perhaps even all of Asia. All crammed in this little spinning wheel.

"There's no place like this on Earth anymore," Omesh said.

"I know," Hjalmar said. "I'm Earth-born myself, I know the shock you're feeling. It's been years since I felt it, but I remember it well. Like I said, this place has been overrun with riffraff. Chandi V is still a proper corporate satellite. It's not like this place at all."

"About that," Omesh began, for although he hadn't lied when he said he was going to Chandi V, he hadn't meant exactly the same place Hjalmar was thinking of. It was getting awkward not correcting the misconception. But Hjalmar was already heading down the stairs, hands in his pockets. Omesh picked up his trunk and tried to hurry after.

It was a long way down; he lost count of how many staircases, each more crowded than the last. When they reached the bottom, they were in the thick of it. People pressed up against him, some shouting into his face, apparently selling things, but he couldn't focus on the words. Then Hjalmar was back at his side and the people fell away, giving them a little bit of space.

"Do they know you or something?" Omesh asked.

"No, I've never been here," Hjalmar said. "I'm not sending out the 'please take advantage of me' vibes you are, though."

"So, where are we heading?" Omesh asked.

"A spice trader on the far side of the station," Hjalmar said.

"Is there a tram or something?" Omesh asked,

trying to look around. The sight of all those people was still too stomach-churning.

"We're hoofing it," Hjalmar said. "This way." He disappeared into the flood of people, and Omesh took a breath and plunged after.

The trunk was actually a help to him; the effort of keeping it close at his side, rolling over the seams in the floor and through puddles he didn't want to think too much about, let him narrow his focus and tune out most of the crowd. But not all of it; he soon became aware that a group of boys was walking with them, seeming to stroll casually, munching on sorry-looking fruit or passing a careless hand over some stall's wares, but always maintaining a sloppy circle around Omesh and Hjalmar.

"Hjalmar," Omesh said in a low voice.

"I see them. If we stay in crowded areas, they'll probably do nothing."

"Probably? But you know where we're going, right?"

"My maps seem to be outdated. There have been some significant structural changes. I can steer us mostly in the right direction."

"Can your contact send us help?"

"He's going to consider getting us off this scrap heap favor enough, I'm afraid," Hjalmar said.

"Some people are easily swayed by my family name, but this fellow isn't one of them."

"You've been talking with him?"

"Messaging." An exuberant vendor lunged at them, waving something roasted on a spit that Omesh had the sudden fear was rat, and Hjalmar brushed him aside, catching Omesh's shoulder again to make sure the two of them were staying together in the pressing crowd.

Then the people around them began to thin out, and they found the long passageway blocked by stacks of shipping containers.

"What's this?" Omesh said. "I thought this atrium space went all the way around."

"It's supposed to," Hjalmar said with the barest hint of a frown. "This is new: an apartment complex."

"People live in there?"

"Lots of people."

"Can we go the other way?"

"Not at the moment," Hjalmar said, and Omesh noticed the ring of boys had become a line blocking off any retreat.

"These kids are goondas, aren't they?" Omesh said. "I mean gangsters. Hoods."

"I know what goondas are," Hjalmar said, "and yes."

"So where do we go? Into the apartment

complex?"

"That's almost certainly their territory," Hjalmar said. He looked around slowly, as if he were scanning the image for some software in his head to analyze.

"We'll be seeing what's in that trunk now, I think," the tallest of the boys said, tossing an apple core aside.

"It's just personal stuff, nothing of value to you," Omesh said.

"You know what I value now, do you?"

"Omesh, let them take it so we can be on our way," Hjalmar said.

Omesh was about to object, but he noticed something glinting in the tallest boy's hand. At first he thought it was a knife; then he saw it was just a piece of scrap metal. Then he saw how the piece had been sharpened to a fine edge and went back to his first assessment: knife. All the boys had them; some were smaller than others, and some had handles covered with layers of duct tape, but all were honed to a sharp edge.

"That's a wise decision," the head boy said. "But we'll be needing everything you have on you as well."

"There you're out of luck, I'm afraid; I haven't anything."

"I doubt that very much," the boy growled,

and with a jerk of his head, he sent two of the other boys closer to investigate. They moved cautiously, but when Hjalmar made no attempt to keep them away, they grew bolder, patting down all the places where pockets might be, before turning back to their boss with a shrug.

"Hey Rocco, his clothes might be worth something," one of the others said. "Personally, I like the shirt."

"They are nice," Rocco agreed. "A bit too nice. This fellow thinks he's too smart to walk through our part of the station with money on him. But he's not so smart as all that. He doesn't need to have money on him; he *is* money."

"Huh?"

"Ransom, you idiot. Tell me, boy: who's your daddy?"

"You'd be wiser to let me go," Hjalmar said, perfectly calmly.

"You're going to be difficult?" the boy asked, brandishing his knife.

"I'm going to be very difficult."

"Fine. Boys, let's get off the street, shall we?"

The trunk strap was ripped from Omesh's hand and one of the smaller boys carried it into the maze of passages between the containers, holding it high like a war trophy. Two more boys grabbed Omesh by the arms and propelled him after. He twisted and fought, but the wiry boys were stronger than they looked. He managed to look behind him long enough to catch a brief glimpse of Hjalmar passively following, hands in pockets.

Omesh hoped he had a plan. But he didn't look like he had a plan.

The boy with the trunk ducked inside one of the shipping containers and the others followed. The space within was larger than Omesh had expected; the dividing walls between three containers had been removed to leave a meeting space for a gang ten times the size of the group that had kidnapped them. A large gang that broke into packs to prey on the crowds in the station marketplace... it made sense. It also made Omesh feel sick to his stomach. They were already outnumbered, and if they'd ever had any intention of taking Omesh's trunk and letting him go on his way, it looked like that was a thing of the past now.

The boys holding him dragged him across the room and pushed him down into a chair of sorts; it looked like it had been made hurriedly from pieces cut from one of the missing container walls. Then his arms were pulled painfully tight behind him, and one of the boys lashed his wrists together with a plastic zip tie while the other used more zip ties to secure his ankles to the legs of the chair. The raw edges of the chair legs bit deep into the flesh of his calves and his bonds were so tight he could feel the blood flow being cut off.

"Shirt, please," Rocco said, and Hjalmar carefully unbuttoned it and took it off, holding it out to the boy who had said he liked it. Rocco snatched it before the other could take it, though, shooting Hjalmar a look of annoyance before running probing fingers over every inch of the fabric, examining the seams and the collar most closely.

"You won't find any chips there," Hjalmar said, but that only made Rocco search again even more thoroughly before tossing the shirt aside in disgust.

"Pants," he said with a commanding gesture.

"I have no identification on me," Hjalmar said.

"Pants."

"I do have identification *in* me, but I rather doubt you have the technology to access that."

"This gets inside things," Rocco said, waving his shiv in front of Hjalmar's nose.

"Yes, but if it gets inside my skull, where my ID is, I rather lose my value as a ransom victim, don't I?"

"No one puts an ID chip inside someone's skull," the boy scoffed.

"It's not just an ID chip. But that is where it's located."

This didn't seem to mean anything to the gang members, which struck Omesh as extraordinarily odd. Everyone on Earth knew about brain chips. They were held out as the ultimate reward for those who worked their way up the A&MC ladder. Omesh himself had spent his entire life up until three weeks ago studying hard to someday earn one himself. These kids acted like they didn't even know the technology existed; more, like they had never even imagined it.

"It's in his forearm," one of the other kids said. "That's where they inject it."

"You mean here?" Rocco asked, and he slipped the point of his handmade knife under Hjalmar's skin. Hjalmar growled in pain but still made no move. Omesh was beginning to find him more than a little creepy.

"Can't you just tell them your family name?" Omesh asked. "They're not even on this station, so what difference does it make?"

"None at all," Hjalmar said with a crazy grin that seemed to even creep Rocco out. He pulled the knife out of Hjalmar's arm and stepped back, regrouping. Hjalmar looked around the room, his eyes finally stopping on his own shirt in the hands of the boy who had wanted it. He snatched it out of the boy's slack grip and wrapped it around his bleeding arm, holding one sleeve in his teeth as he tightened the bulky bandage.

"Anything worth anything in the trunk?" Rocco asked, and Omesh realized for the first time that the smallest boy had snapped off the lock and was going through Omesh's things. The clothes his mother had so neatly folded away were strewn everywhere, his handmade computer was in two pieces on the floor, and the boy was holding in his hands a shiny paper kite.

"This is pretty cool," he said, turning it around in his hands.

"It's useless," Rocco said, stomping over to peer inside the trunk and check the lining for hidden compartments himself, but there was nothing more. This was all Omesh owned. The kite was a surprise; his mother must have slipped that in when he wasn't looking. He had spent months designing that kite with the intention of flying it at Uttarayan, but his sudden departure had spoiled those plans. Now he'd never fly kites again; there was no wind in space.

The sudden wave of homesickness overwhelmed him. He had known he was leaving the most perfect place in the solar system and life would never be so good again, but he had never expected it to get this bad, this quickly. He hadn't even met his uncle yet.

"They're both worthless," one of the other boys said with just a touch of recrimination.

"No, that one's not," Rocco said, pointing at Hjalmar with the still-bloody shiv.

"He'll never talk. He didn't even scream when you stuck him. I don't think he's entirely human."

"Don't talk nonsense," Rocco snapped. "Maybe he can't be hurt, but I doubt the same is true of his friend."

He seized a fistful of Omesh's hair and yanked it back with such force it brought spots to Omesh's vision. Then he pressed the wet blade of his knife to Omesh's throat. It was only there for a moment, and Rocco never said a word, although Omesh was certain that more threats and demands were meant to accompany the gesture. Instead, there was a scuffle, a grunt, and a shrill scream.

The grip on his hair fell away, and Omesh righted his head. He wished his hands were free so he could touch his neck; he felt a trickle there but didn't know if it was Hjalmar's blood or his own. The shiv was lying on Omesh's lap, staining his new kurta. Rocco was now crumpled on the floor, clutching his knee and whimpering as he tried and failed to get up.

The reason for that was soon clear, as Omesh

finally spotted Hjalmar dodging the clumsy stabs of two other gang members. He caught the wrist of one, guiding the boy's own momentum to bring him close and then striking with the speed of a cobra, a short kick that made a horrid crunching sound as it impacted the boy's knee.

Once there were two people on the floor in as many seconds, the others disappeared. The smallest boy lingered for a moment, tempted by Omesh's kite in his hands, but when Hjalmar turned to look at him, he quickly overcame his indecision, dropping the kite and scampering away.

"Why didn't you just do that in the first place?" Omesh asked. His neck was twinging every time he moved his head in a way that promised to be worse in the morning.

"I don't really enjoy hurting people. I try to find other options."

"To the point where you let them stab you?"

Hjalmar looked down at his shirt-wrapped arm as if he'd forgotten it. "I've had worse."

"It will need stitches. Can you get that here?"

"Sure. With every teenager armed with shivs, I'm sure there's a robust business to be had in stitches and antibiotics. But we should get to our destination first."

"And hurry. I don't think that was the whole

gang. They probably just ran to get the really big guys."

"I agree." Hjalmar stepped over the boy still moaning at Omesh's feet and picked up the shiv to cut away the plastic ties. The sudden rush of blood back to Omesh's hands and feet brought a rapturous pain.

"Take a minute," Hjalmar said. "I'll repack your trunk."

Omesh rubbed at his ankles first and then stood up, taking a few limping steps around. He wanted to be able to run as soon as possible. Hjalmar gathered up the scattered piles of clothing, stuffing them back inside the trunk. Then he looked at the two pieces of the computer.

"It's all right; I can fix that," Omesh said, limping over to pick up the kite.

"I've never seen a computer like this," Hjalmar said as he nestled the pieces in with the clothing.

"It's built from scraps, so I guess you could call it one of a kind."

"You built it?"

"Yeah. I wasn't allowed to take any A&MC technology with me, so I built that. Technically, it's just junk, so I can keep it, but it works. Faster than my school tablet, actually." He leaned down to gently arrange the kite over the top and Hjalmar shut the lid, then used one of the zip ties to hold the latch down in place of the smashed lock.

"I'll carry the trunk, you just keep up," Hjalmar said and led the way out of the room.

Omesh came after, slowly at first, but more quickly as his feet recovered. He could feel eyes on them as they passed through the narrow alleyways, small children or sometimes women or old men watching them from the dark doorways. No one tried to stop them or even speak to them, but he was sure when the rest of the gang started the pursuit, the bystanders wouldn't hesitate to point out which way they had gone.

Then they were out of the complex and back in the open space of the station marketplace. Back in the crowds and the hundred mingling smells. Funny what just ten short minutes could do to rearrange a person's idea of what was terrifying and what felt safe.

"Not far now," Hjalmar said. Then he stopped suddenly, staring off into space.

"What is it?" Omesh asked, looking around but seeing nothing out of the ordinary. "Are you getting a message or something? Is there a problem with your contact?"

"You said you were going to stay with your uncle on Chandi V," Hjalmar said.

"Yes, about that—"

"There are no scheduled arrivals to Chandi V except my family," Hjalmar went on. "What's your uncle's name?"

"Prakash Goyal," Omesh said, "but he isn't a corporate employee. He won't be in your... head."

"Barnacle Town," Hjalmar said. "You're going to Barnacle Town."

"I guess that's what they call it."

Hjalmar set down Omesh's trunk. Then he straightened, his face as unreadable as ever.

"What's going on?" Omesh asked.

"I can't take you with me."

"OK," Omesh said, feeling anything but. "OK, but can you take me as far as the *Dauntless,* anyway? My uncle is waiting for me there."

"No, I really can't."

"OK. OK." Omesh didn't know what else to say. Hjalmar was looking around, his arms crossed over his bare chest. A trickle of blood was worming its way out from under the shirt bandage. "What do I do now? I don't have any money. And those boys will be back."

"You're clever," Hjalmar said. "You'll think of something. Anybody who can build a workable computer out of bits from a junk heap can find a way to make a living in a thriving community like this one. They're all illegal squatters, but they aren't all out-and-out criminals. You'll be fine."

"What? I don't understand what's happening," Omesh said.

"Yeah, sorry about that. I've got to go. Good luck." Then he turned and walked away. He was tall, and he had silver-blond hair; it took a very long time for him to disappear in the crowd.

Omesh Rashid Nasrin had grown up on a farm on the edge of the Thar Desert, twenty miles from the nearest neighbor and more than a hundred from the nearest village. He was an only child, and his parents worked from sunrise to sunset every day of the week, which left little time for them to spend with him. But now, surrounded by people packed around him in all three dimensions, now he felt truly isolated.

CHAPTER TWO

RABIA

"Shouldn't you be in school?"

Rabia looked up at the guard. She couldn't remember the last time one had actually spoken to her. "You're new, aren't you?"

"Answer my question first." He leaned forward as he said it, something merry in his eyes. Rabia barely checked herself from stepping back. She would swear he was flirting with her, except that was impossible. She was Rabia; no one flirted with her. He must just be colossally bored. Rabia raised her hand, fingers spread wide, then touched it down on the palm reader built into the desk. Her handprint remained for a moment, then turned bright green.

"Not a truant," Rabia said.

"You work the night shift somewhere, then?"

"Hardly! I'm only seventeen."

"Early graduation?" the guard ventured. That flirty vibe was starting to fade away.

"Nope. Dropout. I'm learning in the school of life now, and life is just a little bit beyond this airlock. See you later!"

This wasn't fair to her father, who was technically her teacher now, but telling people she studied all the usual subjects just on her own always led to question after question. Plus, saying she was a dropout just sounded cooler.

Rabia completely ignored the ladder in favor of leaping over the edge to the lip of the open airlock some eight feet below, then started down the long, steep path into the heart of her home away from home.

Ah, Barnacle Town. A place with a smell like no other. Rabia breathed it in, closing her eyes as she sorted and labeled each component. Greasy food cooked over an open flame. Stray dogs and doglike children doing their business wherever. Families of ten or more packed into a space no bigger than her bedroom with the only available method of bathing a bucket carried up from the community tap—or more commonly bathing at the tap itself, modesty be damned. Closer to the market, the smells of ripe fruit and spices took over. Nothing back home in Chandi V ever smelled like anything in particular. Not even the food.

She didn't mind that her days as a corporate resident were numbered. She didn't even mind that she had no idea what she would do that last day she walked past the security gate, the day when she wouldn't slip back through just as curfew was sounding. Living life from moment to moment, doing whatever work was available just to keep the meals coming—the thought rather excited her.

But it scared her mom. She had been acting weird for weeks now, but last night Rabia had gotten up in the middle of the night to pee and heard her mother's tears from the next room and her father's deep voice murmuring sounds of comfort. She didn't have to hear the words to know she was the one behind her mother's quiet weeping. It was a long-established rule of the universe that her sister Teresa was incapable of doing anything to upset their mother. No, it had to be Rabia and her rapidly approaching eighteenth birthday.

It was far too late to attempt making herself over as just another piece in the corporate machine, even if she wanted such a fate. She didn't think that would please her mother, anyway; as a human resources analyst, she knew better than anyone how ill-suited Rabia was for such a life. Still, perhaps it was time to come up with a plan. If she knew what was going to happen next, perhaps her mother wouldn't worry so much.

She would talk to Si Fu about it. He always had lots of ideas. More than that, he had a way of bringing them out of Rabia with pointed looks and smiling silences rather than speaking them himself. An afternoon of kung fu and tea would be more than enough to get her going on the road to having a plan, she was sure.

"Look here, Tom. Jumpsuit is back."

Too much woolgathering; she should have noticed all the urchins crawling out of their little hidey-holes before she was surrounded. They weren't moving too close to her, but they didn't need to. Their job was to get her to where Alain and Tom lurked under the awning of the coffee stand, and she saw no reason not to keep walking since she had been heading that way, anyway. There were always more of them about than she could see, and she honestly did try to avoid fights when possible; she would have taken a different lane if she had noticed them.

The urchins that ran with the gangs had the advantage in this little game of theirs. They blended in with the rest of Barnacle Town, not just the other people but the very walls: nondescript hair, dingy T-shirts and faded jeans, canvas sneakers so old and battered and full of holes they could almost be called sandals.

She, on the other hand, in her bright indigo jumpsuit with the prominently displayed Chandi Corporation logo, was a little hard to miss, especially in the middle of a workday when few corporate residents were out and about. The fact that her hair was one long braid of vibrant pink probably didn't help, either.

"Hey, boys," she said as she stopped a nonaggressive few paces away from Alain and Tom. She could remember when they had both been urchins as well. Alain could nearly pass as a corporate higher-up now, with his white silk shirts and polished shoes. She had no idea where in Barnacle Town he got his clothes or who did his laundry. She did appreciate that he didn't favor the loud colors and flashy jewelry of the other gang boys. But then Alain always did do things his own way.

Tom, on the other hand, looked like he had only half molted from urchin status. His clothes were nicer than those of the boys who answered to him, but they were already showing signs of neglect. And of sloppy eating habits.

"Didn't we tell you not to stray down our lanes again, Jumpsuit? Didn't we, Tom?"

Once upon a time Alain had called her by name, back when she had ripped out of her jumpsuit and stashed it in a hole in the wall before going to Si Fu's. Then one day, he had followed her after class and saw her getting back into her mandatory corporate uniform. Rabia didn't know why he had spied on her. Perhaps someone else had seen her first and told him; Barnacle Town was full of eyes. But for whatever reason, he had called her only Jumpsuit ever since. She wore her corporate clothes openly now; there was no one left worth hiding things from.

Rabia fixed her gaze on the middle of Alain's nose. Looking into his eyes brought that moment back in too-sharp clarity, and she would not let him see again just how much dumping her as a friend had hurt her.

"Yes, you did mention. Then I kicked both your asses, and four of your friends' asses. I rather thought that had settled the matter," she said.

"Well, it didn't."

"Do we really have to go through this every time I come to Barnacle Town? Because honestly, my fists get tired." She thought about adding something about how the definition of insanity was repeating the same actions and expecting different results, but she decided they wouldn't really get the humor.

"Tom and I actually have a proposition for you," Alain said.

"Is that right, Tom?" Rabia asked.

Tom raised one eyebrow but said not a word.

"The boss has put me in charge of the Saturday fights," Alain began, but that was all she needed to hear.

"Not interested," Rabia said, all humor and sarcasm gone.

"Come on! You were a mainstay when my brother Luc was running it. And it can be worth serious coin to you. I'll give you a cut on what my bookies make. Everyone is dying to see you fight again."

"Do I look hard up for cash to you?"

Tom snorted and mumbled something only Alain could hear.

"Well, that was the carrot," Alain said with a dramatic sigh. "Would you like to see my stick?"

"Is it bigger than your carrot?"

"I know Si Fu isn't teaching anymore, leastwise no one but you goes up there. He lives smack-dab in the center of my little territory; I know everything that happens in my lanes. He isn't teaching anymore, and that's an awfully big space for one frail old man."

"Is this a threat?" Rabia asked, not quite suppressing a laugh. After the last lesson she'd taught his little gang, one would think they would be reluctant to take on her si fu. Of course, Si Fu had been very disappointed in her for her part in that little ruckus, but they didn't know that.

"You're not always here, are you? Every night at curfew, you have to scuttle back to the corporate part of the space station, don't you?"

"Technically, the corporate part *is* the space station. The rest of this is just junk welded to the outside. Or didn't you know why they call it Barnacle Town?"

"Am I not being clear?" Alain asked with a glance at Tom.

"You're being perfectly clear," Rabia said. "It's just that I'm not worried about your stick. I, the student, have already thoroughly spanked both of you and a nice selection of your toadies. That's nothing compared to what my teacher can do to you."

"I don't know, Jumpsuit. I've seen the man around and he's moving pretty slow these days."

"Why don't you go ahead and rely on that, you ass," Rabia said and turned her back on him. Not the smartest move, perhaps, but neither he nor Tom made an attempt to jump her from behind, and the urchins were keeping their distance. She would have to walk the streets more alertly from now on, though. Alain and Tom would favor ambush for the next encounter, and they would cer-tainly bring weapons.

It could be fun.

As she turned, she saw the reason the two of them were loitering outside the coffee shop: Alain's older and taller brother was hassling the owner of the curry stand across the lane, shaking him and growling right in the man's face.

"Hey," Rabia said, stepping forward. Si Fu loved vindaloo, and Prakash's curry stand made the best vindaloo in Barnacle Town. Not that he had a lot of competition. But still, Prakash was a good man who looked out for Si Fu when she couldn't.

"Stay out of it," Alain growled, but she easily slipped out of the hand meant to restrain her and marched across the lane into the curry shop.

"Let Sri Goyal go," she said.

Alain's brother Luc looked over at her coolly. He had been running the fights before she had quit; she didn't have to make any threats. "This doesn't concern you."

"That's funny, because I feel concerned," Rabia said, taking another step closer.

Luc thought over the situation, glancing past her in a way that let her know Alain and Tom were standing in the doorway behind her. She ad-justed her mental picture of her surroundings but made no outwardly defensive move, not even so much as a shift of her weight. Something in the kitchen was starting to burn, a caramel smell just turning to a smoky one. Then Luc let Prakash go with a backward thrust that was just short of knocking him down, as if he had calculated the limit to how aggressive he could be without Rabia feeling compelled to treat it as an attack.

"It's fine, Rabia," Prakash said, although he looked far too pasty to be fine. "Please, there is no need to fight here."

"Yeah, save it for the ring. Yes?" Luc said.

"I think I've earned you enough coin for one lifetime," Rabia said. "Get lost. And don't hassle my friends."

"I'm not hassling anyone, missy. I'm here on official Barnacle Town business."

"Official? That's funny. It implies anyone here actually holds an office," Rabia said.

"Watch your step," Luc warned.

"You don't scare me."

His lip curled up in a humorless sneer. "Indeed. Safe every night beyond the airlocks, snug in your corporate apartment, with your corporate mom and corporate dad. But who says it's you we'll be after?"

Then he reached out and grasped the nearest support beam. The curry stand, like the rest of

Barnacle Town, was welded together from bits of space debris. The kitchens had once been a storage container, with a door formed from the jagged hole left from a collision with some meteor or piece of space junk that rendered it useless for its old purpose but quite sufficient for its new one. Prakash and his wife lived over the curry stand in a long, narrow pod, which had once been a sleep compartment for one of the tiny space stations that had first housed humans in space. The pod was long indeed; it overhung the storage container by a considerable margin. The addition of a few mismatched support beams to hold up the pod overhead had made an open space for tables and chairs. Dining areas were almost nonexistent in Barnacle Town, and the curry stand was as popular for being a place to sit as for its cuisine.

Watching Luc shake the beam, Rabia wondered for the first time just who had put this place together. Prakash was a fine cook, but as the sleeper pod above them began to sway, Rabia doubted his abilities as an engineer.

"Stop it," she said as calmly as she could.

Luc just grinned, his hand on the beam still rocking it back and forth. Alain gave a chuckle, and Tom joined in.

"Stop," Rabia said again.

"Please," Prakash added as the sound of his

wife's sudden cry of alarm echoed from above them. "Please."

Luc just grinned and kept at it. So Rabia hit him.

He staggered back, hands to his face. Rabia shook her hand. There are better places to hit a guy than right in the mouth, but that grin had pissed her off. Teeth hurt, though, and it wouldn't be a complete surprise if she got some sort of disease.

The hand that fell on her shoulder wasn't a complete surprise, either. She let Alain spin her around, using the momentum to drive an elbow right under his ear. She was just turning to face Tom when she heard her name. It was softly spoken, but somehow it filled her with more shame than her mother's loudest rebukes.

"Si Fu," she said, stepping back and lowering her hands.

Huo Fei Li crossed the narrow lane, leaning heavily on his walking stick. By the time he stepped into the curry stand, Tom, Alain, and Luc had all made themselves scarce. Prakash was gone as well.

Si Fu stepped up to the counter and set down the empty cook pot he had been carrying.

"There was a reason," Rabia began.

"Yes, there always is," Si Fu said, and she said

no more. Rabia stepped around the counter to the kitchen, turning off the flame under the enormous wok and fanning the smoke away as best she could. Whatever had been cooking in there was interestingly shaped charcoal now.

Prakash came back down the stairs, all but carrying his very pregnant wife, Anjali. He went over to the loose beam and inspected the damage.

"You will need some strong help to reset that," Si Fu said. "The butcher near my house has two apprentices who are always looking for an opportunity to make an extra coin or two. I'll send them your way, yes?"

"Yes, thank you," Prakash said, leading his wife to one of the chairs, but she shook her head.

"I'm fine, Prakash, really. Vindaloo, Mr. Li?"

"Always divine; thank you," Si Fu said. Empty pot in one hand and the other curled under her belly, she disappeared into the kitchens.

"What did they want, Prakash-ji?" Rabia asked. "He said it was official."

"It was. I don't know who the dons are that are running this place now, but they want to make it just like the corporations we've all worked so hard to avoid."

Rabia was puzzled and must have looked it, but Si Fu understood.

"The baby," he said.

"Indeed, the baby," Prakash said. "We have room enough for him, food enough for him, but apparently 'all of Barnacle Town' feels we will be taking more than our share of the water and air."

"That's nonsense," Rabia said. "None of you pays for either; it all comes from Chandi Corporation." Not legally, either, but that wasn't a thing which needed to be said aloud.

"This is bad," Prakash said, sinking into a chair, head in hands.

"I can speak to them for you," Si Fu said. "They will understand."

"But it's more than just the baby now," Prakash said. "My nephew is coming. He's been expelled from Earth and I told my sister I would take him in. How could I not? He has nowhere else to go. I'm going to pick him up tomorrow. When they find out..."

"Please, don't worry," Si Fu said, resting a hand on Prakash's shoulder. "I'll speak to them. They will understand."

"I..." But Prakash clearly had no will to argue. "I am grateful."

"Vindaloo, Mr. Li," Anjali said, setting the steaming pot on the counter. There were more red chilies in there than meat pieces, just the way Si Fu liked it. The fact that it would soon have her in tears in no way diminished her appreciation for the bright color of the dish. Nothing she ate at home was ever this pretty. Rabia shut the lid, then slid her sleeves down over her hands to pick it up without burning herself.

"I didn't know you knew the dons," Rabia said as they made their way farther down the narrow lane to the blind alley which hid the door to his former school.

"I don't, but I know their type. They can be talked to and negotiated with if you speak their language," Si Fu said.

"What language is that?"

"Politics, child," Si Fu said with a little chuckle.

"But they're thieves," Rabia said.

"Why do you say that?"

Rabia blinked. "Because they take money that isn't theirs?"

"Ah, but with that money, they provide all of us with energy and water."

"I guess it started that way," Rabia said. The history of Barnacle Town was an oral tradition that varied widely, depending on who was doing the telling. "The merchants who were a little more prolific than the rest elected themselves representatives between the people of Barnacle Town and the Chandi Corporation, and they collected the bribe money and negotiated on everyone's behalf. But it's bigger than that now. And I know they collect more than they're spending; the stories I hear here and the stories I hear inside just don't match up. I call that theft."

"All right, Rabia. They are thieves, by your definition. But they're not just thieves." He stopped at the end of the alley to fish out the enormous key from within his robes. The butcher's shop and home were made from a collection of half-destroyed cargo pods all welded together with a ferocity that made the joins look like particularly brutal scars. Beyond the butcher's was a cul-de-sac formed by the back ends of many other ships forming an extremely irregular space. Barnacle Town was very far from a planned community.

Si Fu reached his hand with the key inside the gap between the back of the butcher's and the wall that was the end of Barnacle Town, a wall made entirely of welded-together scraps. There was a click, and a door twenty feet over their heads swung open.

Si Fu turned to her as he put the key back into his pocket. "Barnacle Town has grown since I first came here; it has grown a lot. People brought their families here to live within the protection of the space station's magnetic radiation shield, to take advantage of the gravity to walk upright. This is a good thing. But too many people in one place create trouble. You need a way to agree on how to get along besides fighting with each other. That's politics. The corporation has its own structure, but out here we have the dons."

"They're getting more powerful," Rabia said.

"Yes."

"Too powerful?"

Si Fu thought about this for a moment, and when he did speak, it was—as usual—not a direct answer.

"I've lived a long time. I've seen the human race decimated, the remains scattered across the solar system. We so nearly died out sixty years ago. Now we are beginning to get our strength back. I see people starting to move beyond just surviving the plague to really living for themselves.

"The corporations control the big space stations. They think that means they control humanity out in space. The dons are thieves of a sort —I will agree with your assessment there—but the dons are also the ones in a position to show the corporations just how untrue their assumptions are.

"Now, come. Let's get upstairs and eat before the food gets cold."

He may have walked on level walkways leaning heavily on a stick, but when it came to shimmying up that wall of welded joints and strange outcroppings of girder ends and enormous screws, Si Fu still moved like a young master. He lowered the hook, and Rabia hung the pot from it so he could slowly hoist up his dinner as Rabia made her own way up the wall.

Yes, Alain would be a fool if he thought her master was an easy target. She had no reason to worry about him. Any home that involved scaling a twenty-foot wall to get in the front door was very nearly ambush-proof.

So why was she so uneasy?

The doorway was narrow, as was the hall beyond, almost uncomfortably so, but its size was deceptive. From the lane below, the door seemed to lead to a tiny crawlspace, but once inside and past that narrow hall, it opened up into a tremendous amount of open space for Barnacle Town. It was extravagant even by Chandi Corporation standards, where most of the large spaces had been converted into many smaller units to house the refugees fleeing Earth decades ago. Once upon a time, Si Fu had used his open space to teach kung fu, tai chi, and chi gang to anyone who wanted to learn. When Rabia had first come here, he had anywhere from twelve to twenty students practicing at any given time of the day, all spinning and punching, advancing and retreating, and still there had been room for more.

But Si Fu wasn't teaching anymore, and only Rabia still came to see him. Some days he was so tired he just sat in his dangerous-looking rocking chair made of scrap metal, dozing and waking with little difference between the two. Other days he was as alert as ever, and on those days he was still Rabia's teacher, watching her as she drilled forms over and over and correcting her technique.

Rabia followed Si Fu across the open practice yard, steaming vindaloo in her sleeved hands, to the rickety staircase that led up to the loft that was his living space. It looked out onto the practice space and was the usual Barnacle Town size: barely big enough for a table and two stools, and the stools had to be put up at night before he could lay out his bedroll. But for such a tiny space, it was filled with wonders. Rabia set the vindaloo on the table and Si Fu opened the lacquered cabinet tucked under the table, taking out two gorgeous china bowls, matching round cups with no handles, and lacquered chopsticks.

Even after putting all the chilies in Si Fu's bowl, Rabia could barely manage the spiciness, and when she was done her eyes and nose were both streaming. Si Fu gobbled his down like it was so much porridge. When they were done and she had helped clean up and put everything back away, Si Fu sat back in his chair and looked at her intently.

"I know," she said, hoping to circumvent this conversation.

"You threw the first punch," Si Fu said.

"But didn't you see what he was doing?"

"Yes, I did. He needed to be stopped; this I do not argue. But what you did, you didn't do to stop him. You did it because you were angry."

Rabia looked down at her hand, at the cuts and scrapes his teeth had left behind. She remembered that grin, that superior I'm-the-one-in-control-here grin. It made her blood boil all over again just remembering it. And, she was certain, if she had turned her head at that moment, she would have seen Alain grinning at her in just the same way.

"I should have just pushed him away, I guess," she said with a sigh.

"Perhaps. There were other options you could've tried before touching him at all."

"But there is no talking to a guy like that. You don't know him."

"Perhaps this is true, perhaps not. The problem here is not his character, it's yours. I want you to know, when you do something, that it is the best course of action for the circumstances. I want you to have this knowledge at the time you make the decision, not after."

"How?"

"You need to remove the thing that is keeping you from seeing clearly. Your anger."

Rabia laughed humorlessly. "I think that's pretty much irremovable."

"Nonsense," Si Fu said. "You just need to focus. It is an opponent like any other. Figure out how it fights, when it will strike, and how it will attempt to counter you, then use that knowledge to flow around it."

"That sounds kind of impossible, Si Fu," she said.

"Luckily, I know some tricks," he said with just a hint of a grin.

Rabia went back home that night with lists of book titles to search the corporate library for and breathing exercises to practice. It was only when her mother looked up from her computer to say hello that Rabia realized she had let another day go by without coming up with a plan for her future.

Surely she would remember to do something about that tomorrow.

CHAPTER THREE

TAKASHI

Tak didn't think you could properly call what he had arrived on a ship. Someone had built it piece by piece from whatever bits of junk would serve for the sole purpose of pushing cargo containers from space station to space station, but only those near Earth and the moon. He was quite certain that when the pilot and copilot were going through their preflight checklist, the thing they called the "life support system" was made of repurposed coffeemakers. The fact that the three of them had made it to Barnacle Town still breathing was a minor miracle.

It had made him terribly homesick.

But now he was back inside a corporate space station, although not one entirely taken over by riffraff like Haven was. This one was all corporate on the inside, but a layer of riffraff clung to the outside. The ships docked at the center of the hub, and his destination was the farthest point from where he now floated, one hand clinging to a cargo net bulging with weird objects. The pilot had shoved him and his duffel bag out of the ship and then promptly disappeared. Tak looked around for some clue as to where he was meant to go. There was a lot of cargo secured against the walls, but very few people.

Then he saw one, an angry one coming his way, pulling himself from cargo net to cargo net with great efficiency.

"What are you doing here, boy?" If the man was put off by discovering that Tak was both a foot taller and a foot wider than he, he didn't show it.

"Tak O'Reilly," Tak said, putting out a hand, which the man scowled at but didn't deign to touch.

"You're not getting into Barnacle Town. I don't know what your pilot promised you, but the town is closed. We can't fit another shiftless drifter inside our hulls."

"Well, that's a relief," Tak said with a smile. "Where can I catch a ride out of here?"

"I don't arrange rides," the man growled and

kicked away, propelling himself back down the long cylinder of the cargo bay. Tak's smile grew wider still, and in his mind he began composing the letter to his mother, explaining why even the effort she'd gone through to put him on a nonstop flight hadn't been enough to get him all the way to her father's beloved sumo school. The fact that the blame couldn't possibly be his was an added bonus. She couldn't say he hadn't tried.

Tak secured his duffel bag on his back and began poking around the cargo bay, completely at home in the null gravity. Most of the ships were slapdash affairs like the one he had come in on, not built for more than moving from space station to space station. You could probably crash one on the surface of the moon and walk away from it, but you'd never get it back up into space again. Which was a shame; Tak was rather partial to the lunar cities. They were horribly overcrowded, of course, and every trip he had made there had involved at least one series of painful inoculations against whatever latest epidemic was sweeping through the population, but there was a music scene there, and he loved live music.

Further down the bay, he saw a ship with a logo he recognized. It was from one of the floating cities of Venus, a mining colony. It didn't look luxurious enough to be from one of the pleasure cities. That might be a good option, Tak thought. He could find a job on the ship to take him to the mining colony, then find a job there. And maybe, someday, crash a party in one of the pleasure cities.

It wasn't likely, but a boy could dream.

"Hey, kid!" This from a guy scarcely older than himself, although they were nearly of a size. "You doin' anything? Wanna give us a hand?" He was towing a crate out of a decent-looking ship, one that looked sturdy enough to handle atmo and massive enough to go down a gravity well and get back out again. Maybe it was Earth bound.

"Sure," Tak said, launching himself into the ship's cargo hold and releasing the mechanism on the next crate to let it float free after him. "Where are we going with them?"

"You've done this before," the other kid said, impressed.

"Since before I could walk," Tak said, which was very nearly true. "I can fly ships and fix them, too."

"You sound like you're angling for a job. We're locking down these crates over here." He pointed, and Tak followed. "The name's Owen," the kid said, locking down his crate on the platform before extending his hand.

"Tak." He never gave his full first name; the

shorter version involved less explaining. Half of his blood was Japanese, but none of it showed. "Maybe I am looking for a job. Where are you headed?"

"Back to Mars. Ever been?"

"Yeah, once or twice." He didn't add that he hated it there. The deserts were gorgeous, no question about it, but the fascist rules the people of the domed cities lived under held no appeal for him. It was going to be hard enough in six months' time when his mother expected him to join her there. Of course he could stay working on the ship, always on the move. That life had suited him fine once before.

Tak and Owen unloaded a dozen more crates. Though the crates weighed nothing here in the center of the satellite, they massed quite a bit and could be awkward to work with, but the two of them both had the confident touch of experienced cargo haulers.

"Here," Owen said, slapping a few round coins into Tak's hand. "You still thinking about that job? I could talk to my captain."

"Thanks," Tak began, but he was interrupted by a long stream of what seemed to be cursing, although the English was too thickly accented for Tak to quite understand. It was the pilot who had originally brought him here, and he seemed irked.

"Come!" the man said, pulling on his arm. "Come!"

"I guess you gotta go," Owen said.

"Guess so. See you." With a sigh, Tak followed the pilot down the length of the cylinder, away from the ships and toward the surly man who had already told him he couldn't stay.

"What's all this?" the surly man asked, clearly put out at being interrupted, although to Tak's eyes, he hadn't been doing anything much.

The pilot gave a long explanation that Tak didn't bother to try to follow. Then he grabbed Tak's arm again. "Give. Give the..." His hands fluttered and Tak had not a clue what word was escaping him.

"You've got a message of some sort?" the man said with a sigh.

"Oh." Tak unzipped a pocket and dug out a small silvery disk hanging from a thin chain. The man took it, turning it over in his hands.

"You need a computer to read the file," Tak offered.

"I don't need to read the file; this mark here is good enough for me," the man said, examining the Japanese character engraved on one side. Tak couldn't read it, but he supposed it was the name of the man who owned the sumo school he was meant to be enrolled in.

"Good enough for what?" Tak asked with a sinking feeling.

"You should have said before that you were here for the school," the man said. "That's a whole different situation."

"So I can go in?" Tak asked.

"Yeah. But keep that handy, will ya? I'm not the only one's going to make the mistake of thinking you're just a drifter."

Tak nodded, zipping it back inside his pocket before following the direction of the man's finger to an elevator.

So close.

Once out of the elevator, the Japanese character got him past a pair of corporate security guards, who quickly escorted him out of the satellite airlock into what could only be Barnacle Town.

He was certain he had been in more squalid places, although he would be hard-pressed to name one at the moment. It was not nearly so crowded as the lunar cities, but it was far more chaotic. There were no streets or buildings like in a city, nor were there hallways and rooms as in the smaller space stations like Haven. No, here was nothing but a twisted wreck of ships all welded together, with people crawling over, around, and through them, passing through every busted-out window, doorway, and hole blown through the hull by space debris. It was like a human ant farm, only instead of building in sand, they had built in space junk.

He loved it at once. He put his hand into his pocket, pulling out the disk on its chain and slipping it around his neck. There was gravity here and little risk of losing it. But his fingers had brushed against something else: the coins he had been paid for helping to unload the Martian ship.

Now Tak had a choice to make.

His mother had intentionally sent him here on a nonstop flight with no money and no possessions worth trading. She had meant to make sure he had no choice but to go at once to the school and stay there. It had cost her so much to get him in. Not in money—she had never had much of that. No, she had paid in pride. She didn't have much of that left either, not after having to return to her father, young Tak in tow, husband gone to the far side of the solar system. His grandfather had worn her down with his constant criticisms of everything she did. Now that he was suddenly dead, her plan to leave Tak with him while she completed her probationary period at her new job was shot. So she had done what she thought was the only thing left: called up her father's old friends and begged and groveled until Tak had his place at the sumo school.

His grandfather had once gone to this school. He had often regaled Tak with long tales of his former days, happy days spent in the sumo stable. He had had a bright career ahead of him at one point. To hear him talk, you'd have thought that point was still ahead of him, some shiny thing just beyond the horizon. He had never even noticed with what horror Tak listened to his stories. Being mentally traumatized in pursuit of a goal that could be gone in the blink of an eye—or the blowing out of a knee—was not Tak's idea of how he wanted to spend his life. The fact that his grandfather had never gone on to do anything else afterwards, never pursued any other job, let alone dream, was something Tak considered unforgivable.

Tak knew his mother hadn't wanted to send him here. She didn't like the idea of such strict discipline any more than he did. But she liked less the idea of Tak out on his own, especially in Haven. He could see her point; he had become one of the security team's scapegoats. A few of the things they had picked him up for he had actually done: gambling and a petty theft when he was too young to know better. But now they picked him up for all sorts of crimes just because they always knew where to find him, and because it made the coalition of merchants that ran Haven happy to know their security team could always catch a culprit, even if it wasn't the right one. Without his grandfather's corporate ties, Tak would have spent a lot more time in custody. Now, with his grandfather gone, even Tak could see the merit in leaving Haven and starting over somewhere else.

They had no other family; there really was nowhere else for him to go. So his mother had tracked down friend after friend of her father, playing the game of favors promised and favors remembered. She had kept these conversations out of Tak's hearing, but he saw in her eyes afterward how much they had upset her. She had known these people before, had lived in their upper-level corporate world, and had left it all to be with Tak's father, free, and to live in a world where the give and take between people wasn't so scrupulously accounted.

Even remembering that look in her eyes, could he force himself to go to that school, just because it was what she wanted? Now that, with those coins in his hand, he had another choice?

But was the school really what she wanted for him? Or was it just for him to be OK without her for six months?

Tak didn't even bother inquiring as to the location of the school. And finding a game of chance in progress didn't require asking for directions; any out-of-the-way alley would do. Soon, a few lucky throws of the dice had his two coins up to twelve.

"I like this town!" Tak said, putting his money down for one last throw. He had enough for a couple of meals, his usual stopping point. Getting greedy made enemies.

"Do you now, stranger?" said one of the other kids. No one huddled around the dice was any older than twelve and all were much smaller than Tak, but they had a sharp look to them. He guessed they were all concealing weapons of some fashion, and they were starting to glance at each other as if they didn't trust his luck. When the dice came up boxcars again, there was grumbling.

"Hey, they're your dice, you know," Tak said, collecting his coins and disappearing them into pockets. "Is there a place I can get a room and some food?"

"No," one of the kids said. "We don't have space for strangers."

"OK, no room, but some food? I'm famished," Tak said. He wasn't concerned about the lack of room; he had slept in streets and hallways before.

He would just have to be sure to secure his money in the bag around his neck first.

"Where you from?" the kid persisted.

"All sorts of places," Tak said.

"You gotta give us a chance to win our money back," another kid said.

"Tell me where I can get something to eat and I will," Tak said. "Well, I'll eat first, but then I'll come right back."

"I think you're too lucky," the first kid said, picking up the dice and examining them.

"Don't be a sore loser. Those were your dice."

"Maybe you switched them," the kid said.

"Look, you're being ridiculous. I'm out of here."

Tak put his coins in his pocket, zipped it shut, and headed back out into the crowded lanes. People were everywhere, climbing up and over wings and defunct engines and hulls, carrying baskets on their backs, as the climbing frequently required hands as well as feet. Tak looked back once or twice, but no one was following him.

He found a vendor selling falafels from a cart. He slipped off his duffel bag and dug out his bowl, then negotiated how many coins it would take to fill it with the spicy patties plus generous dollops of baba ghanoush and yogurt and enough pita bread to soak it all up. It was most of his money, but as Tak savored the spicy goodness, he declared it well worth it.

The LED panels strung throughout the town began to dim—some sort of community-mandated nighttime. The lanes were still full of crowds, and businesses that liked the dark were beginning to show signs of life. Tak found what he guessed served as Main Street, a mostly straight, fairly long and open stretch of space built on the back of a single rocket-shaped ship, the other ships stacked to arch over this road rather than fill it. Tak saw a few people gathering things up off of spread blankets or taking down little display stands. The marketplace, then. A good place to search for work when it opened in the morning.

Tak saw a gap in the fuselage of one of the smaller ships sitting on the back of the rocket where a panel had broken away, not too visible from the street. He climbed up to get a better look. It was tight, but scavengers had removed enough components from within to leave a space just large enough for him to curl up in. He still didn't think anyone was following him, but caution was never a waste. In that niche he could see without being seen and, unlike a lane, there wasn't a back side that would also have to be watched. He would still have to sleep lightly, just in case.

Once he had pulled himself up into the little cubby, he secured his coins in the bag around his neck and tucked it and the silver disk under his shirt. Then he pillowed his head on his duffel bag, gazing down along the length of the marketplace. There were a few phantom smells still lingering in the air from whatever had been for sale under his niche that morning: overripe fruit and fried bread overwhelming other, subtler smells that gave him a vague sense of machinery, solvents, and oils maybe.

Going to bed with a full belly was always the way to end a day well spent. His mother hoped for more. She had spent the last three years slaving away in the corporate part of Haven to earn qualifications as a lab tech just so she could have more. But Tak thought this a fine life. There were days without food, but they only made the falafels more satisfying when you got them.

He had just drifted off to sleep when a dozen hands emerged from the darkness, reaching in from all around him and pulling him out of his niche. He hit the rocket ship with a dull thud, landing mostly on his shoulder but his skull still impacting hard enough to leave him a bit dazed, dazed enough to still be wondering how what seemed to be an intact rocket had gotten into space, before there were other smaller thuds around him. Then it was hands and feet in the darkness, kicking and striking him all over his body. Tak curled into a ball, arms around his head and knees to his chest to protect what he could, but more than one sharp-toed shoe found his kidneys or the back of his head. He tried to get up and fight, but there were just too many of them.

Then the hands were on him all at once, turning him over and pulling his arms away so they could get at what was hanging around his neck. Tak struggled, managing to get to his knees this time, but two boys holding tight to each of his arms were more than he could handle.

"We don't like strangers in Barnacle Town," someone said. Tak raised his head, focusing blurrily on the kid in front of him. No, not a kid; this guy was a year or two older than Tak.

"Yeah, I got that impression."

"The money is around his neck. I saw him put it there," one of the other kids said.

"Is it, now?" the kid in front of him asked, stepping closer.

"I suppose you're going to call it a tax?" Tak asked. This wasn't his first mugging.

"I don't need to call it anything. I'm just going to take it." His hand closed around the bag and pulled, snapping the bag cord and disk chain both. "What's this?" he said aloud, turning over the silver disk. "It's you. You're the one we're looking for."

"Yeah, I guessed that," Tak said, mopping at his nose with his shirtsleeve. The only light was from some sort of drinking establishment on the opposite end of the marketplace, so it took Tak's groggy mind a minute to work out that the slick of black on his cuff was blood from his nose.

"No, I don't mean that. Forget that. The boys know that when you gamble, sometimes you lose. Right, boys?"

There was a murmur that was meant to be assent, but to Tak's ears they sounded as confused as he was.

"Who am I again?" Tak asked.

The boy sighed loudly, then picked up the silver disk from Tak's chest to dangle it before his eyes.

"You're meant to be someplace today. Do you remember that?"

"What's it to you?"

"I've been asked to find you and make sure you get where you're going."

"You're from the sumo school?"

"No. Let's just say we're associates."

Tak rubbed at his nose again, then grimaced as

he twisted the sleeve of his sweatshirt to find a clean spot. "Can you be more clear?" he asked at last. "I hate speaking in code. Particularly if we aren't speaking the same code."

"All right," the boy said, leaning in close and putting a hand on Tak's shoulder. "You came here to Barnacle Town for one purpose: to go to the sumo school. That is the only purpose you will be fulfilling in Barnacle Town. We will be escorting you to your school now, and if we come across you again in future, it had better be because you've been given permission to visit our humble town, or we will escort you back again. Also, this 'escort' can be a with- or without-violence experience; that's totally up to you. Is that clear enough for you?"

"I think so," Tak said, struggling to keep the fear out of his voice. Not fear of what the boy had said—Tak had been on the receiving end of much more explicit threats in his time—but fear of what the boy was doing with his hand on Tak's shoulder. He didn't seem to be pinching or squeezing anything, but Tak's whole arm had gone numb and cold, and the feeling was spreading into his chest.

"Good," the boy said, and that hand gave a friendly slap before falling away. Tak pulled his arm in close to him, rubbing it back to warmth. "The school is this way. I guess you got lost, huh?"

"Something like that," Tak said. Cursing fate. Clearly, there was no way he was not going to go to this school.

But that didn't mean he had to stay.

CHAPTER FOUR

OMESH

OMESH PULLED THE BENT GRILL BACK INTO PLACE AS well as he could from the inside, then crawled farther in, stopping after the first bend to slump against the wall of the duct. If they knew where he'd gone, he'd just made a very bad mistake. Worse than leaving the atrium for the narrower hallways had been. But if they didn't, if they kept on hunting him in the hallways, he might have bought himself a little time. He concentrated on slowing his breathing, ignoring the sharp stabs under his rib cage that had been there since he'd run up all those staircases, and listened.

The old man was still jabbering away to himself in what sounded to Omesh's ears to be a made-up language. He had been alone in this stretch of hallway, and Omesh suspected that was less from the apparent madness than from the stench coming either from the man himself or from whatever he'd been poking at inside his cook pot. Omesh hadn't wanted to get a better look after he'd seen that it was still twitching.

Then he heard other footsteps, closing in from both directions. They met at the old man and argued briefly in what Omesh guessed might be Spanish or Italian. They pestered the old man with questions, but his crazy monologue never changed rhythm or inflection.

Then the footsteps went away again, and Omesh released the breath he'd been holding. He was safe for the moment. But he didn't reckon they'd be fooled for long; they knew this was the place they'd lost him, and they'd notice that bent grill when they circled back. He was desperately thirsty and wanted nothing more than a cool drink of water and a long sleep, but instead he got back up into the low crouch that was all he could manage in the small space of the utility tunnel and made his way deeper into the world within the walls of the space station.

He had thought his anxiety dreams in the weeks running up to leaving home had been bad, but clearly his imagination had focused too much on how the physics of living in space could kill him. He hadn't even thought to consider what the people would be like.

He reached an intersection, ducts crossing at right angles horizontally and vertically. The space between was too large to step across from a crouching position, but he could get to the left or right easily enough. Two such hops would keep him going straight, but turning was probably a good idea, so he went to the right and kept following that tunnel. He could see other short tunnels branching off to his left, ending in grills like the one he'd crawled in through, but for the moment these ducts felt safer than those hallways, crowded with people and crawling with goondas hunting for him. The people were living in the hallways, cooking over camp stoves or even makeshift hearths and bedding down in faded blankets or old coats. The few rooms he had peered into had been just as crowded. Now he understood the pressure the Agriculture and Mining Collective put on farmers like his father to meet quotas; there were so many people up here to be fed.

At the next intersection, Omesh decided to change levels. When he'd first been chased out of the marketplace, he'd taken the stairs all the way up to one level short of the airdock entrances, so down was the best option. He swung his duffel and threw it to the duct that was down and on his left, then hung from the lip of the floor on his left, swinging his body into the lower tunnel to land next to the bag.

The first thing he'd done after finding himself alone in the marketplace, abandoned by Hjalmar, was to sell his trunk. He couldn't run with it, and it made him easy to identify. He had also sold his kite and most of his clothing, buying the duffel bag with the straps he could use to carry it on his back and keeping only as much as he could fit inside it. He had also bought a faded Yankees baseball cap to cover his hair and had put on his oldest T-shirt. It hadn't been disguise enough, and the walking he had hoped would take him into a rival gang's territory hadn't been far enough. That loose circle of boys had formed around him in the marketplace crowd and he had known he was trapped and had to run.

Clothes were replaceable, and he had a little money in his pocket now—which he was going to need—but he regretted giving up the kite. His only comfort was how enchanted with it the woman who had bought it had been. Her eyes had glowed as she hung it in the corner of her tea stand, like a flower in an island girl's hair. Better there than in the hands of some young goonda, he supposed.

Omesh unzipped his duffel and slid out his computer. He had been searching for a wireless signal when the boys had found him. He knew there was some sort of network working here; Hjalmar had accessed it with his chip. Some outside source had told him that Omesh wasn't recognized as an arrival at Chandi V, that was the only thing that could explain his sudden desertion. But Omesh's computer wasn't finding even the weakest of signals, not earlier in the marketplace nor here in the ducts. This place should be bathed in signals, and yet it wasn't.

Someone had deliberately disabled all wireless access. Omesh could see an easy way to make money by doing that: keep just a few access points and charge to use them. He had seen people paying goondas to use the water coming from the taps; Omesh was surprised they hadn't found a way to goonda-tax the air.

Thinking about water was making him too aware of the thick mass of his tongue cleaving to his mouth. He continued along the cramped tunnel, duffel in one hand, open computer in the other. Perhaps he'd get a flash of signal somewhere in here. If he could just find a hot spot they'd missed, back here in the walls.

Then he found something better: an open access panel. He pulled a multi-tool out of his back pocket, using it to cut the ties holding the cables together and sorting through them until he found what he wanted: a communication line. Then he sat with his computer on his knees and plugged the line into the port. He remembered when he had installed that component. How Ali had teased him: what was next, two cans and a string? Everything on Earth was wireless, but Omesh had guessed that in space the equipment was older, and he had decided not to take any chances.

The icon on his computer lit up to show he was connected, and Omesh fired up his communication program. He should call his uncle and tell him he was delayed; perhaps he could catch him before he even left Barnacle Town and save him the needless trip. He should call his parents and tell them he was OK, even though he wasn't sure he was.

Omesh paused with his hands over the keys. He didn't know how either conversation would go, how he would keep his own fear at bay long enough to answer all the inevitable questions calmly, so he didn't cause anyone any worry.

In the end, he called the top contact in his list, his best friend Ali. He doubted there'd be any signal delay here. He didn't know where Haven was exactly, but judging by how much—or, rather, little—time had passed before the shuttle broke down, they hadn't even gone as far as the La-grange point L1. The clock on his computer was still on India time, 3 a.m. No wonder he was so tired. But knowing Ali, he was still up.

The screen opened up, and he saw Ali, hair impressively tousled, blinking at him. "Hey. Miss me already, yaar?"

"Did I wake you?"

"Nah. Well, yeah, but I wasn't in bed. Working on this thing..." He looked around his desk, then found a mug of something and took a long swig. Then he grimaced. "Gah, how long has that been there? I think the dog's been in it. So what's up? By my calculation, you can't have even reached your destination yet. You should still be on the shuttle."

"Something broke on the shuttle and now I'm stuck on this space station that isn't anywhere on the route I was supposed to be on."

"Seriously? Yaar, what are you going to do?"

"I have no idea. None." He swallowed hard. "That's not the half of it. This place is full of goon-das, and apparently I'm a walking target."

"It's those curly locks of yours, yaar," Ali said, rubbing at his own hair. Under normal circum-stances, it was completely straight; at the moment it was a living sculpture. "It's not just girls from Goa who can't resist."

"She wasn't from Goa," Omesh said under his breath, then aloud: "I'm hiding in an access duct, and I think I'm sort of stealing internet access."

Ali sat up straighter, the teasing look gone from his eye. He glanced to one side, to another of his many computers. "You think you're not on a clean line?"

"Yaar, I don't know. How would I know? That's your thing," Omesh said.

"I'm going to run a program here. It might make a visual glitch." The crispness of the picture pixelated and became herky-jerky, but when Ali spoke, his voice came through as clear as before. "OK, so what's your plan?"

"I don't have one."

"Yeah, tell me another one. The great Rashid Nasrin has no plan? Not likely."

"Well, I figured I'd have to get a job here and earn enough to pay my own passage the rest of the way."

"How could they just dump you without taking you where you paid to go?"

"I don't know. But all the passengers were in the same situation and they acted like it was nothing. I guess this happens all the time."

"Your parents can't help you?" Ali said. Through the glitches and static, Omesh could see him still dividing his attention between two screens.

"No, nor my uncle." The economy on Earth was entirely run by the Agriculture and Mining Collective, to the point where there was no currency, only numbers in the A&MC computers, numbers not recognized as meaning anything outside of the Collective. What little money his parents had didn't even exist up here. And his uncle was not a rich man; sharing what little he had with his nephew was sacrifice enough. Omesh wouldn't ask him for more.

"I wouldn't worry about it too much. You can fix things; there's always money to be had in that."

"Like you know," Omesh said, trying not to sound bitter. One of them was hiding in a duct, and the other was safe, warm, and well fed in his own bedroom. "Did I mention the goondas? I wasn't exaggerating..."

"I didn't think you were," Ali said. "Although the goondas might just be the tip of a much more sophisticated iceberg. I think it's likely someone knows where you are."

"What?"

"The security system is aware of you and is busily installing a tracker program inside your computer."

"It's what?!"

"Relax, I've already downloaded a little thing of my own that will remove it once you're offline. They'll think they have you tagged when you unplug, but that program of theirs will never get a chance to run."

"Thanks."

"Don't mention it. But they'll still know where you accessed their network."

Omesh looked over his shoulder. Was he being paranoid, or were those whirring sounds growing closer? Still, he heard no sounds of people in the ducts with him.

"I should run."

"Yes, I think you'd better. Find a way to call me again, though."

"Yeah," Omesh said, lost in thought. "My parents—"

"I'll call them. At a decent hour," Ali added. "I'll tell them a modified sort of truth so they won't worry. But yaar, call me back so *I* don't worry."

"I will. Thanks."

"That's what best friends are for, yeah?" Ali said. Then the screen winked out. Omesh detached the cable.

It was awkward trying to run bent over, computer in one hand and bag in the other, but there wasn't enough room to put the duffel on his back.

He paused to listen each time his duct crossed another, but the whirring sounded the same everywhere. What was he hearing? Some sort of air movement, fans or something? It couldn't be following him; it was too pervasive.

At least Ali hadn't rubbed it in—that perhaps Omesh had made the wrong choice going into space. Not that he'd disagreed that Omesh had needed to leave home, not Ali with his tremendous love for his own kid sister; that Ali had understood. But taking the Collective's alternative of leaving Earth struck Ali too much like giving in to a battle that ought to be fought. Omesh couldn't do it; he couldn't make a stand that would put his family in even more trouble with the Collective. Just disappearing hadn't been an option.

As much as Ali liked to tease him about the girl they'd met in Goa, Omesh knew that, at the heart of it, he was right. If Omesh found her, she would do anything she could to help him. It was just that the Collective would need absolute proof that he was no longer alive and on Earth, and the only absolute proof they'd accept was their own. So he'd taken the shuttle ride. But he was glad Ali wasn't rubbing it in; at the moment, squatting in the smoldering remains of Mumbai sounded like heaven, and if he closed his eyes, he could just taste the tangy, tamarind taste of her kisses.

The whirring sound intruded on his memories, growing suddenly louder to his left, and he turned to see a small, flat form moving towards him down the duct. He looked the other way and saw another to his right, boxing him in. Omesh pulled his multi-tool out of his pocket and opened the small blade, the closest thing he had to a weapon.

Then he realized what the whirring was: little rotating brushes on the bottoms and sides of the approaching objects. They were cleaning robots. Omesh laughed to himself, closing the blade and putting the tool back in his pocket. The cleaners stopped just short of him and he had the distinct impression they were watching him like little dogs.

Then he saw the camera eyes flush with their front panels. They *were* watching him. No—someone, somewhere, was watching him through these robots. He remembered what Ali had said about the security on the network; too sophisticated to be goondas. Omesh picked up his bag and stepped over one of the cleaners. It didn't make a move, but he could see another camera eye on the back panel, and as he moved down the duct, both cleaners followed him, keeping a respectful distance much like the goondas had.

Where robots spied, men would surely follow;

he needed to get out of the ducts, and fast. But every grill he passed was firmly secured. He ran up and down the shorter tunnels, trying to find a grill that was at least loose or wiggled a little, when two more robots appeared before him down the main tunnel. He could step over them again easily enough, but he was getting anxious to get out of this rat's maze. He went back down the short tunnel to the last grill he'd checked and rattled it again, but still there was no give. Desperate, he set down his duffel bag, laid on the floor of the duct, and began to pummel the grill with both feet.

"Hey, whatcha doin' in there?"

Omesh lifted his head to look between his feet. A young kid was looking back at him through the grill.

"Can you let me out?" Omesh asked.

"It's screwed shut," the kid said with a shrug.

"I have a tool," Omesh said, pulling it out of his pocket. The kid snatched it from him when he poked it through one of the holes in the grill and Omesh had a sudden fear that he was going to run off with it, but he only turned it over in his hands until he found the proper screw attachment and opened it up to set to work on the screws.

"Thanks; you're a lifesaver," Omesh said as the boy worked.

"You're new here," the kid said, his eyes intent on his task. "It's tough here for new people."

"You should have some sort of welcoming committee. Help us settle in," Omesh said half jokingly.

"I'm guessing you've met the welcoming committee already," the kid said. "I let you out, where are you going to go?"

"I don't know. I'm not even supposed to be here; I need to get a ride to the *Dauntless*, or better yet, to Chandi V."

"I know people," the kid said as one screw fell to the floor with a clatter and he started on the next. Omesh looked back to see the robots watching him from the end of the tunnel. "Rides are expensive."

"I don't doubt. I'll have to earn money first," Omesh said.

"That's not easy, either," the kid said.

"I can fix things."

The kid paused at that to look him in the eye. "What kind of things?"

"All kinds of things. Machines and computers and engines."

"Cool." He focused again on his task and the second screw dropped to the ground. "I make you a deal."

"What sort of deal?"

"I help you, you help me. I know people. I can find someone to sell you a ride who won't rip you off much. And I help you find fixing jobs. You can stay with my family. We can hide you from the gang-bangers."

"That's a lot to offer. What do I do for you?"

"Teach me," the kid said. The third screw came free, and he swung the grill on the remaining screw until there was enough space for Omesh to crawl out. He closed the multi-tool and held it in his palm for just a moment with a look of such longing before handing it back.

"Teach you what?"

"How to fix stuff. I collect broken things, and I try to fix them, but I don't know what I'm doing, really."

Omesh looked him over. He was easily the skinniest kid Omesh had ever seen, the button-up shirt hanging off him. "How old are you?" he asked.

"My name is Manoj and I'm nine. Well, almost nine."

"Manoj, you've got yourself a deal."

Manoj nodded solemnly, then led the way farther down the tunnel to a large, open space. It didn't have the height of the atrium, but the far wall was somewhere beyond what Omesh could see in the flickering lights of cook fires and random LEDs. The floor was scuffed and scarred, but there were occasional painted lines running over it, faded but just visible. Omesh guessed this had been some sort of vehicle storage bay, wheeled vehicles to traverse the endless hallways of the space station. That was just a guess; there were no vehicles to be seen now. People were clustered in groups around light sources, but there were no walls between, only the faded lines on the floor. But Omesh would swear from the way the groups were clustered that the people were using the lines as boundaries.

"This is my mom," Manoj said, walking up to a large group around one dying cook fire. There were two women there, Manoj's mom and another woman who didn't seem to be any relation. There were no men there, only children. Omesh counted seven, none older than Manoj. "Mom, this is—"

"Omesh Nasrin," Omesh said, bowing in namaste out of habit. The woman smiled a weary smile and gave him a gracious salaam, which he returned. Manoj walked right up to the cook pot, ladling out a portion into a dented metal bowl and handing it to Omesh as he rattled away what Omesh guessed was the story of how they'd met and what they'd agreed. Omesh could read a little Arabic, but he couldn't possibly follow this rapid monologue, although Manoj was an animated speaker and Omesh could work out the high points of the story.

He looked around but didn't see any utensils, so he dug out his multi-tool and used a knife to spear the bits floating in the soup. There was no meat, and the veg had been cooked down to the point of losing its identity as a distinct item of foodstuff, and the entire thing was mostly hot water, but Omesh pounded it down. He hadn't realized how hungry he was until he'd slaked his thirst on the broth. He handed the bowl back to Manoj, hungrier than ever, but saying nothing but thanks. Manoj, the skinniest boy he had ever seen five minutes ago, was downright meaty next to his siblings. In the morning, he would find a food vendor and spend the money he had left over from selling his things to buy breakfast for all of them.

Then he and Manoj would get to work. Perhaps it was a good thing, this little delay in his trip. It would take some time to earn the money he'd need, and he'd fill every possible minute of that time teaching Manoj everything he knew about fixing things. If Ali was right and there was always money to be had in repair, Manoj's family would never be so lean again.

CHAPTER FIVE

RABIA

"Wʜᴀᴛ's ᴡʀᴏɴɢ, Rᴀʙɪᴀ?" Sɪ Fᴜ ᴀsᴋᴇᴅ.

Rabia blinked and focused her eyes on her teacher, sitting across from her on the floor. "I'm doing something wrong?"

"Are you?" he countered.

She didn't know how to answer that; she was sure she had been practicing her breathing correctly.

"What are you feeling?" Si Fu asked.

"Relaxed?"

"Hmm." He was fussing with his clothes, adjusting the cuffs of his worn old shirt. He didn't have to say out loud that he didn't believe her; it was clear enough.

"Well, my head aches, I'm not sure why. And my eyes are achy, too," she admitted.

"Silly girl," Si Fu said. "When I told you to focus on the end of your nose, I meant focus your mind, not your eyes."

"How do I look at the end of my nose with my mind?" Rabia asked.

"Not look—focus!"

Rabia bit her lip. She got that there was a distinction, but she had no idea how to actually do it.

"And your head aches because you keep holding your breath," he went on.

"No, I'm not. I'm going slow, in and out, mouth and nose, just like you said to."

"You need to let it flow naturally," Si Fu said. "But you don't; you try to control it. You need to relax your mind first. Your body will follow."

Rabia nodded absently. She was trying to will herself to relax, and she knew that was wrong. You couldn't make an effort to do something effortless. She just wasn't sure how else to go about it. She kept hoping she would just do it once, by accident. Then maybe she could do it again.

"Enough work for today, I think," Si Fu said, reaching for his staff to get up from the floor. But once on his feet, he wobbled as if about to faint. Rabia jumped up to steady him, but he had already recovered and warded her off with an up-raised hand.

"Are you all right?"

"Well enough," Si Fu said, but Rabia thought he looked a bit gray.

"Can I get you something? Tea?"

"I'm fine," he said and straightened up. "But if you like, perhaps you can fetch me some vindaloo?"

"Sure. I'll be right back." She ran upstairs for his covered pot, then back down and out the hidden doorway, jumping to the alley behind the butcher's. He had just gotten a load of something in; she could hear his cleaver thwacking away and a thin rivulet of gore was running through a gap in his wall and across the alley to disappear in another gap between ships. She wondered where that ended up and had a sudden vision of a vast reservoir of all sorts of nasty pooling at gravity's end. She could almost smell it. She shook the image out of her head with a shiver. Then she headed to the curry stand, swinging the pot as she walked, happy at least to be done with chi gung for the day.

Rabia didn't feel like she was making much progress. Si Fu had taught her chi gung meditations, and she had been practicing them every day for more than a month, focusing on her breath as she moved oh so slowly through the forms or, like today, doing a still meditation. He had also told her of things he had read once, long ago when he had been a young man studying medicine in Beijing, articles about the physiology of anger, the genetics and body chemistry involved.

"Anger feeds on anger," he had told her. "The longer you let it go, the harder it is to stop it."

Rabia nodded along. She had a deep suspicion of pithy phrases. And the books he remembered never existed in the library archives when she searched for them on her computer back in the station. The archives were spotty when it came to fiction, but in a field like science or medicine it was surprising to look for something and not find it, even if the original was in Mandarin.

Si Fu was unbelievably old. If he had really lived in Beijing when it was still a crowded city with medical schools, he would have to be well past one hundred now. Perhaps his memory was fading. It certainly seemed like his stories of his angry youth were filtered through some sort of lens. How could Si Fu, who never got so much as annoyed as far as she could tell, have been a talks-with-his-fists teenager? She suspected he was either making it up or remembering it as more than it had been.

Not that she said so. A year ago, she would have argued, or at least scoffed and teased. But Si Fu was talking more and more of his youth these days, even as he looked more and more tired. She hadn't yet talked to him about what she would do when she reached her birthday and had to leave home, but in her mind, she had already planned to move in with him. He needed someone there with him, and it was a not-too-scary first step away from home for her. If not for the fact that she knew it would break her mother's heart, she would move to Barnacle Town now. She didn't like thinking about how Si Fu got by on the days when she couldn't come to see him.

"Hello, Prakash," she said, hefting Si Fu's pot up on the counter.

"Hello, Rabia; always nice to see you," Prakash said, but Rabia's eyes were on the boy next to him. She had never seen him before. "This is my nephew, Omesh."

"Omesh, you've finally arrived!" She beamed at both of them, knowing how worried Prakash had been when his nephew had been stuck in Haven for so long, out of reach of any of his family.

"Yeah, just last night," Omesh said. He didn't look much like his uncle. Prakash was tall and wiry with a hawkish nose and tightly curly hair.

His nephew was just her height and rounder in the face. She bet he got his cheeks pinched a lot when he was a kid.

"How's Anjali doing?" Rabia asked.

"Well, but tired. I was just heading upstairs to check on her. Omesh, you have things?"

"Yes, uncle; I'll be fine," Omesh answered.

"I'll be back down before the dinner rush," Prakash said. He ran up the first three steps but paused and turned back again. "If a redheaded samurai orders, see his money before he eats!"

"Yes, uncle," Omesh answered. After a moment's musing, though, he turned to speak to his uncle again, but Prakash was gone. "Is that a Barnacle Town proverb?" he asked Rabia.

"Doubtful," Rabia said. "This isn't really the proverb-generating crowd. There's a sumo school here. Maybe he's talking about one of the students. Although they are very strict about the Japanese-ness of their students. I know some local boys who tried to apply for admission but were turned down. I doubt they'd let their students color their hair either. They're a conservative bunch."

The boy nodded, still mulling it over.

"So you're Prakash's nephew, the one from Uttar Pradesh?" she asked.

"Gujarat, actually, but I spend my summers in UP with my grandparents, Prakash's parents. Or I used to."

"Where's Gujarat, then?"

"Just south of Pakistan."

"I suppose none of that matters much now?" Rabia asked.

"You mean 'All Countries Are One'?" Omesh asked. "That may be the official policy, but erasing the lines on a map tends not to affect people's hearts much. My parents' farm is on the western edge of the Thar Desert, if you prefer natural landmarks."

"My Earth geography isn't very good," Rabia admitted.

"I bet you know more about Earth than I know about space."

"It's hard to tell. Most of what I 'know' I suspect is propaganda."

He clearly didn't know how to answer this, and she suspected she was making him uncomfortable. Well, he wasn't the first.

"I'm here for vindaloo, as spicy as you can make it, please," Rabia said. "It's for my si fu. I don't think he can taste much anymore except your uncle's vindaloo. He loves it."

"My mother follows the same recipe, I think,"

Omesh said. "Very fiery, even for a Desi like me." He was in the kitchen, but she could still half see him as he stirred something. He was wearing a brilliant green shirt that went down to his knees over jeans that still looked new and thick-soled sandals. Very far removed from either corporate jumpsuits or Barnacle Town hand-me-downs. He looked more like a character from a movie than a real person.

He brought out the steaming pot full of vindaloo and Rabia dug out the mishmash of coins that were the usual Barnacle Town currency. Omesh dropped them into the reader one at a time, each coin causing a green light to flash briefly.

"What happens if you get a red light?" she asked.

Omesh looked up as if to answer but said nothing, looking past her intently. Rabia turned to see Alain and Tom loitering in the doorway.

"Not today, boys," Rabia said, setting the lid on the pot and latching it down.

"Not for you, Jumpsuit, no," Alain said, and Tom smirked. "Where's your uncle, boy?"

"Upstairs. My aunt isn't feeling well and—"

"We all weep for you," Alain interrupted. "I guess you'll have to take the message."

"I can do that," Omesh said uncertainly.

"No," Rabia said. "He won't."

Alain sighed dramatically. He slumped against a support beam, arm flung over his eyes. The beam shifted slightly.

"Is this the one?" he asked, looking up. Tom nodded.

"Come on, man," Rabia said. "If you touch that, you know I have to kill you." None of Si Fu's tricks were going to help her now, she could see. Closing her eyes and focusing within might keep her from getting angry, but it would also make her foolishly vulnerable. And she couldn't stay calm while she watched Alain tear the curry stand down. What did Si Fu expect her to do in this situation?

Alain leaned back a bit, and the beam shifted another inch or so. Rabia sighed and stepped forward. She didn't raise her hands or make an aggressive move, but Alain knew her well enough to know that by the time she did, she'd already be hitting him. He straightened up, putting his hands up in a defensive stance, and Tom moved to cover the doorway.

"I don't think I understand what's going on here," Omesh said, breaking the moment. Alain was making little come-hither motions with his hands, and Rabia was tempted to take him up on it. But he was no longer touching the beam. She decided that was victory enough for now and went back to Si Fu's pot of vindaloo. Omesh was looking at her expectantly.

"Barnacle Town has no government," she explained. "These two hoods work for bigger hoods who have taken it upon themselves to make rules for the rest of you."

"Which doesn't really concern you corporate types, Jumpsuit," Alain added, hands still up and moving, as if he didn't trust her to not strike him at any time. Omesh was looking her over, noticing her bright blue jumpsuit for the first time.

"You are the authority here?" he asked Alain.

"Yes," Alain said at the same instant Rabia said, "No." She glared at him, but he stared right back at her, not backing down.

"What rule did Prakash break?" he asked at last.

"The problem with these rules, they don't tell you what they are until after they've decided you've broken them," Rabia said. Alain ignored her.

"He's added to our already overly large population without permission," Alain said, finally dropping his hands. Tom resumed leaning against the doorway, arms folded.

"Oh," Omesh said, glancing up at the sleeper pod above them, then back down at himself. "Oh."

"Oh indeed. We all share this space, and it's a small space," Alain said. "Someone needs to start taking a lead on these issues before we end up eating each other like trapped rats."

"I don't disagree with that," Rabia said. "But your methods?"

"Do you have any idea what's going on these days?" Alain asked. He took a step closer to her, but it wasn't a threatening move. He was talking to her almost as if they were still friends. Funny that should make her feel so lonely. "The cost of bribes to keep the air and water flowing has sky-rocketed. Who do you think pays these bribes in a town with no taxes? Whoever can afford to. Namely, the dons."

"I would figure their own self-interest is dri-ving this," Rabia said.

"Self-interest, really? The bribes they pay give air to everyone, get the food shipments through the station hallways," Alain said.

"And now they want the power over everyone in return." Rabia shook her head. "No, you're going about this all wrong."

"No, you've never understood. We are nothing to you people, nothing. Only the dons are strong enough to negotiate with your corporate leaders," Alain said.

"You're the one not understanding," Rabia

said. "You have no idea what it's like on the other side of that airlock. It's not nirvana, there."

"I've seen more than you think I have," Alain said.

"What have you seen?" Rabia asked. Perhaps that had come out too sarcastic; Alain crossed his arms and refused to say more. He didn't take a step back, but he might as well have. The distance between them was back. He was out in the streets threatening people on his own now, not just playing backup to his brother. Rabia knew they would never be friends again.

"What about me?" Omesh asked.

"There's no point in kicking his ass; it's not like he has anyplace else to go," Rabia pointed out.

"It was more about setting an example to others. Which was why we were supposed to kick Prakash's ass."

"I can't let you do that," Omesh said.

"Nor I," Rabia added. "Why don't you convince your boss to let this one go?"

"Yeah, I don't think that's going to work," Alain said.

"Make it a trade. I'll dig around my end of things, look for information that could be useful to the dons."

"From where? You don't work, don't attend

corporate school. You're not exactly in the loop," Alain pointed out.

"But I know someone who is in all the loops, including the ones she has no business being in. I'll have *her* dig into it. Deal?"

"I'll present it to my boss. He's the one to say deal or no deal," Alain said. "Of course it would grease the wheels if you'd agree to fight again."

"No, no, and no," Rabia said, pulling a thick pair of gloves out of one of her pockets and sliding them on before picking up the pot. "My arena days are over."

"You'll cave," Alain promised, but he and Tom left for the time being.

"Dons," Omesh said. "That's funny."

"It's an Italian thing."

"Yeah, but not just. That's what they called themselves in Mumbai back in the day as well." He slumped onto the tall stool behind the counter with a weary sigh. "My uncle says I'll grow to like it here, but I don't know."

"Hey, you're just having a rough welcome. Barnacle Town has lots of good points or I wouldn't be coming here every day," Rabia said.

"It's better than the last place I was, but different. It all feels so temporary, so tenuous," Omesh said, looking around at the curry stand.

"Well, if you're thinking you should get that

support fixed, I wouldn't disagree with you," Rabia said. "The butcher's boys reset it last time, but that's only going to hold until the next time someone decides to start pushing on it."

"If I had materials and tools, I could anchor it more firmly," Omesh said. "But I've been to the markets here and there's nothing useful."

"No, not in the regular markets. Boy, I'm going to have to teach you how to shop."

"Huh?"

"There's an art to finding what you need in Barnacle Town." Rabia considered the implications of her next offer for a fraction of a second, but no longer. If it was for Prakash... "I tell you what, make me a list of what you need and the next time I'm here, I'll have it all for you."

"For real?"

"Yeah. Just don't ask where it came from. And you'll have to write it by hand, no computer trail."

Omesh looked around for something to write on, then wandered back into the kitchen. When he returned, he was holding a large scrap of canvas from a potato sack. "Just to fix the beam, or can you get me things to fix the space upstairs as well?"

"Write it all down and I'll get what I can," Rabia said. This was going to be tricky. Anything that involved her sister was always tricky. But she owed it to Prakash. He watched out for Si Fu when she couldn't.

"How much will we owe?" Omesh asked as he handed over the list. Rabia caught herself just in time from praising his penmanship. She'd sound like a total dork, but she'd never seen such an elegant script before, and written on a potato sack, of all things. Writing by hand was not a skill particularly valued in the corporate schools and hence was just barely taught. She had assumed Earth schools would be much the same.

"It's not going to cost me anything, so nothing," Rabia said at last, slipping the list into her pocket. "Give my regards to your uncle." Then she hoisted the vindaloo and started down the lane.

She called for Si Fu to lower the hook for the vindaloo as soon as she had popped open the door behind the butcher's, but he didn't answer. Rabia sighed. She wanted to tell him all about how she had not picked a fight with Alain, had actually had a semi-intelligent conversation with him, but if Si Fu was napping, it would have to wait. She scaled the wall, then lowered the hook, swinging it back and forth until she snagged the pot handle and hoisted it up.

She crossed the practice yard with its racks of staffs and wooden swords, the delicate fans and tasseled tai chi swords hanging from the walls, and up the staircase to the loft. She was halfway up the steps when she saw him lying on the floor surrounded by broken china. The vindaloo fell from her hands to bounce and roll down the stairs as she ran forward to drop to his side, turning him over.

He was still warm. She laid him flat and tried to revive him with CPR, counting and pumping, then stopping to blow breath into his lungs over and over. His ribs cracked under her hands and his mouth tasted sour, but his heart refused to beat. She kept it up long past the point where she had any hope of doing any good.

Finally, it was the table that made her stop. It was too close over Si Fu's body, and she kept hitting her head on it as she pumped at his chest. When it caught her just under her eyebrow, making her vision gray out, she had had enough. The adrenaline rushing through her body wasn't doing anything to bring Si Fu back. It was just building and building. Throwing the table over the side of the loft to smash on the practice yard below didn't bring him back either, but it burned off some of that adrenaline before it could drive her completely mad. The chairs soon followed, then the bedroll, but that wasn't satisfying at all the way it fluttered down. What else could smash? She needed the sound of it, the feel of things breaking apart.

Then a sudden thought struck her. What would Si Fu say if he could see her now? Rabia collapsed on the floor among the already broken bits of china, tearing at her hair as she sobbed.

But they were sobs of anger and frustration. The grief would have to come after.

CHAPTER SIX

TAKASHI

THE OTHER RIKISHI MAY HAVE BEEN TAUNTING HIM, Tak wasn't sure. He had learned more Japanese in the last six weeks than he would have ever thought possible, but the more colloquial speech he heard outside the classroom in the bathhouse and during practice was harder to pick up, particularly when it was being mumbled out of the corner of the mouth by someone who didn't necessarily want the instructor to hear. Tak didn't let it bother him; he already knew that no one in the school was his friend.

The instructor spoke the word, and the match began. Tak and his opponent both charged at each other. The other rikishi got his arms around Tak and attempted to lift him up off the sandy floor, but Tak dropped into a crouch, slipping under one massive arm. He caught hold of his opponent's sumo belt and pulled. The rikishi tried to pull away but stumbled over Tak's foot and fell to the ground with a dusty thud.

Tak returned to his starting position as his opponent got up from the floor and their instructor made some comments about the match. Tak didn't really listen. The nuances of sumo didn't interest him, so long as he had a place to sleep and food to eat. The food was too much of a bland thing for his tastes, but he had never seen such a beautiful place.

The sumo school was inside the hold of one of the big cargo haulers, the kind built to go to the moons of Neptune and back. This gave the school a large open space that was completely gated off from the rest of Barnacle Town. The hold was filled with wooden buildings and gardens, all lit from above with silk screens, both to hide the ceiling of the hold and to diffuse the light. The gardens were a decadent delight; Tak had never had the pleasure of drifting off to sleep to the sweet aroma of night-blooming jasmine before.

The identity of the school's patron was a closely guarded secret, but Tak had no doubt it was a corporation. No one else could afford to spend so much on beauty to be seen by so few.

The practice broke up as the white-belted sekitori entered the training ring. They were fresh from bed, their longer hair neatly combed and tied back. Several of the more experienced ones, the ones who had already won several tournaments, had little cabals of apprentices who followed them about, fetching water or helping to tie the massive sumo belts. Tak found the fawning stomach-turning, but there was no being a sekitori unless you had done your time as an apprentice.

Tak trailed behind the other blue-belted young rikishi to the bathhouse, filling a bucket at the faucet and finding a few square tiles of floor to call his own as he washed away the dust and sweat. The other rikishi laughed and joked together. Sometimes someone would look his way to see if he was sharing in their joke, but Tak seldom listened closely enough to know why anyone was laughing.

He tried not to hate his mother for sending him here with a mere handful of words in her native tongue. She must have known English was forbidden; funny, she had never mentioned it. He had spent a few miserable days letting it all just wash over him, getting cuffed about the ear or smacked with wooden swords for not following directions he hadn't understood. Then he had packed up his bag and walked back out the door.

He hadn't been out long. He had had the feeling of eyes on him from the minute he passed out of the school gates, and the eyes had been more numerous by the time he finally found some proper food—a really excellent chicken korma. By the time he had finished eating, the eyes had become entire bodies, street urchins loitering all around the curry stand, not bothering to pretend not to be watching him. As he got up to pay for his food, he saw the older boy, the one who had been in charge the night they'd given him his beating. Tak had tried to ignore him, focusing on counting out the coins. But the man behind the counter had a coin scanner, and it had flashed red for every coin he had. His gambling winnings weren't solid money, just a thin layer of shiny over a core of garbage.

"I'm sorry," Tak had mumbled, searching his pockets for anything of value he could offer, but there was nothing but the disk that was his sumo school admission.

"Here," the leader had said, appearing beside him and handing a few coins to the man behind the counter.

"Thank you, Alain," the curry-man had said. "And you, from now on, you pay in advance."

"Of course," Tak had said, deeply embarrassed.

"You'll keep that in mind the next time you're

out on a day pass," Alain had said, "from the school."

Which might not sound like a threat, but Tak had known it was. He was unwelcome in Barnacle Town, and very outnumbered. So he had gone back to the school and begun the work of trying to fit in. Mostly, he wasn't succeeding.

Tak dumped the last of the bathwater over his head and shook his hair vigorously. After toweling off, he pulled on his lightweight yukata. It was far too big, hanging from him like a sheet. He guessed this was meant to inspire him to get larger faster; he was one of the smallest wrestlers at the school.

Eating was definitely part of the job of being a sumo wrestler. He didn't really care for chankon-abe, the fattening-up stew that was the staple of sumo wrestlers. There was a rotating list of ingredients, so it was never the same stew twice. One day, the meat was chicken or beef, the next fish or pork, and the vegetables were always a hodge-podge of whatever could be bought at the market that day. Sometimes there were noodles in it; those were the best days. But mostly Tak had had enough of anything that tasted like miso to last him a lifetime. The solar system was full of spices, and he missed them.

Tak ate as much as he could stand, stuffed in a

bit more rice, then joined the other junior rikishi in spending the afternoon cleaning and scrubbing and mopping as the older ones shuffled off to their long baths and longer naps.

Except for Kenko, of course. Kenko would never choose soaking in a tub or dozing over tormenting Tak. All those cuffings and whacks he'd gotten for not understanding Japanese? Kenko had been the administrator of nearly all of them.

"What is this I've found, Takashi?" he taunted from the doorway of the kitchen. The other rikishi all carefully put their heads down, working furiously and hoping not to be noticed. Tak looked up with a sigh and saw Kenko waving a magazine about.

Wait, not a magazine. A catalog. A ship catalog.

"Give that back," Tak said, reaching for it. But Kenko was both taller and wider and easily whisked it out of reach.

"This is not on the list of approved personal items for rikishi," Kenko went on.

"It's reading material; it's allowed," Tak said, trying to catch it again. Kenko again kept it out of reach, but this time followed up with a ringing slap to Tak's ear.

"If it were in Japanese, it would be allowed. This is not in Japanese."

"Come on! None of the ship manufacturers print up Japanese catalogs."

"Did you check?"

Tak fumed. He had not in fact checked, but he hadn't needed to. They would as likely had catalogs printed in Latin. Japan was one of the hardest hit regions of the world during the plague, and its language was fast becoming a dead one. The sumo schools might be working hard to preserve it, but the world of commerce had long since let it go.

"Give it back."

"Or what, little rikishi?"

Tak had no answer. He could scarcely threaten Kenko without making the bigger rikishi laugh. But he wanted that catalog back.

Aside from the general unfriendliness of Barnacle Town, there was just one other reason to stick it out in sumo school: he was pretty good at the actual sumo. And being pretty good at it, he stood the chance to make some coin on his own. Not enough for a ship, maybe, but when his father returned in five years from his trip to the far moons, they could pool their money together and get a nice one, nicer than the one his father had lost.

But that was far in the future. Tak felt each one of those five years stretching out before him like each was its own infinite line. In the present, he was alone, far from either of his parents, having to make life-changing decisions all on his own. Like how much more humiliation he was willing to subject himself to.

While Tak was struggling with indecision, Kenko leaned around him and dropped the catalog into the wash water. Tak lunged for it, but the cheap synthetic paper was already pulp. He looked down at the morass of gray fluff occasionally dotted with the more stubborn of the inks, interspersed with the bubbles and oil slicks of the dishwater after too many chankonabe cooking pots.

Yes, he had kept that catalog hidden in his bedroll, taking sneaking looks at it whenever he could. But he didn't really need the pictures to keep his dream firm in his head, did he? He had long since memorized every ship's specs. The catalog was superfluous at this point. Wasn't it?

Strangely, he felt the pain of Kenko's blows before he even realized what the other boy was doing. But it had been worth it. Yes, he could close his eyes and see those ships anytime he wanted to. He could also close his eyes and remember the sight of Kenko blinking through the pulp and soap bubbles. It had clung there like a facial mask even as he had beaten Tak, then turned and cuffed the other rikishi who hadn't been able to restrain their laughter.

But Tak had had enough beatings for one day. When Kenko stopped smacking the others and swung the shinai back in Tak's direction, Tak put up a hand and caught the bamboo blade, tore it from Kenko's grip, and tossed it through the paper screen wall. Even though Tak would surely be the one laboriously re-papering the screen later, Kenko clearly found the idea of crashing through the flimsy wall to retrieve his weapon inconceivable. His face went from red to purple, but Tak didn't hang around to see what would come out when he finally stopped sputtering and started speaking. He left.

Not that he thought of really escaping. He would just be caught and returned by the street thugs again if he tried. But it was a free day for the older students; perhaps he could blend in so long as he was back by curfew. He had some real money now, won off his fellow students in an illicit late-night card game. He could deal with this place much better after he'd filled his belly with some tandoori chicken.

Tak was dressed in the yukata and geta that was the only clothing his lowly station allowed him. The yukata wasn't so bad; yes, it was basically just a bathrobe, but it said something about

Barnacle Town that it didn't raise any eyebrows. The geta, however, were elevated wooden sandals designed for walking over muddy ground, not for clambering up and over through the lanes of a town of derelict ships. They were hard to walk in, and everyone heard you coming.

There was a line of people at the curry stand already waiting to order. Tak took his place at the end, trying not to feel conspicuous, which is hard to do when you're wearing tall wooden sandals and a silk robe. Having spent half his life in free fall, he was acutely aware of how utterly impractical this outfit was, but how one dressed was just another aspect of sumo he had to fall in line with. It wasn't like he was going to be floating again anytime soon, as much as he missed it.

"What can I get you?" the kid behind the counter asked. Tak was relieved to see the man was nowhere in sight, but even so, he dropped his handful of coins on the counter.

"You should probably read these first, and then tell me what I can get," he said.

To Tak's embarrassment, the kid laughed out loud. "Sorry," he said, picking up the coins. "I just understood something."

"Oh, yeah?" Tak said as the boy dropped the coins into the reader. Each one got a green light.

"I can give you a bowl of anything, a basket of roti, and a pot of tea for that," the boy said.

"Tandoori chicken?"

"Surely."

Tak sat down at one of the tables and the boy brought him the pot of tea and a cup. He set down the teapot but paused with the cup halfway to the table as a procession of clopping feet in geta marched past. Tak didn't have to turn to know who it was: a troupe of older students, each chanting his name in a singsong. At least they weren't trying to haul him back to school; taunting Tak could handle.

"What's that they're saying?" the boy asked, frowning.

"O'Reilly," Tak said with a sigh. "My name. They are playing up the accent, with the *r*'s and the *l*'s. I assure you they all speak English just as well as you or I."

"O'Reirry," the boy repeated, then looked down at Tak and flushed. "Sorry."

"You almost had it," Tak said. "Shape your mouth like you want to make an *r*, but make an *l* instead."

"O'Reirry," he tried again, then laughed. Not a mocking laugh, more of an "isn't life absurd?" kind of laugh. Tak liked him at once. And not just because he hadn't had anyone remotely like a friend to talk to in weeks.

"My first name is Takashi. That they can pronounce. I prefer Tak, though."

"My name's Omesh Nasrin. Hard to butcher that." Then he was gone, back behind the counter to take the next order. It was the tail end of dinnertime, and most of the customers came in with their own pots to bring the food back to the nooks and crannies they called home and share it with their families.

There wasn't much to see in Barnacle Town, Tak remembered from his last trip out, so he lingered over his food, enjoying eating something that wasn't chankonabe. The others passed by a few more times with their taunting calls, but Tak didn't react, so they soon tired of that game.

He was the only one sitting at a table when the man came back out of the kitchen, looked around, then said something to Omesh in Hindi. Omesh answered and the man wiped his hands on a towel and went upstairs.

"Still hungry?" Omesh asked, bringing out another basket of roti. "Come sit at the counter and you can help me finish off the leftovers so I can scrub the pots." Tak didn't need to be asked twice. Omesh set out two plates, and they went pot by pot, sampling more dishes than Tak could even name.

"Your uncle is a good cook," Tak said.

"Nearly as good as my mother," Omesh said, sopping the last bits of sauce off his plate with a torn chunk of roti. "You're new to Barnacle Town too?"

"I've been here a couple of weeks, but they don't let us out of school much," Tak said. Which was a bit dishonest; it implied he'd been let out this time. "Before that, I lived on my father's ship. He did small deliveries around the inner solar system, so I grew up all over. So you just moved to Barnacle Town yourself?"

"Yeah," Omesh said. He seemed about to say more, but something in the street behind Tak distracted him. Tak turned to see a girl passing by the shop, a girl in a corporate jumpsuit with a long braid of bright pink hair that started from a top-knot and fell all the way to the small of her back.

"You know her?"

"Sort of," Omesh said. "Her name is Rabia. I've only talked with her once. She hasn't been in the shop for over a week."

"You sound worried. Does she normally eat a lot of curry?"

Omesh glanced over at him, as if unsure if he was joking. "I think those guys are following her."

It took Tak a moment to pick out what guys he was talking about. The one trailing behind was a tall, lanky fellow that didn't look particularly threatening. But the one in the lead was Alain.

"Should we help her?" Tak asked. Damsel in distress—that would be a good enough excuse for getting back to school after curfew, wouldn't it?

"She can take care of herself in a fair fight, I think," Omesh said, sounding uncertain.

"They're being awfully sneaky for guys looking for a fair fight." He didn't mention his past encounter with Alain, but it had been clear then that fair fights weren't really his modus operandi.

"Yeah. Let's catch up with her and warn her." Omesh led the way out of the shop and through the twisting lanes. Tak struggled to keep up in his clunky geta. The girl had already passed out of sight. They just caught a glimpse of the end of a shiny shirt flapping loosely from someone's shoulders as they ducked around a corner: one of her pursuers. Omesh jogged to chase it.

"Are you sure it's them?" Tak asked.

Omesh didn't answer, just kept running along.

They were in a part of Barnacle Town that Tak wasn't familiar with, with more residents and fewer shops. The lanes twisted, divided, and re-joined, sloping up or sloping down in no real pattern, and always they would catch just a glimpse of their quarry before losing them again.

Then they took one last turn into a courtyard between several tall stacks of shipping containers that had once been a multitude of colors, but whose paint had long since faded to a sort of vague sameness. The space was narrow but tall; looking up, Tak couldn't see the top of it, just stacks and stacks of containers fading into darkness. The containers had been divided into far too many apartments, holes welded through the walls every few feet marking the divisions. There was the sound of people all around them, but the courtyard was empty.

"Did they go up?" Tak wondered, looking up at the ladders and balconies that hung treacherously from the open ends of the containers. Some had people sitting in front of their doorways, women peeling vegetables or children playing games with balls or tokens. A few looked down at the two of them, but no one gave any sign of having just let someone inside.

"Have you seen a girl go by here, one with bright pink hair?" Omesh asked the nearest woman. "I'm afraid she might be in trouble."

"They'll all be in trouble if the corporation catches them. Not that anyone ever listens to me," the woman grumbled, then gathered up her sewing and went back into her apartment, shutting an irregularly shaped door with a bang.

"What the hell is she talking about?" Tak asked.

Omesh shrugged, tugging at his lip as he walked around, searching the courtyard.

Tak was just about to suggest that maybe they had lost them a turn or two back when an extremely dirty little boy with flinty eyes stepped out of the shadows, hand held out.

"If you want to see the fight, it's going to cost you some coin, brothers," he said.

"The fight?" Tak repeated.

Omesh leaned in to speak close to his ear as the boy waited with hand out. "Those two guys who were following her? I recognized one of them. He had a friend who wanted her to fight for his brother. She refused, but..."

"Maybe they weren't following her to ambush her then," Tak said. "Maybe they just all happened to be going this way. And they always walk like suspicious creeps."

"Well, I'm going in. You coming?"

"Sadly, I spent all my money on curry."

Omesh pulled some coins from his pocket and pressed them into the boy's palm. "Enough for two?" he asked.

"Yeah, sure," the boy said with a grin, the coins

disappearing from his hand, although Tak saw no pockets in the ragged shorts which were the only thing the boy wore. More than enough for two, by the looks of that grin. It occurred to Tak that Omesh was a bit of a rube.

"Which way?" Omesh asked.

"Through that hatch and straight on to the core," the boy said.

Tak looked at the hatch. It was like a cupboard door; there would be crawling involved, and he was not really dressed for it.

"What's the core?" Omesh whispered to him.

"The core of the space station, I assume; the hub of the wheel," he whispered back.

Omesh opened the door and got down on his knees, and Tak squatted to peer over his shoulder. It was pitch black inside. "That means this passage goes through Barnacle Town *and* through the corporation. Tell me, boy, does your secret entrance have a secret elevator?"

"Kinda," the boy said.

"What's that mean?" Tak demanded, but the boy just grinned.

"Coming?" Omesh called back, already lost in the darkness.

Tak looked back over his shoulder. He should be heading back to school. If he got back after curfew, he would be punished, worse than for just sneaking out. And worse than the punishment would be Kenko's glee as he administered that punishment.

"Yeah, I'm coming," he said, trying to tie the ends of his yukata out of the way before dropping to his knees. And here he'd thought there was little chance of having to wear this outfit in free fall. But he had to go. He had a pretty good idea what was taking place here, and Omesh would stick out like the rube he was. If he had any more money on him, he would likely lose it, either to a pickpocket or to a small-scale grifter. Someone should have his back.

The crawling passage was nowhere near as long as he had feared, but that was only because it ended in a small room at the bottom of a vertical shaft just large enough for the ladder it contained. At least there was light here, a few dim red bulbs set just far enough apart for no part of the shaft to be in complete darkness.

It was a long way up.

"This doesn't look safe," Omesh said. Tak thought at first he was talking about the ladder that stretched on into infinity. Then he saw what was on the floor, a sort of platform attached to the side rails of the ladder by pairs of wheels like a car on some crazy vertical roller coaster.

"Kind of an elevator?" Tak guessed. Omesh

dropped to one knee to examine the mechanism. It looked sturdy enough to Tak, but then Omesh cast a surreptitious glance his way and the cause of his worry was clear. Tak had the sudden urge to point out that he was still the smallest rikishi at the school. Instead, he looked up again. "I think there's another one on its way up. I can see more lightbulbs than before."

"I guess we hold on to these straps up here and stand on the platform," Omesh said.

"I think the straps are for coming back down," Tak guessed. "If this goes all the way to the core, we're going to need something that will tow us back down to gravity."

"Good point. Ready?" Omesh pushed the obvious button on the mechanism and they began to move up with a frightening velocity. Omesh jumped back away from the ladder rungs whizzing by and Tak tried to make more room for him, but the walls rushing past were already tickling at the hem of his yukata.

The line of lightbulbs overhead was getting shorter and Tak had the horrible thought that they were about to ram into the underside of the elevator platform that had gone up before them. Then a face appeared over the edge, suddenly enough to make him jump. The head pulled away again as the platform reached the end of the ladder and promptly stopped. As neither of them had been holding on to the straps, they both kept moving, past the boy and out into the unlit expanse of the core. Tak let the momentum take him, glancing back over his shoulder to see what could be the twin of the grubby boy they'd paid at the door tethered to the top of the shaft, calmly removing their platform from the top of the ladder and letting it go just out of the way.

Omesh flailed about, finally catching hold of Tak's sleeve. He seemed to be resisting the urge to climb onto his back like a baby monkey with its mother. Not that Tak wasn't having problems of his own; he had been right about the yukata not being a suitable garment. Aside from floating away from his body to show everyone far more of his increasingly massive thighs than he wanted to share, it was far too lightweight for the sudden chill of the core.

"First time in free fall?" Tak asked.

"No," Omesh said with great dignity. "It's my third."

"No joke?" Tak asked. "I didn't even know it was possible, to go through your whole life without moving in and out of free fall. Not unless you're rich enough to travel in the big cruiser ships instead of shuttles." Tak looked over Omesh's clothes. They were of good quality and new, but not particularly swank. "You don't look that rich. Where'd you live before Barnacle Town?"

"Earth."

"Oh. Well, I guess that would explain it."

"Indeed."

The core was an open chamber crisscrossed with girders, girders which were currently crawling with the street folk of Barnacle Town, from the youngest of urchins to the oldest of crusty old space sailors, all cheering and catcalling at something Tak couldn't quite see. They were wearing the usual Barnacle Town ragamuffin garb and didn't seem to mind the way their breath fogged, almost seeming to shine in the fluorescent light.

The comment the woman had made about the corporation made sense now. They certainly would be irate, to find so many unauthorized personnel in the heart of their station. Someone somewhere had bought off a security guard, and probably more than one. And had doctored sensors and cameras as well, surely.

He thought he knew what was going on here, and it was big money—by Barnacle Town standards, anyway. Tak had been to many free fall fights on many space stations. Most had been held in claustrophobic little arenas made by pushing the shipping containers in the docks as tight against the walls as they would go. Some had been held in unexpectedly empty storage bays after some cargo ship had been delayed en route; those had had the feel of a carnival, all that openness for spacers to spread out and mingle in. But he had never seen one held in a space like this.

"Let's get closer," Tak said, catching Omesh around the collar to help him over to one of the girders. Then they edged their way in and around the other spectators until they could see what everyone was watching.

The crowd, either clinging to girders or free-floating, had left a goodly sized open sphere, the free fall equivalent of a boxing ring. And in the center of the sphere, facing off against a dock-worker three times her size, was the girl Omesh had been looking for.

CHAPTER SEVEN

OMESH

OMESH HAD A SICK FEELING IN HIS STOMACH THAT was only partly due to the horrible sensation of constantly falling. She had told those two hoods she wouldn't fight, so why was she here now? Because of his uncle?

Two weeks had passed since that day, and no one else had stopped by to threaten him or his uncle. But he hadn't seen Rabia either, or her vindaloo-loving si fu. One morning he had found a crate full of the things from the list he had given Rabia waiting outside the curry shop door. Just the supplies, no note. He had been looking forward to talking with her again. Omesh didn't know what had happened to make her just drop out of sight like that.

Now there she was, fighting, her long braid spinning around her like a pink ribbon as she danced out of reach of the man with arms like cannons. She had discarded her bright blue jumpsuit, favoring a skin-tight pair of shorts and a half-top that left nothing for her opponent to catch hold of. Her feet were bare, but so were those of her opponent. Whether this was an advantage in fighting or in bouncing off the girders that marked off the corners of their irregular sphere, Omesh couldn't say. She clearly had hotter blood than he did. He had been cold constantly since leaving Earth; here in the core it was downright arctic. She was working hard, jumping and twisting and grabbing to redirect her motion, but Omesh doubted any amount of exercise would make him inclined to take off his shoes and shirt here. It felt like he would lose flesh just touching one of the metal girders.

"She's good," Tak said appreciatively. "That fellow is never going to land a blow, mark my words. She's done this before."

"I don't know," Omesh said. The guys in the curry shop had seemed intimidated by her, but he had never actually seen her do anything aggressive. At the moment, she looked horribly outmatched. But as she sailed across the sphere, she looked back over her shoulder at her burly opponent, a mischievous grin lighting up her face. She wasn't worried at all.

Omesh had never met anyone remotely like her; not even that girl in Goa had been this bold. Her devil-may-care attitude was frightening and appealing all at once. She turned herself about to face her opponent, long, bare arms extended like bird wings, legs already curling back in preparation for her next move.

The dockworker waited for Rabia to make her move. She barely touched off one of the girders at the edge of the sphere, sending herself back out into the center, arms wide and braid trailing along behind her. Then he launched himself off his girder, sailing like a juggernaut through the open space. Omesh gauged his trajectory, then gauged Rabia's. He was going to hit her, and there was nothing she could do to change her path now.

"She's got him now," Tak said. "Overconfident ass that he is."

"What?" Omesh asked, but he couldn't take his eyes off the point where their two paths would meet. Rabia didn't even seem to notice the large man about to barrel into her; she certainly wasn't looking his way.

What exactly happened, Omesh couldn't say; it went by too fast. The man had reached her, just as he had intended, but she caught him and swung herself onto his back, letting his own greater momentum carry both of them. Then her hands did something subtle to the back of his neck, something short and jabby, and the man just went limp. He didn't even attempt to stop himself from ramming the girder on the far side, taking it right on the top of his head with a loud crunch.

The long, narrow space resounded with the cries of the crowd—cheers from those who had bet on Rabia and loud taunts from those who had not. Rabia spun away from the dead weight of her dazed opponent, a move almost like a floating dance, her braid spinning around her once more. There was nothing to slow the velocity of her spin and Omesh felt like he was going to puke just watching it, but Rabia kept her wits about her, stopping her motion with a soft touch to the girder above her, proof that even in that tight spin she had never lost her sense of her surroundings.

"Oh yeah. She's good," Tak said. "Maybe the best I've seen."

"Best at what?" Omesh asked, able to turn and fix Tak with a look now that the fight had stopped.

"It's called zero G arena fighting. Every station has a version of it."

Omesh shut his eyes, but that made the feeling

in his gut that he was falling, falling, falling stronger, and he quickly opened them again.

"She's going to fight again," Tak said conversationally.

"Rabia fans, are you?" a man next to them asked. "Personally, I liked her better when her hair was short, spiky, and green. She lacked skill, but man did she have a taste for blood. This is all too pretty for me. It's like she thinks she's a dancer now."

"She won the match," Tak pointed out. The man dismissed that with a wave and a crude sound.

"What changed?" Omesh asked.

"Besides her hair?" the man asked. "Don't know. I heard she had fallen in with some old teacher of the pacifist school. She stopped coming to the fights, anyway. She's back now. Who knows? One hard tap on that pretty little nose of hers and she might get that old bloodlust back."

Omesh felt the bile moving up the back of his throat. It wasn't just the free fall either.

"Who's this fellow?" another spectator asked the man who was talking to them.

"New guy. His name wasn't on the roster; he must be a last-minute addition."

They all watched the next opponent moving

around the arena, getting a feel for the space before the fight began. He had taken off his shirt and
shoes, his skin shining palely against the black silk
of his pants. It wasn't spacer-pasty pale, though;
there was a definite touch of pink to it. This boy
had spent time in real atmosphere-filtered sunlight, not in any artificial simulation. Omesh
didn't need him to turn around to recognize him,
though. Few people had such silvery-blond hair.

"He's from Earth," Omesh said.

"Know him, do you?" the man asked.

"Sort of," Omesh said. He decided not to add
"and he's a dick."

Someone rang a gong, and the fight was on,
Rabia and the boy bouncing from girder to girder,
watching each other closely but not yet attempting to engage.

"I don't know why she wanted to study with a
teacher," the man was going on, having drawn a
bit of a crowd willing to listen to him talk. "This
isn't really about fighting, or not that sort of fighting, the kind you do with both feet on the floor
trying to spill the other fellow. This is all about
intuition. You have to understand how you and
your opponent are going to move and how to
move against him. That can't be taught."

"Certainly it can," Omesh said, more loudly

than he intended. "It's just Newtonian physics. People teach it all the time."

"Oh, I saw you come in here, Mr. Physics," the man scoffed. "Your buddy had to give you a tow."

"I didn't say *I* could do it," Omesh said, feeling his cheeks redden. "I only said it could be taught."

"Perhaps it can," Tak said, "but you'd always be thinking, then moving. For some, it's intuitive, moving and thinking as one. And intuitive physicists make better zero G fighters."

"Well said," the man said, but offhandedly, for the fight had begun in earnest. Omesh could see why the man complained that Rabia was making a dance of it. She dodged away from every attempt Hjalmar made at catching her, but her posture and movement were always more than were strictly needed just to avoid being grabbed. Omesh rather liked the look of it. Then Hjalmar began to mirror her, his moves also pulled off for show.

"That's not good," Tak said under his breath.

"What? Why?" Omesh asked. He was missing something.

"Yep, there he goes." And sure enough, Hjalmar had matched one of Rabia's spins but come out of it before her, catching the end of her pink braid and giving it a hard tug. It clearly caught her by surprise. She moved quickly to recover, getting her feet around and launching herself off his shoulders before he could catch hold of the more fleshy parts of her.

Unfortunately, he still had her hair.

"Are there no rules?" Omesh asked.

"Plenty of rules," the man said with a laugh. "He's not breaking any."

Rabia let Hjalmar tug her hair again, but once she was near enough, she struck him in the face with the palm of one hand while the other caught the wrist of the hand that was grasping her hair and did another subtle move. Her thumb must have found a nerve; he released her, and she flipped away.

Someone rang the gong, and the fighters broke off, retreating to opposite ends of the arena. Omesh saw Alain and Tom on the opposite side, giving Rabia a squirt bottle of water and a towel. She took a short gulp of water but waved the towel away.

"Hey, kid." The loud man who had been talking to Omesh and Tak was now trying to get Hjalmar's attention. "Word of advice."

"What's that?" Hjalmar said in a disinterested tone the man didn't seem to notice.

"Grab her boob."

"What?"

"Grab her boob. It'll drive her nuts."

"I don't follow you," Hjalmar said with narrowed eyes.

"When she's angry, she fights sloppy. She'll lose all technique and just try to whale on you."

"I bet she beats the piss out of you," Tak commented, and Hjalmar scoffed and nodded in agreement.

"She'll fight sloppy and defend sloppy. It's your only chance."

Hjalmar narrowed his eyes again, but before he could answer, the gong sounded once more and he pushed off the girder to float back into the arena.

The two engaged in earnest this time, launching at each other before the sound of the gong had quite faded away and latching on to each other, each refusing to let go.

"It's the opposite of sumo," Tak said. "There's no down here. You can't just knock your opponent down, you really have to take him out."

Omesh wished he would shut up. It was confusing to watch, the two twisting around each other. If Hjalmar wanted to follow the man's advice, he had several opportunities, but he didn't take them, and now that she was in close, he didn't bother using her hair against her either. When the gong sounded and the two broke apart,

Rabia had a big grin on her sweat-soaked face. She seemed to be enjoying herself, anyway.

"Who's winning?" Omesh asked.

"Hard to call," Tak said. "They seem evenly matched to me, but one or both of them is probably holding back. This is the last round; it should be interesting."

This time Rabia did not hurl herself at Hjalmar. She opted instead to hang near the edges of the sphere, watching him closely as if looking for an opening. Hjalmar stayed where he was, waiting for her to come to him. The crowd rapidly grew impatient, shouting at the two fighters to get on with it already, but Omesh rather doubted either was focused on anything but the other at this point.

Rabia finally made her move, launching herself at his back. He was expecting that, however, and arched out of her reach before catching onto her own back. One instant it seemed to be all over for Rabia, but the next it was clear that Hjalmar had done exactly what she had wanted him to do. She reached over her own shoulders, caught his wrists, and easily broke his hold on her sweat-slicked skin. There was another twisting moment, Rabia pulling one way and Hjalmar attempting to redirect her in another way. But when the gong sounded to end the match, Rabia had him pinned, his arms locked by hers and her thumbs on pressure points on the back of his skull. She released him and he floated nearly senseless as the crowd around them erupted in cheers and taunts.

"Pathetic victory," someone behind Omesh was grumbling. "No blood at all."

"You should've grabbed her boob," the loud man said to Hjalmar as he was leaving the sphere.

"What's it to you?" Hjalmar shot back, his voice slurring ever so slightly. Whatever Rabia had done when she pinned him had clearly had an effect.

"I had coin bet on you, boy. Lots of coin."

Hjalmar paused, face half covered with a grubby towel someone had handed him. "She won fair and square; you weren't cheated."

"If you'd done what I said, you'd've won. I'd've won."

"Next time you'll know not to bet on me, then." He pulled a loose-fitting silk shirt over his head. Bits of it stuck to his sweaty skin; other bits ballooned out, free-floating in the lack of gravity. "I don't owe you anything."

"Where you from, boy?" the man demanded.

"Around," Hjalmar answered.

"I know where he's from," Omesh said. Hjalmar fixed his dark eyes on him.

"Do I know you?"

"We've met."

"Have we?" There was no recognition in his eyes at all.

"This boy owes me. Look at his clothes; I know he has it. Tell me where he lives and I'll give you a finder's fee, yeah?" the loud man said to Omesh.

"Oh, for the love of—" Hjalmar dug into the pocket of his pants and came up with a fistful of gold coins. Freshly minted, they glinted in the thousand irregular lights the Barnacle Towners had brought into the core. "Take it and good riddance. I was just looking for a bit of a workout, not another headache. Take it and go."

The man didn't have to be told twice.

"Bank of Dubai," Omesh murmured to himself. He hadn't needed to see the seal imprinted on the coins to know this; the newness of them was enough.

Another fight was about to begin, but the air was suddenly filled with the sound of Rabia loudly cursing. Alain was there with her on the other side of the sphere, and it was at him she was directing her bile. Hjalmar looked up, his face an impassive mask, then launched himself across the sphere past the fighters waiting to begin, heading for Rabia and Alain. Catching hold of Tak, Omesh attempted to follow.

"Let me," Tak said, taking the lead and towing

Omesh behind him. "You piss people off when you use them as launching pads, you know."

"Sorry."

By the time they reached her, she was in the middle of another fight. She had a fistful of Alain's shirt and was beating him mercilessly. Tom floated in to intervene but snapped back, his nose sending out an arc of bloody bubbles as he went spinning away. Hjalmar was at her elbow but only watched. Omesh pushed himself past Tak to catch hold of her.

"Rabia," he said, closing his hand over her arm. She looked up at him, startled. He had expected to see anger in her eyes, but it wasn't there. There was only a crazed grief. The muscles under his hand relaxed and she let Alain go.

"You promised. You gave me your word," she said as Alain floated back away from her, wiping at his face and sending globules of blood, sweat, tears, and mucus everywhere. She still had a hold on his shirt, though. He was still within her reach.

"I think if you play back that conversation in your mind, you'll see I've honored every word of what I actually said," he said.

Rabia swore foully and raised her fist, but Omesh squeezed her arm again and she relented.

"It's too late anyway," Alain went on. "Fifteen families have already moved into your little school. *Families*, Rabia. You were never in the right here, and you know it."

"You lied to me."

"Well, just a little." It was probably meant to be the smile of a charming cad he was giving her, but with his nose a swollen mess and blood still forming globules and floating away from several spots on his face, it came out a frightening leer.

Rabia let him go, still seething. She shook off Omesh's hands and made a lunge at Alain's side-kick, but only to tear the bag from his hands. Then she put a foot in the middle of Alain's chest and used it to push off, working her way through the crowd back to the ladder to Barnacle Town. Tak caught Omesh's collar and propelled them both after her. She didn't look back and Omesh wasn't sure she even knew they were following her, but when she got to the top of the shaft, she stopped, ignoring the boy trying to guide her onto the next platform.

"Hey," she said when the two of them reached her. She didn't look up. She was taking slow, deep breaths, but the anger was still there in the set of her shoulders. Tak caught the lip of the shaft with one hand, then deftly let Omesh go, for which he was grateful. It was hard to look dignified when someone was pulling you around by the collar.

"Hey," Omesh answered. "You OK?"

"Yeah," she said. "Going down?"

"Sure," Omesh said. He tried to follow her to the platform, but he was again reminded how being in free fall was really not at all like swimming. Tak reached a hand around his back and gave him a little push. Omesh just managed to catch one of the loops and stop himself without crashing into Rabia.

"Who's your friend?" Rabia asked when Tak reached between them to push the button. There were only two loops, so he was obliged to hold on to Omesh.

"This is Tak. He's from the sumo school you told me about."

"I'm Rabia," she said, putting out a hand for Tak to shake. Then her eyes went back to Omesh, although she quickly looked away. "I wasn't expecting to see you here. I wouldn't have thought this was your sort of thing."

Omesh wasn't sure how to answer that. Had she been speculating on just what *were* his sorts of things? Mostly it was hard to focus on her words when he could just make out the glints of tears being pulled away from her cheeks to spin away above them, and by the way she kept rubbing the knuckles of her hand against the back of her leg. Her anger was fading into something like shame, he thought. He had the urge to do something reassuring even if he didn't know what would be reassuring to her, but the memory of Alain's face held him back.

"I thought it wasn't yours either," he said at last.

"Yeah, well." She shrank more into herself, hugging her bag and not looking at anything in particular. Tak seemed to notice as well.

"We saw the fight. You're good," he said. She gave a shrug. "No, really. You make much money at it? I bet you do."

"Well, Omesh is right; this isn't usually my kind of thing. These were special circumstances."

"What circumstances?" Omesh asked. His throat felt tight, and he could barely get the words out.

"Oh, no, Omesh," she said, and she looked up at him, reaching out and giving his arm a squeeze. "This isn't about your uncle. It's my Si Fu. Alain promised me if I fought for his brother, I could keep Si Fu's place. I'd hoped to open my own school there or something when I turn eighteen and get kicked out of the corporation. But it was all a lie. They only needed to keep me occupied long enough to steal the key from my bag. Now there are a bunch of people living there and no room for me, and I don't know what I'll do."

Omesh had the urge to be reassuring again.

"You should get a ship," Tak said suddenly.

"Huh?" Rabia tipped her head to one side.

"Keep fighting in these matches. Save the money. I'm going to start wrestling in tournaments soon myself, and I'll save my money. We can go in together and get a ship. Omesh too, if he has money."

"Then what?"

"Then everything!" Tak said, throwing up his arms. There was enough gravity now that he didn't need to hold on to Omesh, anyway. "A ship means freedom! There's always work for ships, but you're your own boss; no corporation, nothing. You take the jobs you want, as many as you want, and the whole solar system is yours."

"I'd love to see the whole solar system," Rabia said with a sigh. "I've only ever been here."

"I was planning to save up for a ship, anyway; I think the three of us should do it. That way, it would only take a third of the time to get the money together. I was going to wait for my dad to get back to do this, but the three of us working together, we could have a ship and be well on our way to being able to pay for another by the time he gets back from the far moons. This is awesome..."

As he kept planning out loud, Omesh sneaked a glance at Rabia. She gave him a smile and a shake of her head. It sounded like an impossible scheme to her too, but wouldn't it be nice to be free?

"If it's our ship, what do we name it?" Omesh asked when Tak's ruminations had wound down to a low mumble to himself.

"Something martial, I think, if we're earning all the money from fighting," Rabia said, throwing her bag over her shoulder. They were nearly all the way back down the shaft.

"Not me; I'll be earning my money slinging samosas," Omesh said.

"It's the three of us, friends, doing this together. We should have a name that says that," Tak said.

"You mean like *Amistad*?" Rabia said. "No, wait; that was the name of a slave ship."

"Seems kind of appropriate to me," Tak said.

They reached the bottom of the shaft, the platform touching down with a jolt. Then they crawled back through the tunnel, emerging in the courtyard where the nearly naked boy was still standing guard.

"It's late," Tak said. The balconies overlooking the courtyard were all empty now, and although the sounds of people could be heard, they were faint and sleepy-sounding. "Damn, I've missed curfew. I'm going to be in so much trouble."

"I'm sorry," Omesh said.

"No worries, it was fun. I'll see you the next time I escape."

"Sure," Omesh said. "See you." He and Rabia watched him run off on bare feet through the twisting alleys, his geta clutched tight against his chest.

"I have to hurry myself or I'll get locked out of the space station," Rabia said.

"I'll walk with you," Omesh said. He hadn't been out in Barnacle Town after dark before, and he didn't like it. Somehow, without the people constantly brushing past him, it felt even more claustrophobic. Maybe that was because he couldn't see anything; it felt like the metal of the ships was close around him on all sides. He tried focusing his mind on the lights he could see here and there—low fires, small LED panels barely seen through windows or doors, and the occasional neon sign advertising nothing that was sold anywhere anymore. He missed seeing the stars.

Rabia kept up a fast clip that got faster as they drew closer to the airlock. She ran around the last few corners and up the long flight of stairs. Omesh slowed to a walk when they reached the stairs. There was no light coming from up above. He knew what she was going to find when she got there. He stopped and waited for her to come back down.

There was something she hadn't said back in the elevator. She had said she'd fought to keep her teacher's space, but they'd taken the key. He guessed something bad had happened to her teacher. That crazed look he had seen in her eyes made sense, then. He had seen the same look in his mother's eyes many times when he was young, when her grief hit her so strongly she simply couldn't let it out and it tore her up on the inside.

Of course, his mother had never beaten the piss out of anyone in grief. He wondered what Alain would look like in the morning, when the swelling and bruising really set in. It would be stomach turning.

Rabia came slowly back down the steps, hugging her bag in front of her.

"I've been locked out," she said.

"Oh," Omesh said. She was looking around as if seeing Barnacle Town for the first time. He looked around as well, remembering all his first impressions, the tenuousness of it all. The almost overwhelming sense of the vacuum of space all around them, of the flimsiness of the barrier that separated this from that. Every unartfully welded join became a thing of menace, as did the smell of cook fires and the danger they represented in an enclosed environment like this one. He had learned to put those things to the back of his mind and just focus on the work at hand, but they were all too willing to rush back up at him.

"I've never spent the night here before," she said.

"Your Si Fu passed on, didn't he?" Omesh asked.

She nodded, not meeting his eyes. If what Alain had said was true, she couldn't go there anymore, either. Apparently, fifteen families were living there now.

"And now I have no plan." She sounded so forlorn, so lost.

"You can come home with me," he offered. "We don't have much room, but I know my uncle wouldn't mind."

"Thanks. I should clean up first, though. I stink. That's the downside of sweating in free fall. The sweat just covers you." Then she looked down at her bloodstained hand as if noticing it for the first time.

"Like on a humid day," Omesh said.

"Huh?"

"When it gets real humid, the air is already so full of moisture that your sweat can't evaporate. So it just stays there on your skin. Makes you feel like one of those rainforest frogs people like to lick."

"I guess," Rabia said, with an air of "don't contradict the crazy person." She had put her hand back out of sight.

"We have water in our kitchen. You can clean up there while I do the dishes."

The sloping lane that ran up to the curry stand was bathed in a bluish light, and Omesh realized that he had left the light on when he and Tak had left. That thought was quickly followed by the much larger thing he'd forgotten to do: lock up the stand. He had left it open and unmanned, money in the box under the counter, rare kitchen equipment lying out for anyone to take.

"Oh no," Omesh said, breaking into a run. Rabia followed close at his heels, so close that the both of them collided with his uncle just coming out of the kitchen door.

"Omesh!" Prakash exclaimed, hugging him tightly, then pushing him back out to arm's length to give him a hard stare.

"Uncle-ji, I'm so sorry," Omesh said. "I don't know what I was thinking. Is anything missing?"

"I'm just glad you're all right. I couldn't imagine what must have happened to you."

"I'm sorry, I left on my own." He looked down at his shoes, thoroughly miserable. If his uncle asked him to explain, he'd have to say something, but he really didn't want to tell the truth with Rabia right there listening.

Prakash seemed to read his mind, looking over at Rabia. "You brought him home? Rescued him from some trouble?"

"Sort of," Rabia said. "I think maybe it was the other way around. I'm sorry too, Prakash."

"Well, nothing is missing, so it's easily forgotten," Prakash said, although he still looked stern. "Mama Polly came upstairs to ask why I was open so late; I guess that wasn't too long after you left."

Omesh nodded, still looking at his own shoes. He doubted that chronology very much; it felt like he'd been gone for hours.

"Don't let it happen again."

"I won't," Omesh said.

"The kitchen is a mess," Prakash added.

"I know. I was just going to take care of that."

"He was," Rabia said. "He just told me he was going to do dishes." She glanced over at Omesh shyly and he felt his ears burn. Now, after having betrayed his uncle's trust in such a huge way, he was going to have to ask for a favor.

"Uncle-ji, Rabia is locked out of the space station," Omesh said. "She needs a place to stay just until morning."

"And I suppose you were thinking your sleep

compartment is big enough for two?" Prakash said. Omesh fought the urge to squirm.

"There are families living in my si fu's place," Rabia said. "I don't have anywhere else to go."

Prakash folded his arms and gave them both a deep scowl. "You leave the compartment door open and know I sleep with one eye open." He pointed to his eye, then at the both of them. Then he softened, reaching out to give Rabia's shoulder a squeeze. "I'm sorry about your si fu, beti. He was a good friend and I shall miss him, too."

"Thank you, Prakash," Rabia said, not quite managing a smile. Then Prakash pointed at the daunting pile of pots waiting near the sink and disappeared back up the stairs.

"I'm sorry about that," Omesh said, afraid to even look at her. "I guess it's obvious what he's thinking we were thinking, even though we were never thinking that."

"Don't worry about it," Rabia said. "You know, you never did tell me what you were doing in the core. I wouldn't have guessed you for a fight fan." They moved into the kitchen and Omesh filled a bucket of hot water for her to bathe with, then started in on the first of an endless row of pots. She had been wearing that outfit all evening, but being alone with her while she wet down her arms and legs with a washcloth, Omesh was suddenly aware of just how bare she was. He kept his eyes studiously on his scrubbing.

"Actually, I followed you there," he admitted. "I saw those two trailing you down the road and was afraid you might be in trouble."

"How sweet," Rabia said. She sounded pleased but also surprised, as if people didn't normally do things for her. "I can handle myself, but it's always nice to have a friend who's got your back."

"There was a man there who said you used to fight all the time."

"I did, once upon a time. I don't really want to talk about it."

"Sorry."

"No worries." She made a sound of annoyance, and Omesh fought the temptation to look up. "This is ruined now, thanks to my mystery opponent. Oh well, it was time for a new look, anyway." There was a thunk as something hit the trash and Omesh looked over to see the long pink braid lying among the vegetable peelings. He turned to see her once more wearing her blue jumpsuit, although she hadn't zipped it up and he could see her fighting clothes underneath. She was running her fingers through suddenly shoulder-length but still pink hair.

"You just cut your hair?"

"No, that was fake."

"But he pulled on it."

"And it hurt like hell," she laughed. "It was anchored in there, supposedly permanently, but there you go. Maybe I'll go the other way this time, get a Mohawk or something." She zipped shut her duffel bag and set it on the prep table and Omesh looked down at her hand. It was clean now, but the knuckles were skinned.

"I think you really hurt Alain," he said as neutrally as he could.

She looked at first like she was going to tell him off, but then she softened. "I think you're right," she said. "Weeks' worth of progress all down the drain. Damn." She slumped back against the prep table. "I suppose you think I'm evil. A bad seed."

"Do you think you're evil?" She looked daggers at him for that. "I think you're upset about your si fu."

"I still need..." But she stopped, shaking her head. With her head bent low, her hair covered her eyes, but he could see from the tightening of the muscles of her jaw how hard she was working not to cry. Then she pulled herself together with a deep breath. "Don't you wish life was really like a story?"

"Huh?"

"Well, if this were a story, it would have been

some rival school that killed my teacher, and I would have a mission now. I would have to go and fight every last one of them, ending with a big showdown with the head of the school, a really long battle that I just barely win. Only no one killed my teacher. He was just old. And now he's gone, and I have no mission. I think it'd be easier, having a mission. I'd know what I'm supposed to do next. Instead, I just feel... lost." She looked around the kitchen. "Do you need any help?"

"No, I'm done," Omesh said, letting the water out of the sink to be pumped back to Chandi Corporation from whence it came. "We should be quiet on the way up; I don't want to wake them."

"I'm already barefoot and in full stealth mode. Lead the way."

It was dark in the stairway and Rabia caught his hand, moving closer to him so she wouldn't bump into the family altar at the top of the stairs and staying close as they crossed the tiny but crowded room. Omesh softly slid up the door to his sleeper and took Rabia's arm to guide her inside before climbing in himself. He closed the door part of the way, balancing the need to follow his uncle's instructions with his desire not to wake his aunt, then crawled across the sleep space to touch the lamp. The sleepers were stacked, his uncle and aunt below him. There was just room enough to sit up, although if Tak had been there, his hair would have been brushing the ceiling.

"We can talk now," he said, "but not too loud."

"This is probably considered a lot of space for one guy in Barnacle Town, I guess," Rabia said, hugging herself as if the walls were closing in on her.

"I think so. But my bed back home is bigger than this whole pod," he admitted.

"I bet you miss your family."

"Very much."

"I have to leave home myself soon. I'm not following the corporate plan for my life, and I won't be an eligible dependent after my next birthday. I'll be out on my own, no parents, no Si Fu." She stopped, swallowing hard. "My parents must be so worried right now."

He could tell by the way she pinched at the bridge of her nose with her fingers that she was fighting the urge to burst into tears. If he put his arm around her, would that help her, or would it just make her break down? He certainly couldn't think of anything useful to say. And if she started crying over her family, he might just start crying over his.

"I have a computer if you want to send them a message," Omesh said, taking it out of his trunk and turning it on.

"You can access the corporate internet?" Her voice no longer sounded muffled by unshed tears; he was helping.

"Yes. I guess it's like the electricity and water, we just take it," Omesh said.

"Someone pays," Rabia said. "Nothing is free, not even if you just take it."

"Here," Omesh said, setting the little computer on her lap. Rabia tapped away at the keys, navigating through screens, then sending her message. When she was finished, she looked more closely at the computer itself.

"I've never seen anything like this," she said.

"I built it myself," he admitted. "Well, my friend Ali helped with the software; that's not really my thing. But that reminds me, thanks for the stuff. I've reinforced the support beams downstairs plus done some repairs on the module. I've got the CO2 scrubbers working, plus the heating and cooling systems. I think it might even be space worthy, although I certainly hope to never test it."

"You did all that?" She sounded deeply impressed and also grateful.

"Yeah."

"That must make it easier to sleep at night," Rabia said, handing him back his computer and hugging her knees.

"It does." Neither spoke for a long moment. Omesh finally broke the silence, setting the computer down on the little ledge in the wall. "Do you want to hear some music?"

"Music would be nice. Thanks, Omesh."

She laid down, using her bag as a pillow, watching him as he turned on the computer's music player and then laid down himself. She turned over after a bit, but if she gave into tears, he never heard them.

CHAPTER EIGHT

RABIA

Rabia woke to a soft but persistent trilling sound.

"Alarm, Teresa," she mumbled, turning her face into her pillow to go back to sleep. But her head wasn't on a pillow, it was on her duffel bag.

The sudden realization of where she was waking up was quickly followed by the imaginings that had tormented her the night before, starting the minute she had found herself locked out of the station, the sensation of all that blackness of space surrounding her, pressing in on her. It was silly; she had been surrounded by space every day of her life. For it to feel more threatening in Barnacle Town was perhaps understandable, but for it not to feel real to her until nighttime in Barnacle Town was just plain silly. "Night" and "day" were little more than a shift change at the security station, a change in the lighting.

The trilling was still sounding, and she turned over to nudge Omesh, only to find that she was alone. She followed the sound to the computer sitting on the ledge. She touched the screen and saw there was a video message in the inbox but no one waiting on a live line for an answer. She touched the acknowledge button, and the alarm fell silent.

Rabia threw her bag over one shoulder and tucked the tablet computer close to her chest before gently easing the door open. There was no one in the living area. Rabia tiptoed past the other sleeping compartment, nearly colliding in the half-light with the small altar at the top of the stairs. She reached her hand out in time to keep the little elephant god from falling over, then she scurried down the stairs to the brightly lit Barnacle Town morning.

After stopping on the bottom step to put on her shoes, Rabia circled around the counter to the kitchen area. The pots Omesh had scrubbed the night before were set out on the stoves, although no fires had yet been lit, and a few bins of almost-fresh vegetables were standing at the end of the prep table.

"Omesh?" she called, working her way further into the kitchen. She could hear a soft murmur of voice that she thought was his, but who was he talking to? She called his name again, louder, as she set her bag and his computer on the table, then saw him in the far corner amidst the great sacks of rice and flour.

He was kneeling on a prayer rug, hands raised palms up as he whispered to himself. There was a crocheted hat on his head, and his feet were bare. Rabia found this very puzzling in light of the little elephant god she had just seen upstairs, but she turned to tiptoe back out of the kitchen.

"Rabia," Omesh said just as she was sneaking out the door.

She turned back, blushing guiltily, although she didn't know why. "I didn't mean to interrupt."

"I've just finished." He turned back to roll up his rug and tuck it away on the top shelf of the pantry.

"You pray, like that?" And if she tried really hard, she could probably come up with a less elegant way of asking.

"Don't you? Rabia?"

"Oh, the name. We're not a religious family in a worshiping sort of way. But my mom has a thing for women saints who had intense, ecstatic love relationships with god. My sister's name is Teresa. As in Saint of Ávila. And I'm Rabia, as in Rabi'a al-'Adawiyya. Although 'rabia' in Spanish means 'rage.' It comes from the same root word as 'rabies.' My mother definitely didn't know that at the time. The look on her face the day I told her..." And the look on Omesh's face as she gabbed away, as if the word "rage" hadn't given them both the same flashback from last night. Rabia caught herself rubbing her knuckles again and forced herself to stop. "So how do you know which way is Mecca?"

"My father gave me this," he said, holding something out on his palm. It looked like a compass, a beautifully crafted one of particularly delicate gold and crystal. But the needle was spinning in mad circles. "Lots of Muslims have compasses like this, all over the solar system. I think it's probably more helpful on Mars or one of the Venus orbiters, though. Orbiting the moon gives too much relative motion between us and Mecca. We're end-on to Earth at the moment; the spin that creates our artificial gravity is doing most of this."

"So what do you do?"

"I try to face Mecca when I start. My father said the intention is the important part." He closed his hand back over the little compass and tucked it away.

He seemed to be acting normally, taking off his hat and putting his sandals back on, but he felt distant. The memory was still in her mind, playing in an endless loop—Alain's face as she pummeled it over and over again. Because if she had stopped hitting him, she'd have started crying, and she was not going to let those guys see her cry. Would she have ever stopped if Omesh hadn't been there?

One touch of his hand had taken the edge off her rage, brought it back into the realm of things she could control. How had he done that?

"You got a message," Rabia said at last, indicating the computer. "Just a minute ago."

"Do you mind if I...?"

"Go ahead. I'm guessing it's from your parents. Can I stay and see?"

"They don't speak English with me," he warned.

"That's fine. It's probably personal anyway, right? I'm just curious to see them. If that's OK."

"You want to see my parents?" Omesh said, as if this were the strangest thing he'd ever heard. But he came around the table, pulling over a stool to sit next to her before keying on the message playback.

His parents had recorded the message on the roof of their house, a sort of garden of potted plants and benches, and all over them was a big blue sky. She was seeing it on a computer screen, just like she'd seen in countless films of Earth, but somehow knowing these were people who had once touched the boy sitting next to her made it seem more real, that sky.

His mother was sitting in a chair, holding a tiny infant in her arms. She looked old, more like a grandmother than a mother, and was weeping even as she spoke. She kept putting her hands together, raising them higher and higher each time, until the man standing behind her with his hand on her shoulder reached down and rescued the little baby. If Omesh's mother looked too old to be his mother, his father looked too young to be his father. How had these two ever even met?

His mother finished speaking at last, reaching up for the baby. His father gently laid it back in her arms before turning to the camera to speak. Rabia was drawn in despite not understanding a word he said. He had a stern way of speaking, but his words had a power she couldn't quite define. She imagined Alexander the Great had had the same power in his words, though. And Napoleon, and Patton. He was a leader of men. Only he wasn't. If he were living on Earth, he must be a farmer.

At last, his father touched the fingertips of his right hand to his forehead and the message ended. Rabia turned to Omesh, but her hundreds of questions died unasked. He was wiping tears from his cheeks.

"Bad news?"

"No, good news," Omesh said. "That was my sister, finally born, and she is healthy and perfect. Good news."

"Oh."

Omesh shut the computer. Then he looked up at her. "Do you want to know why I'm here, and not on Earth?"

"Yes, very much."

"Do you know much about the laws on Earth, the population control laws?"

"No immigration from off planet, only two children per family. And there are rules to space the generations out, right? It's not so different here."

"I am my parents' second child," Omesh said. "I had an older sister I never met; she died when my mother was pregnant with me."

"But that baby..."

"Was not allowed. My parents applied for permission for another child before I was even born, but they were denied. So, after I was born, they both underwent the mandatory sterilization procedures. I was an only child for sixteen years. Then one day my mother announces a miracle has occurred, and she is going to have a baby. Despite her age, despite the sterilization."

"Those are 99.5 percent effective," Rabia mused. Each parent had had it done; multiply it together, that was one unlikely baby. A miracle indeed.

"This violated the two-children-per-family law. The A&MC told my parents they couldn't force me to go, but the alternative was that the baby would go, either aborted or sent out into space to be adopted directly after birth. They were going to have to do that to my baby sister unless I left Earth to make room for her."

"So you came here."

"I came here to live with my mother's younger brother, who had left Earth to find a wife some years ago. I have my name on a list to return to Earth should death or emigration leave an opening, but I'm not hopeful of ever seeing my sister with my own eyes until she is my age or older. I will miss her childhood. I won't ever really be a brother to her. I'll be a stranger."

Rabia put her arms around him, pulling him

into a tight hug. She could hear the sounds of choked-back sobs.

"What's your sister's name?" she asked.

"My mother calls her Chandra, the same as my older sister," he said. "My father has named her Jabrayah. He had named the first Qiyyama, but then my mother feels this baby shares a soul with the one she lost, while my father sees them as two different people."

"Do you have two names as well?"

"I am Omesh to my mother and her family, which includes my uncle Prakash, which is why that's my name here. But to my father, I am Rashid."

"That sounds confusing, having two names."

"And two religions. Two of lots of things, actually," he said. "Perhaps it is strange, but since it's all I've ever known, it feels quite normal to me."

Rabia had more questions—mostly why, why, why—but Prakash came into the kitchen already barking orders in Hindi, and Rabia was sure that Omesh was meant to have a lot more work done by this hour. Omesh handed his computer to his uncle and said something about the message, then took Rabia by the arm to walk her out.

"I'm sorry, I've gotten you in trouble," she said, grabbing her bag. "I'll see you soon, if I can."

"My uncle lets me have Monday nights free," Omesh said as they reached the door.

"I'll be back on Monday for sure, then. Thanks for giving me a place to sleep. And congratulations on your little sister. She's precious."

"She is at that." His tears were all gone now, and he looked genuinely happy.

Rabia hesitated in the middle of the lane, looking toward the now-open airlock, but then turned on her heel and headed the other way, towards Si Fu's school. She had to see. She suspected it was going to make her cry, how his lovely space was now just another overcrowded corner of Barnacle Town, but she had to see for herself.

She rounded the corner of the butcher's and stopped dead in the middle of the lane. The quiet little cul-de-sac was filled with urchins, half naked and grubby, rolling about in some Barnacle Town game. The door to the school stood wide open, a rope ladder hanging from its threshold to the ground below. Two older teens were working together, welding what scraps they had scrounged up to make either a balcony or a staircase; Rabia wasn't sure what they were intending, but she was sure their skills weren't quite up to it.

The world outside her parents' home no longer had a place for her in it. What was she going to do? If only she weren't so bad at making friends, she might have other options now.

"Not what you expected to see?"

Rabia turned at the sound of a voice with an accent she couldn't place, then she saw him in the shadows across from the butcher's. There was no mistaking that long, silver-blond hair; it was her last opponent from the night before.

"Are you referring to the desecrated remains of my Si Fu's lifework, or to yourself?" she asked. She felt herself reaching for the sarcastic humor, though, and it sounded forced to her own ears. What little she could hear of it past the throbbing of her pulse, anyway, and that got louder as he pushed away from the wall and came to stand beside her. They had had one interesting match in the arena. "I didn't catch your name last night."

"Probably because I didn't give it," he said. "You're Rabia."

"My fame precedes me."

"Quite a bit. But after our match, I see your skill was not exaggerated."

"Oh." Not the most brilliant of comebacks, she realized, but it was all she could manage at the moment. Then he reached up and touched the ends of her hair.

"You cut off your braid."

"Time for a change, I guess," she said. Then a

particularly loud shriek from one of the urchins brought her back into the moment. "Probably a couple of changes."

"I have a confession to make," he said.

"What's that?"

"I was asked to draw that last match out to the final bell."

"Are you saying you let me win?"

"Not at all. I fully intended to win," he said, and he was huffy enough that she was sure he was sincere. "Only I think they wanted to tie you up as long as possible, so they could do this. I heard about it after, that this was your teacher's school. I've already been up there. Everyone is all done moving in, and they're putting up partitions and arranging the furniture."

"I was a fool," Rabia said. "You swear the fight was honest?"

"I do," he said solemnly. "But any time you want a rematch, I will gladly prove it to you."

"No, I think I'm truly done with the fights now," she said. "Si Fu was the one who convinced me I was just selling my anger for the pleasure of others. I thought he'd cured me of the need to show off, the need to feel big in others' eyes. But then I did it again, I thought for his sake. I guess I shouldn't be surprised that they stabbed me in the back." He arched an eyebrow, and she desperately wished she could shut herself up just for five minutes and be pleasant and conversational, like a normal person.

"Is this truly your jumpsuit, or did you steal it?" he asked, stepping close to her to touch the patch on her shoulder, the one that said "Chandi Corporation" with their logo of moon and stars.

"I'm no thief." Her breath was catching in her throat again. The only bathtubs in Barnacle Town were within the walls of the sumo school. So how did he smell so good?

"It might be safer for you to stay on the other side of the airlock for the next few days."

"Why?"

He didn't answer right away, just touched the threads of her shoulder patch as if there were some deep significance in it. Then he looked up at her with those dark eyes she remembered from the night before. "Those men who run the fights—if you truly won't fight anymore, they may come looking."

"Nothing I can't handle," she assured him.

"I'm sure. But give it a few days, anyway. Stay out of Barnacle Town for a bit. Promise me?"

Rabia narrowed her eyes. She didn't like the way he asked, as if he already expected her to agree to anything. As if he knew what effect he was having on her because he'd had it on lots of girls before. That wasn't a category Rabia liked to place herself in, the category of "lots of girls."

"Sure," she said, crossing her fingers behind her back just like she'd always done as a kid. "A few days."

"I understand you don't want to fight for Alain anymore, but perhaps you and I could have a rematch on our own? If no money changes hands, it's not like you're selling your anger, is it?"

"No, I guess not," she said, still looking at him suspiciously.

"I don't get many chances to fight in free fall; it's a different set of skills. I expect you can teach me a thing or two." He stepped back, turning away. "Later," he said with a half wave.

"Later," she said, watching until the top of his head was lost in the Barnacle Town throng.

He never told her his name.

CHAPTER NINE

TAKASHI

Tak wondered if the super-caustic soap was what they always used to scrub the baths in the bathhouse, or if they had whipped up a special batch just for him. Whatever the reason, it was eating through the flesh of his fingers. He quickly finished scrubbing the tub he was on and turned on the tap, using his hands to slosh the water down the sides of the tub. The coolness of the water on his skin was so divine he felt inspired to write a haiku on it.

Tak turned off the water to attack the tub again, this time with a softer, sweeter-smelling soap, mostly to wash away the remains of the other soap. This was the last tub, and he was done for the day. The day had beaten him by ending a few hours ago. He gathered up his rags, brushes, and soaps, putting them all back in the bucket he'd gotten them from. 'Bucket' probably wasn't the right word for what he was holding; it was round, too low-walled to be a bucket really but too high-walled to call it just a tray with a handle. He thought it might be made from bamboo, although having never seen any sort of wood before coming to the school, he couldn't say for sure. Whatever it was, it glowed with a soft golden hue. It was a strange world he'd found himself in; even the cleaning tools were objects of beauty.

Tak picked up the bucket and stepped over Kenko's sprawled legs. The older rikishi was meant to be monitoring Tak while he served out his punishment, but had dropped off to sleep hours ago. It turned out that sneaking out of school for a second time and staying out past curfew was a very grave offense. Tak had expected there would be punishment, so he hadn't been surprised the next morning to be summoned to the oyakata's office.

Hiroku had been a yokozuna, a sumo grand champion, long before he had become an oyakata. The other rikishi always spoke of him with great awe. He was seldom seen, leaving the running of the stable to the teachers and instructors who served under him. Tak had thought he had gotten used to going from always being the biggest person he knew to, since he had arrived at the school, always being the smallest. But standing before the oyakata, he had felt downright tiny. The other rikishi, when describing his massiveness, had insisted that Hiroku had lost over a hundred kilos after he had stopped wrestling. Tak could scarcely believe that anyone could be bigger than Hiroku was now. Looking at him now was like looking back on pre-exodus times, when everyone lived on Earth and food was readily available. How, living in space, had anyone ever found enough food to get so big?

Such thoughts had kept Tak's mind occupied while Hiroku berated him for over an hour. Of course, the oyakata had been doing it in Japanese, which made it very easy for Tak to tune him out. Then Hiroku had summoned Kenko to stand beside Tak and had given him a helping of the same. Only Kenko had studiously listened, his face red and his eyes downcast, making apologies whenever Hiroku let him speak. Since that moment, Kenko had been Tak's shinai-wielding shadow. Normally, creeping down the walkway in the dead of night to put a bucket of cleaning supplies away wouldn't be an experience to savor, but oh, to have a precious moment alone.

Tak walked softly on bare feet. The buildings

around him were filled with the sounds of dozens of large boys and men sleeping. Big men, big snores. He rubbed his own growing belly. He didn't put weight on fast the way some of the other rikishi did, but he was already noticing the difference what little he had gained made in his sumo. The change in his center of gravity was making it harder for the other wrestlers to move him, let alone upend him. And Kenko, not able to leave his side, had taken to spending their spare minutes wrestling with him. Tak was loath to admit it, but Kenko knew his stuff, and what was more, he could teach it. Tak was starting to look forward to the first competition.

With everything neatly stored away, he headed back down the walkway to the bathhouse to wake up Kenko. He paused at the doorway, first to admire the way the light reflected off the smooth polish rubbed into the wood of the walkway, then to wonder where the light was coming from. He took a few more steps past the bathhouse, just enough to reach the corner of the classroom and see beyond it. Someone was in the oyakata's office; there was a soft glow of light through the paper walls and the murmur of voices from within. It was not quite dawn, Barnacle Town time. Who was the oyakata talking to? Tak crept closer, hoping to catch a word or two.

He recognized Hiroku's low rumble at once, but whomever he was talking to, Tak was certain he had never heard before. The fellow spoke a Japanese little better than his own, halting and ungrammatical. Tak crept closer.

"I warned you," the man was saying.

"You've given us these warnings before." That was Toyonoshima, the schoolteacher. Tak had fallen asleep to that droning voice many an afternoon. "The dons will speak with saikou keiei sekininsha, and an agreement will be made. Why are you so upset?"

"It isn't up to saikou keiei sekininsha anymore," the stranger said. "Shachou is here, and he has taken over."

Tak wondered who they were talking about. The man was using words he didn't know. As Japanese had no articles, he wasn't sure from what he was hearing if it was "a shachou," "the shachou," or just "Shachou," like a proper noun. But if he was using names, they weren't names Tak recognized.

"Saikou keiei sekininsha is powerless?" Hiroku asked.

"In this case, yes," the stranger said. "Shachou has come to get rid of Barnacle Town, and he won't leave until every last ship is gone."

The conversation continued, but Tak was no

longer able to focus on it; Kenko had caught him by the ear and, twisting it ruthlessly, forced Tak to stumble back toward the bathhouse.

"Silence," Kenko commanded him before he could draw the breath for the curses he'd been learning from the other rikishi for just this sort of occasion. Tak was prepared to go ahead with them anyway, perhaps punctuated with a few slaps of his own—his ear had already doubled in size and was throbbing like a second, hot heart—but the sound of a door sliding open behind him changed his mind. He and Kenko both drew further into the shadows near the bathhouse, watching as a man in a corporate jumpsuit said a few final words of farewell. Then Toyonoshima slid the door shut again. He and Hiroku were still inside the lit office, their voices a low mumble that Tak couldn't make out over the steady shrum-shrum of his ear.

"What were they talking about?" Tak asked in a fierce whisper.

"Do you love punishment?" Kenko whispered back. "Do you have any idea what the oyakata will do to you if he catches you eavesdropping? He expels no one; your punishment will be served right here, under his authority. Look at your hands," he said, grabbing one of Tak's hands and holding it up to the faint light that stretched from the oyakata's office, across the open garden to the bathhouse. "See how chapped they are, and from just one night? You still have six more nights to go. And that's punishment for a minor offense."

"If you're so afraid, why were you listening?" Tak asked.

"I wasn't. I was looking for you."

"But you heard what they said, right? You can explain it to me? Like, what's a shachou?"

Kenko grabbed Tak's arm and pulled him back inside the bathhouse, but when he spoke it was still in a whisper. "A shachou is a corporate official, in charge of all the Chandi Corporation satellites, not just this one. I suppose he probably runs anything they own on the moon or Earth or wherever else as well. And to answer what I'm sure is your next question, Hiroku is one of the dons. The dons and the corporate officials on this satellite often have meetings where Barnacle Town is discussed. You do realize the power and heat and water we use are really theirs."

"I gathered," Tak said. "That man said the shachou was here to get rid of Barnacle Town."

Kenko frowned, then reached up and flicked Tak's earlobe, making him hiss in pain again. "Let the oyakata deal with it; it's not a matter for rikishi."

"It sounds to me like things are going on that people ought to know about. I don't like it."

"The dons represent the people. If the dons know, the people know."

"That's bull," Tak said, then covered his ear before Kenko could flick it again. "It is. They don't call themselves dons in Haven, but we had the same sorts there. The people only know what the dons want them to know. And this feels to me like a big fat secret."

"If it's secret, it's secret for a reason," Kenko said. "Hiroku will bring what he knows to the other dons, and they will deal with it. There's no reason for you to get involved. Considering how much trouble you've already gotten into since joining this school, I would think you'd want to be a bit more discreet."

"Well, you don't know me. I'm not the sit-and-do-nothing type," Tak said.

"You won't be doing nothing," Kenko said. "You'll be practicing in the exercise yard. After that will be class, working in the kitchen, lunch, then more exercise. The baths will need scrubbing again this evening. You'll be doing plenty. What you won't be doing is interfering in matters our oyakata is already dealing with. And I assure you, he is dealing with them. No one is in any immediate danger; this is all just how politics works here. How many more punishments must you have before you learn that things run must smoothly when everyone does the job befitting their station and does it well? Let the dons deal with the dons' business. You are a rikishi; be a rikishi."

"You don't like me much, do you?"

"It's not a matter of liking you or not liking you," Kenko said. "It's my duty to mold you into a good rikishi. That is why you're here, isn't it?"

"To be honest, I don't really know why I'm here."

"That's not exactly a surprising revelation to me," Kenko said with something Tak could almost swear was humor in his eye.

"How will we know?" Tak asked.

"Know what?"

"How will we know that Hiroku has told the other dons, and that they are dealing with things? I can behave like you want me to, but only if I know for sure something is being done."

"I guess we watch. Either Hiroku goes out or one or more of the dons comes here. They always deal with each other face-to-face."

Tak nodded, letting Kenko take that gesture as a promise for good behavior. He was tired, and he needed to think on his own, not argue more with Kenko. The two of them slipped into the dormitory and headed for their respective bunks without a word or a look between them. Tak's head was full of worries and ponderings, but the minute it touched the pillow, he fell into a deep, albeit brief, sleep.

He plodded through the day in a sleepy haze, serving breakfast to the older rikishi before eating himself, exercising and wrestling until lunchtime. Then the real torture: classroom time. Toyonoshima droned on and on about some minor event in the history of Japan. It was hard to get interested when the teacher himself sounded so thoroughly bored with his own material.

Tak was just drifting off when a motion caught the corner of his eye. He knew better than to whip his head around; Kenko and the other older students always prowled the classroom to whack shirkers with their shinai. He sat up straight, looking studiously ahead, more alert than he'd ever been in class before. Not that he was listening to Toyonoshima.

Then he saw it again: someone going by the open door carrying a large sheet of metal. He followed with his eyes, but the man was quickly out of sight. He had thought what he'd seen before had been large and unusual. What was the metal for? The man had been heading to the back of the school, to the torii gate that separated the school from the rest of Barnacle Town.

Tak had a sinking feeling in his stomach, but he forced himself to think it through. After several long moments of thought and four more of the older rikishi passing by with sheets of thick metal, he admitted his first impression was still his only impression. Those metal sheets were from the hull of some ship, and they had seemed intact from what he had seen. Welded into place, they'd be perfect for capping off the alleys that ran up to the school.

Class time ended, and the students wandered out, heading in the general direction of the cafeteria, but not in any particular hurry. Tak hung back, then turned and ran through the gardens to the torii gate. None of the men were in sight, although the sheets of metal had been stacked against the inner wall of the ship. They had been tucked away behind a row of potted plants; not exactly hidden, but they didn't call attention to themselves. Under normal circumstances, Tak wouldn't have thought much of them, if he had noticed them at all.

A long look around showed no one in sight. Tak stepped up to one of the pillars of the torii gate, peeking around it to see the ship's hull beyond. The gate covered the cargo doors, and there wasn't enough room to stick a hand in to reach the control panel behind the pillar, but by pressing his cheek up tight against the wall, he could see the display well enough.

This ship was not a derelict like the rest of Barnacle Town. It was powered up and waiting, the Open Door warning flashing patiently. The atmosphere controls showed full tanks and all checks normal. There were even full tanks of fuel waiting for ignition. Push the gate out of the way and shut the doors and they could just fly away.

"Going somewhere?" Kenko asked, suddenly at his elbow.

"Are we?" Tak flung a hand at the metal plates.

"We've always had those," Kenko said. "They've just been moved down here from the crew quarters up in the ship proper."

"OK, why?"

"It's time to eat," Kenko said, putting a hand on Tak's back and steering him toward the cafeteria.

"You didn't answer my question."

"Takashi, I don't know everything. I do know there's nothing to be worried about. People get nervous, they do things that make them feel safer. Have you been to the marketplace in Barnacle Town yet? They do a booming business in oxygen tanks and water bottles, things no one here would ever need unless the worst happens. And so far, the worst has never happened."

"Are you saying the oyakata is panicking?" Tak asked.

"I'm saying I don't know. All I do know is that it's my job to keep you here and on task, and that's what I'm going to do."

Tak gave him another curt nod, then went to join the other junior rikishi in the food line. Outwardly he was a patient rikishi waiting to be fed, but inwardly he was anything but patient. He tried to map things out in his head. There was no real way to get a sense of geography in Barnacle Town. It was like a series of tunnels in an ant farm, only less organized. But Tak guessed that the sumo school was on the very edge, at a sort of cul-de-sac. It was only barely attached to the rest of the town. He was fairly certain there were no Barnacle Town lanes that extended past the torii gate, nothing that ran up the sides of the cargo ship. And it joined to the adjacent ships at their very tail ends. Most of Barnacle Town was a mul-tilayered train wreck of ship after ship; here, things were downright tenuous. One man with a cutter could separate the two in less than an hour. All the school would have to do was shut its cargo doors.

The school was in a space worthy ship; most of

Barnacle Town was not. Would raising an alarm help anyone at all? Was Hiroku just trying to avoid inciting a useless panic? Don or no, his first obligation was to protect his students; maybe he thought the best way to do it was to sit on this information.

Maybe Kenko was right, and this was all just business as usual in Barnacle Town. He'd certainly been here longer than Tak; he ought to know. But Tak's gut was still sending out danger warnings, and he didn't like to ignore his own gut.

What he needed was more information.

It wasn't the craftiest of plans, but then he was operating with no sleep. It might have even looked like an accident to anyone but Kenko, especially as the bulk of the damage was to his own skin, but the burn of hot chankonabe sloshing over him snapped him awake quite nicely. The boy he had bumped into escaped without harm and, from the way he was apologizing, assumed the blame was his. Tak matched him apology for apology, wiping bits of stew from his yukata as he backed away. He saw Kenko stepping forward, eyeing him suspiciously, and turned to hurry down the walkway to the bathhouse. Kenko moved to follow, but the vat of chankonabe had left a large slick spot on the floor, and a crowd of rikishi had gathered around to gawk at the mess.

It wasn't going to delay him for more than a few seconds. Tak broke into a run, gait echoing loudly off the wooden flooring, then making a more subdued clatter over the dusty garden path that led to the gate.

He had to tell at least Omesh; Omesh could find out more and spread the word from there if need be. He only hoped that when he came back, the school would still let him in.

CHAPTER TEN

OMESH

OMESH CROUCHED OVER THE TANDOORI OVEN BUILT into the floor of the kitchen, waiting for the naan to puff up so he could peel it off and stick the other side of the flat bread to the clay wall. It was hot, sweaty work, and he had long since abandoned his shirt.

"Omesh, why don't you take a break?" Prakash offered. Omesh looked up between pulling two pieces of flatbread out of the oven and saw his uncle standing at the doorway. Beyond him on the other side of the counter was Rabia. He nearly didn't recognize her. She hadn't gone for the Mohawk as she had mentioned; instead, she had opted for short, slender cornrows. Purple cornrows. She smiled and waved.

"Let me just finish," Omesh said, reaching back into the oven for the last few pieces.

"I'll shut down the oven. Just be back before the dinner rush."

"I will." Omesh gave himself a quick wash at the sink before putting on his shirt. Prakash was chatting with Rabia, but she kept looking his way with those big, dark eyes of hers, making him very self-conscious as he did up the buttons. Then he noticed Anjali set down her knife with a sigh and rub at her back.

"Are you all right, Auntie?" he asked. He called her auntie, but she felt more like a cousin to him, being closer to his age than to Prakash's.

"Oh, yes," she said with a tired smile. "My back is just bothering me a bit. I didn't sleep well."

"I can finish that for you if you want to go lie down," he offered.

"No, go see your friend," Anjali said. "I'm nearly done, anyway."

"I'll finish up," Prakash said, taking her by the arm and guiding her to the chair at the counter. "Go on ahead, Omesh. We'll be fine."

"OK, but I won't be long," he promised. Rabia led the way out of the shop and through the lanes at an unhurried walk. "I was hoping to talk to you," Omesh said as soon as they were out of sight of the curry stand.

"I didn't mean to be away so long, but my parents were upset when I got back," Rabia said.

"Did you get in trouble?"

"No, they don't really get upset like that. They weren't angry, just kind of panicked."

"Didn't they get your message?"

"Yeah, they got it," Rabia said, pausing as they climbed over an awkward slope of ship, then slid down the far side before continuing their walk.

"So, why do you have to leave home soon?" Omesh asked. "I thought corporations kept you for life."

"Usually that's true. In my case, not so much."

"What's wrong with you?" Omesh asked, then immediately wished he could take the words back and rephrase. Rabia didn't seem offended, though. She gave him a dreamy smile and seemed to be considering her words carefully.

"Well, I'm sort of the opposite of my kid sister," Rabia said.

"That might mean something to me if I'd ever met your sister."

Rabia stopped in the middle of the walkway, raking a hand through her purple cornrows and bouncing on her toes, clearly reluctant to answer. Omesh was about to tell her it was OK with him if she didn't when she tipped her head back, shook the hair out of her eyes with a loud exhale, and just started talking.

"In Chandl Corporation, once you've finished your basic education, you get evaluated. Your skills are assessed, as well as the needs of the corporation, and your future line of work is determined. Then you start the higher training in your field. Most kids do this at twelve or thirteen; my sister finished off her basic coursework at age ten."

"Genius?"

"Yeah, but don't tell her I said so. She's intolerable enough," Rabia said. "Anyway, my sister tested off the charts in computer skills, so they straight-off put one of those wireless ports in her cranium. And because it's all in the interest of her education, she's actually encouraged to hack into any of the corporation's computer systems. She's already suggested a slew of security improvements they've since made, and she's only fourteen."

"So if your sister has access to everything..."

"She knows everything the corporation knows," Rabia nodded. "But she's a total stoolie. She won't do anything remotely like spying, even for me, her dear sister. Although occasionally she points me in the direction of supply rooms that haven't been accessed in decades. That's how I got that stuff you needed."

Then she started walking again and Omesh had to jog to catch up.

"Thanks for that, by the way," he said. "But I'm not sure how this makes your sister the opposite of you. What did your aptitude test show?"

Rabia laughed, looking across at him. She didn't wear a lot of makeup, but what little she had applied made her eyes look vaguely Egyptian, almond-shaped and exotic. He remembered how little he had slept that night she had spent in his room. It still smelled like her in there.

"You're not going to answer?" he said at last.

"I believe I was recommended for something in the maintenance field."

"Engineer?"

"Not even. Custodial. Now, in my defense, I knew I bombed that test. My reader had been stolen while I was at Si Fu's. We never did find out who took it, and I think it was a big factor in Si Fu deciding not to teach classes anymore. But because I'd lost corporate property—and it was strongly implied by my teacher as well as the head of the school that I must have sold it on the black market so I could buy something terribly elicit—because I'd lost it I had to do community service after class for months until I had paid off the cost of replacing it. So my study time was limited, plus I didn't have my reader with all my notes and stuff. I'm not sure if it would have mattered, anyway; I think my teacher had me down in her mind for custodial for quite some time."

"Well, someone has to maintain the robots," Omesh said.

"I know. And it would be low-stress work and would leave plenty of time for my true pursuit in life."

"Kung fu?"

"Well, that too. But what I really want to do..." She broke off, shaking her head. "I'm talking too much."

"Well, but, I asked."

"It sounds stupid when I say it out loud, but it means a lot to me, you know. I think I've been laughed at enough for my obscure goals."

"Your sister the genius?"

"Good guess," Rabia said, clearly impressed.

"Not being a genius myself, I promise not to laugh."

"All right," Rabia said, walking more slowly and drawing nearer to him, as if about to divulge the sort of secret that got people killed. "I want to collect stories."

"Collect stories?"

"I told you—"

"I'm not laughing. Explain, please."

"Do you have any idea how many stories were lost in the plague and exodus? All those people fleeing with just what they could carry, seeking refuge in corporate stations."

"Nobody brought novels with them, you're saying. And the corporations aren't exactly famous for their libraries."

"Exactly," Rabia said, giving his arm a squeeze of solidarity. "I know at the time these space stations were built there was still an internet that reached all of Earth's orbit as well as the moon. And signals could be sent to Mars and back. There is tons of free space on the servers on this space station, room enough for millions of text files. But no one ever bothered to copy things over before the networks crashed."

"The books must still exist, in the cities," Omesh said.

"On Earth, where I can never go."

"And even if you were on Earth, they don't let you in the old cities." A flash of memory of the girl from Goa. She had claimed to have been inside Kolkata, to be on her way to meet others like herself inside Mumbai. Somehow, she seemed more remote now. "They're still under quarantine except for a few places, like Dubai. Which, again, is not exactly famed for its libraries. Well, you've picked an impossible life goal for yourself."

"It certainly seems that way," Rabia sighed.

"But you don't go to school now," Omesh noted.

"No, I'm on my own. After my assessment came back, my parents had a long talk with me. I was all for going right into job training, such as it is, and work. But my parents didn't think that was the best path for me to achieve my goal. So they took me out of the corporate school entirely and I've been learning on my own ever since. I study what I find interesting and show my dad what I'm doing, but there are no tests or papers unless I feel like writing one."

"What do you study if you can't find the stories?"

"Sometimes you can find stories in unusual places. History textbooks sometimes talk of the myths and folklore. Sociology and anthropology books have a few as well. But my dad feels like I should have a well-rounded education, so I do math and science, too. I learn in spurts; I'll do a ton of math for a few weeks and then nothing for months. It's weird, I guess."

"It sounds like Earth school, actually. We get to design our own curricula and our teacher monitors our progress and suggests avenues for further study. We all live too far apart to have actual classrooms, so it's all by computer. There's still a global internet on the surface."

"What do you study?"

"I *did* study agriculture and machinery. Everyone on Earth has to farm or mine, but I was also intending to do some engineering, improving farm equipment."

"Did?"

"Well, I'm not part of the system anymore. I'm not on Earth."

"So you're on your own, like me."

"Yeah."

"Cool," she said with a big grin, and Omesh had to look away. She glowed. Then he realized they had somehow come full circle and were nearly back to the curry stand. He could see a line already forming at the counter; he couldn't very well suggest they turn around and keep walking. But he really wanted to.

"Say, I wanted to ask you for a favor," Rabia said.

"Sure. What?"

"Do you remember that guy I was fighting? The one with the really long silver-blond hair and the really dark blue eyes?"

Omesh felt his heart drop down to his feet. Her glow had just kicked up about ten notches, and she was practically hopping in expectation of his answer.

"I remember him."

"Do you ever see him around? Most of Barnacle Town comes through your curry stand at some point."

"I've seen him." He felt disconnected, as if he were floating far away listening to someone else answer Rabia's questions.

"I really want to see him again, to talk to him, but I don't even know his name or how to find him. I thought I knew every fighter in Barnacle Town, but I know I've never seen him before. Teresa says he isn't corporate, so he must live out here. You seemed like you recognized him that night. Do you know his name?"

"Hjalmar..." But something kept Omesh from finishing. "Hjalmar something. I'm not sure where he lives." He felt like the grubby remains at the bottom of the sink after washing all the vegetables, all dirt and peelings and substandard bits of veg.

"Well, if you see him again, will you let him know how to find me, and find out where I can find him?"

"Sure," Omesh said.

"Thanks," Rabia said and squeezed his arm again. It felt less companionable this time. "Hey, isn't that your friend, the redheaded samurai?"

Tak saw them too and raised his hand, all the greeting he could manage, as he was red in the face and winded.

"Did you run here?" Omesh asked.

"Yeah," Tak managed, hands on knees as he tried to catch his breath. He kept looking back down the lane he'd just come from. Then he noticed Rabia's jumpsuit.

"I thought you were a Barnacle Towner. You work for the corporation?" he asked, still breathing hard.

"No," Rabia said. "But I live there."

"Maybe you should hear this too, then," Tak said.

"Hear what?" Omesh asked, but his eyes were on the curry stand. Prakash was just visible in the kitchen, moving from pot to pot. Anjali was sitting on the chair behind the counter, but she looked wan. He should really get back so she could go lie down.

"Someone in the corporation is planning to get rid of Barnacle Town," Tak said. "To dismantle it, I think. They said every last ship."

"What? Who said?" Rabia exclaimed. Omesh was too stunned to speak. The image of all the ships of Barnacle Town floating freely through space loomed in his mind's eye.

"Someone in a jumpsuit like yours; I didn't catch his name," Tak said, looking again back down the lane.

"Is someone following you?" Omesh asked, looking as well.

"Probably. I wasn't supposed to leave the school. I've been trying to sneak out since morning, but I only just managed it."

"Was his jumpsuit exactly like mine?"

Tak shrugged. "It was dark; I couldn't see his patches, if that's what you're asking. It wasn't blue like yours, though. I think it was green."

"Green means engineering," Rabia said, pulling at her lip.

"How did anyone from the space station get here in the middle of the night? They shut the airlock," Omesh said.

"That door to the core might not be the only secret entrance," Tak said. "For that matter, who's to say he didn't use that one?"

"He might have done," Rabia said.

"What do we do?" Omesh asked. "I can tell everyone I meet that Barnacle Town is in danger, but without proof, I don't think I would be listened to."

"Definitely not," Rabia said soberly. "There have been scares before. You'd be taken for the boy who cried wolf. Tak, what did you hear specifically?"

"Not much, and they were speaking Japanese," Tak said. "I couldn't understand all of it. But the corporate man said we didn't have much time. The school is already prepared; they'll just shut their doors and leave."

"What does this mean?" Omesh asked, glancing from Tak's worried face to Rabia's uncharacteristically serious one.

"I don't know yet," Rabia said. "It might be nothing, honestly. Rumors of these sorts of threats have come up before, and it's always been nothing. Let me go find out and come back."

"Go where?" Tak asked.

"Back home, inside the space station. I have to talk to my parents. Maybe my sister. If something is going on, one of them will know. Then I can come back and tell you."

"I can't wait," Tak said. "I have to get back to the school."

"You've done what you could," Omesh said. "We can take it from here." He didn't add that the sumo school was the safest place for anyone to be.

Not like the curry stand. The sleeping module upstairs was as space worthy as he could make it, but it was still precariously perched on the pillars over the dining area. One panicked mob sweeping down the lane would be enough to smash it all.

Rabia was watching his face closely, as if his thoughts were on display there. "Is there anything more you need from me?" she asked.

"I've sealed it up, got the life support working. It never had flight capabilities; there is really nothing more I can do with it," Omesh said. But he couldn't help chewing his lip as the back of his mind worked on the problem. How were they planning to remove Barnacle Town? Would the ships be sent off into deep space, left in the same lunar orbit as the space station, or plunged down to the moon surface? Was there any way he could influence which fate was theirs? Was there anything he could build to deal with any of those outcomes?

"Keep thinking about it," Rabia said. "I'll be back as soon as I know anything. If you have a list for me then, I'll try to fill it right away. All right?"

Omesh nodded.

"Maybe this is nothing," Rabia said, but she didn't sound convinced. As Omesh watched her and Tak go, he remembered Hjalmar when they had met back on Haven. He ran back every word, every gesture like a film in his head. By the time he reached the curry stand counter to take Anjali's place, he was sure.

Hjalmar had known this was coming. It was why he was here. Somehow, Hjalmar was a part of it.

CHAPTER ELEVEN

RABIA

Rabia jogged up the irregular staircase, vaulted herself up out of the airlock, and slapped her hand on the screen at the guard station. The guards on duty didn't even glance over at her. A group of men were signing out at the opposite desk, heading into Barnacle Town for a night of rabble-rousing and procuring all those things the corporation didn't provide for them. Rabia had always assumed that the corporation had seen the need for this and that was why Barnacle Town was there. The cities on Luna and Mars were built as cooperative ventures between many corporations, and noncorporate people had filled the space under the domes around the corporate buildings. People needed to get out of the boss's sight now and then; it was a basic human need. Only on a space station, there was nowhere to go. Unless you had a Barnacle Town.

But if what Tak had heard was true, and they were getting rid of Barnacle Town, would the employees object? There were as many people on board the space station who complained about the constant presence of vice as there were people who enjoyed a little vice when off duty. But even the anti-vice crowd would be chilled at the idea of sending thousands of people off to a slow death in space, wouldn't they?

Rabia headed out of the security building and down the narrow street. The space station had been designed to house ten thousand people comfortably, with enough gardens and farmland to keep them fed and self-sufficient. The streets were meant to be lined with green trees, buildings interspersed with gardens and parks. But when the plague hit Earth, people had crammed into any ship that could get them off the surface. Few had had any destination; it had just been panicked fleeing. The space stations had taken pity on the overcrowded passenger ships and opened their holds. A station meant for ten thousand was suddenly holding twice that number. Shelters were built to hold them, taking up space meant for growing food.

Some had died from a variety of diseases in the first year, some perhaps from a weak form of the Earth plague; no one really knew for sure. But after that first year, the population began to grow, and the refugees had never gone back to Earth. After the plague had run its course and communication with Earth was restored, the A&MC were in charge, and they wouldn't take back anyone who had fled. Chandi V, like many other space stations, had to make tough choices. It held more people than it could feed, more than three times as many now.

Rabia didn't know who exactly the Agriculture and Mining Collective was—although the word "collective" creeped her out a bit—but she knew they must be fabulously wealthy. They could name the price for any food item and the spacers would simply have to pay it. No one had the room to grow it themselves.

Not unless they pushed half their population out of an airlock. Rabia was pretty sure those stories were just rumors. And anyway, it could never happen here.

Only suddenly, it felt like it *was* happening here.

Rabia's palm also opened the door to her family's apartment. It was hard not to think of the day in the near future when her palm would no longer open any doors for her. If there was no Barnacle Town, where would she go?

"Hello, Rabia, dear," her mother said, looking up from her computer to give her a quick smile. Her mother went to an office on the other end of the space station in the mornings, but in the afternoon she was always working from home so she could be there when her daughters came home. Rabia was never envious of her sister's brains, but she was envious of the way Teresa favored their mother in looks. Both were tall with the lean build of a runner, a pastime they used to share; both had the same darkly brown skin. Rabia favored their father, short and curvy, and her lighter brown skin was covered in freckles. Her father blamed his grandfather's Scottish blood for the freckles.

Rabia had hoped that Teresa cutting off her long braids would even up their looks, but it turned out that Teresa with a tight cap of hair was even more ethereally beautiful than Teresa with braids down to her butt.

"Hi, Mom," Rabia said, giving her mother a kiss on the cheek. "Busy?"

"Nothing that can't wait if you need to talk."

"I do, but I want to talk to Dad too."

"Sounds serious," her mother said, that worried line forming between her eyes.

"It's not about me, it's about Barnacle Town."

"Why do you need to talk to us about Barnacle Town? Never mind, you wanted to wait for Dad. He's on his way here now. He was just stopping to pick up our dinner. Why don't you and your sister wash up so you're ready when he gets here?"

"OK, Mom." Her mother saved her work on the computer, then folded the desk against the wall and turned her chair around so that it stood at the dining room table with the others. Their apartment was only three rooms: her parents' room, the room she shared with her sister, and this room that was dining room, living room, and home office all in one. After dinner, they'd collapse the legs and drop the table down into the floor, then recline the chairs to watch a movie on the computer or sit on the floor with pillows and play games.

Or they used to, before her sister had gotten her implant. Now she spent all of her time in her room, seemingly staring off into space. Which was what she was doing when Rabia opened the bedroom door.

"Hey, Teresa," she said, flopping down on her own bunk.

"There's weirdness in the core," Teresa said, only half focusing on the words even as she said them.

"Sounds like a mantra."

"Do you know anything about it?"

"No comment."

"I thought as much. If I find anything, I have to report it, even if it implicates you."

"How could it implicate me? What do I know about dodging security measures?"

"This is true."

Rabia heard the apartment door open and her father come in. "Mom said wash up," she said, hopping to her feet and pulling the sink down from where it waited folded against the wall with the toilet. Showering required a trip down the hall to the bath they shared with all the other apartments on their floor. Neither of her parents was ever going to get promoted to a level that allowed in-apartment showering.

Her father was already spooning steaming casserole into their bowls when the two came out of their room, Teresa fully aware of her surroundings for the one time of day her parents absolutely required she not access her implant. It was typical corporate fare; warm, nourishing, but only spiced to a level that no one could possibly object to. Total blandness. But the bread was filling.

"Rabia wanted to talk to us about Barnacle Town," her mother said when the food was mostly gone.

"Is that so?" her father said.

"I want your advice on something," Rabia said, then gave them the whole story of what Tak had overheard. Then she told them of the things Alain had been hinting at that day in the curry stand. Her parents' smiles became ever deepening frowns.

"It's all true, isn't it?" Rabia said, studying their faces. "You know it's true."

"It's consistent with some other things," her father said slowly, looking over at her mother, who nodded.

"What does that mean?"

"Someone is here, but not officially. There were no announcements or corporate-wide meetings, but it's one of those things everyone knows," her father said.

"Who?"

"Someone from the Chandi family," her mother said. "From Earth. Probably the patriarch himself."

"But how would he get rid of Barnacle Town?"

Her father sat back in his chair and rubbed at his jaw as he thought it over. He worked on the team that maintained the growing conditions in the greenhouses. He never dealt with Barnacle Town and seldom went there, but Rabia knew he had engineering knowledge enough to make a good guess.

"The easiest thing would be to shut the airlocks, cut off their water and air supplies, and wait," he said at last.

"And if they were in a hurry?"

"Cut the ships off the hull," he said. "But that would be problematic in other ways. Barnacle Town grew slowly, ship by ship. There were a lot of little adjustments to the ship's spin to compensate for the added mass and keep us at one G. Losing all those ships at once will affect us in one big blow."

"We'll get heavier?" Teresa asked, just when Rabia was certain she had tuned them all out in favor of a virtual world.

"I don't really know," he admitted. "Not my field. But some sort of compensation will have to take place. And the engineers in that field will surely know this."

"If they're consulted," Rabia said. Then she remembered that Tak had said the man he'd overheard had been wearing a green engineer's uniform.

"They will have been," her mother said suddenly. "They've been in a closed-door meeting for the last two days."

"Is that unusual?" her dad asked.

"Somewhat. I didn't think anything of it at the time, but I imagine now our mystery guest called it for just this purpose."

As Rabia saw it, there was only one question left to ask.

"Can we stop it?"

"I don't see how we could," her dad said.

"Then we have to warn them," Rabia said. "So many people, and the ships are derelicts. They aren't space worthy. They can't survive."

"They aren't dead yet," her mom said. "There are still things we can try. Long shots, but still..."

"Talk to people," her dad said. "People who care about Barnacle Town, people who just care about the lives of thousands of people. We'll start with the other Jeffersonians for sure."

"But if they're corporate employees—"

"They can still protest, Rabia," he said. "A person doesn't sell their soul when they join Chandi Corporation, no matter what you've been listening to them say in Barnacle Town."

"But will it help?"

"I hope so. I really do," he said. "Will you two clean up?"

"Yeah," Rabia said, but she felt dead inside as she watched her parents leave the apartment. Who cared about the dishes at a time like this? Danger loomed like a specter over the entire space station; what did it matter if she herself wasn't at risk? Others she loved were Omesh, Prakash, Anjali and the baby she was so nearly about to deliver. Hjalmar.

"I can do it," Teresa said when she saw that Rabia wasn't even stirring from her chair. She stacked the plates, bowls, and flatware on the tray, then set the tray outside the door for the kitchen crew to pick up. "Do you want to lie down?" she asked.

Rabia looked up, startled by the genuine sound of concern in her bratty little sister's voice. "No, I don't think I could," she said.

Teresa dropped down the computer desk and clicked through the commands to send the table down into the floor for cleaning and storage. Then she clicked another command and Ted, their floor-cleaning robot, zoomed out of his cubby, zipping around the room to suck up any crumbs from dinner. He bumped against the feet Rabia didn't bother to pick up from the floor. It didn't bother Ted, he just worked around her.

"Do you want to watch something? Play a game?" her sister asked.

"No."

Teresa sighed, opening the cabinet and tossing several pillows out into the room as Ted turned himself about to back into his cubby so the mechanism in the far wall could empty his pan and recharge his battery. Rabia slid out of her chair, lying down with her head on a pillow to stare at the ceiling. Teresa lay down beside her. Rabia remembered how often they had done this when Teresa had still been little, telling each other stories and giving each other the giggles.

"You asked me about that guy yesterday," Teresa said after an eternity. "I have an answer for you, but you're not going to like it."

"You said his description didn't match anyone in the station," Rabia said.

"He didn't. He's a new arrival."

"Then he's corporate? Truly?" Rabia asked, sitting up. That was one friend safe, anyway. Or sort of a friend. "He seems kind of young to be a new employee. Is he a Wunderkind like you?"

"Oh, he's more than a corporate employee," Teresa said. "His name is Hjalmar Chandi. His father is the operational manager of this space station. And his grandfather is the patriarch. He's the CEO of Chandi Corporation."

CHAPTER TWELVE

TAKASHI

Tak was lost in the rhythm of the movement: crouch low, lift one leg high, bring it down with a stomp and a clap of hands on thighs, then repeat with the other leg. It looked simple enough, but the bigger he got, the more difficult it was to keep the flexibility. It was hard work lifting his increasingly massive legs up into the air, and his body was slimy with sweat.

"Hey."

Tak looked up, startled. It was Rabia, looking very subdued despite the purple hair. Her jumpsuit was unzipped to the waist, the sleeves tied around her like a belt, and the black tank top she wore underneath was completely nondescript. Was she intentionally hiding her corporate logos?

"Who let you in?" he asked.

"The guy at the gate. I've been here before with Si Fu, and he recognized me," Rabia said.

"Did you learn anything?"

"You were right; something is up," Rabia said. "The patriarch of the Chandi family is here. All the space station engineers are behind locked doors. The official reason is some sort of team-building exercise, but no one believes that."

"They're figuring out how to get rid of Barnacle Town without damaging the space station," Tak said.

"That would be my guess."

"What do we do?"

"I've been thinking about that all night. There are a lot of ways this can go down incredibly badly. Most of them involve people panicking. We need leadership, to keep people organized and working together."

"But who?"

"The dons," Rabia said with great reluctance. "They have a system in place, people—well, boys, mostly—in charge of particular neighborhoods. They aren't anyone's favorite people, but they are recognized as an authority of sorts. I don't like it, but I think they're our best shot."

"So we go to the dons," Tak said.

"There's a problem with that," Rabia said. "You

can't just meet with the dons. No one I know even knows who most of the dons are."

"Come on; someone knows," Tak said. Then he flinched as a shinai blade came down on his head.

"I doubt very much that there is a good explanation for this," Kenko said.

"She's a friend—" The shinai rapped off his skull a second time.

"Hey, don't do that again," Rabia said. Kenko didn't even look at her.

"It's all right, Rabia," Tak said. "I'm supposed to be exercising here, not talking to you."

"That gives him the right to hit you?"

"It's what I signed up for," Tak said, touching his scalp and looking at his fingers. No blood. It felt like it ought to be bleeding.

"Send her away," Kenko said. "Now. Unless you want me to take her out of here."

Rabia didn't understand a word of Japanese, but Kenko's tone was clear enough that she took a step back, settling herself almost imperceptibly into a fighting stance. Tak thought it would almost be worth it to see what she could do in gravity, but there were more important matters at hand.

"She came here to tell me more about what the man was telling the oyakata yesterday," Tak said. Then he switched to English; it was rude to talk as if Rabia weren't there. "The station engineers are in a closed-door meeting, figuring out how to remove Barnacle Town without damaging the station. Once they know, this whole town will be gone."

Kenko's face was inscrutable as he processed this information. He looked from Tak to Rabia. Then slowly, almost toad-like, he blinked his eyes and opened his mouth. What came out was a strangely accented English, and Tak realized for the first time that Kenko was not a native speaker of Japanese, no more than he was. He always sounded so much like Hiroku and Toyonoshima when he spoke his flawless Japanese, but when he spoke English, his accent wasn't Japanese but something else, something Tak hadn't heard before. "The oyakata is already working on this situation, as I've told you. Our place is to do our own jobs as well as we can. Our job is still sumo."

"The oyakata has a responsibility to this school, but not to this town," Tak said. "He will act in the best interest of the school."

"Which is to let the rest of Barnacle Town die," Rabia said. "Look at this place, this gorgeous place! Take out these buildings and plants and lights and you'd have enough space in here to take half of Barnacle Town to safety."

"And where is safety, exactly?" Kenko asked. "This is a cargo hold; it doesn't have the life support systems to maintain a hold full of breathing, warm-blooded people. If safety isn't close by, we will be rescuing your townspeople from a fast death in exchange for a slow one."

"A slow one buys us more time," Rabia said.

"Time for what?"

Rabia had no answer, but she was clearly thinking just as fast as she could. "Can you talk to your oyakata?" she asked at last.

"No," Kenko said firmly. "He will never open up this space to refugees. It's not his ship; it's not his place to do so."

"But he's the only don we know," Tak said. "Isn't there some way we can convince him to talk to the other dons, or let us talk—"

"No," Kenko interrupted. "It would be admitting to eavesdropping."

"Well, I know why I was out there, listening in," Tak said. "Why were you?"

Kenko went red again but showed no other signs of temper.

"Is it that regimented here?" Rabia asked. "You can't even talk honestly with your si fu? I mean, sensei?"

"Oyakata," Tak said.

"Yes," Kenko said. "It's that regimented here. There's more at stake than you really know."

"So tell me," Rabia said.

But Kenko just shook his head. "You have to go now. Visitors are allowed to observe practices but not to distract the rikishi."

"What will you do? Nothing?"

"I will follow my oyakata's orders. He meets with the dons today; surely after that I will be told, I will know what I'm doing. Takashi as well," Kenko said.

"Letting you hit me with a stick is one thing, but standing idly by when a massacre is in the offing?" Tak said.

"So leave," Kenko said.

"No, stay," Rabia said. "At least for now. There's nothing you can do out there, anyway. I'm going to go talk to Omesh. We'll figure out something. I'll be back to talk to you again. You just stay near the one don we know. Watch and listen."

"I will," Tak promised. Rabia shot Kenko a warning glance, then gave Tak a quick hug, not bothered at all by his sweaty flabbiness. Then she jogged out of the exercise ring back toward the gate, purple cornrows bouncing with her step.

"We're being watched, you and I," Kenko said, returning to Japanese.

"So?" Tak crouched down low, lifted a leg, then stomped and slapped.

"It's my duty to see that you keep to your place here," Kenko said. "Whatever happens in the next few days, there is still a tournament coming up, one in which you must do well."

"Or what?" Tak asked. At this point, getting kicked out of school would be something of a relief. He could stop justifying to himself why he was staying.

"Do well," Kenko reiterated. "And don't meddle. Stay out of the oyakata's business. And stop breaking rules. Winning matches won't make them any more lenient about the rules."

"Why do you care? I would think you'd be relieved if I got expelled."

"No one gets expelled," Kenko said, and Tak nearly shivered at the coldness of his tone. "This place has a future, if you want it. Work hard and you can accomplish it. That's a rare, rare thing these days."

Tak didn't know what to say. What Kenko said was very true. His father had worked hard every day of his life, but he'd lost everything in one bad deal. If Tak worked hard, he would win tournaments, and winning meant cash and other, less tangible benefits. As long as the sumo schools existed, he would have those things. And sumo had been around for centuries. Not even the decimation of the human race had stopped it.

Still, Tak would keep his eyes and ears open around Hiroku. His success would be meaningless if it involved turning his back on thousands of doomed people. And Rabia was right about the hold. If only they had somewhere to go, they could save half of Barnacle Town.

"Crouch lower, leg higher," Kenko said, rapping him with the shinai, but it was a soft blow, a mere reminder. Tak crouched lower.

CHAPTER THIRTEEN

OMESH

Omesh woke to the soft chime of his computer announcing a new message. He felt like he'd just shut his eyes a moment ago, and what sleep he'd gotten hadn't been restful. He pawed the computer closer to him and cracked open one eye to see who the message was from. Ali, answering his rather long message from the night before. He pushed the computer away and sat up to dress. He could sort of guess what Ali would have to say, anyway. Something worthwhile about Omesh's problems with making the pod space worthy, and something very much not so about his problem with his uncle.

He had tried everything, every argument, but nothing would make his uncle believe that Barnacle Town was in danger. If steps were going to be taken to prepare for that emergency, Omesh was on his own taking them. The memory of his uncle's red face and his struggles to keep his voice low so that Anjali upstairs wouldn't hear him... Omesh knew that whatever steps he did take, he'd have to be very sure he wasn't caught taking them.

Through the thin door at the end of his bed, he could hear the low rumble of his uncle's voice, the softer sound of his aunt answering. He couldn't make out the words, but he sounded worried, she tired. Omesh ran his fingers through his hair, then slid the door open. He swung his feet out, reaching down to slip his sandals on. He had expected today to be one long awkward silence, but although the mood in the room was strange, it wasn't remotely one of simmering anger.

"Omesh, can you open the restaurant by yourself today?" Prakash asked.

Omesh looked up, startled. Had his uncle changed his mind? He looked from Prakash to Anjali and back again, uncertain. Prakash not only had dismissed Omesh's worries about Barnacle Town, he had made it very clear that it was not even to be discussed in the presence of Anjali. But if he wasn't going out to talk to others about the problem, then what was this all about? Given that Anjali was right there, he couldn't ask.

"Certainly, Uncle-ji," he said. Then, very carefully: "Is there a problem?"

"No problem," Anjali said. She looked worse than Omesh felt after his own near-sleepless night, as if she hadn't slept properly in days. She had her hands folded in her lap, her head bowed so that the loose strands from her braid concealed her face.

"Are you all right, Auntie?"

Anjali lifted her head and gave him a smile. "Yes, just tired."

"So she says, but I'm going to find the midwife and have her come and check on her," Prakash said with a worried frown.

"Don't worry about things here. I can take care of it," Omesh said, trying hard to keep the panic from showing in his face or voice. On his own?

"Just do your best; our customers are very understanding," Anjali said.

Prakash gave Omesh one last hard stare, clearly reminding him of what was not to be discussed. Then he softened, reaching out to give Omesh's shoulder a squeeze. "I'm glad you are here with us. I know you miss your family, but we're grateful that our little one will be born already having a big brother to look out for him."

"I always will," Omesh said.

Prakash fussed over his wife one last time, although she was already settled as comfortable as she could be with a tall glass of mango lassi near at hand, which she dutifully sipped from for him. Then he went out the door, sliding down the rails of the narrow stairway like a sailor in an old naval movie.

Anjali gave a soft sigh that struck Omesh like an alarm set to full volume.

"Are you...?"

"No, not yet," Anjali said, rubbing her hands over her belly. "We expected him days ago, but he's not ready yet. I don't think the midwife can do anything except possibly make Prakash feel better."

"There used to be a drug for this sort of thing, something that would get the process going," Omesh said, trying to remember where he had read that.

"It will happen when it happens," Anjali said. "Still, it's a shame we don't have those drugs anymore. Is it true on Earth you still have vaccines?"

"You mean you don't have them here?"

"No. Sometimes you see them in the black markets, but who knows where they came from or if they even are what they claim to be? When Prakash and I were first married, we lived with my family on the moon. We moved here because Prakash had heard that it was better for babies to be born here than on the moon."

"Oh, the low gravity?" Omesh guessed.

"More the diseases. Things are very crowded on the moon. Many children die every year from one epidemic or another. Barnacle Town is safer. I've heard others say there is something in the water we take from the corporation, something that helps keep them from getting sick. I don't know; that sounds like magical thinking to me. But I've only seen a few children die since we've moved here, so there must be something. I miss my family, but I'm glad Prakash brought me here."

Omesh bit his lip hard. He couldn't imagine a place more crowded than Barnacle Town, or one that felt less safe. But Anjali was completely sincere.

"You should get downstairs; I'll be all right alone until Prakash gets back," Anjali said.

Some time later Omesh was hurriedly peeling potatoes, racing to have the dum aloo ready for the lunch rush, when Rabia appeared in the doorway. His heart lifted at the sight of her, then crashed back down. If she asked about Hjalmar, was he still going to lie? If he swore to himself not to, would he end up doing it, anyway?

Well, he was entitled to have two conflicting natures, wasn't he? He already had two names.

"Can I help?" Rabia asked, snatching up a potato and just as suddenly dropping it. "Hey, these are hot!"

"Freshly boiled. The peel sloughs right off. Mostly."

"Good thing I have tough fingers," Rabia said, watching him peel away the skin of the potato in front of him and put it over in the done pile before tackling one of her own.

"Thanks," Omesh said. "Prakash is fetching the midwife for Anjali. I thought I had this under control, but in hindsight, I should probably have started things in a slightly different order."

"Running a restaurant isn't really a one-man job," Rabia said, "as your uncle well knows. He won't be mad."

"I can still be mad at myself, can't I?"

Rabia shrugged and went on peeling her potato. "Sure, suit yourself. But I need to talk to you."

"I'm busy." That came out grumpier than he had expected.

"And I'm helping. We can talk and work at the same time, right?"

"Sure," he said, trying for a more cheerful tone.

After all, it wasn't her fault he couldn't look at her without remembering the way her whole face had changed just speaking about Hjalmar. She wasn't deliberately tormenting him when she brushed his arm reaching for another potato.

"I have a plan, but it's not working out too well," she said at last.

"What's your plan?"

"I want to get the dons involved. I know they have relations with some of the higher-ups in the corporation. I think they might have some leverage. Maybe they can prevent this whole thing from happening."

"I don't know," Omesh said. "Tak said his stable master was a don, and he already knew and wasn't telling the others. They sound like a pretty self-interested bunch. Saving Barnacle Town isn't in the stable master's self-interest, apparently. Who knows if any of them will care?"

"Maybe they won't, but I have to try."

"I guess. The only other option is to tell everyone ourselves—"

"—and that could lead to a riot," Rabia finished. "Believe me, I know."

"Of course, there is the problem that no one knows who the dons really are," Omesh said. "Tak's stable master aside."

"I was just there, at the school," Rabia said. "It doesn't seem hopeful that we can get to the other dons through him." A sudden flush of color climbed her cheeks. "Do you have any idea how they treat Tak there?" Omesh shook his head, but she didn't even pause for breath. "I've been there before. I know they're tough on the young students, but they are downright sadistic with him. And he just takes it!"

"Well, he has to," Omesh said.

"If it were me, I'd have taken the wooden sword out of that punk's hands and smashed his own skull in. See how he likes it."

"That's not very mature."

Rabia shot him a dark look but then shrugged a partial agreement. "True enough."

Omesh got up to check the oil in the fryer, nodding to himself when the water he dropped from his fingertip sizzled and danced. He started gently dropping potatoes in, one by one. The mental image of Rabia beating Tak's fellow student with his own sword brought another thought to his head. "If you're going to find the dons without going through the stable master, you're going to have to go through Alain."

"I know," Rabia said, studiously not looking at him. It wasn't hard to guess why she'd be reluctant to talk to Alain. "I can find him easily enough. Getting him to listen to me? To agree to help me?" She shrugged again, peeling the last of the potatoes with a few quick strokes. She handed it to Omesh, and he slid it in with the others.

"Do you want me to go with you?" Omesh asked.

"You're busy," Rabia pointed out.

"If you wait until after lunch—"

"No. I should go alone anyway."

"Why?"

Rabia didn't say anything for a long time, just pushed potato peelings around the tabletop with a fingertip. "I just should."

"Well, come back afterwards and tell me what he said. I'm going crazy here, peeling potatoes when I should be upstairs figuring out a way to make that pod safe."

"You said it was space worthy."

"Well, yeah, but it would be like the story of Perseus and Danaë. Do you know it?"

Rabia nodded. "Cast at sea in a wooden chest."

"Without Zeus to guide us to shore. I need a way to get us somewhere safe, but I just don't know how to do it."

"Keep thinking about it. Anything I can get for you, I will. In the meantime, I'm going to keep trying to make it a moot point. If I can't reach the dons, I have one more card that might be worth playing."

"What's that?"

"Hjalmar. Remember him?"

Omesh gave his very best noncommittal shrug.

"His full name is Hjalmar Chandi. His father is the operational manager of this satellite."

Omesh focused on his potato. He had already guessed as much when he'd realized Hjalmar had a chip in his head. Of course, he was a corporate son; he was practically a prince by modern standards. No wonder Rabia liked him so much.

"How is that going to help?" he asked at last. "I doubt his father considers the advice of his teenaged son before doing things. Hell, he's probably on his father's side." He remembered Haven. Hjalmar had practically fled when he found out where Omesh was heading, as if avoiding exposure to some fatal disease.

"I know it's a long shot. That's why I'm going to the dons first. I'm not even sure how I'd get to him; his family's apartment is in a part of the satellite I don't have security clearance to, and since he doesn't actually live here, his e-mail isn't listed in the directory."

"You've already checked."

"Well, yeah. I had to do something besides quietly going nuts while waiting for the airlock to open this morning. Look, I've got to get going, but I'll be back later. Good luck with lunch."

"Lunch!" Omesh said, hurriedly fishing potatoes out of the deep fryer. They were a little past golden brown.

CHAPTER FOURTEEN

RABIA

Rabia was getting impatient. She had been to all of Alain's usual haunts, flashing the corporate logos on her jumpsuit as much as possible, but there was no sign of him. She tried approaching some of the urchins she was certain were runners for the gangs, but they bolted when she came near or simply refused to acknowledge that she was speaking to them. At last she found herself in the alley behind the butcher's, standing at the base of the rickety staircase the new tenants had built. She put her foot on the first step but changed her mind, turning and walking briskly away, hands deep in the pockets of her jumpsuit.

It was just that she missed it. She missed how it felt to push herself to make the drops lower, the punches snappier. She missed having something besides the inside of her own mind to focus on for a few hours. There was no room at home to practice more than stationary chi gung meditations. There were no open spaces anywhere in the space station. She never noticed how many people she brushed against just walking through the lanes until moments like this, when she desperately wanted the space.

Or moments when no one was brushing against her. Rabia lifted her head, taking her hands out of her pockets even before her eyes confirmed it: she was alone in the middle of an apparently empty lane. But the lanes were never empty.

"Go ahead and come out," she called. Urchins materialized all around her, mostly boys and mostly teenagers, although a few were girls and a few were far too young for this sort of work. Alain's gang took all comers, apparently. But then that was Alain, wasn't it? The egalitarian. Corporate people excepted. "Take me to your leader," Rabia said. No one laughed. "Well, you're my escort, right?"

"Do you surrender?" one of the bigger boys asked.

"Oh, don't say it like that," Rabia said. She knew Omesh was right. She knew she was immature when she said in Tak's place she would fight rather than take it. She guessed he'd say the same thing to her now. What did a few words cost her? But she couldn't say them.

And Alain knew it. What was he playing at?

"Do you surrender?" the boy repeated, pulling a blackjack out of thin air—certainly his shirt was too threadbare to have hidden it—and slapping it significantly against his palm.

"Is that how it is? Come on, then," Rabia said. But even as she settled into her stance, she was purposefully calm. She focused on her breathing, desperately hoping she could control her emotions as easily. She had never been struck with a blackjack before, but she had little doubt it would hurt. It was going to take a miracle, containing her anger.

Then she saw him. Alain was there, a little further down the lane, well out of her reach with all his gang between them. He was leaning against a wall, watching her coolly with arms crossed, Tom as always right behind him. His face was a riot of colors, the purples and blacks just beginning to fade to yellows and greens. There was a kink in his nose that hadn't been there before.

Rabia didn't care how much the blackjack hurt; she vowed to hold her anger. She would meet the urchins' aggression, surely, but she would not be the one to escalate it.

Then they fell upon her, attacking her in twos and threes. Not a bad strategy, considering how long it had been since Si Fu had held a proper class and she'd had other students to practice defending against multiple attacks with. But her mind focused only on her breath, leaving her muscles to remember moves that, though not practiced recently, had been practiced repeatedly.

The boy with the blackjack did manage to get a shot in, and when she staggered, the others fell back, thinking they had her down. But Rabia judged it a glancing blow; he had struck her from behind and she hadn't seen it, but it certainly felt like it had grazed rather than hit her full square. She didn't wait for her vision to clear of the exploding black balloons before she stepped back and caught him in the throat with an elbow strike. She distinctly heard the blackjack hit the hull of the ship below them with a dull thud, then the boy followed. Her vision was still swooping back and forth as if she were on a sailing ship on high seas, conflicting with the information her inner ears were giving her. Not that they were still; they were mostly swooping the opposite way, and not at the same frequency. Rabia closed her eyes, tuning out the vertigo and focusing on where she remembered the blackjack lying as she squatted low and swept her fingertips over the hull. When she straightened, the weapon was in her hand. She hoped that looked intimidating enough; she couldn't quite get her eyes to focus on any of the other urchins around her yet.

"Hold," Alain said.

When Rabia's vision at last cleared, the two of them were alone in the lane. Or rather the three of them, Tom a discrete distance back but still present.

"What do you want, Rabia?"

Rabia reversed the weapon in her hand and held it out for him to take. Tom stepped forward and took it, stuffing it into a pocket before fading back once more.

"Well?" Alain prompted.

"I need your help," Rabia said.

"That seems unlikely."

"I need to talk to the dons."

"I stand corrected. It's not unlikely; it's impossible."

"Please, Alain. It's important."

Alain looked at her, studied her, really. Two fingertips reached up to rub at the bridge of his nose, a gesture of his she knew well, but he desisted with a hiss of pain.

"I'm sorry." It sounded so small. But there weren't words big enough.

"We were friends once," he said.

"I didn't change that."

"No, you were pretty consistent in your dishonesty, weren't you?" Alain shot back. He reached for his nose again but thought better of it. "Because we were once friends, I'll hear you out. I'm not promising any more than that."

"This is because we were once friends, not because you feel guilty about what you did to Si Fu's school?" Rabia regretted the words as soon as they were out of her mouth, but as usual she couldn't take them back.

"I feel no guilt," Alain said. "Speak."

Rabia touched the back of her head gingerly. There was blood on her fingertips when she pulled them away. No wonder her thoughts were refusing to line themselves up. As best she could, she told him everything: what Tak had overheard, what her family had told her. Her words trailed off uncertainly at the end, but she had gotten her point across if the grave look on Alain's face was any indication. He made a motion with his hand and Tom stepped forward again, this time with a towel in his hand. Alain took it and pressed it to the back of Rabia's head, placing her own hand over it before stepping back.

"You should get back home. I'll take it from here."

"I want to help," Rabia said.

"There's nothing for you to do. I'll speak to my boss, and he'll speak to the dons."

"Then what?"

"They'll find a way to verify your story first. Do you realize what it means, if this is all true?"

"Well yeah," Rabia said with deep sarcasm. "Bye-bye Barnacle Town."

"No, I don't think that's likely," Alain said. "That can be prevented. No, the real problem here is that one don is acting against the others. If what you tell me is true, that is."

"What does that matter, compared to the rest of it?"

"If the dons start openly fighting each other, it could very well end up being a bloodbath."

"But it's just the one acting against the others. How many are there, anyway?"

"I'm not telling you that. But the balance of power is a very complex thing. One little nudge here and a lot of people are going to start flapping their arms to get that balance back."

"But you think they can save Barnacle Town? And they'll do that before they start killing each other?"

"The dons will take care of their own."

"Will you tell me when you hear anything?"

"Why don't you ever take my advice? Go back inside your space station and stay there, safe."

"I have people here," Rabia said. "Can I ask you one more thing?"

"You can ask."

"That guy you got to fight me—did you know who he was?"

"Who is he?" Alain asked.

"His name is Hjalmar Chandi. His dad is the CEO of Chandi V. Are you saying you didn't know that? Did you approach him to fight or the other way around?"

"The other way around," Alain said distractedly. "That is interesting."

"Have you seen him since?"

"No, but then why would I?" Alain said.

"I guess he's probably not going to come back to Barnacle Town now. He must know more than we do about all this."

"Do you really think so? I've noticed the better off a family is, the more extended the adolescence of their children."

Rabia was sure there was a dig at her in there somewhere, but she decided to let it pass. "I want to know what's going on; will you keep me in the loop here?"

"Why can't you just stay home?"

"Look, you know I won't do that. So let me help. Omesh in the curry stand can get messages to me even when I'm in the space station. Will you tell him when you know anything?"

"Fine, whatever."

"Good luck," Rabia said.

Alain smirked, then he and Tom disappeared down the lane.

Rabia headed back to the airlock, but her feet slowed as she approached the long stairway. She listened to the sounds of the people around her, breathed the smells in deeply. She had the horrible premonition that this time when she stepped through the airlock, there would be no stepping back. Surely they had more time, a few days at least. So her mind said, but her heart felt differently.

She wanted to stay. She wanted to be here when things started happening, helping out in any way she could. But she had no way to help, really. She knew getting meaningful help from Hjalmar was a long shot, but she had to try.

She felt guilty, though. With everything that was at stake here, she felt her blood warm just at the thought of being near him again. It wouldn't remotely be a romantic moment, but with Hjalmar, she would take what she could get.

CHAPTER FIFTEEN

TAKASHI

IT WAS THE MIDDLE OF PRACTICE, BUT NO ONE'S heart really seemed in it. The wrestlers were more playacting than truly trying to best each other, and the advice and cajoling from the coaches were vague, as if they were only half watching themselves. Tak found it frustrating; he very much wanted to lose himself, to focus just on the art of sumo and forget all else, but if no one else was focusing, it was impossible. Sumo was not a one-man sport.

"The tournament is coming up soon," he said to one of the other rikishi as they drank from the water bucket. "Doesn't anyone want to train hard?"

"There's not much point," the other wrestler

answered. "This one is on Mars; we never do well on Mars."

"But it's the same wrestlers at every tournament. What difference does it make if it's on Mars, Luna, or one of the space stations?"

"Spacers seldom wrestle well in real gravity," Kenko said. Tak hadn't even heard him approach, but his shinai was out of sight.

"I'd think we'd have an advantage, training in higher gravity. We're stronger," the other wrestler said.

"Your reflexes are honed to this environment," Kenko said. "If it were just a matter of strength, there would be no problem. But we will only be on the surface for two days before the tournament, not enough time to relearn how to move. Walking is going to be challenge enough."

"Plus there's the Coriolis effect," Tak added. "As a spacer, you're accustomed to compensating for it. On Mars, you'll be compensating for something that *isn't* there. It's a small thing, but you'd be surprised how many little ways you'll feel its lack."

"You've been to Mars?" Kenko asked.

"I've been everywhere but Earth."

Kenko grunted and nodded, the shinai behind his back slapping lightly against his leg. "You have experience in adapting to different environments."

"Since I was a baby."

"It will be interesting to watch you fight." Tak didn't know what to say. From Kenko, that came scarily close to being a compliment. "Enough water. Back to practice."

Tak was just squaring off with another wrestler when he saw his teacher Toyonoshima come out of the door at the far side of the practice yard. The door that led to the bridge of the cargo ship. Then the other wrestler's charge hit him and knocked him to the sand with a whoosh.

"Mind elsewhere?" Kenko taunted.

"What was Toyonoshima doing on the bridge?" Tak asked as he got back on his feet.

"Not our business."

But Tak tuned him out, eyes on where Toyonoshima had met Hiroku. The two were too far away for Tak to overhear anything, but the startled look that swept across Hiroku's famously stoic face gave Tak a very bad feeling.

"Something is going on."

"When we need to know, they will tell us. Get back to fighting," Kenko said, but something had the other rikishi in a stir.

"Do you hear that?" one of them asked.

"Hear what?" Kenko countered, patience worn thin.

"Listen."

They all stood silent, straining to hear. The stable master and schoolteacher had left the moment before, and every wrestler and coach stood rooted to the spot, heads tipped as they listened intently. Tak was just seeing the humor in the scene they were making when he heard something, too. A banging.

Every rikishi looked down at where their massive feet touched the sandy floor.

"Someone's outside," one of them whispered.

"Impossible," Kenko said, but he was whispering too.

There were a few more sounds, sometimes light and sometimes heavy. They were moving.

"Someone is out there," Tak said, dropping to one knee to spread a hand across the floor. He, of course, felt nothing.

"Who?" one of the younger rikishi asked.

Kenko's eyes met his, and he knew they were both thinking the same thing. He looked around at the other rikishi, some of them not more than twelve years old. He should tell them. They should know.

But before he could speak, Hiroku was back,

clapping his hands to end a practice session that had ground to its own halt some minutes before.

"Coaches, come with me. Rikishi, wait here for further instructions," he said curtly, then was gone. Kenko and the other older students went with him. Tak crept to the edge of the sandpit to watch them go. Hiroku was gesturing as he walked and Tak's eyes followed the direction of one of his pointing fingers, to where Toyonoshima was moving aside the potted trees from the back of the garden near the torii gate.

They were taking out the sheets of thick metal plating.

Tak bolted from the practice ring, ignoring the cries of surprise from the other rikishi. Pausing only long enough to fetch his robe and geta—because his wrestle belt was a tad more revealing than he liked to be in public—he headed out the door of the school. The coaches taking up the metal sheets mostly had their backs to him, but even the ones looking his way didn't bother to stop him. Hiroku had been throwing a lot of orders around, and rikishi were hustling about on missions in all directions; even heading out of the school, Tak didn't look suspicious.

He was out the gate and nearly to the end of the lane where the coaches were stacking the metal plates when a hand on his arm stopped him.

"Takashi," Kenko said with the barest shake of his head.

"It's happening," Tak said, taking advantage of the moment to put on his geta and properly belt his robe.

"No, it isn't. Not yet. They are only laying the explosive."

"Only?" Tak scoffed.

"It's politics, Takashi. This is their move, like a threat. But they will wait for the dons' response before taking the next step."

"Well, I'm not going to wait. People need to know."

"Know what? They've heard the same sounds you have."

But Tak didn't stay any longer to argue, and Kenko didn't stop him again, just turned back up the lane to help bring down another metal plate. If Tak wasn't back in time, he knew they wouldn't hesitate to seal him out, but a warning had to be raised.

Or did it? There was a weirdness in the air in Barnacle Town. People were racing about just as he was, acting as if they were searching for something but all too readily interrupted in their search to cluster into groups and speak together in earnest whispers. Lots of people had heard the sounds coming from outside, but no one seemed to know what it meant.

Then Tak rounded the corner to cross the large lane that lay between him and the curry stand, the one that led up to the airlock into the space station. The lane was packed with people, all shouting and pushing to get past each other and get a better look. What they were trying to see Tak had no clue, but it was clear that at any moment the tense worry could erupt into violence. It only needed one person pushing a little too hard.

He would have to force his way through. There was no other way to the curry stand, short of storming through people's homes.

"What's happening?" someone near Tak asked.

"I can't tell," Tak said.

"They've closed off the airlock." The boy who gave this answer looked like he had just emerged from that shoving crowd, clothes torn and disheveled and a lip just starting to turn puffy.

"Why?" the man behind Tak asked. "It's not like they ever let any of us in."

Tak didn't answer. Things were close enough to panic without him pointing out that shutting an airlock had a pretty obvious purpose: to contain atmosphere, not people.

"I need to get up there," someone else said. This

man was wearing a Chandi Corporation jumpsuit, just some guy looking for a little after-shift fun. "They must know they've locked me out. I signed out at the guard desk, but I haven't signed back in."

"You might want to get off the street," the puffy-lipped kid said.

"But I have to get up there!"

"It's up to you, but if it were me, I wouldn't be plunging into that crowd wearing those clothes," the kid said with a shrug.

"The guards on the other side of the airlock have no way of seeing you," Tak said. "There are a hundred people already knocking on that door, and they're not opening. Take the kid's advice; get off the street."

"Maybe you're right," the man said uncertainly. Tak didn't hang around waiting for him to make a decision, though. He still had to find Omesh. Cinching up the belt of his yukata, he pushed his way into the crowd. His girth came in handy; even the few young men he jostled who seemed inclined to make something of it quickly changed their minds when they saw the size of him. Getting back across with Omesh's family was going to be a bit of a trick, but if they stayed close in his wake, it might be doable.

The lane on the far side was empty and Tak

broke once more into a run, geta clanking loudly on the uneven metal ground. Omesh was alone in the deserted curry stand, an odd assortment of electronic parts spread out on the counter before him. He looked up, frowning, as Tak ran in.

"It's time, then?"

"They've shut the airlock in the middle of the day, and someone is outside on the outer hulls of Barnacle Town, laying down explosives," Tak told him. "It's not panic out there, not yet, but it will be soon. I think you should get your family and come with me."

"What?"

"There's plenty of room on the freighter. And not just for you. If we throw out the buildings and the garden plants, we can fit a lot of people in there."

"Not everyone," Omesh said.

"No, but a lot."

"This is your teacher's plan?"

"No, it's my plan, but they're damn well going to do it."

Omesh looked down at the parts on the counter. His aunt emerged from the kitchen and leaned against the doorway, her gaze sweeping from Tak to Omesh. She looked worried.

"My uncle isn't here," Omesh said to Tak at

last. "He went out to fetch the midwife, but he hasn't come back yet."

"You want to wait for him? They were starting to seal off the lanes around the sumo school even as I ran out; I'm not sure how much time we have," Tak said.

"Auntie," he started to say.

"I'm not going anywhere without Prakash. You've fixed up our sleeper module; I will wait there. When Prakash comes back, we'll all go together," she said.

"Auntie, the sleeper is not our best choice. It's like a lifeboat, we can't live long in it. The freighter is our best hope," Omesh said.

"Prakash knows to find me here; he doesn't know about the freighter."

Tak was nearly hopping up and down with impatience. If only they had comms like corporate employees, this would be a non-issue. One call to Prakash to tell him to meet them at the freighter and they'd be done.

"I'll go out and find him," Omesh said. "You go with Tak to the freighter and we'll meet you there."

"No, Omesh. I'll wait here."

Omesh grumbled to himself for a moment, then took Anjali by the arm, leading her upstairs. Tak waited at the bottom of the stairs while he explained to his aunt how to seal up the compartment and the signal he'd use to tell her to open up and let him back in.

"Will you move this inside first, Omesh dear?" she asked, indicating the little altar that stood just outside the compartment door. Tak came up the stairs to help, as clearly they weren't going anywhere until Anjali felt safe. There was scarcely room inside for the table with the elephant god and his bowl of offerings; Anjali's chair had to go to make room. After Omesh had taken it out, he found Anjali leaning against the wall of her sleeper pod, breathing hard.

"Auntie?"

"Find Prakash. Hurry."

"You want me to leave you here alone, now?"

Tak shared Omesh's incredulity. He had never seen a woman in labor before, but he was pretty sure this was it.

"I'll be fine." But she didn't sound fine; she sounded like she was in pain, and there was fear in her eyes. "Please hurry." She let Omesh help her into her sleeper pod, but quickly shooed him away afterward.

Omesh and Tak ran down the stairs and stopped. The lane was packed with people, and Omesh had no idea where to even begin searching.

"Isn't there anyone we can send to sit with her?" Tak asked.

"On a normal day, sure. Now?"

"Do you know how long it takes to weld three panels into place, then cut through the joins that hold the freighter to Barnacle Town?" Tak asked.

"Probably less time than it's going to take to find my uncle," Omesh answered, eying the crowd still gathered around the airlock. "Perhaps you should go on ahead. Hold them as long as you can. I'll be along as soon as I find my uncle."

"That's a good idea," Tak said. "I doubt they are planning to take on Barnacle Town passengers before they jet off. I have to be there to be sure they do."

"How are you going to do that, through the power of words?"

"It's all I have to work with at the moment."

"I hope to see you soon, then," Omesh said. There was an awkward pause between them; Tak had no idea what to say. Finally, he just gave a short nod and turned to go. Then Omesh caught his arm, pointing. Tak looked down the lane, the opposite direction of the crowd at the airlock.

"Good God, is that Alain? Your girlfriend certainly did a number on his face."

"What's he doing?" Omesh asked. Tak watched as the raccoon-faced Alain crossed the lane to where Tom was slouching, chewing a nail as he waited for him. Alain opened his jacket, showing Tom something he had inside. Then the two set off together.

"It can't be good," Omesh said.

"What could be worth doing now? In the midst of all this?"

Omesh looked at him. Neither of them had any idea. But as Omesh had said, it couldn't be good. And there was only one way to find out.

"We have to hurry," Tak said, slipping off his geta. The situation was going to call for fast and quiet.

CHAPTER SIXTEEN

OMESH

"I think I know where they're going," Omesh said, in the short spurts of words he could manage while also running up and down the uneven surface of the lane.

"I'm afraid I do too," Tak said. "But surely they would've locked that as well?"

"Not if they never knew it was open," Omesh said. They rounded the last corner to find the courtyard of shipping containers filled with people. Families were bustling together, gathering children and belongings, only there was nowhere to run to.

"You should just gather these people and take them back to the sumo school," Omesh said. "I don't see Alain or Tom anywhere."

"I have a bad feeling, though. Let's check the hatch first and be sure they aren't up to anything worrisome. It's just over there," Tak said. The access hatch wasn't particularly hidden, but it was off the main courtyard, at the end of a short dead-end alley, easily monitored by one ratty kid acting as a doorman.

Or two burly hoods acting as guards.

Tak and Omesh snaked their way through families with overloaded baskets to the mouth of the alley. The two hoods were not much older than Omesh and Tak, but they were large and broad, and clearly not going to let anyone pass.

"Alain sent for us," Omesh said to the one he took to be the alpha male of the two. They both wore the same black pants and shiny shirts, but this one also had a gold hoop in one ear, a recent piercing not too cleanly done to judge by the lobster-red color of his earlobe. The guy just snorted, and they both ignored him.

"The door is still open, isn't it?" Tak asked.

"No one's getting in," said the kid without an earring.

"If the door is open, let everyone in," Omesh said, stepping closer and speaking low. The people around him were three steps away from being a panicked mob; they didn't need any dashed false hopes to push them over the line.

"Not going to happen," Earring said.

"There's plenty of room in the core for every-one. There's air in the core," Tak said.

"At the moment. How long do you think that will last after the corporation discovers we're in there?"

"So what are you doing, then? You talk like you've got a better plan," Tak said.

"Well, if Alain sent you, you must know it."

"I think I do," Tak said, praying he was wrong. "He's getting leverage with the cor-poration."

"What?" Omesh asked.

"The dons want to be in a position to negotiate for Barnacle Town. Apparently that opportunity has passed. If it ever existed."

"We still have a chance," the hood said. "If we act fast. If everyone stays calm and lets the dons do their business. We have enough air to last us for several hours."

"Have enough... they've already cut us off?" Omesh asked.

"Air and water. We think they're tapping into our lines to power their equipment outside or we'd be in the dark already, too."

Omesh thought of his aunt all alone, sealed up in the sleeper pod, in labor. She was safer than most in Barnacle Town, but how afraid was she right this moment? How much more afraid would she be when the lights went out?

"What's the leverage?" Tak asked, stepping closer to Earring.

"Like I'm telling you," he scoffed.

"Then I guess we'll have to go see for ourselves, won't we, Omesh?"

"I should warn you, I'm a kickboxer. So's my brother."

"Fascinating," Tak said, then dropped into a crouch and drove his head right into Earring's solar plexus. He staggered back, gasping for breath.

"Omesh, door," Tak said.

"Right." Omesh slipped past as Tak squared off against the remaining guard. The hatch door had been left ajar, a small, flat metal bar holding it open. Omesh swung the door wide open, catching the bar before it fell to the ground. Tak was backing towards him, the remaining guard's eyes darting from Tak to his gasping brother and back again. His sense of duty won out, and he advanced on Tak, a blackjack appearing out of nowhere in his hand. Tak lowered his head, preparing to take whatever blows were necessary to bring down his man.

Omesh took advantage of that moment Tak was in his crouch to throw the metal bar in his hand. The guy ducked and batted the metal away, just managing to give Omesh a look of intense annoyance before Tak tackled him to the ground. The blackjack sailed through the air before landing in the corner of the alley with a clatter.

"Hurry," Omesh said, still holding the door open. Tak dove through first, and Omesh bent to crawl after him.

There was something ominously final about the way the door clicked shut behind them. Tak heard it too, looking back over his shoulder with a puzzled look on his face. Omesh turned around and pushed on the door.

"Well, damn," Omesh said.

"Brilliant."

"Can we break it down?"

"Oh, so very doubtful," Tak said.

"But I have to find my uncle. Anjali..." Omesh kicked at the door again, choking back a sob of rage.

"I know, but there's nothing we can do here. We have to go up. Even if Alain and Tom didn't need stopping, it's our only way out now."

Omesh nodded and Tak went ahead, moving down the tunnel in as fast a crawl as he could manage. Omesh followed behind, studiously ignoring the view of Tak he was being subjected to.

He tried to remember the night of the fight. Had he ever seen the door shut? He didn't think he had. Somehow, someone had gotten that hatch open without the corporation security system knowing and had just never let it shut. He wondered how long that situation had been maintained. Months? Years? And he had undone it at the worst possible moment. Sure, the corporation would know if the people of Barnacle Town were swarming into their core and hiding out there, and sure they would meet that challenge with as much callousness as they were exhibiting even now, but it could have bought a whole lot of people just a few more hours if only he hadn't tossed the metal bar the ruffians had been keeping wedged over the door's locking mechanism.

The elevator platforms were still there, stacked at the bottom of the endless ladder. Tak was already aboard, holding out a hand to help Omesh up, as the stack was quite a bit higher than it had been on fight night. They switched on the motor and began the long climb up to the hub.

"Help me with my geography here," Tak said suddenly. "The ship I came in on docked in the hub, but the fights weren't at the docks."

"No," Omesh said, consulting his own mental map. "The station is a torus with a long spindle, right? If you stand it on its spindle like a top,"—he gestured with his hands—"the ships dock up here, on the non-spindle side of the hub. Where we're headed is the opposite side, the spindle side."

"The space was so massive I couldn't see to the end. I guess we were looking down the spindle?"

"Yeah. I've been reading up on it since I got here. This space station was originally built as much to take advantage of zero-gravity industry as to house a community in space. But the exodus came before they got the industry underway. Which was probably a good thing, actually; they were at a minimal occupancy and had a lot of space for refugees."

"You could fit all of Barnacle Town in that spindle. Twice over, I bet," Tak said, and once again Omesh regretted the door.

This time they were prepared; Omesh kept his hand on the motor and started slowing them down when their growing weightlessness became apparent. He brought them gently to a halt at the end of the ladder.

"It's dark in there," Tak whispered. The shaft they had been in was lit with emergency lights, as were the low, narrow corridors that branched off from it every dozen meters or so. The passages were meant to be used by space station engineers performing maintenance and were lit and kept warm to a point that was almost but not quite comfortable. The core itself was unlit and, without the crowd of Barnacle Towner bodies, much colder. If there were lights in there, Omesh saw no way to turn them on from where they were.

The darkness did make it easier to find their quarry, however. Just follow the faint glow of a flashlight much further in.

"Let's move close, but not too close," Omesh suggested. "I want to see what they're doing before they see us. If we can avoid another time-consuming fight, all for the better."

"Assuming they didn't hear us coming up after them," Tak said. The motor had made a soft hum, but without it, the silence was nearly absolute.

"If they had heard, wouldn't they have ambushed us by now?"

Tak shrugged. Then, grasping the collar of Omesh's shirt, he jumped out into the open space. The girders that crisscrossed the space made frequent course correction possible, although Omesh was constantly worried they were going to collide with one in the near-total darkness.

Alain and Tom had gone much deeper down the spindle than where the fights had been staged. Tak and Omesh floated through the darkness for several long minutes. Occasionally, a sound would echo back to them, a clang of metal or a muffled curse. But then the light started getting larger faster and Omesh realized that Alain and Tom were coming back towards them. He started to move out to intercept them, but Tak caught him and pulled him behind a girder.

"Let them pass," he hissed in Omesh's ear, and Omesh nodded. It wasn't like they were going to go anywhere; all four of them were locked in together. Two of them just didn't know it yet.

Tom was carrying the light, and as they passed, he swung it up towards Alain, waiting for his response in whatever half-whispered conversation they were having. Alain waved the light away and Tom trained it back in front of them again, but it had been there long enough for Omesh to get a gruesome, up-close look at the remains of Alain's face.

If he hadn't actually seen it done, he would never believe it was Rabia's handiwork. It just didn't jibe with the happy glow that was so much more her. Of course, considering the guy who was making her glow the brightest and his own martial tendencies, maybe it made perfect sense.

"Come on," Tak said when Alain and Tom had gone.

"How are we going to find where they went? We don't have a light," Omesh said.

"There's still a light ahead of us. Can't you see it? Just barely red."

Omesh strained his eyes but didn't see what Tak was talking about until they were much further in. He didn't like contemplating the sorts of things that glowed red like that.

He liked it even less when he saw it. And when he realized what it was.

"Looks like a bomb," Tak said, but there was a question in his voice, a question hoping for a negative answer. But Omesh couldn't give it to him.

"Yes. A crude one, but definitely a bomb." Omesh looked it over as carefully as he could without touching it.

"Are you guessing like me, or do you know for sure?"

"I know for sure. This is C-4, a plastic explosive. On Earth for a month of every year, we have to do civil service. For most of us, it's what they call urban reclamation; destroying what's left of the towns and cities so we can use the land for more farms. My father is certified in explosives, so instead of being on rubble removal duty, he brings down the buildings."

"And you got to help?"

"Well, I got to watch. But I was in training."

Omesh frowned, leaning in closer. There was little to be seen in the dim light, especially as that dim light was coming from the digital readout on the top and the rest of it was out of reach of the light. The counter read just under two hours.

"Why here? Why not in the center of the space station?"

"It's not big enough to destroy the space station anyway," Omesh said. "And even if it were, they would have put it in the hub, not out here. They aren't trying to destroy the station; they're doing something else. But what?"

"You said this space was for industry, but no one ever uses it," Tak said.

"True," Omesh said, tugging at his lip. He was missing something.

"It's on the hull. Are they hoping to punch a hole, vent the atmosphere out into space? Maybe they picked this place because it's so out of the way the corporation won't be able to respond as quickly."

"Aside from the fact that this area is already sealed off from the station proper, I don't think the explosion would be enough to breach the hull," Omesh said. "Not enough to do more than damage these cables here, maybe."

His mental picture of the space station suddenly loomed back up before his eyes, pivoting around to stop spindle up. When he had seen it from space, his eyes had been full of the massive torus, and of Barnacle Town, but the constant glinting at the far end hadn't escaped his notice.

"The solar panels. They're going to knock out the power to the whole space station."

CHAPTER SEVENTEEN

RABIA

Rabia felt like shaking her sister until that implant rattled right out of her head, but she restrained herself, taking deep breaths. Lots of deep breaths. Enough to start getting a little dizzy.

"I know you know where he is," she said at last.

"And I know you know I know," Teresa said, far too pleased with herself.

"He's been to Barnacle Town, more than once. And he's in a position to do something actually helpful. I have to talk to him."

"Since he came here with the group that is even now jettisoning Barnacle Town into space, I think your sense that he's on your side might be a bit misguided," Teresa said.

"Just tell me where he is so I can talk to him and he can tell me that himself."

"Sorry, no." A frown passed over her face and her eyes grew even more unfocused. It was disconcerting. When she was more passively accessing her implant, she tended to look like a blind person trying to look at you, but not quite able to make eye contact. This deeper thing she did was like talking to a someone who was communing with deities like the oracle at Delphi or something, like Rabia wasn't even there as Teresa just tossed words out to the universe at large.

"What is it?" Rabia asked.

"I don't know. Nothing is setting off any warning systems or anything, but there is definitely something not right in the core. Fluctuations in the readings, within the normal range, but still..."

"People in the core?" Rabia guessed.

"Shouldn't be possible."

"It is. There's a hatch," Rabia admitted with a sigh. However this shook out, there would be no more zero G fights. She might have sworn off fighting herself, but she hadn't meant to deny everyone else the opportunity.

"Access hatch," Teresa said, sitting forward in her chair. "I see it now. It's secured."

"Did you lock anyone in?" Rabia asked. "Lots

of Barnacle Town know that door is there. They could all fit in the core if they tried."

"That many people would have set off the alarms," Teresa said. "But just a few, the size of a maintenance crew, wouldn't."

"More than that can get by, and routinely do," Rabia said. "We've been having fights in the core for years."

"We?" Teresa asked, her gaze turning sharp all at once to pin an accusing glance at her sister. Rabia just shrugged. "I'm going to have to dig deeper. Sorry, no more conversation."

"Tell me where he is first," Rabia said, but her sister was already gone, pupils dilated down to mere specks in that way Rabia always found so creepy. She reclined her sister's chair, putting a pillow under her head. Teresa would lose all track of time once she started picking apart programs to examine the code. Teresa had told their parents that the implant was only a computer link, but Rabia had her doubts. Something was working to slow Teresa's heartbeat and respiration, to diminish her need for food, drink, or the call of nature for long periods of time. Such things could be learned through meditation or yoga, Rabia knew, but Teresa never did either of those things. Something in her head was giving her a shortcut.

Rabia pulled Teresa's favorite quilt off her

bunk and carried it back to the living room to spread over her, then left her alone in the apartment. She was going to find Hjalmar if she had to go door to door to do it.

Although she was aware of people all around her, crowded together in the apartment buildings or the makeshift shelters, the streets of the space station were empty. But Rabia had the strong sense that no one was sleeping. It was nearing midnight, but there was an energy in the air. It felt like fearful expectation, but perhaps she was only projecting her own feelings. She headed toward the community center. It was late for anyone to be about, but it was as good a place as any to start.

She wasn't technically allowed in the building with the high-end apartments where the Chandi family would be staying. She would probably get dirty looks just for walking in that neighborhood. She could get in through access ports easily enough—before her days of roaming Barnacle Town, she had passed the time exploring the elaborate system of tunnels that connected all the space station buildings through their sub-basements—but there would be hell to pay if she were caught there now. And she surely would be.

Despite the hour, there was a gathering of people in the center's sports room. She paused in the doorway, eyes scanning the crowd for a head of silver-blond hair. He wasn't there, but she rec-ognized her father near the center of the tight cir-cle. Then she saw more familiar faces; the Jeffersonian Christians were all there, and it looked like they'd each brought ten more people with them. These were the people her father had managed to gather together, then. It was a good-sized crowd, but they didn't look like they'd be much help. Despite the fire in their eyes, they were just middle-level employees like her parents. She stepped back out of the room, letting the door softly click shut behind her.

She poked through the cafeteria, dark and abandoned, and the games room where a few teenagers were lurking, not playing games. One of them saw her and waved her over.

"I know you," the kid said when she was close enough to hear a low-pitched voice. "You used to be a Jeffersonian, but you don't come to meetings anymore."

"I'm still a Jeffersonian, thank you very much. I'm just not a big-group-meeting kind of girl," Rabia said.

"You go to Barnacle Town all the time. Do you know what's going on?" he asked. The whole group was looking at her anxiously, and one girl had the end of one of her braids in her mouth, chewing her own hair mechanically.

"What have you heard?" Rabia asked.

"Are they really massacring all of them? The corporation?"

"In a manner of speaking."

"Man, that sucks," one of them said. "No more bathtub gin."

"Who cares about that? My girlfriend lives there," said another.

"Lots of girlfriends live there," Rabia said. "Although clearly we must also save the gin. Life around here is going to be beyond dull without Barnacle Town."

"What can we do?" the girl with the braids asked.

"Storm the airlock and force them to open it back up?" the gin boy suggested.

"Considering they're in the process of removing Barnacle Town as we speak, I think that would be a very bad idea. You'll have no way of knowing if it's Barnacle Town or the vacuum of space on the other side."

The kid didn't like having his idea axed and showed it. "Well, what are you doing about it, then?"

Rabia carefully didn't let his aggressive tone get to her, unless putting extra perk in her own voice was letting it get to her. "I'm looking for a guy with silver-blond hair. Have you seen him?"

The guy that had called her over scoffed loudly, but another sat up straighter. Rabia could almost see the lightbulb going on over his head.

"Are you sure you aren't looking for a chick?"

"Definitely a guy. Why?"

"Because there's a girl with hair like that in the observatory. She's been there all night, just staring at the starscape screen. I've never seen her before in my life; she must be from the other side of the station or something."

Rabia was halfway out the door before she remembered to shout back a thanks. The observatory was across the quad, but since what was meant to be an open space of lawn was now home to several dozen families, she had to take the long way around. She was just running around the corner of the observatory toward the front door when she collided with someone coming the other way, knocking them both back like pool balls.

"Watch it," the girl snapped, flicking an immaculately styled wave of hair out of her eyes. She had exceedingly fair hair, and her skin was paler still, with just a hint of pink that suggested time in real sunlight under a real sky, but her eyes were incongruously dark. Also, familiar.

"You know Hjalmar," Rabia said excitedly.

"Somehow I doubt you do," the girl responded, brushing at herself as if Rabia had somehow gotten her dirty.

"But I do, and I need to see him."

"He's terribly, terribly busy."

"I'm sure you Chandis are all very busy, killing off thousands of inconvenient people."

"You're quite rude."

"Thank you."

"That wasn't a compliment."

"Wasn't it?"

The girl wrinkled her nose, then attempted to brush past her. Rabia caught her arm. The girl looked down at her hand as if it were an insect.

"I need to talk to Hjalmar," Rabia said. She knew she sounded like a simpleton, over-pronouncing each word, but it was all she could do at the moment not to lose her temper.

"I don't see that happening," the girl replied, freeing her arm with a sharp twist. Hjalmar wasn't the only fighter in the family, apparently.

"Please—he does know me."

"We've only been here a few days, and my brother is a notorious recluse. How could he possibly know you?"

"We fought each other in the zero G matches." It was a risk; Rabia's parents didn't know she did that, and the other corporate types who had entered the matches hadn't told their nearest and dearest either. It was likely Hjalmar had kept it a secret as well. Yet the girl's eyebrows slowly rose.

"You're Rabia?"

"Yes!"

"He said you had pink hair."

"Well, this week it's purple." The look on the girl's face said more than words about what she thought of that.

"I'm going to regret this," she said with a sigh, then turned and led the way down the street, toward the more opulent apartment buildings. Rabia had to jog to keep up with her, which was annoying since the girl seemed to be just walking herself. And it was a walk of sheer elegance; a book on top of her head wouldn't fall off. How'd she move so fast like that? How long were her legs under that ankle-length black skirt?

The lobby of the apartment wasn't particularly swank. The furniture in it was worn and everything looked just a little dingy. No, it reeked of luxury just because it *was* a lobby. The building Rabia lived in had had a lobby once. Now three families shared that space and everyone came in through the back door.

"You know what's happening?" Rabia asked as they went up the elevator.

"Better than you do."

"And it doesn't feel wrong to you?"

"This may come as a surprise to you, but no one actually asked me how I *felt*."

"But still..."

The elevator doors opened, and the girl shot Rabia another annoyed look before stepping out. The guard at the station glanced up but said nothing as the two girls passed him by.

Rabia had had a picture in her mind of what a nice apartment on the station looked like: bedrooms for everyone with room enough for a bed and a chair and a toilet in a whole separate room. Separate sitting rooms and dining rooms. Its own kitchen and a bathroom or two. At the first step inside the apartment, she realized just how small she had been imagining.

The girl realized Rabia was still standing in the doorway and reached back to pull her through with a barely contained sigh. "Surely you've seen this all on *Homes of the Corporate Princes* or whatever you folks call that program."

"Haven't seen, not my sort of thing, and what do you mean 'you folks'?" Rabia rattled off automatically. What she was really thinking was more along the lines of "Wow—wow—wow." The ceiling soared far above her, with lights dangling on chains at the proper level. The room may have been designed as a sitting area with pillows and chairs and even couches, but they were strewn over such an expanse of space a person in one chair would be hard-pressed to carry on a conversation with a person in the next chair.

What a waste of space. What a fabulous waste of space.

"Come along, my little gawker. Hjalmar and I share the apartment in the back."

Rabia followed, somehow resisting the urge to bend down and touch the thick, colorful carpets that showed no sign of ever being walked on before. This place was nothing like the lobby below. The furniture of brightly polished wood was covered with china vases, small sculptures of stone, wood, or metal, bowls of flowers she just knew were fresh. That temptation she did give in to, bending to smell a gorgeous bouquet of pink and red roses. Yep, they were real.

"Hjalmar, company," the girl called as they passed another set of doors, these standing open.

"Not tonight, Ulrika, I told you."

Rabia followed the voice to a chair in the corner, facing away from the door. She could only see the top of his white-blond head.

"Sorry, Rabia, but you heard what the man said," Ulrika said, but made no move to lead her out. Hjalmar jumped up from the chair and turned to face them.

"Well, I'll leave you two to it," Ulrika said and

retreated from the room, her feet noiseless on the lush carpeting. Rabia watched her leave almost wistfully. Now that she was here, she had no idea what exactly she should say. She realized she had never really thought she'd find him.

"You're safe," he said at last.

"No, I'm not one of the twelve corporate residents trapped on the wrong side of the airlock," Rabia said. "Neither am I one of the thousands of Barnacle Town residents your family has condemned to death."

He looked shocked, as if her words came as a blow. She was beginning to wonder if he hadn't actually known what was going on when he turned away from her to pick up a glass that had been sitting on a table near his chair and drained its contents in one long swallow. "It's more complicated than you think."

"People are going to die. Nothing complicated about that."

"I saved you."

"How do you figure that?"

"I told you to stay away from Barnacle Town, and you stayed away."

"No, actually, I didn't," Rabia said. "I'm not in the habit of doing what I'm told, particularly not when the person telling me what to do is so very carefully not telling me his name."

"So it's just luck that you were home?"

"Pretty much. My sister says I signed back in less than five minutes before they sealed the airlock."

"So the one thing I tried to do turned out to be superfluous. Typical," Hjalmar said. He sat down on the arm of the chair and picked up a small sculpture off the end table to fidget with.

"I guess it's time to try a second thing, yes?" Rabia prompted.

"Hey, I risked a lot just warning you," he said.

"Did you really?" Rabia scoffed. "And would you call it a warning? 'Hey Rabia, Barnacle Town is going to be blasted into space, tell your friends' is a warning. What you gave me was a bit more like a command."

"If I had told you what I knew, you would have told others."

"Certainly."

"And what would they have done? The ones who could afford shuttle fare would leave, maybe, but the rest would be trapped and panic would set in. In that scenario, you've managed to save maybe a dozen or so of the rich dons. In exchange, you've put a lot of corporate lives at risk. Or don't you think your Barnacle Town friends would plan some retaliation?"

"You've forced them into a no-win scenario. What would you do?"

"That's a nonsense question. I would never put myself in such a tenuous position."

"Because Barnacle Towners chose to be there."

"You think Chandi Corporation scoured the skies, finding ships at the end of their lives and forced them to weld themselves to our hull, I suppose."

"Don't play stupid with me," Rabia said, stepping forward to snatch the statue from his hands. He hadn't once looked at her, and it was starting to annoy her. "Barnacle Town is the result of a lot of people facing a long series of 'I do this or I die' choices. Yes, that sequence ends at a very tenuous position indeed. I'm sorry it inconveniences you and your family. But don't characterize it as a choice you'd never make. As if you were the death-choosing type."

"Why did you come here, Rabia?"

"To talk to you."

"To me or at me?"

"You're in a better position than I am to help."

"I can see why you might think so," he said, snatching the statue back out of her hands to set it back on the table. "But honestly, I'm not."

"You won't even try?"

"Try what? Do you even have a plan?"

"You can't talk to your family. Can't stop this?"

"My father has been trying to stop this day from coming for ten years. He had to lie to do it, to hide the reasons this station cycles through so much more air and water and energy per capita than any other Chandi Corporation—"

"The dons pay for that."

"—to hide in the bookkeeping the bribe money he's accepted that never quite matches the actual cost," Hjalmar went on as if she hadn't just interrupted. "To downplay the wear and tear on the engineering of this space station that carrying an extra, improperly balanced load causes. It lost him his marriage; my mother hasn't spoken to him in years. It's just now cost him his job. Can you grasp the implications of that?"

"Yes," Rabia said. Facing a life outside of the corporation herself, she had an inkling. Of course, looking around the apartments, it was clear he was giving up much more than she was. "Your grandfather would do that to his own son?"

"Not his son. Son-in-law," Hjalmar said. "And yes, he would. He will."

"Why did he bring you and your sister with him to do it? That seems a little heartless."

"Why do you think?" Hjalmar asked, looking straight at her for the first time. There was so much pain in his eyes, Rabia nearly staggered back.

"It's a test," Rabia guessed.

"Indeed. Grandfather needs to know if we stand with our mother, with our family, with the Chandi Corporation, or if we stand with our father."

Rabia felt bad for him. She really did. That pity was the only thing that kept her from telling him to man up already. But she wasn't going to back down, either. "Well, which is it?"

"You're the one who brought up 'do or die' decisions. Which do you think?"

"You're telling me if you side with your father, you'll be vented off into space?"

"No. I'll be dropped in one of the cities of Luna, or maybe Mars, with no cash and no prospects."

"That seems like death to you?"

"Look, if I side with my father, I gain nothing. Nothing," he said when she started to scoff. "I will not be able to stop Barnacle Town from being cast off into space to either float away or crash down to the moon. I won't be able to stop my father from being banished to the far moons to find his own way back or not, more likely not. Despite what you might think, I'm not actually being offered a choice here."

"Maybe that's not true, though," Rabia said. "Life isn't a series of A or B choices."

"You just said it was. Do or die, you said."

"Forget what I said; this is more complex than that." She stared at him hard until he gave a small shrug that she decided to take as him conceding the point. "There must be some other choice no one is seeing. Barnacle Town can't stay. If you say that's true, I'll accept it as a starting point. But does it follow that they all have to die? That you have to get rid of Barnacle Town like this? It's inhuman."

"Where would you send them? What city would take on that many refugees all at once? And how would you get them there? This station has already been a financial sinkhole for more than a decade—who is going to step up to pay to save thousands of useless people?"

It was probably the word "financial" that did it. Rabia slapped him, hard. He didn't even flinch. She slapped him again, but still he made no move to stop her. Her hand had left a red mark, vivid on the milky paleness of his skin. He shook the hair back out of his eyes and fixed her with his dark gaze, and almost as if it were an image he had sent directly into her mind telepathically, she saw Alain's bleeding face. Then Hjalmar raised his chin just a notch, inviting her to hit him again.

Rabia spun around and stormed out of the room, past the other rooms filled with roses and chandeliers and shelves of little costly nothings. He knew as well as she did that if she had wanted to hurt him, she would have hurt him. A slap was meant to shame. The look in his eye, the tilt of his chin—he could no more feel shame than Omesh could feel a murderous rage.

Rabia, thinking of Alain, thinking of all of Barnacle Town, felt both.

CHAPTER EIGHTEEN

TAKASHI

"So, do you know how to disarm a bomb?" Tak asked, going for levity. It was hard to tell by the dim red light of the counter, but Omesh was looking a little gray.

"No," Omesh said. He sounded gray as well.

"Me neither." Tak was actually a bit afraid to touch it. He didn't know what jiggling it about would do.

"If the counter is accurate, we've got nearly two hours. I think we need to get some help."

"I'd have more trust in the accuracy of that counter if I knew who'd built this thing," Tak said, desperately hoping it wasn't something Alain and Tom had cooked up together. "I can't argue about going for help, but we are, in fact, still locked in here."

"We're locked out of Barnacle Town, but no one in Barnacle Town is going to be much help right now," Omesh said.

"So, what do you think?"

"We go back down the ladder and take one of the cross passages."

"And hope to run into an engineer?"

"Or find a door out."

"You don't think it will be locked?"

"If we're loud enough, someone will come and investigate."

"At the very least, they'll get us out of their service halls and toss us back into Barnacle Town." Tak sighed. "I guess that's our plan, then."

Tak took the lead back through the now-dark spindle. The ladder shaft was dimly lit, enough that he could see what he was aiming for, but not enough to even get a sense of how far away it was. It was like a will-o'-the-wisp in a fairy tale, always just a little farther on. Plus, his yukata was really a summer robe. Outside of the lowest level of rikishi, anyone who wore one was just looking for something to wrap up in while at a steaming bathhouse. It wasn't designed for the temperatures the core was kept at. If he had more light, Tak was sure he would see his breath clouding.

When they reached the top of the ladder shaft, they could just hear the sounds of Alain and Tom pounding and cursing at the door back to Barnacle Town, an angry, echoing murmur.

"Our elevator platform is gone," Omesh said. "They know we're here."

"If we're quick, they won't find us," Tak said. "Hold on to my back."

Omesh obeyed, catching hold of fistfuls of the robe at Tak's shoulders. Tak, still holding his geta in his hand, caught a ladder rung with his toes and pushed, caught another with the toes of his other foot and pushed again. It took a few steps to find a rhythm, and Omesh too was adjusting himself on Tak's back to flow with the motion, but after a few levels, he was nearly up to a run.

They had to go quite a ways down to get to the first cross passage, far more than half the length of the shaft. Tak guessed by the weight of Omesh on his back that they were at about half normal gravity at that point, and his steps were less about running and more about slowing their fall. Tak stopped their motion with both feet and a hand on the ladder, and Omesh let go of him, pushing off the wall to land in the corridor with a stumbling clatter. Tak jumped and landed somewhat more gracefully beside him.

"Where is this, do you think?" Tak asked,

hands on knees both to catch his breath and because the corridor was too low-ceilinged to stand up in.

"There is a sort of tower that runs through the space station. It looks like a skyscraper to the rest of the space station, or so I've read, but it runs from the hub to the airlock at Barnacle Town. When you came in through the cargo bay, the elevator went down through this building," Omesh said.

"What else is in it besides the elevators?"

"I don't know. Offices?"

"Here at half G?"

"Storage then?" Omesh shrugged. "Does it matter?"

"So if we follow this passage, we'll be going past storage or maintenance rooms, not living quarters. It's past midnight station time; no one is going to be around to hear us."

"We'll find someone once we get out," Omesh said. "But we really have to hurry."

They started down the long corridor. The light was dim, only a series of low-illumination LED strips placed as far apart as possible. The sounds echoed and re-echoed around them deceptively, but Tak had the feeling that Alain and Tom had given up on the door and were coming back toward him and Omesh.

Walking along the passage was preferable to climbing down a near-endless ladder, but not by much. It was not quite tall enough for either of them to stand upright while they walked, but too tall for crawling to be necessary. Running in a crouch quickly grew tiring. Other, similar corridors crossed theirs at regular intervals. Tak took the first turn, just to get them out of sight from the ladder in case Alain and Tom were looking around while they were bickering with each other, but after that he kept on straight.

"Do you know where we're going?" Omesh asked after several long minutes.

"Not really. I'm hoping we find another ladder that will take us farther down."

"Or a doorway out," Omesh said.

"Whatever works." Tak wished he had some way of measuring time, but perhaps it was just as well he didn't. There was little he could do with the knowledge if he had it. And even if he knew exactly how much time he had before that bomb exploded, he had no way of measuring how much time remained before the sumo school freighter left him and the rest of Barnacle Town to their fates.

One problem at a time.

"What's that?" Omesh asked, pointing up ahead. There was a little space set off from the main corridor. As they reached it, they saw it was some sort of computer station, with CPUs stacked against the wall, complete with cooling systems and lots of screens of readouts.

"What's it doing here?" Tak asked, poking his head back out to look farther down the corridor. Still no sign of a door; who would work here?

"It's probably some sort of security measure, putting backups where none of the corporate employees know they are."

"Someone must come down here or everything would be covered in dust, don't you think?" Tak said.

"You can get some*thing* to take care of that without some*one* ever knowing about it," Omesh said. "Cleaning robots."

"Swank," Tak said. "I don't think this helps us."

"Unless there's a way to call up a map to guide us out of here, or to send a message for help."

"Maybe you can contact Rabia."

"Maybe," Omesh said, looking over the screens. There was no visible means of interacting with anything, no mouse or keyboard or stylus. "Internal port only? Doesn't seem likely; those are so rare."

"We don't have a lot of time," Tak reminded him, wrapping his yukata more closely around him. It was no warmer here than it had been in the core. Omesh reached out and touched the computer screen. The charts of CPU usage and heat readings disappeared, replaced by a field of blue.

"State command," a voice from nowhere requested.

"Contact Rabia," Omesh said.

"Full designation is required."

"Damn, I don't know her last name," Omesh grumbled.

"Call up a map then," Tak whispered back.

"Give me a map," Omesh said.

"Invalid command."

"Provide map?"

"Invalid command."

"Map!"

"Invalid command."

Omesh tried several more phrases, some not even in English, and Tak suspected cursing was involved near the end. "There's a bomb! Do you understand? Bomb!" He punctuated that last one with a sharp rap of his fist on the screen.

"Invalid command."

Omesh took a deep, calming breath. Then he started peering more closely at the panels. "I think I can crack this open."

"And do what? With no tools? Come on, I think we should just keep moving," Tak said.

"Invalid command."

"I guess you're right," Omesh said, leading the way out of the computer space and back down the corridor. Worry over bombs and fleeing ships was beginning to recede in Tak's mind; now he would give just about anything to be able to stand fully upright. His back was screaming at him.

Suddenly, the lights all around them flickered and went out. Somewhere far off in the darkness, someone—Alain or Tom—yelped. Tak tried to peer back down the corridor, but the darkness was absolute. Still, it had sounded like Alain and Tom were in their corridor. Why would they climb this far back up the ladder rather than try any of the scores of corridors they would've passed first?

"What's happening?" Omesh whispered. Tak turned back toward Omesh. Before he could formulate an answer, he saw a light wink back on, much farther down along the corridor.

"Come on," he said, hurrying on once more. It was impossible to speed up to so much as a jog unless you liked your head repeatedly banging against the ceiling. When at last they reached the light, they both just stood and stared at it.

"It's one of the runner lights," Omesh grumbled.

Tak looked around. But if this section was any different from any other part of the corridor they'd been moving through, the difference was too subtle for him to see. "What now?" he demanded, of whom he couldn't really say.

"Maybe we should just find our way back to the ladder," Omesh suggested.

"In the dark? I wouldn't be able to find the turn we used to get here with the lights off," Tak said. He probably should have figured out a way to mark it just in case, but he really hadn't intended to have to backtrack.

As silently and inexplicably as before, all the lights came back on. Then a line started to trace itself on the wall under the light that had been their guide.

"What's that?" Omesh asked.

"A door," Tak said as the outline finished forming. "Sealed so tight it's invisible. That's just evil."

"How many doors do you reckon we've run past?" Omesh asked. Tak just placed his hand on the door and pushed. It swung open easily. The two stepped through it, into a closet filled with boxes and crates. The door swung back shut behind them. Tak spun to catch it, but too slowly.

"There's no knob or pull or anything," he said, trying to pry it back open with his fingertips. "How do you get it open?"

"With a computer," Omesh said. "This is all very *Alice in Wonderland,* always losing the path behind, always having no choice but to go forward."

"Huh?"

"Never mind. We seem to be in another dead end," Omesh said, looking around at all the crates. He touched them with his fingertips, reading the labels and lifting the lids off a few. "Rovers. Why would they need rovers?"

"Apparently they don't, since they're sitting here under several inches of dust," Tak said, fighting a sneeze. He lost. There was a soft click and another door finally swung open. "Come on, there's a door. Let's keep going."

The half gravity was more noticeable here, where they had the space to bounce when they walked whether they wanted to or not. Getting out of the closet wasn't too much trouble—plenty of handholds and an unlocked door—but the corridor beyond was long and empty.

"Left or right?" Omesh asked. Both directions seemed to continue on for eternity. All the lights went out again, and the two waited in the darkness until a few lights winked back on, forming a sort of dotted line along the left-hand corridor.

"I guess we go that way," Tak said. "But at the end of this, I better get some cheese."

Omesh nodded. He looked pale, washed out, and Tak didn't think that was just from the dim light. "We're nearly there," he said, squeezing Omesh's arm.

"Nearly where?"

"I don't know. Where someone can help us. I think it's only been about half an hour since we left the bomb. We have time."

Omesh nodded again, but it was clear his thoughts weren't on the bomb; they were on his aunt alone in the sleeper pod, about to deliver a baby while a riot unfolded around her.

Tak led the way down the hall. At least he could put his geta back on now; the floor was carpeted, unlike the service passages, and the sound of his loud wooden shoes wouldn't echo over and over and drive them both mad.

The irregular lights led them down the corridor, then down a cross corridor to their right, then down another corridor to the left before ending in an elevator lobby servicing twelve separate elevators. Tak reached out to push the down button, but it lit up moments before his finger could touch it.

"All right, then."

One of the elevator doors opened, and they stepped inside. Neither made any move for the rows of buttons. Momentarily, the doors swished shut and one of the buttons lit up.

"It's like having a ghost for a guide," Tak said,

leaning back with his hands on the rail. Elevators were not pleasant things, elevators that carried you through incrementally greater levels of gravity even less so.

"Ghost in the machine, I think," Omesh said. Tak watched as Omesh's knees buckled under him before he finally realized there was a point to what Tak was doing and staggered to grasp the nearest rail.

The elevator doors opened up on yet another corridor lit only by a few, spaced lights.

"Who's doing this?" Tak asked as they walked down the hall. "Friend or foe?"

"What if we tried another corridor?"

"We'd be in the dark," Tak said. "And we can't try to open a door; they're all palm locks."

"I noticed," Omesh said. "No people around either. This is kind of creepy."

The corridor brought them out into a lobby. There were no more lights to follow, but glass doors opened out into an open square. A square lit dimly, strangely, from above. It reminded him of the domed cities of Mars, and he rushed forward to get a close look.

"It's like a city out there!" Tak cried, pressing up against the glass. "And look at that sky! You can see little clouds moving through the black.

Haven was nothing like this. This is what Earth must be like."

"There aren't any stars," Omesh said. He sounded almost sad. "Come on, we're running out of time."

The doors opened to reveal a row of massive pillars, and beyond the pillars was a long flight of steps. Tak guessed someone had been going for grandeur, but it was hard to get a sense of the real scale because everything was covered in makeshift buildings. Squarish huts filled the spaces between the pillars and the building, some stacked up to three stories high, looking no sturdier than the handiwork of the first two of the three little pigs. The buildings on the steps were more precarious still, starting flat on one step but using blocks of concrete or old office desks to fill in the spaces between the floor of the hut and the steps dropping away below.

"They live like this?" Omesh said in a whisper. "It's no better than Barnacle Town."

Tak nodded. The doorways around them were covered with curtains of various sorts, not proper doors. Here and there were the sounds of a fussing infant, or children whispering together. Not everyone was trying to sleep, though; at the bottom of the steps, a crowd had gathered around a vending cart, eating something deep-fried out of paper cones and talking together.

"Should we ask them for help?" Omesh asked.

"I don't think telling just anyone about the bomb would be helpful. But how are we going to find someone who can do something about it?" Tak asked.

"They must have a security department, maybe even a headquarters we could go to. Someone down there could direct us to it."

"They'll know the minute we ask that we don't belong here."

"They probably know already. They don't recognize us, and we're staring at everything like we've never seen anything like it before."

"I'm not that bad. It's not too different from Mars, really."

"Well, I feel incredibly out of place," Omesh said. "Let's go down. If they have us arrested for trespassing, that still gets us to the right people."

"You're right." They headed down the steps, Tak once more carrying his geta. The nearer they drew to the crowd, the less Tak wanted to ask them for anything. They were speaking together in low voices, constantly looking around, and while they were all holding the paper cones, none of them were actually eating.

"What do you think is going on?" Omesh asked, staying close to Tak.

"Not a clue."

Then the men fell silent. Tak thought at first it was the two of them approaching that made the men stop speaking, but then he heard a whir of sound coming down the street. A little green robot was hard at work cleaning the street curb with its whirring brush attachment. The men watched the robot with hooded eyes, and some seemed to be making an effort to look like they were really eating.

The robot kept cleaning until it was directly in front of Omesh and Tak standing together on the bottom step. Then it stopped and turned to face them. The little red light on its front panel winked at them.

"Um," Omesh said.

"Maybe it's like the corridor, and we're supposed to follow it," Tak guessed. The robot winked again but did not resume cleaning.

"Where's it taking us?" Omesh asked.

"Only one way to find out," Tak said, stepping down into the street. The robot spun away from the curb, then zipped down the street, red light winking away. Tak glanced over at the men, who were all staring at him and Omesh. Then he followed the robot.

"Is this what Earth cities are like?" Tak asked as they walked through the streets.

"There aren't many cities left anymore," Omesh said. "Everyone is a farmer and lives and works on a certain parcel of land, and everything you need, like food and clothing, is shipped to you from the A&MC stores. We don't congregate much. This is a bit like a pre-plague city. Those are all being torn down, though."

"You must have a lot of space," Tak said. There would be a lot of space here if people lived only in the buildings, but other shelters had been put up everywhere, some only tents, others built from leftover construction materials, still others from shipping materials. It really wasn't so different from Barnacle Town. It did *smell* cleaner.

The robot stopped suddenly, spinning around to face them again. It winked its red light, then spun to face the building to their left.

"Is this our stop?" Tak asked.

The robot winked.

"Thanks for the guidance, little friend."

They walked up to the front door. The handles had been sawn off, and the doorjamb sealed. It was made of glass, but all they could see beyond it was a heavy curtain.

"Do we knock?" Omesh wondered.

"Maybe there's another door," Tak said. "I'd

hate to wake someone up at this hour; we should at least check first."

They circled around the building and found a smaller, metal door in the back, an ugly little plastic gnome holding it open. The downstairs corridor was dark, but upstairs there was a light.

"Are we back to this, then?" Tak said, and headed up the steps. After another sequence of corridor, turn, another corridor, another turn, they finally saw a point where the path of light ended. There was an open door.

The room beyond the door was small and carpeted to match the hallway. Pillows and quilts littered the floor in a way that seemed vaguely homey, although there was no family present at the moment. Only a girl of maybe fourteen sitting alone on the floor, her legs in a lotus position. She was wearing a jumpsuit like Rabia's, but she had added a beaded scarf around her hips to make it a touch more feminine. Her dark hair was cut close to her head; the enormous earrings that hung down to her shoulders seemed meant to compensate for these missing locks. Her head was tipped back as if she were looking at the ceiling, but as Tak stepped closer, he could see that her eyes were rolled back in her head and twitching ever so slightly. It was creepy. He was about to back out of the room again when her eyes dropped back down and she smiled at both of them, a knowing sort of smile.

"So, you two are looking to contact Rabia?"

CHAPTER NINETEEN

OMESH

It could only be Teresa. She had the same almond-shaped eyes, even the same makeup that gave her an Egyptian look. Her skin was darker and her hair was short and naturally black, but there was the same mischief in her hint of a grin.

"Is Rabia here?" he asked at last.

"Will be soon. She's heading down right now. Mightily pissed off about something, to judge by the security footage," Teresa said. "Do you guys want some tea?"

"There's a bomb," Tak said. "We need to contact someone in security. Someone who can defuse a bomb."

"A bomb in the core," Teresa guessed, frowning. "Man, I hate it when I'm right about security failures."

Omesh began, "Can you—"

But she held up a hand to stop him from talking, and her pupils contracted to pinpoints. It happened rapidly, startlingly so, and it gave her an eerie, empty look. But only for a moment; then they zoomed back to normal size, and she regarded him.

"As I thought; it's already taken care of," she said. "Tea?"

"What's taken care of?" Tak asked.

"Your bomb. From the chatter I've been monitoring, it wasn't a very sophisticated device."

"It's been disarmed already?" Tak asked.

"Yes. Tea?"

Tak let out a rush of air, rubbing his neck and rolling his shoulders.

Omesh was not at all relieved. His stomach felt full of acid, eating away at the walls, on the verge of spilling out and filling his entire chest with its acrid burning. Tea wasn't going to help.

"We need to get back to Barnacle Town," he said.

"I wouldn't recommend it. The panic has ramped up several notches since you left. Lots of violence; it wouldn't be safe."

"How do you know?" Omesh asked at the same moment Tak said, "Since we left?"

"Trust me," Teresa said with that same knowing smile. "The explosives have nearly all been placed, but the order to carry on with the demolition has not yet been issued. It might not be given at all. At the very least, you do have some time."

The door behind them slammed open and Rabia stood there, hands in fists and hair in wild disarray. Then she saw the two of them there with her sister. "Omesh!" She flung herself against him hard enough to knock him back a few steps, squeezing him tight. It was a little disconcerting; he had never had a girl press her whole body up against him like that before. Except his mother. But she did it differently. "You're alive!"

"But we need to get back," Tak said, and Rabia let Omesh go.

"How did you even get here?" she asked.

"Through the core. Alain and Tom put a bomb on the power lines running from the solar panels."

"What?"

"It's been taken care of," Teresa said.

"But how did you get here, to my house?"

"That was me," Teresa said. "You remember I said there was something wrong in the core?

Someone has done an incredibly elegant job of hacking the security systems. They really seem to be working appropriately, only they're not."

"Huh?" Tak said.

"It's technical," Teresa said, and Rabia rolled her eyes. "You can call it intuition if you like."

"It's because of her implant," Rabia said.

Teresa gave a shrug of agreement that said "more or less."

"So that's how you found us?" Omesh said.

"Whoever did the hack only concerned themselves with your little arena area, but you followed the other two quite a bit deeper. That was the point at which the alarms went off in security. You would've been arrested in the tunnels with the other two if you hadn't shouted my sister's name at that outmoded computer backup."

"You heard me?"

"Certainly. Although I couldn't really answer except by leading you here."

"Is your family OK?" Rabia asked, looking back at Omesh.

"My aunt is sealed in the sleeper pod," he said. "I don't know where my uncle is. I was looking for him when we saw Alain and Tom with what turned out to be a bomb." How long had he been gone already? An hour? Would his aunt have had her baby by now? Maybe not. Maybe Prakash was back with her. He needed to get back and get them on the sumo school freighter.

Assuming it wasn't too late for that.

"Tea is here," Teresa said just before the door chimed. Rabia took the tray from the cafeteria worker with a murmur of thanks.

"We need to get back," Tak said again. "A lot of people are going to die, and maybe there's something I can do to help. Now that you know about the bomb, our job here is done. As much as I appreciate the hospitality, I can't just sit here sipping tea."

"Nor I," Omesh added.

"You can't get back to Barnacle Town through the airlock," Teresa said. "The access port you used to reach the core is similarly sealed against you now. Honestly, your best hope is to wait here for the security team to come for you."

"Then what?" Omesh asked.

"Then you play on Chandi Corporation's gratitude for being heroes."

"Will it be enough gratitude to save Barnacle Town?" Tak asked.

"Not likely. But if you're determined to get back, some sort of transportation will surely be arranged."

"You can't go," Rabia said. "It's a death sentence."

"I can't leave my aunt to face it alone, either. She's in labor."

"The crew working outside reports that they're placing the last of the detonating cord on the joins that hold Barnacle Town to the space station," Teresa said, her gaze fixed as if reading text only she could see. "They are working slowly, making every effort to maintain atmospheric integrity within Barnacle Town, but the closer they get to the airlock and the original ships, the harder that becomes. The ships are just parts of ships there, fragmentary. The hope had been to blast Barnacle Town into a squadron of discrete ships—"

"Whose hope? Someone who's never even *seen* Barnacle Town?" Omesh asked, his voice nearly cracking. Most of the space station residents never went to Barnacle Town, but hundreds did. Hundreds knew the ships were not space worthy, and the plan to blast them apart was just scattering the massacre.

"Barnacle Town holds more secrets than you know," Teresa said. "It's full of lifeboats for just this eventuality."

"Really?" Omesh said. "Then how come I don't know of any? And if I don't, who does?"

"But of course you do," Teresa said. "Your own home and Tak's freighter are your two lifeboats."

"But—"

"Did you think you were the only nervous Towner with engineering skills?"

The door opened and a man and a woman came in. Their conversation cut short as they saw Tak and Omesh standing there.

"Mom, Dad, this is Omesh and Tak," Rabia said. "And these are my parents, Sean and Ghubari Paxton."

"Paxton," Omesh said to himself as he shook hands with both of them. So that was her last name. Her parents were both tall, but while her father was a wiry kind of tall, her mother was built like an Amazon. Sean was a shade or two lighter than his daughters, Ghubari a shade or two darker.

"You're both from Barnacle Town?" Ghubari asked.

"And we need to get back," Tak said.

"I'm not sure how to do that," Sean said with a frown. "How did you even get here?"

"Me," Teresa said. "Security will be here shortly to detain you. You're being tagged in the files as terrorists, but don't worry. I'm sending out memos detailing all the evidence that clears you. If Mr. Gupta is still awake, he'll surely intervene."

"He's awake," Ghubari said. "Everyone else is."

"Who's Mr. Gupta?" Omesh asked.

"The operational manager for Chandi V. Tea?" Teresa offered again. With a sigh, Tak sat down and let her pour him a cup of tea.

Omesh sat beside him but only took a single sip from the cup she gave him. It was sweet and fragrant and hot and the last thing he wanted when visions of his aunt alone in the cold dark haunted him.

"We're doing all we can," Ghubari told him, taking his hand and squeezing it. "Mr. Gupta has promised to meet with us within the hour. Perhaps Suresh Chandi as well. He's the CEO of Chandi Corporation."

"The one who's here to get rid of Barnacle Town," Tak said.

"Yes."

"Ah," Tak said, nodding as if suddenly understanding something, but he shook his head at Omesh's questioning look.

"I know that doesn't sound like much, having a meeting, but considering it's the middle of the night, we're taking it as a very good sign," Sean was saying. Then he turned to his wife and conferred with her in a low voice, and Teresa's pupils were once more mere dots. Rabia turned to Omesh and Tak.

"Is it bad?" she asked.

Omesh played with his teacup, moving it this way and that on the saucer. He didn't trust himself to speak.

"It wasn't when we were still there," Tak said. "The airlock was closed, and we could hear people moving outside the ships. It was more uncertainty than panic when we went through the door to the core."

"It's worse now," Teresa told them, her attention once more back in the physical world. "The computer links haven't been severed yet and the dons are sending message after message. They're getting desperate, and the news isn't good."

"I can't believe this is happening," Rabia said, rubbing furiously at her face, then having another go at her hair. If she tousled that up any wilder, she would look like an anime character come to life. Omesh fought the urge to laugh; it would not be a good sort of laugh, and he doubted he'd be able to stop.

"Security is here," Teresa said just as the door chimed.

"Hello, Georg," Sean said as he opened the door. The man who answered his greeting with a nod wore a jumpsuit with insignia declaring him the head of space station security. Two other guards followed behind him, taking positions near the door. The two guards were young and lean. Georg was not exactly fat, but he was definitely soft, with baby-fine hair just covering his pate. He looked like Omesh's math teacher back on Earth.

"Hello, Sean," Georg said. "Providing succor to outsiders, are we?"

"I'm afraid so. They're just kids."

"I can see that," Georg said. "And Teresa keeps pinging us that they found the bomb; they didn't set it. I saw it on a video link. It was pretty crude, and our explosive expert doubted it would have damaged the hull."

"It wasn't meant to," Omesh said. "They were going to knock out your power, that's all."

"That's quite an 'all,'" Georg said with an uncomfortable laugh. "Look, there's no reason to be unpleasant about this since you're trespassers, not terrorists, so why don't the two of you just come down to the security cells with me? I won't lock you up. We'll just sit and have coffee and sandwiches until my team finds the real culprits."

"We're in a bit of a hurry to get home, actually," Omesh said.

"Home? Barnacle Town?" He shook his head regretfully. "I don't see that happening."

"Check your orders, Captain," Teresa said suddenly. "They've just been updated."

Georg nodded, not at all bothered with having a teenaged girl talk to him as if he were an underling. "Can I use your computer, Sean?"

"Please do."

"You're going to the Civic Center," Teresa said even as Georg clicked through screens on the computer. "All of us, actually. Not only did the Jeffersonians get their meeting with the operational manager and the CEO, they got a meeting that will be broadcasted all over the station, attendance mandatory for all employees. Omesh and Tak are to be there as firsthand Barnacle Town witnesses."

"Indeed," Georg said, turning away from the computer. "Shall we?"

Rabia caught Omesh and Tak by their sleeves, holding them back as the others trooped out of the apartment.

"I'm sorry," she said. "I tried."

"Tried what?" Tak asked.

"Hjalmar," Omesh guessed.

"Yes, Hjalmar," Rabia said. "I just don't understand how someone can know what's happening and not care, but he doesn't. He just doesn't care."

"I doubt there's anything he could do even if he did," Omesh said. "Don't beat yourself up over it."

"Yeah," Rabia said with a scoffing laugh. "Wouldn't want to do that."

"So what's with the security guy?" Tak asked as the three of them left the apartment.

"What do you mean?"

"Most places I've been, if you break a rule, the security team ambushes you with stun weapons, or just a blow to the head if clubs are all they have, and you wake up locked out of the community. Which is particularly harsh when the outside of the community is a vacuum. Too many people, not enough space; no one tolerates anything anymore."

"Just like that, no trial or anything?" Rabia said. "That sounds horrible. What sorts of places have you been?"

"All sorts. The lunar cities, Mars, some of the other space stations..."

"Security people on Earth are pretty laconic," Omesh said. "Like statues, really. But well-armed statues. I don't think anyone messes with them."

"So how come your guy is so nice?" Tak persisted.

"Well, Georg isn't part of the police force that maintains order in the living areas," Rabia said. "Although even those guys don't ambush you and toss you out an airlock. Georg is in charge of the security of the station itself, and I don't think we've ever had a threat to the station itself before. Mostly his job is signing people in and out of the corporate buildings to keep track of their work hours."

They went out the door, around the apartment building, and into the street. People were coming out of all the other buildings, bustling down the street in twos and threes. They were all heading the same way, and at every cross street, more people joined them. Maybe Tak was right; maybe this meeting could accomplish something. His aunt would spend a few scary hours alone in the dark, but if in the end they were all safe, it would be worth it, wouldn't it? He tried to form that mental image, all of them safe at home again, Prakash there bringing Anjali's chair back inside, Anjali lowering herself into the chair, a little cousin wrapped in blankets nestled in her arms.

He couldn't quite see it. No matter how tightly he squeezed his eyes shut, he couldn't make the vision come. All he saw were ships floating off into the black.

Rabia caught his hand, lacing her fingers between his and holding tight. He didn't dare look over at her, just kept his eyes shut, letting her guide him down the street, desperately willing the happy ending to come true.

"It's going to be OK," Rabia said to him.

"Yeah. This meeting—isn't this part of a plan to stop things?" Tak asked.

"Well, they mentioned the two of you as 'witnesses' from Barnacle Town. I'm guessing that means no dons are coming." Rabia sighed. "I'm afraid they are going to let you talk for appearance's sake, but they aren't going to listen."

"We have to try. There must be something we can say that will stop all this. Otherwise, why meet with us at all?" Tak said.

"I just need to get back," Omesh said, and the lump was back in his throat. "I left my aunt there all alone. I *have* to get back to her."

"I'll make sure they do that much for you," Teresa said. "Two space suits and whatever supplies you can carry shouldn't be too much to ask in return for saving the solar power. If that bomb had gone off, we would have been in a fix; we don't have the supplies to make a repair, and who knows how long we'd have to wait for more cable from another space station?"

"If this meeting is pointless, can't you convince them to let us go now?" Omesh asked.

"It needs to be done. Things need to be said. They won't be heard now, but they'll be remembered later," Teresa said.

"Remembered by whom?" Omesh asked, but she didn't answer. The crowd was closing in on them now, bottlenecking at the entrance of some enormous building like a coliseum. The hallways leading into the building and circling the perimeter were meant to be spacious, but like everywhere else inside the station, the space was filled with makeshift shelters, making it difficult for the crowd to move through. Some of the taller structures were swaying when jostled, and Omesh shut his eyes. Strangers were pressed up against every inch of him, and there was no escape. If something should happen, were one of those buildings to fall or a fire to break out, there would be nothing he could do. He would die in a churning mass of panicked humanity.

"This way," Rabia said, holding tight to his arm and guiding him off to one side. He let her pull him along, only opening his eyes when they suddenly tumbled into open space. A man behind them quickly slammed shut the door they had just come through.

"Where are we?" Tak asked.

"Backstage," Teresa said. "Mr. Gupta wants to meet you privately first."

"Continue down the corridor to the greenroom," the man at the door said. He was wearing the same red jumpsuit as Georg. Omesh assumed this meant he also worked in security. "Help yourself to whatever while you wait."

"Thank you, Mr. Eliot," Teresa said. The man looked startled, but just nodded. There was the quirk of a smile on her face; clearly she got a thrill out of knowing everyone's name and having the contents of their personnel file just a thought away. Omesh was glad he wasn't an employee. If someone were going to know everything about him, he'd prefer if they had to put a little effort into digging the information up first.

The room at the end of the hallway was long but narrow, with tables laden with platters of food on one side and a long row of empty chairs down the other side. A man stood alone, hands in his pockets, looking at the plates as if finger food were the most depressing thing in the solar system.

"Mr. Gupta?" Teresa called.

The man turned and gave a small but genuine smile. "Teresa," he said, shaking her hand, then touching her shoulder, something too long for an affectionate pat but too short for a hug. "I knew giving you that implant was a good idea. You've saved us all."

"Thank you, Mr. Gupta," Teresa said, sounding far more comfortable talking to the man in charge of hundreds of thousands of lives than Omesh thought any fourteen-year-old ought to. "But even if I hadn't been watching, these two gentlemen from Barnacle Town were intent on finding someone they could give a warning to. They deserve your thanks more than I."

"Yes, thank you, gentlemen," Mr. Gupta said, shaking hands with each of them in turn and looking at them intently. He was not particularly tall, not particularly handsome, and decidedly swarthy in appearance. But if he was the operational manager, that meant he was Hjalmar's father. Omesh didn't see it. Either Hjalmar really favored his mother or he'd had the sort of appearance-altering work done that only a corporate prince could afford.

"We'd like to go home now," Omesh said.

"I'm afraid that's not possible just yet," Mr. Gupta said.

"Why are you having this meeting without the dons?" Tak asked, to Omesh's surprise. He could never be that direct with someone with a rank like operational manager.

"Not by my choice, I promise you," Mr. Gupta said. "Do you work for the dons?"

"No," Tak said. "I'm just your ordinary Barnacle Towner."

"I *am* sorry," Mr. Gupta said. "I did everything I could, but—"

"Mr. Gupta? You're needed onstage. The meeting is about to begin."

"Thank you," he said with a dismissive wave, then turned back to Omesh and Tak. "I'm going to do everything I can for you, I swear it. In the meantime, please eat something. You're here as witnesses for Barnacle Town, so please keep your attention on the monitors."

"We're here to witness *you*?" Tak asked. "We thought we were here as witnesses to what you all are doing to our home!"

"I'm sorry," Mr. Gupta said. "I really am." He looked at each of them in turn, then left the room.

"This is bull," Tak said, crossing his arms and glowering.

"Don't worry," Teresa said, "I'm working on getting someone permission to speak."

"Who? One of the dons?" Omesh asked.

"Hiroku?" Tak added.

"Na, it'sna..." Her voice slurred into nothingness and she wandered off toward the stage, her pupils down to pinpoints, fingers tracing their way along the wall as she stumbled down the hall.

"She does that when she's not really here," Rabia said, slumping into a chair with a sigh. "You might as well eat."

"I don't think I can," Tak said, still fuming. The monitors set in the walls every few meters were showing images of people finding their seats in the massive Civic Center. The seating areas were free of people's homes, although the floor of the arena was a village of shanties up to the very foot of the stage. As they watched, Teresa came on-stage and took a place in the back of a crowd of standing people. Mr. Gupta was already sitting at the right hand of a man who could only be Mr. Chandi, the CEO. No one else could give off such an imperial aura just by wearing a business suit rather than a jumpsuit. He was pretty pale for a guy named Suresh, Omesh thought, and his hair was practically blond. Maybe Hjalmar's looks weren't fakery.

"Where are your parents?" Omesh asked, realizing for the first time that the three of them were alone.

"They lead the Jeffersonian Christians, so they'll be on the stage there somewhere," Rabia said.

"What's a Jeffersonian Christian?" Tak asked, and Omesh was relieved he didn't have to be the one to ask. And if he could do nothing but wait, he'd rather spend the time listening to Rabia than old men in suits.

"Oh, that's a long story," Rabia said, sitting back in her chair, feet sprawling. "It goes all the way back to when this space station was shiny and new. My great-grandparents, every single one of them, were employees here on Chandi V, working with the crew that were finishing off the station before it was sent off to its final destination in the asteroid belt. Of course, the plague and exodus changed those plans. Anyway, Chandi Corporation was a multinational, and it brought workers here from all over the Earth. And because everyone lived here as well as worked here, little communities of like-minded individuals sort of gravitated toward each other. This usually fell along ethnic or religious lines. My great-grandfather, by which I mean my father's father's father, wasn't a particularly religious man. In fact, he had little patience for anything he considered hokum or superstition. So he set up a group of his own, the Jeffersonian Christians."

"Your father's father's father's name was Jefferson?" Tak asked.

"No, they're named for Thomas Jefferson, one of the founding fathers of America. Way back then, he had wanted a way to introduce Christian ideas to the Native Americans, but like my great-gran, he didn't hold much with improbable things. So he sat down with a couple of Bibles and a pair of scissors and he made his own version of the New Testament. No virgin birth, no resurrection, no miracles, just a message for how people should treat each other. It's a good message, and my great-gran thought it was one that anyone could get behind. Hence his group here. He was a pretty charismatic fellow, and so was my grandfather. The group has gotten pretty big since."

"Are you part of it?" Omesh asked.

"Well," Rabia said, tucking her feet back under her and fidgeting with her hands. "I get my great-gran's point. It is a good message, but..."

"But what?"

"Well, I told you before how I am with stories. Thomas Jefferson cut all the *story* out of the story. I think things are true in a story that don't necessarily have to be physically real. It doesn't mean they aren't true, like, psychologically. True in your heart, I guess." She stopped, looking up at the monitor where her father was speaking at a microphone. Mr. Gupta had told them to be witnesses, but he had never bothered to turn the volume on. "I don't know. It's just something I think about a lot."

"So they are speaking on behalf of Barnacle Town because it's the right thing to do?" Tak asked.

"Yes. Did you think no one would?"

"But it's not going to help?" Omesh said. He barely managed to inflect it as a question.

"It's not like Mr. Chandi doesn't already know that killing thousands of people is wrong. No, I don't think explaining it to him in great detail is going to help at all."

"Maybe Teresa's mystery guest..." Tak began, but Omesh raised his hand to silence him. Someone else was coming onto the stage, his hands bound before him.

Alain.

CHAPTER TWENTY

RABIA

R ABIA WATCHED ON THE MONITOR AS HER MOTHER put her hand to her mouth, shock widening her eyes. Her father leaned forward to speak angrily into the microphone on the podium before him.

"Volume, volume!" Omesh was saying, and Rabia stood on her chair to reach the monitor controls.

"...before he was taken into custody," Georg was saying when they could finally hear.

"Noted," Mr. Chandi said curtly. "Let the accused speak."

Rabia's parents stepped back from the podium, her mother still gaping at the Technicolor display that was Alain's face. Rabia covered her face with her hands, trying to will the shame away. They didn't know it had been her, they couldn't possibly know it had been her.

"State your name for the record," Mr. Chandi said.

"Alain," he said, with a hard stare. "I have no surname."

"Of course not. Mr. Alain, will you tell the crowd gathered here today why you are bound?"

"I put a bomb on the power lines running from your solar panels to the station proper," Alain said, enunciating clearly into the microphone and making eye contact with several faces in the crowd.

"Did the dons tell him to do this?" Tak wondered.

"Plant the bomb?" Omesh asked.

"No, confess!" Tak said.

"And why did you place this bomb, Mr. Alain?" Mr. Chandi asked when the crowd's murmurs had quieted down.

"I was asked to by my don."

"Which don is 'your don'?"

"Please, Mr. Chandi, you know full well I cannot answer that question," Alain said.

"And why not?"

"Because the dons are like the Three Musketeers."

"And what does that mean, Mr. Alain?"

Alain let his face show surprise that the CEO of a major corporation would miss a literary reference. "One for all and all for one, Mr. Chandi. Whichever don I, as you call it, 'work' for, my actions reflect the will of all the dons."

"And what positions do these dons hold in Chandi Corporation, Mr. Alain?" Mr. Chandi asked.

"None. They all reside in Barnacle Town, as you well know."

"And as they have no position in my corporation, they have no right to ask my corporation for anything. Wouldn't you say that was true?"

"No."

"Of course not," Mr. Chandi said as if the answer delighted him. "Because your dons think they are men of power. They think they have the might to make their own rights. And my son-in-law in his time here as operational manager has indulged them in this little fantasy. He has dealt with them as if they were clients, people of equal position to be negotiated with. People who had something to offer Chandi Corporation in exchange for what they take."

"The dons have paid for every service Mr. Gupta has provided. It's all been recorded in the corporate accounts. It is, by any standard definition of the term, an entirely legal agreement," Alain said.

"Does he usually talk like this?" Omesh asked.

"I guess..." Rabia said, but it didn't sound at all like the Alain she knew. The soul of his words she knew well. They were classic Alain. But the delivery of them? This was something quite new. How much she had lost, the day he had decided to quit talking to her.

"My son-in-law was not empowered to make those sorts of decisions," Mr. Chandi said, looking down as if consulting something on the electronic notepad before him. Rabia got the sense that most of what this man said and did was very studied. He knew exactly what image he wanted to project, and every gesture furthered that end. "And he has not been acting with the best needs of Chandi Corporation in mind. I hereby inform all of you that Mr. Vijay Gupta is no longer operational manager of Chandi V. I will perform those duties until such a time as a worthy replacement can be found."

"Teresa is going to be crushed," Rabia said. "She loves that man like an uncle."

"Did he know? When he was talking to us before?" Omesh asked.

"How could he possibly?"

"I think he suspected," Tak said. "He was so nervous."

"Teresa didn't suspect," Rabia said. "Or she would have done something."

On screen, Rabia's parents were both earnestly speaking, although as they were no longer at the podium, the microphone didn't pick up their voices. Mr. Chandi could hear, however, and he listened with exaggerated patience, hands folded on the table before him.

"Are you quite finished?" he asked at last.

Rabia's father gave a curt nod; her mother turned away. Was it anger she was swallowing, or grief? Rabia wasn't sure.

"Fine, then listen to me. This is not a democracy. You people are employees, not shareholders. If you do not wish to fulfill the requirements of your jobs, you may terminate your employment at any time. If you do not fulfill the requirements of your positions, Chandi Corporation will terminate your employment."

He stood up and walked to the center of the stage to look out over the rows upon rows of faces. The arena was almost completely silent, so silent that when he spoke again, he was heard, despite no longer being near a microphone.

"I am well aware what the state of things has been, and why. Our grandfathers and great-grandfathers made difficult choices. They made sacrifices. They did the best they could to hold everything together. We must honor them for that; it is not hyperbole to say they saved the human race.

"Our fathers inherited this state of things and did the best they could with it. That was little enough; humankind was near starvation, barely holding on. But they got us through, and we should honor them for that.

"Now, the state of things is in our hands. The specter of famine no longer looms over us; since Earth has been turned over entirely to farming, there is enough for all of us to get by. It is no longer needful for us to just hold on. No, I would say what is required of us is to move forward. That is the mission of Chandi Corporation: to help humankind move forward. What humankind needs most desperately is more space. More specifically, more space stations. This space station was built to go out to the asteroid belt and to refine and use resources there to make more stations. It is time that she was allowed to fulfill her destiny.

"Our engineers give a target date of five years to build the first station. Then half of you will remain here, and half will move to the other station. Do you understand the implications of this? Each of you in five years will have twice the space. In ten years, there will be four stations; you will have four times the space. No more family size restrictions, more freedom to train and apply for jobs that interest you. This is our future.

"Our future," he repeated, and took a long, dramatic look at Alain still standing, hands cuffed before him, at the podium. "In time, it will benefit others. I have said our mission is the advancement of humankind, not just ourselves, and I meant it. But right now, anyone who isn't working with us is holding us back, holding the advancement of humankind back. It cannot and will not be tolerated."

"That's some nice rhetoric, Mr. Chandi," Alain said. "You almost have me believing it. Almost. If only everyone I know and love didn't have to be cast out into the black in order for humankind to advance."

"You were meant to be gone years ago, young man," Mr. Chandi said. "But I arrived to oversee the removal of this space station from lunar orbit to the position in the asteroid field that our scouts indicate as optimal for our needs, and there you all still are—and now there is no time to do it nicely. You do have my sincere apology."

"You can keep it," Alain said.

"As for all of you, my employees, if you do not

share my mission, now is the time to act. If you cannot do what is asked of you, turn in your resignations now. There will be no more protests, no more meetings that do not pertain to the work before you. I realize you all were born into your position as Chandi Corporation employees, and you were assigned jobs based on the station's needs and your skills, and not on your own choice. This is your moment for choice. There are shuttles here now to take away those who choose to terminate their employment.

"The rest of you, get back to work."

Then he turned and left the stage.

"That was horrible," Omesh said.

Rabia nodded her agreement; she didn't trust her voice not to warble if she tried to talk.

"And now the workers dismantling Barnacle Town are going back out of the airlocks to finish the job," Tak said with a bitter laugh. "I guess it's detonation time."

"We have to get back now," Omesh said.

"And you will," Georg said, appearing in the doorway with Alain and Tom walking behind him, still cuffed. Rabia wondered where Tom had been this whole time. On stage, or in the wings? She thought it was only in Barnacle Town that he had the power to blend in with his surroundings, but maybe not. "The airlock into Barnacle Town proper isn't useable now. Have either of you worn a space suit before?"

"Yes," Tak said, but Omesh shook his head.

"One of you has, anyway; that will help," Georg said, turning to speak into a communicator. Alain and Tom wandered over to the food tables and began to stuff the delicate finger sandwiches and other crudités into their mouths, ignoring the security men who trailed behind them, watching their every move.

"Teresa," Rabia said, sitting up from her low slouch and then getting all the way to her feet as her sister drew nearer. The aimless quality of her walk had nothing to do with her implant this time, if the tears on her cheeks were any indication. "Are you OK?"

"Oh, yes," Teresa said. "I'm quite fine. Nothing can touch me." Rabia reached to pull her sister into a hug, but Teresa stepped back, shaking her head. "No time for that now. They are sending these four out the nearest airlock just as soon as they can stuff them into suits."

Rabia glanced up at the monitors. The people in the crowd were not leaving the auditorium. Some were too stunned to move, but most were milling together in small groups. Her parents were still on the stage arguing some point with the other Jeffersonians.

"Look, aren't they still trying to stop things?" Rabia said. "Maybe it isn't too late yet."

"Didn't you hear that speech?" Teresa asked. "He's not kidding about the shuttles. Anyone who won't do what he expects will have to leave."

"To where?" Tak asked. "Where are the shuttles heading?"

"Well, that's just it, isn't it?" Teresa said with a laugh that bordered on a sob and a cry of rage both. "We have nowhere to go. The dons have sent messages everywhere. The lunar cities, Mars—they've even tried Earth. No one wants refugees, not even refugees with corporate skills. A few employees might find places with family members elsewhere, but for most of us, this place is all we know. Banishment from here may as well be a death sentence."

"So all that talk about choices..." Omesh began.

"Was just talk," Teresa finished. "Think it through. He's moving a station that is dependent upon Earth for all of its food supply out to the asteroid belt. Getting rid of Barnacle Town is just the first step. Any excuse to cut down on the number of people here, he'll take. He has to, if he wants to see this mission of his through. I've been crunching some numbers, just estimates really, but what I'm seeing... I don't know how he's bankrolling this at all. It's—" She broke off, wrapping her arms around herself as if suddenly cold.

"Teresa, are you sure you're OK?" Rabia asked.

"I'm fine," Teresa said. "Thanks to this implant in my cranium, I'm un-fireable."

"That's not what I meant," Rabia said.

"Your friend there, cramming his face with puff pastries. He's got a pair of nice shiners. I wonder how he earned those?" Teresa said, and Rabia's face burned as if she'd just been slapped.

"Hey, now," Omesh said, but he almost flinched back when Teresa turned her uncanny eyes onto him.

"Yes, Omesh. Tell me, are you forgetting anything?"

"I don't think so," he said with a nervous glance at Rabia.

"I did promise you any supplies you could ask for," Teresa said.

"I don't think I need anything," Omesh said, looking up and to the right as if consulting a mental checklist. "The sleeper pod is as space worthy as I can make it. No, I don't think I need anything."

"Was there anything you noticed on the way here? Something that might come in handy?"

"What's with the guessing game, Teresa? If you want to give him something, just give it," Rabia said. She knew her sister had only said what she'd said about Alain as a defense mechanism against any sisterly shows of concern, but that didn't make her any less angry with her.

"I need to be trusted," Teresa said, hugging herself again. "He has to ask me for it, so that I can reluctantly agree to provide it. Otherwise, my loyalties might be questioned."

"What?" Rabia asked. Sometimes it was hard to tell when her sister was being serious and when she was playing games.

"The rovers," Omesh said, and Teresa smiled ever so slightly. "They have airbags."

"Why would you need airbags?" Rabia said, drawling out the last word as she understood. "The moon. They're sending Barnacle Town down to the moon."

"That's the plan," Teresa said.

"Will airbags be enough?"

"I thought the plan was to get to the school," Tak said. "It has engines."

"Auntie might not be able to make it," Omesh said.

"Then carry her, for Pete's sake," Tak said. He was going to go on, but they were interrupted by Georg.

"It's time," he said.

"I'll have what you need sent down to the airlock right away," Teresa said. "I hope you don't mind if I skip the long goodbye, but I do have a lot of tasks waiting for me. Busy day." She gave Omesh and Tak both a tight hug, and Rabia thought some of the tearstains on her cheek were a little fresher when she turned away and disappeared back up the hallway leading to the stage.

"Do your sister's emotions always bounce around like that?" Tak asked.

"No," Rabia said. "Quite the opposite. Until today, I thought they'd removed them to make room for that chip." Then Georg and the other guards were there, with Alain and Tom. "I'll go with you to the airlock," she said to Omesh and Tak. She felt far away, as if hearing someone else speak. Someone else was moving her body as well; she certainly didn't feel like she was the one walking out of the Civic Center to the nearest station access building and taking the elevator down to the airlock. This time, Omesh took her hand and gave it a squeeze. As if she were the one in need of support, when he was the one about to leave and die.

Rabia bit her lip until she tasted blood. Once they were gone, she would cry. Right now, she would only make things harder for them if she let despair take her.

Georg and the security team brought them to a

locker room, opening doors and holding out suits until they found four that looked to be the right size or close enough. Tak was, of course, the hardest fit. By the time they found a suit big enough for him, Alain and Tom were already dressed with their helmets on and the airlock worker on duty in his bright yellow jumpsuit was checking their seals. The two of them touched helmets, sharing a private conversation or maybe just a look. Rabia didn't know what to make of it; their body language wasn't what she would expect of two would-be bombers. Tom grasped Alain's arm and gave it a squeeze and Rabia looked away, feeling intrusive watching them. They, too, were going to near-certain death.

"How does this go?" Omesh asked, struggling with his fastenings. Rabia brushed his hands away, sealing him in with a few quick movements. "You've done this before?"

"No, but we all get the training," she said, blinking hard.

"Hey," he said, "didn't you tell me it was all going to be OK?"

"And you believed me?" She tried to make it sound like a joke.

"I still believe you," Omesh said. "We haven't run out of things to try. There's still Tak's school, if I can get my family there. Maybe they're there already, wondering where I am. Failing that, thanks to your sister, I stand some chance of getting our pod down safely."

"And then what?" Rabia asked.

"I'll have enough oxygen to last the three of us a day," he said. "I don't imagine my little cousin will change that too much."

"But you won't be able to move or do anything."

"Nothing but wait."

"Wait for what?"

"Wait for... whatever comes next." His dark eyes fixed on hers with an intensity that nearly made her stagger back. He meant her; he would be waiting for her.

"Omesh," she cried.

"I want you to take this," he said. His hands in the suit gloves were awkward, but he managed to press something into her palm, folding her fingers over it.

"Wha—"

"You can give it back to me when I see you again," he said.

"This way, gentlemen," Georg called. Tak stood beside him, looking surprisingly at ease in the awkward suit. "It's nearly time for the detonation; if you have a specific destination in mind, you have to go now before it's all free-floating bits."

"Goodbye, Rabia," Omesh said. "And thank you."

"Thank me? For what? I've been useless."

"Thank you for what you do next," he said. The smile he gave her trembled a bit at the corners and she didn't think he had nearly as much faith in things working out as he was pretending to have. Then his helmet with its reflective visor was over his head and she couldn't see his face anymore. Her fingers worked automatically, sealing the helmet to his suit. Men had arrived with a large box of what she assumed were rover landing airbags; it was time for them to go. She put her arms around Omesh for one last hug, and his hand in its oversized glove patted her back awkwardly.

Then the security team led the boys into the airlock and the door shut between them and Rabia, leaving her standing alone in the locker room.

She put her cheek to the door. He was still inside; it would be half an hour of breathing pure oxygen before the airlock would depressurize, she knew. She wondered if he was just on the other side, if he would hear her if she knocked, but that was silly; the metal was too thick for that. She stood uncertainly for a moment, then looked down at the object still in her hand. It was his compass, the indicator now describing lazy loops back and forth. They were at an angle to Mecca now, apparently.

"What I do next," Rabia said, watching the needle dance. "I have nothing new to try. So I guess it's square one all over again. But this time he's damn well going to listen to me."

CHAPTER TWENTY-ONE

TAKASHI

Tak had bounded through the cities of Luna and Mars, floated through the massive cavernous towns carved out of asteroids in the belt, peered out of the windows of the floating villages of Venus. But his favorite place was this: the vacuum of space. He loved the feeling of being detached from everything.

Of course, they weren't detached from everything. If they were, Barnacle Town would go speeding away from them with the rotation of the space station. They were proceeding in pairs along a tether that had been installed for the use of the deconstruction crew; it led straight to Barnacle Town and then up the side. Tak and the others were still feeling the effects of the station's centripetal force, albeit backwards from what would be convenient. They made their way like monkeys, hand over hand along the cable with feet dangling, always feeling the pull that wanted to spin them away into the black. The tethers kept them attached to the cable, but that pull still had a sinister feel. When they reached Barnacle Town and started their downward descent, Tak finally had a chance to take in the view.

The moon was freaking huge. The Chandi space station kept a relatively distant orbit, but still the moon loomed so large over everything it felt like it was curved outward, containing them.

Then he saw the sliver of Earth, just visible now but growing larger the closer they got to the end of Barnacle Town. The sun was behind him, behind the space station, and everything before him was bathed in its light. The moon was nearly too bright to look at, and the Earth was like a blue-green jewel.

The guard assigned to him touched his helmet to Tak's. "The one projecting out there?" he asked. Before they had put their helmets on, Georg had told them they would have to maintain radio silence. The fact that they were going back to Barnacle Town was not something the security team wanted the space station at large knowing about, Tak guessed.

"I think so. The plaque on the bridge says it's called the *Hakudo Maru*. Can you see its markings?"

The guard pulled away again, touching something on the side of his helmet. Their suits were different from the generic ones they had given to Tak and Omesh; Tak suspected the guard's helmet had some sort of magnifier over his eyes.

Then he turned to touch faceplates with Tak again. "It says something, but the writing is in Japanese. I'm going to assume that's the one."

"It must be," Tak agreed, but the guard had already pulled away. Tak took one last look around, but mostly all he could see this far down the tether was the outside of Barnacle Town, blocking his view of the moon and of Earth.

The electronic panel next to the airlock didn't respond, but there was a manual wheel, which Tak helped the guard to turn, slowly raising the door until they had room enough to scramble inside. Omesh and Georg followed, then Alain, Tom, and their guards. The last two guards worked together to turn the inside wheel to lower the airlock door. The inside electronic panel also was inert, but there was an emergency lever and Tak pulled it. Just like when they'd gone out the corporate station airlock, they had to sit for thirty minutes and breathe before they could open the other door, but at least they could take off their helmets. Alain and Tom were murmuring to gether, and the guards must have had computer links in the pads embedded on their suit sleeves, so engrossed were they in whatever they were looking at. Omesh was chewing his lip in worry. The time passed slowly.

"That's it," Georg said when something in his suit chimed. "I'm afraid we need to take the suits back..."

"Oh, sure," Tak said. He and Omesh both struggled out of their suits, but Alain and Tom took their time about it. The air was frigid, and each breath burned Tak's lungs, but that was nothing compared to how the floor felt under his bare feet. He belatedly realized he had left his geta behind in the locker room. Omesh didn't look happy either, tucking his hands under his armpits. It went beyond shivers; the boy was shaking. Of course, he had spent his life in one of the hottest places on Earth.

"Let's get this open," Tak said, turning the last wheel. Omesh crawled through as soon as there was room enough for his body, then Tom and then Alain, but Tak had to wait longer. There was a downside to his sumo physique.

"Good luck to you," Georg said.

"Do what you can for us, please?" Tak said.

"You didn't get to see much of us normal folks while you were on our station; I'm sorry for that. But believe me when I tell you the whole station is pulling for you. I know it looks like everyone gave up on you, but it isn't so. The religious groups are having prayer meetings or spell circles. Anyone with connections outside of our station is spreading the word as far and wide as it can be spread, and the rabble rousers are..."

"Rousing the rabble?" one of the other guards offered.

"And risking termination for it," Georg added.

"Thanks," Tak said as sincerely as he could. Then he slid Omesh's box under the door and slipped through after it before lowering the door back down and sealing it so Georg and the others could leave. Everything they had just mentioned was all well and good, but what Barnacle Town really needed was not an outpouring of love and sympathy. It was for a few key people to refuse to do their jobs.

Was revolution really so much to ask for?

"Thanks for that," Omesh said, hands still in his armpits, but he indicated the box with a nod of his head.

"Not a problem. I'm built for the cold," Tak said. "I guess we have another half an hour anyway, since they'll have to pressurize again before they leave the airlock here."

"Seems risky, doing that twice in a day," Omesh said.

"No one has the tech to build new space suits these days," Tak said. "They are rare and valuable things." He turned to face Alain and Tom. They were huddled together, although whether for warmth or from fear of retribution, it was difficult to tell. "Did you really think you were helping?" Tak asked.

"The dons needed leverage," Alain said, but he sounded completely miserable.

"That's your leverage? A bomb?"

"It was a bluff."

"Your bluff was ticking."

"I have to find my uncle," Omesh said through blue lips.

"Let's check if he's already here first," Tak said and led the way aft to the cargo area. Alain and Tom trailed behind.

Tak had had the image fixed in his head for so long of a hold full of refugees all escaping together that stepping out into the sandy arena and green gardens of the school came as a shock. But of course it was all still there. He had not yet done anything to change that.

Omesh, Alain, and Tom trailed behind him as

he made his way to the gate. A few of the younger students gaped at him as he walked past, but no one said anything. All the older students, as well as Toyonoshima and Hiroku, were out in the lanes, working to put the last scrap of metal in place and weld it tight.

"Stop!" Tak yelled. They all looked up at him in surprise, then annoyance. So they had known he was gone, had perhaps even vocalized a little good riddance. Hiroku's eyes then passed on to Alain. But Hiroku said nothing to him, turning his attention back to Tak.

"We only speak Japanese here, rikishi," he said.

"I have to—" Omesh whispered.

"Yes, go," Tak said. "Let him pass, please," he said to the others in his very best, most polite Japanese.

The ones holding the scrap metal stepped back and made enough space for Omesh to squeeze through with the box. Beyond was a throng of people who all started pushing forward at once, yelling and crying. Omesh disappeared among them, in too much of a hurry to let even an angry mob stop him.

Hiroku was staring fixedly at Alain.

"I failed," Alain said. His tone was one of a mere reporting of facts, no sense of shame or defiance or anything. Hiroku didn't say a word. "We should go as well," Alain said at last.

"I suppose you should," Hiroku said, dismissing both him and Tom with a wave. Then the older students set the metal back in place and held it fast while Toyonoshima fired up the welder. The mob didn't stand much chance at getting in, not past rikishi as strong in their sumo as they were. Still they surged hard against the metal plates and the students struggled to get them in place so that the welding could be completed.

"Why won't you let them in?" Tak asked. "There is room enough here." He waved his hand over gardens and practice arenas.

"Not for all of them," Hiroku said.

"Then we take as many as we possibly can."

"No. This is not my home that I can invite all the guests I want. I'm a steward only," Hiroku said.

"The man who does own it is thousands of miles away. Decisions have to be made without him, and they have to be made now."

"They have been. Now you can either go back with the others and wait or you can leave through that mob." Toyonoshima stood waiting, welder ready but still. Only a handful of the biggest sumo wrestlers stood between their school and a desperate mob.

"We can't just leave them all to die. It isn't right."

"We can't take them with us either," Hiroku said. "This is a freighter, not a passenger ship. It can't handle that many breathing bodies; we don't have enough food or water. There is only one toilet facility."

"I didn't say it would be easy," Tak said.

"I agree with Takashi," Kenko said, stepping forward. If that admission had cost him anything, if it came at the end of some long internal struggle, no sign of it was on his face. He looked just as severely earnest as ever. "We must do this. We are all here to preserve the last remains of our culture. This is important work; we are a people who've nearly died out. But we're not dead yet. And Japan isn't the only culture we belong to. We set up this school within another culture, and they have embraced us. We can't abandon them."

"Again, we simply cannot take them aboard. We would never make it to Mars with a cargo bay full of people."

"We're going to Mars?" Tak asked.

"We do not yet have a destination," Hiroku said. "Our benefactor is finding a place for us."

"So, in the meantime, we fill up our hold with people and take them down to Luna," Tak said.

"Luna won't take them either."

"Once we land and have them off the ship, I doubt very much that Luna will turn them out into the vacuum. But that's what's about to happen to them right now."

"Luna does not want them. Do you think we haven't communicated with every possible port, from the very moment we suspected this would happen? No one wants a freighter full of refugees. Particularly not Barnacle Town refugees. They are known for their low work ethic and high sense of entitlement."

"Now that's not fair—" Tak began, but Kenko talked over him.

"Think of how our school will be spoken of. The stories will spread throughout the solar system. All sumo wrestlers will be considered heroes or villains depending on what choice we make here today."

That argument seemed to reach Hiroku. His face was as impassive as ever, but his long silence showed how carefully he was thinking it over. Tak chastised himself for not thinking of it sooner; he knew how anxious the stable masters were to get more publicity. Sumo needed corporate sponsors for money and for prestige. Mr. Chandi was trying to change the future of the human race, but most corporate leaders were little more than the rich, bored princes of yesteryear. They were frivolous with their money, and there was nothing they loved more than a good story.

But when Hiroku finally answered, it was a cold "No."

"Then I will leave," Kenko said. "I'll throw my lot in with the rabble. You'll have to make it through the next competition without me."

"Are you certain?" Hiroku said. Kenko was one of his best wrestlers, not just in his own bouts but in improving the morale of his stablemates, encouraging them on to better performances. If he weren't there, the entire sumo stable would feel the lack.

"Yes, I am," Kenko said. This time he did look like the words cost him something, but still he said them.

"Very well," Hiroku said.

"I will go as well," Tak said.

"You I invite to leave," Hiroku said, not even looking at him.

"And I," said another student. The three of them looked around; none of them had realized how closely their conversation was being followed. Even Toyonoshima with the blowtorch had killed the flame, listening intently to all that was said.

"Me too," said another voice in the crowd, and then there were so many voices they couldn't be distinguished. Not one of his stablemates was willing to huddle in safety while thousands within arm's reach were left to die a horrible death.

"I can seal the way out now. What could any of you do about it?"

"Try it and see," Tak said, although in that moment he was again very aware of just how big Hiroku was.

Hiroku didn't answer. Tak felt his hands sweating and resisted the urge to look at the other rikishi to make sure they were still with him. He kept his gaze fixed on his stable master and waited him out.

"We will open this door only," Hiroku said at last. "All rikishi fall back to within the cargo hold. Move furniture, make room. Toyonoshima, I want you standing at the controls. The very instant the atmo starts to bleed out, or the mob turns ugly, shut the freighter doors."

"The lights will go out before they start the detonation," Tak said to Toyonoshima. "That will be the warning sign to shut the doors."

His teacher gave a curt nod and took his position. The students pulled back and Hiroku gave the sign to take the barrier down. The mob pushed forward, but Kenko and a few other of the largest students caught them, slowing them down and directing them into the ship. Hiroku barked orders at the crowd to stay calm and move quickly, but in an orderly fashion.

Having each person touched by one of the sumo wrestlers was a genius idea, Tak thought. In their robes and geta, they didn't look as fierce as when just wearing wrestling belts; they were almost teddy bear–like and were a reassuring presence. But there was no denying that they were big men, and anyone looking to start a riot was well aware of just how many terribly big men were standing not more than a few feet away.

There was some pushing and shoving but no fighting, and it was almost eerily quiet. Takashi stayed near the door, watching the people go past. Families clung together in groups, and soon the wooden buildings were filled with bodies and people were finding what space they could on the walkways or in the gardens and practice arenas.

But when the lights went out, the crowd still waiting to get in shrieked and rushed forward, climbing over each other to reach safety. Arms and legs were stark black outlines against the red of the emergency light glowing over the cargo doors.

"We must get these doors closed or we're all lost!" Toyonoshima shouted, barely intelligible over the screams of the crowd. All the students pushed forward, their faces grim in the red light. It took all of them together to fight back the surging crowd and keep them back so that the door could close. The wailing all around them was louder than ever and Tak knew that families had been separated, but there was nothing more they could do.

He hadn't seen Omesh or his family. A lot of people had gone by in just a few minutes, but he was certain he would have seen them if they had been there.

"Be safe, friend," Tak whispered. He hoped that box held everything Omesh had needed, and that he had gotten it to his aunt and uncle's place in time.

Tak felt a rumble, something he felt in his chest more than heard. It grew louder, drowning out the screams around him. Tak dropped to the floor, covering his head with his arms. Their little world was being ripped apart and its death cries were terrible. He couldn't block them out, could only wish that they would end soon. If only he weren't so sure what getting that wish would mean.

In the end, he screamed along with all the others.

CHAPTER TWENTY-TWO

OMESH

Omesh tried to keep his head down and focus on moving one step at a time, but wayward elbows, fists, and feet struck him from all sides. His left ear was ringing from one such strike, and he was afraid to lift his head to look around lest he lose an eye. There was scarcely enough room for him, let alone the massive box he was lugging. But the worst was when the crowd surged like an ocean wave and picked him up off his feet, carrying him along in the wrong direction, then dropping him again with a thump. He stumbled but didn't fall.

At last he fought his way through to a larger lane, one less crowded. The people here were running in all directions. The noise was oppressive, echoing and reechoing against all the ship hulls. Omesh set the box down and leaned back against the wall with his hands on his knees, fighting to get his breath back. His ribs felt bruised. He heard a constant keening and looked up to see a girl of about five standing at the junction of two lanes, a baby nearly as big as she was in her arms. The girl's eyes were shut tight as she screamed for her mother over and over again. The baby on her hip looked at her with mild alarm.

How was he ever going to find his uncle now?

Someone jostled him from behind but caught him until he had his balance.

"Sorry," Alain said, nearly out of breath.

"I have to find my uncle," Omesh said.

"He'd be at the curry stand, wouldn't he?" Alain said, eyes sweeping over the scene Omesh had already taken his fill of.

"He wasn't when I left."

"He'll be back by now, I'm sure," Alain said. "I'll put the word out to the gangs to watch for him. Anyone sees him, they'll send him on to you there. Good luck."

"Good luck," Omesh said. He watched as Alain and Tom jogged to the end of the lane, then stopped at the girl. Alain scooped her up, baby and all, then disappeared around the next ship.

The shortest path to the curry stand ran

through the marketplace, but as he drew nearer, the sounds of people around him were increasingly drowned out by an ever-louder roar. The people running towards him were battered and bleeding, their clothes torn. Some clutched sacks or containers against their chests, but most were empty-handed. A few eyed the box in his arms, but no one made an aggressive move. These were all people coming out on the losing end of a fight; Omesh didn't think he'd get past the winners so easily.

He climbed over the last ship and stood looking down the long open space that was the marketplace. The stalls were smashed and people were picking through the ruins. Others were fighting over things they'd found, hitting each other with anything handy. He saw a woman snatch what looked like a sack of flour from a little boy, knocking him to the ground with a hard shove, then turn and take the swing of a metal pipe right in her face. Her nose exploded and Omesh shut his eyes, but the image of her facial bones giving way wouldn't leave him. He stumbled back the way he'd come. He would have to take a longer route; he would never make it across the marketplace in one piece. He certainly couldn't do it with the box.

The smaller lanes Omesh now took were quieter. There were others besides him jogging this way or that, but more and more, he was seeing people just sitting. Some had their belongings packed in boxes or backpacks with them, some had nothing at all. He passed one of the late-night establishments, its doors open for business, the loud thump of dance music pouring out into the lane, as if this were just another night. He could even see people inside dancing. Their movements were crazed and energetic, as if they hoped to dance themselves into an endorphin high before they died.

He was nearly all the way home when someone leaped down on him from an unseen nook in one of the ships above him, landing on the box and driving it down to the ground, Omesh with it. His chin connected with the edge of the box and his teeth slammed together hard, just nicking the end of his tongue. The man standing on his box was holding a cricket bat, and Omesh scrambled back as the bat whistled down at him. He felt it pass through his hair. The air coming off it was like a mini shock wave pressing on his scalp. If that had hit him square, he'd be dead.

The man gestured with the bat, hoping to scare him off, but Omesh couldn't go. Without that box, he and Anjali would die. He had to get it back.

He leapt up, tackling the man's legs. Omesh was sure he had caught him off guard, but the man didn't fall. He crouched down low, one hand holding the bat and the other out for balance, but he didn't fall. He caught Omesh by the hair, pulling him up until he was on tiptoe; Omesh covered his attacker's hand with both of his own, trying to pull it down closer to his head to make the pulling stop. The man didn't say a word, just cocked back the bat to give it a one-handed swing. Omesh locked his eyes on the man's. If he was going to die, he wasn't going to die with his eyes shut.

Suddenly, the air was full of missiles. A few hit Omesh, glancing blows that left his flesh stinging, but most hit the man. He dropped Omesh and backed away, arm and cricket bat up to protect his head. Omesh ducked down behind the box. Next to his foot was a small slug of misshapen metal. He looked back over his shoulder. There were three street urchins standing behind him, firing away with slingshots. He looked forward again in time to see the man take a swing with his cricket bat. There was a loud crack as he connected with one of the slugs and sent it whistling back down the lane. One of the urchins, a girl who looked too old for the pigtails she was sporting, pressed back against the wall, but the slug caught her on the shoulder and she yelped in pain. The other two took careful aim and fired back, both hitting the man square in the forehead, one after the other. He dropped his cricket bat and stumbled away, blood flowing freely from between the fingers pressed to his head.

"You Omesh?" one of the kids asked.

"Yes."

"Alain sent us. We're to be sure you get to the curry stand OK. You OK?"

"I am now," Omesh said. "Thank you."

"OK, we'll walk you the rest of the way. Need a hand with that box?"

Omesh and one of the boys carried the box between them. The other boy trailed behind, slingshot in hand and eyes watchful. The girl did the same at the front of their troop, her upper arm already sporting a sizeable welt.

When they reached home, there was no one in sight, although he could hear the sobs and cries of people all around him. Everything in the curry stand that hadn't been welded down was now gone. The beam he had repaired was askew again, the sleeper pod above now listing to one side.

"You need help with this?" the boy asked, indicating the box with a tap of his toe.

"Do you have the time? Don't you all have to head to the sumo school?"

"The sumo school?" the boy repeated.

"It's a working freighter, with engines and life support and everything."

"We have a place," the girl said, peeking into the kitchen, then crossing the dining area to look up the stairs to the sleeper pod. "I'm going to see if your uncle's here. You two better hurry with the whatever; there isn't much time."

Omesh threw back the lid of the box and started unpacking the contents. There were tools nestled against one side of the box. The parachute and heat shield were useless to him and he tossed them aside, but there were enough airbags and rockets mounted on pivots for four rover landers. The sleeper pod was more than four times bigger than a rover, but they were landing on the moon, which was almost certainly lower gravity than what these rover landers had been designed for. He hoped; there simply wasn't time to crunch the numbers and nothing he could do about it if the results weren't good.

"Your uncle isn't here," the girl said, coming back down the stairs. Mama Polly was making her way down behind the girl, one careful step at a time. "Plus there's a baby. I guess that's new."

"It is," Omesh said, looking from her to Mama Polly.

"Mom and baby are both fine," she said.

"They're resting. There was some bleeding; it'd be best if she didn't have to walk about just now, but these aren't times for expecting the best. You didn't find Prakash?"

"No," Omesh said.

"I'm heading to the don's place now. If he's there, I'll send him on back. God be with you, all of you."

"And with you," "Thanks, ma'am," "Thankee," the urchins answered at once. Omesh nodded and mumbled something even he didn't catch; his mind was already on the process of mounting the airbags and rockets to the sleeper pod. Even as he worked, focused on bolting the airbags into place, the back of his mind was racing. He knew the sleeper pod wasn't actually attached to anything but the pillars that held it up, and as Alain's brother had shown, that was flimsily attached at best. It rested on top of the shipping box that was the kitchen, but the only thing holding it there was gravity. When the det cord ignited, blasting apart the ships around them, they should be left free-floating.

He hoped. There were far too many variables to say anything for sure.

The lights flickered off, then back on as he worked on the last of the rockets. The urchins looked nervous.

"Go on," Omesh said, looking away from his work long enough to make sure they heard him. "Thanks for everything."

"See you on the other side," the girl said with a sort of salute. Then they were gone.

The lights went out three more times as Omesh worked. The third time they stayed out for several long seconds, and the wails of people all around him had his heart in his throat. They flickered back on, but Omesh was sure that time was short. He finished, tossed the tools into the empty box, and ran up the steps to the sleeper pod.

His aunt met him at the door, moving slowly, as if her whole body ached, but deliberately.

"He didn't come?" Omesh asked.

Anjali merely stepped back to let him in, lifting the edge of the sari she was wearing to hide the show of her emotions from him. He had never seen his aunt wearing anything other than jeans and long kurtas, like his, but older and less well made. He hadn't even known she owned a sari. It was a bright red, and he supposed she had worn it for her wedding and then stowed it away. It was strange after all he'd seen running through Barnacle Town to find her at the end of it, dressed in bright colors and wearing all of her jewelry. A jeweled bindi dotted her forehead, and she had put vermillion in the parting of her hair.

She was practically screaming wife-not-widow at him.

The lights went out once more, and the air was filled with panicked screams. Omesh stepped forward, closing the door behind him and locking it shut before turning on the battery-powered lamp he had left near the door. Anjali crossed the slanted room to gather up the bundle she had left on her bed.

"There are other places in Barnacle Town which are safe," Omesh said. "I'm sure Prakash found one of them." He didn't say what he was really thinking. Prakash had been gone for hours, in streets full of random violence. The likeliest reason for his not being there was that he had been caught up in one of those fights. Perhaps he had been hurt and someone had taken him somewhere safe, or he had stumbled far on his own power but could go no further. Or perhaps he had been hurt and was still lying wherever he had fallen, exposed.

"I pray you are right." But the weary anxiousness of her voice said she had had all the same thoughts.

Omesh looked around. Someone had been busy, either his aunt or the old woman or the girl-urchin. Who or whatever had tipped the pod had made quite a mess, most of which had been merely piled into the sleep coffins and left there. All the food from the kitchen was stacked in boxes and sacks against the walls, even the things like rice that Omesh had no idea how they could even begin to cook now. The table she used as an altar had been broken, but the little statue of Ganesh was still intact and stood in a new position, in a nook in the wall that had once housed a first aid kit. A new bowl stood before him, filled with milk and flowers, and incense sticks burned to either side of him.

"You did all this? Mama Polly aid you weren't supposed to move."

"I did it before," Anjali said. "It helped to have something to do."

"While you were in labor?"

"I would take a break when a contraction came. Mama Polly and her son were on their way to their don's place and stopped to help me finish. Then Mama Polly stayed to help with the baby. Then you were here, with your friends."

Omesh looked around. He was jumpier than the day he and Ali had tried double espresso, or rather espressos, and his mind was racing, but it couldn't seem to find a task that he should be doing. He set the control box for the rockets on the end of his bed. There were cameras in the rockets that took pictures of what was below them, comparing distances and firing when needed, so there was nothing for him to do there, either.

"Do you want to see your cousin?" Anjali asked.

"Of course," Omesh said. She had crawled into what room was left in her sleep coffin among the household goods she had packed in there earlier. Omesh just managed to squeeze in beside her.

Anjali pulled back the corner of the blanket. "This is Raj."

His cousin was purple and wrinkly and his black curls were dotted with something white and waxy-looking. He opened his dark brown eyes and looked up at Omesh, his gaze steady. He was beautiful.

"Hello, Raj," Omesh said, touching his cousin's cheek. "Welcome to the world." Anjali smiled.

Then the explosions began.

CHAPTER TWENTY-THREE

RABIA

Rabia could taste blood on the back of her tongue. She darted off the road, running past empty playground equipment into the shadow between two buildings. She huddled close to the wall for a moment, but apparently no one had chased her. She leaned forward, hands on knees, and let the blood drip from her nose, hawking and clearing it out of her mouth. Her stomach was protesting the little bit that had run down the back of her throat.

This was not going well.

Teresa should have been able to find Hjalmar for her. They both had implants; for Teresa, that meant always being online and reachable. Even during the few minutes she ate dinner with the family, she was never completely offline, just reachable for emergencies only. Teresa had been shocked that Hjalmar's implant was completely off the network. Rabia hadn't been. No one who sneaked through Barnacle Town to get to the zero G fights in the core could possibly be as rules-conscious as Teresa.

Rabia straightened back up, testing her tender nose with the back of her hand. It was sore as hell, but the bleeding had stopped. Time to find another way to Hjalmar. The front door, so easily accessible when Ulrika had walked beside her, was clearly off-limits on her own. And the men guarding the Chandi family building weren't remotely like affable Georg.

Rabia continued down the alley between the two buildings. She could smell plants, flowers, and something fruity but past ripe. She really was in the swank neighborhood. The alley ended in a low wall, but she easily hefted herself over it and into the garden. A quick glance around showed her what she needed: a watering can half filled with water. She dipped her hand in, hissing in pain as she scrubbed at her face. It wouldn't do to roam these streets with blood on her face. That might fly in Barnacle Town, but...

A sob bubbled up in her throat, and she had to squeeze her hands into fists, biting down hard on her lip to get it back under control. By now, the detonation had started. Somewhere out there Omesh was in a tin can, floating off into the black with his aunt, his only hope a social maladjust who couldn't talk her way past a bunch of blank-faced security types without losing her temper and taking a swing at one.

Boy, oh boy, had he ever swung back.

Rabia took a deep breath, then got back to the work of cleaning herself up. She had one last thing to try: the tunnels. It was risky. If she were caught, they'd surely throw her into the brig and she'd never find Hjalmar then. But short of going back to Teresa and waiting for Hjalmar to get back online, she saw no other options.

Another cleansing breath. The sort that Si Fu had taught her to keep her temper in check, not to deal with the guilty feelings after, but there you go. A few more, then she closed her eyes, remembering. It had been many years since she had explored the tunnels, but it was not like they would have changed. She had been everywhere, and that had to include the Chandi V building. She just had to remember how she had done that.

Five blocks away was a library. She could get to the tunnels through the basement.

Rabia hopped back over the garden wall and slipped back down the alley to the street, trying to look nonchalant, like she belonged. The purple hair made it tough. That and the blood all down her front. She unzipped the front of her jumpsuit, rolling down the top half and tying it around her waist by the sleeves. She wasn't the only teenager to sport that look.

She reached the library only to find the door locked. That was odd. More than odd; with the corporation rotating everyone through three equal-sized shifts over a twenty-four-hour day, the library was always open. Except today, it wasn't.

"Not a coincidence, then," Rabia mumbled to herself, but she went around the corner to try the side entrance. Locked as well. Either the librarians were on strike or some corporate missive was closing all places large enough for people to gather in, Rabia reckoned.

A pair of guards were coming toward her down the street. They didn't seem to take any particular notice of her, but that could change when they got close enough to get a good look at her. Rabia turned away from the building and started walking in a random di-rection, hands in pockets, trying to look like someone who had desperately wanted to download new materials onto her reader and had just been denied. She doubted she was pulling it off since she wasn't actually carrying a reader.

She could hear the two guards talking to each other. She couldn't make out the words, but they were definitely following her. She picked up her pace, burying her hands deeper in her pockets and hunching down. Not that that would make her hair any less purple. She was just considering breaking into a run when she stumbled. There was a man on a bench near the sidewalk at the edge of a tiny park—the sorts of parks and benches they had long since pulled out of her part of the space station to make room for more homes —and although he was hunched up to be unnoticeable more effectively than she, the feet she had tripped over were not so discreet.

"Pardon me," Rabia said, trying to hurry away, but the man caught her arm.

"Aren't you Teresa's sister?" he asked.

"Mr. Gupta?" she asked, recognizing him now that he was sitting up.

"Yes," he said, running a hand over his hair. So he didn't need her to tell him he looked terrible, then. "It's all right, gentlemen. She's with me."

The two guards exchanged a long look, and Rabia sensed that Mr. Gupta's word had plummeted in value of late. Then the taller one shrugged, and they both went on their way.

"Teresa has been trying to reach you," Rabia said.

"Yes, I know. Or rather, I suspect." The hand on his hair moved to the nape of his neck and he winced just a little.

"They took your implant?" Rabia asked. She'd never heard of such a thing being done, but he nodded.

"I'm scheduled to leave for Neptune within the hour."

"Can't you refuse?"

"Not if I want any hope of seeing my children again," he said. "Not that they'll see me now, but perhaps in a few years they'll feel differently."

"I've met your son," Rabia said. "And your daughter, too, but briefly."

"Did you?" His eyes lit up. "What did you think of him?"

"Excuse me?"

"Teresa tells me you've a way with people, an instinct. She says you're nearly always right about someone, even after meeting them only once."

Rabia didn't know what to say. It didn't sound like something Teresa would say about her. She'd certainly never thought of herself that way. Unless she had meant knowing someone she'd fought with? Si Fu always said you could know everything about a person's true nature from their kung fu. But then how could Teresa know, never having met any of Rabia's opponents?

Rabia sat down next to him to think it through. Mr. Gupta waited patiently, but never took his eyes off her. They were disconcerting, those anxious eyes.

"Hjalmar hides himself," she said at last, focusing on the hands in her lap and trying to tune out his watchful gaze. "He has a... facade, I guess you could say, but I don't think it's like a thin shell. It goes deep. It has layers, and they overlap. I'm not sure even he knows how deep you'd have to go to find the true him. I think, deep down, he's a decent, honorable sort. He wants to do the right thing, but the layers get in the way. They tell him how he's supposed to act, or think he's supposed to act, and it gets in the way. I mean, he and I fought. Sparred. Well, fought. I saw his honor then. But it's under a lot of layers."

She bit her lip, not certain how he would take what she had said. She wasn't even sure exactly what she meant; the words had sort of formed themselves on their way out of her mouth. "That makes sense," he said in a faraway voice. "Oh, my son. What a life you have had." The way he said it, it almost sounded like a question. *What life have you had?* "Mr. Gupta, can't you do something?"

He knew what she was talking about. That

was clear from the look of agony that passed over his face. "They've already detonated the charges. It is done."

"I know, but I'm certain there are people still alive out there."

"I'm certain too."

"But can't we do something to help them? They're going to die out there."

"I'm afraid my days of bucking authority are through. It was different when I was young. I have too much to lose now."

Rabia had never seen a man who looked so much like he'd already lost everything. It only started with the chip gone from his head and the children who wouldn't speak to him.

He got up suddenly, brushing at his pants as if they were covered in crumbs. "It's time for me to go. My shuttle awaits."

Rabia nodded, her mind already elsewhere. Perhaps she could break one of the library windows and get inside. She could be in the tunnels before the security team responded.

"I do have to stop by my apartment first to fetch my bag and say farewell to my children."

Rabia nodded again, still not really listening. Did she remember the path through the tunnels that would take her to Hjalmar?

Mr. Gupta leaned down to put his face close to

hers. "If you were to tag along, I don't know who would object."

Now he had her full attention. But of course, he must have known what she was doing so far from her own neighborhood. She jumped to her feet, walking beside him down the street. She was afraid to speak lest he change his mind. He looked just as forlorn as when she'd first seen him hunched up on the bench. They passed the point where she had been stopped before, but the guards were nowhere in sight now. Just as they'd been invisible when she'd come this way with Ulrika, but this time she felt watching eyes on her.

Mr. Gupta hesitated outside the apartment door, then pressed his palm to the lock. It flashed green, and the door clicked open. "I wasn't sure that would still work," he said with a sad little smile. "There is a washroom just through there if you want to clean up. There's aspirin in the cabinet too; please help yourself. I've left your sister a lengthy message, but she won't receive it until after I've gone. You can tell her, if you see her." He caught her hand suddenly, pressing it tightly in both his own. "Good luck to both of you."

Rabia murmured thanks and squeezed his hand back, keeping her real thoughts to herself. She didn't want well-wishes; she wanted *help*.

Rabia went down the hall to the washroom.

She supposed he wanted the chance to say goodbye to his family in private, although why he offered her aspirin, she had no clue.

The bathroom was bigger than her and Teresa's bedroom. Two people could fit in that tub, and not just bobsled style. Rabia sighed, tuning out the luxury while she ran some water into the sink, then looked up into the mirror.

Oh dear. One punch and she was nearly as brightly colored as Alain. And her cleanup job with the watering can had not been anywhere near as thorough as she had assumed. There was a crustiness to the front of her tank top where blood had soaked through her jumpsuit, but at least she was wearing black today and it didn't readily show. She rustled through the cabinet until she found the aspirin. Now that she'd looked at it, her face had become a steady throb of pain.

When she opened the door, she found Hjalmar in the hallway, waiting for her.

"Hey," Rabia said.

"What happened to you?"

"My fault," Rabia said.

"Are you telling me you fell down the stairs?" Hjalmar asked with a halfhearted quirk to his lip. As if the spirit were willing to be sarcastic, but the flesh was weak.

"No, I behaved like a brat and got smacked down like a brat."

"No brat deserves that," Hjalmar said.

She waved her hand, dismissing his words. This wasn't what she needed to be talking to him about. "You have to help me," Rabia said. "Help me help them. I know you can."

"What do you know?" Hjalmar said, managing with a simple straightening of the spine to suddenly be looming over her. "What do you know about what I can do?"

"You have to be able to do something," Rabia said, resisting the urge to cower. "I can't stand being this powerless. They need us."

"I think I know just a little bit more about it than you," Hjalmar said in a low rumble.

"What's that supposed to mean?" Rabia asked.

"This," Hjalmar said, giving his own head a loud smack. "Thanks to this lovely piece of technology in my head, I can't not know. It's all there, just waiting for me to look at it. Like a gap where a tooth has just fallen out, and you have to keep touching it with your tongue to feel that little twinge of exposed nerve. That pain."

"Well, what is it?" Rabia asked, but softly. His look of anguish was surely real.

"You know they set off the detonations, right? Your sister told you."

"Yes."

"Did she tell you about the live feeds from the crews working outside? The cameras they have on their helmets, recording everything?"

"Well, that's how she knows."

"Did she tell you about the bodies? I can see the bodies, drifting in the black. I can't hear the screams, but I see their faces as they scream. I see their eardrums burst in little explosions of blood, their lungs collapse—"

"They aren't all dead," Rabia said, catching his hand and squeezing it hard until he focused on her again. "Some of them had places to weather this out, like lifeboats. But lifeboats can't make it to shore. They have to be rescued."

"By whom?" he said.

"I'm thinking by you and me," Rabia said.

"How?" Hjalmar said. He dropped his face into his hands, slumping against the far wall, and was quiet for several long minutes. Rabia thought he might be crying, but when he lifted his face again, it was the same as before, exhausted but dry-eyed. "Come on."

He led the way back down the hallway but stopped at the room that seemed to serve only as an entrance to the apartment.

"I think I made you angry, when you were here before," Hjalmar said.

"You think you made me angry," Rabia repeated, incredulous. If he wasn't sure, what did he think that slap had been, a come-on?

"What I said—it came out wrong." There was a disconnect between his words and his eyes, Rabia thought. Was he saying something he didn't mean, or was he simply unable to find the words to say exactly what he did mean? Was it insincerity or just inarticulateness she was dealing with? She had told Mr. Gupta that Hjalmar had many overlapping layers, but she hadn't told him that she suspected the facade layers overlapped the truth layers and she wasn't sure which was which. She was suddenly too tired to even care. It had been a long day, or rather, two days. She rubbed at her face to wake herself up and hissed again in pain. Funny how she kept forgetting about the nose.

"Whatever," she snapped. "Look, if you aren't going to help me, I'm going back home. My parents and sister could probably use my help. You see, we're still trying to save what you call the useless people."

"Hey, I just said that came out wrong," Hjalmar said.

"How could it possibly have come out right?" Rabia asked. "It wasn't a matter of word choice; your whole point was reprehensible."

Hjalmar sighed, then reached past her to open a door to another room. Then he waited for her to step in first.

Rabia couldn't hold back the scoffing noise as she realized what he was doing. Being the gentleman. As if she cared. People had died, people were even as they walked still dying; she wasn't in the mood for chitchat or other old-world pleasantries.

He grumbled something she couldn't quite make out, then grabbed her shoulder and steered her ahead of him through the door. She spun her shoulder out of his grasp, then grudgingly walked beside him through the still-empty rooms of his home to the apartment he shared with his sister. She was there now, sitting in the chair where Hjalmar had been before, curled up with a reader on her lap, eyes half closed.

"Do you want anything to drink? A soda or something?" Hjalmar offered.

"What? No! People are running out of air even as we speak. We have to do something."

Ulrika looked up from her reader, then sat up a little straighter, eyes a little wider. "What happened to you?"

"I don't know, Ulrika. Just how many security checkpoints did I not see when you brought me here last time?"

"You can call it ten," Ulrika said with a smirk and snuggled back down into her chair.

"You really look a mess," Hjalmar said, giving a little wince.

"Can we talk in front of her?" Rabia asked, a bit more aggressively than she had intended.

"What? Oh, sure. Honestly, Rabia, I don't know what you expect me to be able to do. It's too late, anyway." He held up a hand when she started to retort, and she bit her tongue, letting him go on. "I know there were people there who were tremendously important to you, that you made connections there that you didn't make with the people here. So I'm sorry about what I said. Again."

"The people who are important to me are mostly still there, you know," Rabia said.

"There were a lot of bodies when they broke the town off our hull," Ulrika said, not looking up from her reader. Rabia supposed she had an implant as well. She would have seen everything Hjalmar had already described.

"My friends knew how to keep themselves safe," Rabia said with all the confidence she could muster. "They are still out there, waiting for rescue."

"Rescue by whom?" Hjalmar asked again. "No one wants them." He passed a hand over his silvery hair, then stopped with it pressed against his nape. A gesture eerily like his father's.

"What did your father do?" she asked suddenly.

"What?" they both said at once.

"He told me a minute ago that he bucked authority in his younger days. I was wondering what he did."

Hjalmar and Ulrika exchanged a long look, so long that Rabia first suspected and then became convinced they were communicating with each other through their implants.

"We don't know," Ulrika said at last, turning back to her reader.

"It was when we were very young," Hjalmar said. "He was banished from Earth and sent here. In case you thought we Chandis were immune from sanctions."

"You won't help because you might be banished from Earth? Sorry, you'll have to do better. I've never been to Earth and I'm just fine without it."

"It wasn't so much banished from Earth as banished from us. And our mother—he's not seen her since," Hjalmar said. Ulrika pinned a very dark gaze on him, but he lifted his chin a fraction of an inch in an "I regret nothing I've said" gesture.

"So?"

"I'd help if there were anything feasible to be done," he said. "But there just isn't. I won't risk my grandfather's wrath in some pointless stunt. Even if there were people out there still alive, waiting for rescue. What then?" He dropped off, rubbing at his chin distractedly. "Where could they go? They could, I suppose, try to separate into smaller groups and get into different cities."

"They don't have propulsion, they can't go anywhere on their own," Rabia said. But she sat forward, ready to engage with him. He was willing to brainstorm; she had to show support for the effort, even if she nixed the first few ideas, just to keep the process going. She certainly didn't know what they could possibly do. He had a whole different set of knowledge and experience to draw from, if he just *would*.

"The moon is handy," Ulrika said out of nowhere.

"Not enough different cities for that many people," Hjalmar said, shaking his head. "And they are all fighting overpopulation as it is. I doubt they would take the refugees in even if they found their way to the harbors; they certainly aren't going to expend resources fetching them."

"If they could get to the surface safely, maybe they could just stay as they are, their own city,"

Rabia said. "They could join together again, make another Barnacle Town."

"A city without water or power or—" Hjalmar listed, counting off on his fingers.

"All right, all right," Rabia said. "There must be somewhere they can go."

"They could live anywhere on Earth if they survived reentry," Hjalmar said. "They'd have to hide from the A&MC, but it's a big world with lots of places to hide."

"Again, except for the sumo school, they don't have propulsion. Plus, nothing I saw in Barnacle Town was designed for reentry. No heat shields. Can't you get some corporate tugs out to bring them down to the moon? It's not a great chance, but it's a chance."

"That would involve my grandfather, and he isn't going to do anything unless it's of tremendous benefit to Chandi Corporation. Unless you can come up with a plan that saves your friends and serves corporate interests both, the answer will be no."

"You won't even ask?"

"I won't even ask."

Rabia sat down on one of the plump chairs, looking down at her hands. She felt like she was going to cry again, but for once she had no anger to summon in its place. She just felt empty.

"If anyone's interested, I've come up with a plan," Ulrika said.

"What sort of plan?" Hjalmar asked, sounding dubious.

"This sort of plan," Ulrika said, turning the reader around. Hjalmar and Rabia both moved in closer.

"A list of Chandi stations," Rabia said.

"Grandfather isn't going to get rid of them here just to let them attach somewhere else," Hjalmar said.

"They're not just space stations. Take a look at this one, for instance," Ulrika said, pointing to something on the screen.

"Oh," Hjalmar said with the air of sudden understanding, straightening.

"Oh what? This means nothing to me," Rabia said.

"It's a station on the moon surface," Hjalmar said.

"Chandi Corporation has a station on the surface? I don't remember that from corporate school."

"Probably because they never would have mentioned it," Ulrika said. "It's empty. It was a plague hot spot, sealed off like most of the cities on Earth and never reopened."

"It still hasn't been. No one wants to risk there

still being something infectious in the air system," Hjalmar said.

"But everything there would still work?" Rabia asked.

Hjalmar shrugged.

"I'll go talk to Grandfather," Ulrika said. She got up from the chair, tucking the reader under one arm and sauntering out of the room.

"She'll convince him," Hjalmar said, watching his sister go with something very like jealous admiration in his eyes. "She can talk him into anything. She's good like that, good with rapport."

Rabia suspected what he was really saying was that he wasn't. But now was the time to let that sort of thing just go. "What if the life support systems don't work on the moon? We'd be selling them false hope," she said instead.

"Do you have some other way of figuring out if it works without sending them there to find out?" Hjalmar asked.

"Could we go?"

"How?" Hjalmar asked. Rabia was beginning to hate that question.

"Look, your grandfather, in his speech, mentioned a bunch of shuttles standing by to take anyone who quit their jobs off the space station. Was that a bluff, or were the shuttles real?"

"Both," Hjalmar said. "There were really shuttles, but he knew no one would take them. The only possible place to go would be a station like Haven whose corporate structure collapsed two generations ago. It would be like living in Barnacle Town, and who would choose that?"

"Me, for one," Rabia said under her breath, but Hjalmar had finally figured out the answer to a *how* question on his own.

"You want to steal one of the shuttles," he said.

"Is it stealing if you do it?" she asked.

"Technically? Yes. In my grandfather's eyes? Definitely yes. That whole 'corporate prince' thing is just a figure of speech, you know."

"So it's stealing, then," Rabia said. "Are you with me or not?"

"I'll help you," Hjalmar said. "But please, don't get your hopes up. There is surely a reason this lunar station has never been reopened."

"We'll soon know," Rabia said. "Let's go."

CHAPTER TWENTY-FOUR

TAKASHI

Tak had forgotten that after the detonation, they would all be weightless. People all around him were crying out, holding on to whatever they could reach. The buildings had been anchored down to the cargo hold floor, but the plants and paving stones, all the objects in the schoolroom and bathhouse, and everything the rikishi owned was floating free. Worse, the sand from the arena was everywhere. How had it spread so fast?

Tak, still near the door, was able to see in the red glow of the emergency light, but further in, the people were floating in darkness. The lights would come on when they fired up the engines. What were they waiting for?

"We should move among the people, try to keep them calm," Kenko said to the other rikishi.

"Keep them calm?" one of the younger students said. "I've never been in zero gravity either. Who's keeping me calm?"

"A little floating is all it takes for you to lose all your discipline?" Kenko said, moving up the wall to hover over them. "Share out what food we have, and blankets. Anything anyone needs."

The rikishi tried their best to give him the requisite bows, but the motion had counter-motions that many found alarming. Kenko gave a small smile but waved them on their way.

"And you?" he asked, settling closer to Tak, who hadn't moved.

"They've got it covered," Tak said.

"And if I made it a firmer order?"

"No good. I'm pretty sure at this point I'm expelled. Sort of kills the motivation for following orders."

"You don't even want to see if your friend made it here?"

"I'm certain he didn't," Tak said. He was about to bury his head in his arms in a hint even Kenko couldn't ignore when he saw Hiroku and Toyonoshima awkwardly making their way toward the two of them.

"The engines won't fire," Hiroku said.

"But they were tested," Kenko said.

"The test was a simulation," Hiroku said. "Obviously we couldn't actually fire the engines while still attached to Barnacle Town."

"What do we need to do?" Kenko asked.

"We're still attached to Barnacle Town," Tak said, repeating Hiroku's words. "That's the problem, isn't it? Something that someone welded onto the hull is blocking some sensor somewhere."

"That is our best guess," Toyonoshima said. "The systems are all operational, but something is stopping the ignition sequence. The computer keeps telling us it's an error and gives us a numerical code—"

"—but none of you are trained pilots or engineers," Tak said.

"So we don't understand what it means, yes," Toyonoshima said.

"We need you to go out and cut off the last of whatever is still attached to us. Then we can try firing the engines again," Hiroku said.

"You don't know that will work," Tak said. "It could all be for nothing."

"It's our best guess," Hiroku said.

"Why me?" Tak asked.

"You have experience with these things. The information your mother submitted when she applied for you to be a student here indicated you do."

"Not this exactly, but I've worked EVA before."

"Also," Toyonoshima said, "you're our littlest rikishi. You're the only one who can fit into the suit we have up on the bridge."

"If you fit at all," Hiroku said.

"Let's find out," Tak said.

Hiroku and Toyonoshima went first, lighting the way with flashlights they'd brought with them from the bridge. Tak kept his eyes on the two of them, trying not to look at the people all around them in the dark, huddled together in groups watching them pass with wide, scared eyes. It was only when they reached the bridge that he saw that Kenko had followed, too.

"Here is the suit," Hiroku said, pointing to something that looked like a relic from the first Apollo missions.

"You're sure it's up to spec?" Tak asked.

"It tests out."

Tak sighed and started the work of wedging his body inside the suit. They had thought the engines had tested out, too.

The others helped him with everything above his waist. It was a very snug fit, but the suit wasn't quite as old as he had thought. It had a readout pad on his left forearm that indicated temperature, oxygen, and water levels. Kenko sealed the helmet to the suit and Tak clambered back into the airlock. At least waiting to pressurize, he got a little nap in.

He had been helping his father make repairs on their family ship since he was old enough to hand him tools. That had involved working in a suit in a vacuum, but never out in the open of space. When Tak had gone out with his father, it was always in an enclosed harbor mesh at one of the bigger space stations, and they had stayed on their own ship's hull and not gone free-floating. Tak pictured that in his mind, imagining his father somewhere just out of sight but there if he needed him. After he had turned the wheel to open the far door of the airlock, he latched his safety line and gave it a few tugs to test it. This time, he didn't admire the moon or Earth; it was too dizzying. He kept his gaze focused on the hull before him and imagined the skeletal struts and solar arrays of a harbor around him.

They had to be free of the rest of Barnacle Town. Toyonoshima had said that the joins would come away easily under the cutter, but he had to be careful not to damage the hull or inadvertently cut through his own suit. He also had a limited amount of time before the suit was out of oxygen.

The tether they had followed before was long

gone. Tak made his way along the rungs that ran along the side of the ship until he reached the first join with Barnacle Town. He was still connected by his first tether to the airlock, but now he connected a shorter tether to the nearest rung, so if he started to float away, he wouldn't have to start all over at the airlock and make his way aft again.

The cutter did indeed slice through the knotted, welded join with frightening speed. A bit more resistance would make it easier to control, but Tak gritted his teeth and kept his focus on moving slowly.

He was well on his way through the second join when something bumped into him. He looked up, the cutter taking advantage of his momentary loss of concentration to hop up in his hands. He had gouged a deep slice in the man's leg before he regained control. By then, the space around him was a rain of floating droplets of blood.

What was more terrifying was the man himself. The vacuum hadn't just killed him, it had turned him into a horror show of ruptured ears and eyes. Tak shoved him away so hard he sent himself away to the end of his short tether.

Now that he was looking, he saw more bodies floating like snow in a snow globe all around the remains of Barnacle Town. Here and there he saw a light in a port window or an old but functioning running light on a ship. The people on board the *Hakudo Maru* weren't the only survivors, then, but many people had died. And the other survivors were just floating, waiting helplessly for whatever would happen next. Fast and horrible might be preferable to slow and horrible, but they were both still horrible. Perhaps if they found a place to drop off the refugees, they could come back and pick up more. Somehow. Tak wasn't exactly sure how they could go about it with only one space suit.

He lowered his head and got back to work. The suit was built to dispense water, but when he tried sucking on the tube, it was dry. He went from mildly thirsty to completely dry-mouthed before he stopped the cutter to take a break. It felt like he'd been at it for hours. His mouth was cottony, and he had to pee. He reckoned he was about three-quarters of the way through the work, though. He could hold out.

He glanced at the indicator panel on his forearm as he was about to fire up the cutter, then stopped and took a closer look.

The O2 level still read as full.

That was impossible. He might be overestimating how long he'd been out, but even if he cut that time in half, the gauge should still show some usage.

"Broken," he said to himself with a dry, humorless laugh. "It's broken."

Three-quarters of the way through. He should be able to finish. He fired up the cutter before the horrible thought hit him.

He had no way of knowing if that tank had even been full when he started.

But they weren't leaving until they were free of Barnacle Town. He had no choice. Or rather, his choice was to potentially die alone outside the ship or to definitely die with company inside the ship. He preferred alone. Not as much as he preferred not dying, of course. Grimly, he got back to work, ignoring an ever-growing headache that seemed to particularly enjoy tormenting the backs of his eyeballs.

At last he broke away the last join, revealing the passage beyond the cargo door, cluttered with bodies that had not made it on board in time. When they ignited the engines to pull away, all these bodies would be cooked. Tak would have preferred to move them all out of the way, just in case anyone ever came out here to retrieve them and give them all the funerary rites they would have desired. But it was doubtful anyone was coming out for the survivors, let alone the dead.

And the cheery feeling stealing over him was frightening him. The fright was a detached feeling, as if he were a happy little cartoon spaceman and fright was in a balloon tied to his wrist. He had to get back inside.

He slipped off the side of the spaceship almost at once, cutter tumbling out of reach. At least he was done with it. He forced himself to focus, grabbing the tether around his waist and slowly reeling himself in. It was a repetitive motion, hand over hand, almost soothing. He caught his eyes trying to close on him and bit down on the tip of his tongue hard to force himself back to alertness.

He reached the airlock and pulled himself inside, collapsing in a floating fetal position for several moments before he remembered to turn the crank to shut the door. The lever to start the flow of oxygen was colossally heavy, and his hands on the helmet fixtures were awkward. He finally managed to pry it off, sending it spinning across the airlock as he fell into a doze so deep he barely felt the helmet bounding back to glance off his forehead.

Kenko shook him awake what he guessed was thirty minutes later. He tugged Tak to his feet to help him out of his suit. They worked without speaking; it was a difficult task in zero gravity, especially as Tak was still feeling thickheaded, and it was made harder when whoever was in the pilot seat finally fired a short burst to take them away from Barnacle Town. Tak tried not to think about the people in the passageway, cooked now.

"We still don't have a destination," Kenko said. "The plan is to stay in this lunar orbit until we hear from our benefactor."

"Do you know who that is?" Tak asked.

"I don't think anyone but Hiroku knows. Not even Toyonoshima."

"It must be someone both rich and Japanese. I can only imagine that's a pretty short list," Tak said.

"It depends on how Japanese they are," Kenko said. He'd finally pulled the last boot free from Tak's foot. As Tak tried to pull his yukata around him in a way that wouldn't float right back up, Kenko stowed the suit back in the cabinet near the airlock.

"I don't think a half-Japanese benefactor would be so strict on who they allow in the school," Tak said. "I've been told that the benefactor hasn't been told the whole truth about me or I wouldn't be here. But Hiroku owes a debt to my grandfather, who made a place for him in his school when Hiroku was the young rikishi."

"I know the story," Kenko said. "I've not been around much, but from what I've seen, the people most concerned about purity tend to be the least pure themselves."

"So, the benefactor is someone who feels their own mixed heritage is a defect, and he or she is overcompensating?"

"I think Hiroku was given very specific instructions on not letting the riffraff on the ship," Kenko said. Not quite answering the question, Tak noticed. "If you hadn't said anything, it would just be us here now."

"Why didn't you say anything?" Tak asked.

"I couldn't. My position here is even more tenuous than yours."

Tak didn't know what to make of this. Kenko seemed to be king of the world to him, the golden child who could do no wrong. He oversaw practices, he kept discipline during school lessons, he doled out chores and punishment. His position seemed pretty far from tenuous.

"Kenko," the older student went on, "is my fighting name, not my birth name. You will lose your name when you appear on your first banzuke, I'm sure. I lost my name the first day I came to this school."

"What's your real name, then?" Tak asked.

"Naranbaatar Khan."

"No part of that is Japanese," Tak said.

"Indeed. But then, no part of me is Japanese."

"I don't understand."

"I'm Mongolian," Kenko said. "From Mongolia, on Earth."

"How did you end up here?" Tak asked.

"My parents died when I was young, too young to take over our camel herd, so our land was redistributed by the A&MC. My younger brother and I went to live with my mother's sister, but they have children of their own. When we reach our majority, we'll be forced to leave Earth."

"But you're not eighteen yet. Why didn't you stay as long as you could?"

"Leaving Earth is hard, but leaving Earth with no job, no prospects, is even harder. I took the one opportunity I had to enter a vocation off of Earth, but it involved leaving at once, at the age of twelve."

"Sumo?"

"Of course. Was our benefactor our benefactor then? I don't know. Perhaps they were in charge, but cared less about such things. Perhaps Hiroku hid certain truths, as he is doing with you. Whatever the case was, I was given the fighting name Kenko before I'd even learned the shiko."

Takashi didn't know what to say. There must be a reason Kenko was telling him all this now. Just as there must be a reason—

"I suppose, in light of all that, you are wondering why I've been so hard on you?"

"Yes, I was wondering just that."

"My younger brother will be old enough to start sumo school soon, provided Hiroku will accept him. I've done my best to show him that foreigner though I am, I can conduct myself with attention to every detail of Japanese culture. Because this isn't really a sport, sumo, it's the last way the remaining Japanese have of holding their culture together. I appreciate that. I respect that."

"And you think I don't," Tak said.

"I think you focus on the sport and miss the deeper purpose."

"You could've just said so."

Kenko made a face that said maybe yes, maybe no.

"How did you get in in the first place?" Tak asked.

"I've had three members of my family become yokozuna, distant ancestors back before the time of the plague. I sent videos of myself wrestling and a long letter to all the stable masters all about what I could bring to the culture of sumo. I had already taught myself to read and write Japanese as well as to speak it, which put me ahead of most full-Japanese boys these days. Hiroku was impressed."

"You really wanted this," Tak said.

"You don't?"

"To be honest? I just want a ship," Tak said. "A ship and freedom. But I don't expect to get something from nothing; I know I'll have to work for it."

There was another blast from the engines that sent them tumbling. They exchanged a look and agreed without words to make their way fore to the bridge.

"Did we hear from our benefactor?" Kenko asked.

"No," Toyonoshima said.

"And time grows short," Hiroku said, tapping a gauge. "At the rate we are using up our oxygen, we'll be lucky to last another six hours."

"Six hours?" Tak repeated. They had mentioned finding a harbor on Mars. Had taking on refugees changed things so much? He had expected to have a few days to figure out the next step. What could be done in six hours?

"You have friends inside the space station," Kenko said. "The girl with the purple hair."

"Yes," Tak said. "I just hope there is something she can do, and fast."

CHAPTER TWENTY-FIVE

OMESH

AFTER THE EXPLOSION, THERE WAS SILENCE. OMESH had expected to hear something—the sound of metal rending, people screaming—but sealing in their air supply also sealed out the ambient sound. They were no longer touching anything, then, or he'd hear something conducted through the metal walls. His stomach felt like it was floating up into his throat. The feeling grew stronger until he really was floating. Anjali stayed curled around Raj, the two of them nested among the furniture, sacks, and boxes in her cell. Omesh clamored out to deal with the chaos of floating objects, but everything was exactly as his aunt had left it.

"You packed this well," Omesh said, just then

noticing the straps that she had secured to hold the boxes and sacks against the walls.

"The girl you sent up helped. The straps were her idea. I glued down the offering bowl and Ganesh-ji as well," she said. She pointed toward the little altar but then turned herself into a sitting orientation, putting a hand over her head to keep herself from bumping against the roof of her sleep coffin. "Omesh, look at the milk."

Omesh turned, expecting to see the air filled with white globules, but it wasn't. He leaned in to see the last of the milk simply disappearing, leaving behind the sad little space-grown marigolds. Only they were looking a little less sad, the petals losing their droop and brightening in color.

"He drank our offering," Anjali said, struggling with her sari. Omesh made his way over to help her tie the ends together, making a tight sling for the baby in the process. Raj was far too little to be left to float on his own.

The pod gave a slight shimmy. Anjali clung to Omesh with one hand, holding Raj close against her with the other.

"It's all right," Omesh told her. "No more explosions. The parts of Barnacle Town are just breaking away from each other now, floating free.

We might bump into bits now and again, but our hull is strong. We'll be fine."

Anjali gave him a smile, more in thanks for trying to reassure her than any actual reassurance. Omesh forced a smile back. Now there was nothing for them to do but wait until someone sent ships to rescue them, or until they crash-landed on the moon, or until air or water or heat gave out. It could be a long wait.

To Omesh's desert-loving blood, it felt cold already.

"We will be all right," Anjali said, although whether she was speaking to him or Raj, he wasn't sure. "Ganesh is the remover of obstacles. I imagine he will remove them one at a time, when the moment is right."

Omesh didn't answer. He was pretty sure the flowers were the reason the milk had disappeared, but if thinking otherwise kept his aunt hopeful, it would be mean-spirited to contradict her.

Time passed in agonizing slowness. Anjali mostly slept, as did Raj, leaving Omesh on his own to check and double-check things that didn't need his monitoring and to wait for something to happen. He floated into his own sleep coffin. His aunt had put all of his things back into his trunk before packing the space with furniture and boxes, so he knew his computer was safe. He tried to nap and found it impossible to sleep. But he didn't feel awake either. He merely floated somewhere in between the two, aware of his surroundings but not really, as if only half his mind were paying attention.

Omesh knew they had been floating for hours; his watch still chimed for every prayer, and he dutifully covered his head and did his best. But he had given his compass to Rabia, so he had to guess which way faced Mecca, and he had to hook his feet under his trunk and keep them flexed, pressing the trunk up against the roof of his sleep coffin, in order to prostrate himself. Awkward as it was, there was still some peace in it. He could almost smell the air of his home at the edge of the desert, almost feel the heat of the sun, almost sense his father there beside him.

Then he finished and was alone once more in the cold silence.

He should have sent his parents one last message before he lost his connection to the corporate internet. They didn't even know that Barnacle Town was in danger. What would they think when their video letters went unanswered? He worried about his mother. Anjali reminded him a bit of her, with her stubborn refusal to let a little thing like going into labor stop her from doing a massive amount of work. His mother was stubborn like that. But he was afraid no amount of work would take her mind off losing another child.

Omesh forced his mind to take a more positive track. He wasn't lost yet; he was just waiting. He wished he could get at his computer; some music would be nice. But the trunk was too buried behind other things, and he didn't want to risk waking Anjali with a lot of loud digging around. Instead, he tried to pass the time by remembering the poems his father used to recite. His father could barely read, but he seemed to have entire books of poetry in his head and could dip into them any time and come up with the perfect poetical response to anything from an inconveniently large rock that needed to be dug out of a field before planting to getting his wife to smile with a lighthearted couplet. Rumi had been his favorite. Omesh closed his eyes and heard his father's voice reciting ghazals. But on his own, he couldn't remember more than a few couplets here and there.

He was beginning to worry that they weren't going to crash down onto the moon. What if they had been sent out into the black instead? Not that it mattered much; either way, they could do nothing but wait for rescue.

Mostly he thought about Rabia. He thought counting on her was a better bet than waiting for divine intervention. He knew she wouldn't give up, but that didn't mean she would succeed.

A sudden trilling sound echoed through the pod.

"Omesh?" Anjali called in a sleepy voice.

"It's the rocket controls," Omesh said, silencing the alarm just as it trilled again. "The cameras are picking up something. We must be finally going down to the surface."

Omesh looked at the images that were projected on little screens, each barely bigger than his thumb. He was meant to be viewing all this from a proper command center, surely. He couldn't make out any details, but the gauges measuring the distance were slowly ticking down.

"It won't be long now," he told her. Images of every worst-case scenario kept playing through his mind. The airbags didn't inflate, and they crashed. The airbags did inflate but were too much and they bounced and flipped and then crashed.

He should have done the math.

There was something he could do. In fact, there was something he needed to do.

"This is going to be a hard landing," Omesh said, struggling out of his sleep coffin to the end of hers. "Is this all strapped in place as well?"

"Yes, but will it be enough?"

Omesh tugged at one of the straps. It was canvas, but it seemed sturdy enough. He climbed in with her, bringing the rocket controls with him.

"Make sure the sling is secure and hold Raj tight," Omesh said, watching the numbers tick lower and lower. "I wish we had seatbelts."

"It will be all right," Anjali said, adjusting Raj inside her sari sling and tightening the knot. "You've done well here, Omesh. If Prakash were here, I know he'd be proud. Your parents too."

"Thanks," Omesh said, resisting the temptation to add that they weren't safely on the ground just yet. Then the rockets fired in unison, and Omesh and Anjali both cried out in surprise as they collided with the ceiling.

"Are you OK?" Omesh asked, rubbing his sore head.

"It's fine," Anjali said, adjusting herself so that she sat against the wall of the coffin, feet braced against the side of the box in front of her rather than cross-legged in the middle. "How many times will that happen?"

"I'm not sure," Omesh said, although his words were lost in another quick burst. It wasn't as loud as the reaction control system on the shuttle that had taken him to Barnacle Town, but he could feel the vibration through the walls more and was reminded once more that the rockets weren't built for this sleeper pod, and vice versa.

Some of the pictures on the monitors had little smudges on them, smudges that got smaller even as the features of the moon got larger. They must be other parts of Barnacle Town, parts with no way to fight the gravity, parts that were falling with greater speed down to the surface. When it was all over, he and Anjali would be awaiting rescue at the tail end of a debris field hundreds of kilometers long.

Anjali was singing something under her breath, keeping one arm tight around Raj and the other braced against the ceiling in preparation for the next rocket fire. He thought at first she was singing a Ganesh song, but something in the refrain triggered an image of a couple frolicking in the Alps.

"Sorry," Anjali said when she noticed him grinning at her. "Terrible time for an earworm, but I've had that song in my head all day. My grandmother used to sing it when I was little. I guess it's from a movie, I don't know. But suddenly I can't stop singing that song. Strange that something so inane as singing a song I don't understand can help deal with childbirth."

"I suppose it helps to have something else to

focus on. Not knowing the words probably helps; you're just focusing on the sounds."

"I think you're right," Anjali said with a smile. Even after sleeping the last few hours, she looked monumentally exhausted. His father, after a hard day on the farm, scarcely looked that worn to the bone. She started singing again, a soft murmur.

"It sounds familiar; I think my mother has that movie," Omesh said, hoping to keep her distracted. "You're singing about being up nights, your dreams invaded. You have a restless heart and you think you might be in love."

"Ah," Anjali said with a little laugh. "Of course."

The rockets fired again, longer this time. "Nearly there," he said, trying to sound reassuring. He felt like a kid pretending to be a grown-up, and he didn't think he was being very convincing.

The rockets gave one more short burst, and after a pause, there was a whoosh. All the pictures blanked out; the airbags had inflated.

"Hold on," Omesh said, moving closer to put an arm around her and help her brace for impact and protect the baby.

They hit, Omesh taking the brunt of it when the back of his head collided with the roof. Then they bounced, but not too high. They didn't tip, and Omesh guessed the bottoms of the airbags didn't even leave the surface, or if they did, it wasn't by much. They sank down again, rose up in a smaller bounce, then settled down to stay.

"Omesh!" Anjali said. He felt woozy, and the vertigo was threatening to bring up his meager lunch. He touched the back of his head and his fingers came away bloody. Which only made the wooziness worse.

"Let me see," Anjali said, adjusting Raj and leaning forward, pushing Omesh's head down so she could see his wound.

"I'm OK," Omesh said, but the vertigo was still spinning him around and around.

"Lie down," Anjali said, moving out of the pod so he could have all the room. Then she gave a little giggle as she noticed the gravity they'd been lacking for hours—the decidedly lower lunar gravity. The one she had spent her childhood in.

"Praise Ganesh," Anjali said, kissing Raj's forehead. "I'm home."

Woozy as he was, Omesh still managed a smile.

CHAPTER TWENTY-SIX

RABIA

"We're too late," Rabia said, leaning forward in her seat to peer through the window. Hjalmar didn't answer, but his hands suddenly moving over the controls told her he too had seen. They were flying close to the lunar surface, just high enough to be above the mountain ranges, but close enough to see every detail. Craggy rocky peaks glowing in the sunlight contrasted starkly with the deep inky shadows of vast craters all under a starry sky, and Rabia had let the constant sense of pressure ease up in her mind, basking in her first glimpses of the universe outside of Chandi V.

But now that pressure was back in full measure. Up ahead, the stars were blotted out by what looked like a swarm of large, dark specks. The specks were arcing down to the surface, some falling faster than others. Plumes of dust erupted here and there, eerie in the silence.

The remains of Barnacle Town had made several lunar orbits on their own, but it looked like they would not be making another.

"It's not all going down at once," Hjalmar said at last, looking at a screen to his right that she couldn't see. "But what's raining down is going to make our approach to the station a bit tricky."

"We're nearly there?"

"Yes," Hjalmar said, but he sounded distracted. Then he cursed under his breath and slumped back into his seat, anger lines deeply furrowed.

"What is it?" Rabia asked, unfastening her belt to float behind him and see the screen. "Did something happen to the station? A meteor strike?"

"No, it's not that," Hjalmar said, tapping the screen to zoom in. "There's the station—I've made it red. This gray area is where the debris field is forming."

"All around the station. That's perfect."

"Yes," Hjalmar said. "Perfect." But the way he rubbed at his forehead said he was less than pleased.

"I don't understand."

"It doesn't matter," Hjalmar said. "You're right,

this is good news for the survivors. It will be easier to get them inside the station if they're closer. Granted, I still don't know how you're planning to do that..."

"Something will present itself," Rabia said, without adding, "it has to."

"Strap back in," Hjalmar said. "We'll be landing soon."

"Have you ever landed on the moon before?" Rabia asked.

"No."

"Where have you landed?" she asked.

He gave her a tight grin. "You see, these shuttles practically fly themselves."

"You're joking," Rabia said, but she couldn't keep her hands from gripping the armrests tightly.

"Partly," he admitted. "I've done landings to reach all Chandi properties on the simulator, and my instructor swore it was state-of-the-art and quite authentic."

Rabia bit back a groan. As scary as this was, it was nothing compared to what Omesh was going through. She at least had a window. She could see her fate before it met her.

"I've landed airplanes on Earth lots of times, in all sorts of weather conditions. I'm sure that's trickier."

"I should have been more specific when I asked if you knew how to fly," Rabia said.

"Because you had so many other options," Hjalmar said. "No one else is willing to help you cross my grandfather."

"Except, apparently, your sister. This was her master plan."

Hjalmar didn't answer, busy checking screens and gauges again. It really did look like the computer was doing all the work, but he seemed engrossed in double-checking things.

"You'll be able to see the station in a second," Hjalmar said. "It's going to pop over the horizon right... now."

Rabia leaned forward as far as her straps would allow. It wasn't much. Out the window was nothing but more flat moonscape stretching off to mountains in the distance.

"I don't see it," she said at last.

"When we get closer, the landing lights will come on. Hold on, the RCS is about to fire."

"The what?" But her words were drowned out by a succession of loud booms. Rabia gripped the armrests once more, desperately wishing she'd put her helmet on rather than leaving it off as Hjalmar had done. There had to be a hull breach; something must have hit them or one of the engines had exploded. Nothing normal would be that loud, would it?

"Where are the lights?" Hjalmar asked through gritted teeth.

"It's been decades since anyone was here. Something must have knocked out the power, or someone shut it down before..." Rabia trailed off. She didn't want to think about how this station had come to be abandoned.

"Power and computer control are both out," Hjalmar said. "At this point, the station's harbor pilot program is supposed to be taking over our shuttle and guiding us in."

"But you weren't counting on that to get us down safely, right?"

His answer was lost in another loud blast from the RCS, this one harder than before, bringing them nearly to a standstill before a large piece of shipping container came pinwheeling down in front of their nose.

"Damn, that was close," Rabia said.

"We'll be landing in the hangar, and the sooner the better," Hjalmar said. He was looking very tense and focused. Rabia checked her restraints, pulling the straps as tight as she could.

Another burst from the RCS got them moving just a bit faster now that the danger was past, then different rockets fired individually, controlling the motion of the shuttle as they drifted down close to the surface. A bump in the center of the lunar plain had become a low, flat mountain. As they drew closer, Rabia realized the dimensions were too regular for a natural formation; it was manmade but covered with soil so it blended in with the lunar surface.

Their forward momentum carried them into an opening in the side of the mountain that was big enough to let a dozen shuttles in at once, more if you stacked them; there was room enough to fit three or four vertically. The hangar space within was massive, ten times as deep as the door was wide.

"And here is where the tow hook should be grabbing us," Hjalmar said under his breath. Rabia leaned forward again. She could just make out a groove in the floor: the guide the hook mechanism followed, she guessed. Then they passed out of the last of the sunbeam into the darkness deeper in the hangar. The shuttle had lights, but they were dim, designed to make the shuttle visible to the rest of the world and not the other way around. Hjalmar fired the rockets again, slowing them down further, but not quite to a stop.

"We're running out of hangar here," Rabia said,

gripping her armrests again. Her fingers were going to leave permanent dents.

"Just about..." His voice had the same "my mind's not really here" quality that Teresa's often got. Rabia wasn't sure what that meant; even if his implant contained something like the station harbor pilot program, she was certain it required the tow hook, which required the station to be under power.

Hjalmar's hands tapped at the controls, firing short bursts from first one rocket, then another. They hit the ground and bounced, then again, but not as high. Finally, they came to a stop, one wing grazing the hangar wall ever so slightly, and he sat back with a loud whoosh of released breath.

"What now?" Rabia asked.

"Now we find the power room and bring everything back online."

"Just like that? We just have to flip a switch?"

"Maybe," Hjalmar said, unstrapping himself from his seat and finding his helmet. "I'm going on the theory that the last survivors went through the standard shutdown procedures, in which case, yes, it's pretty much flipping a switch."

"But by standard procedure, shouldn't a remote start be possible? I mean, it would require high-level Chandi passcodes, but I'd assume you have those."

"Yeah, I tried that during our approach. No joy."

"But then your theory—"

"Rabia, we just have to get down there and see what's what."

"Shouldn't we check to see if there's atmosphere first? Even if the systems shut down, there might still be air they didn't use."

"I want to get to the computers in the life support command area and run some tests first. No sense taking chances. This is still a quarantine zone."

"But Barnacle Town is already on the surface."

"Not all of it," Hjalmar said. "Look." He put an image up on the screen built into the window like a heads-up display and pointed. "Parts of it are still in orbit. This here with the bright red heat signature must be the sumo school. There are a few other ones glowing dark orange. They have something keeping them up there, but not much, and who knows for how long."

"I wonder which one is Omesh," Rabia said. "I hope he found his family."

"We will go out for them as soon as we're sure this place is safe. We need to get moving."

They cycled through the shuttle airlock and stood at the edge. It was a fifteen-foot drop to the hangar floor.

"Come on," Hjalmar said, his voice crackling inside her helmet, and jumped over the edge. He arced down in a gentle glide and landed gracefully. "No sweat for a zero G fighter," he said. Rabia jumped. She didn't feel as graceful floating through the air, but at least she stuck the landing. Sort of. Well, there was a slight bounce.

"Look, moon buggies," Rabia said, pointing across the hangar. "If they're still operational, that's how we'll fetch the survivors."

"Rabia, I think any survivors are in the ships still up in the sky. Those bits raining down are hitting the ground hard," Hjalmar said. "The door is over here."

"Do you know where you're going?" Rabia asked. Jumping out of the shuttle had given her an inflated sense of her lunar gravity skills; actually, walking was trickier. She had a sense that running would be out of the question until she had more practice.

"I have access to maps and directories." He stopped at the airlock, opening the panel that held the crank for emergencies. He fit the crank into the cog framed in red paint and started turning it. The door opened inch by inch. The airlock was big enough to drive a moon buggy through, but Hjalmar only opened it wide enough for them to fit through one at a time. Once they were both inside, Hjalmar turned a similar crank on the inside to shut the door behind them.

Rabia looked around, the light on her helmet illuminating whatever she was directly facing but not much else. It looked like the inside of any other airlock.

"There is some air in here, but not much," Hjalmar said, looking at a panel built into the arm of his suit. Then he set to work, cranking open the inner door. "There is an assembly room for pilots, right off the hangar. It will take too long to make the whole station breathable at once, but that room will be large enough to hold the survivors. We can get just that space livable first, then bring the rest of the station up. You can't tell in the suit, but the ambient air is a touch on the freezing side. We're deep enough underground for the rising sun not to change that much, except in the public areas with skylights."

"Sounds like a plan," Rabia said. She poked her head through the growing gap between door and doorframe and looked up and down the hall. This space was also big enough to drive a moon buggy through. Two could even pass each other, but it would be tight.

"This way," Hjalmar said, starting down the hallway to the right. Rabia fell into a bouncing rhythm. They were moving downhill at a gentle, almost imperceptible grade.

"How many people were stationed here before the plague?" she asked. The light from her helmet caught details of things around her—fixtures on the wall and signs pointing out upcoming corridors and doors, the occasional motorized cart parked haphazardly in the hallway—but it wasn't powerful enough to light up everything and give her the big picture.

"A few thousand miners, plus family and support crew. I don't know how many were here after the plague hit, if any fled or if they took in refugees. The logs will show once we get down to engineering."

"It's like a city, then?"

"Yes," Hjalmar said.

There was a cluster of carts in front of him, piled atop each other as if someone had tried to wall this part of the corridor off. Hjalmar looked it over, his light playing over wheels and fenders and seats. Rabia glanced back the way they had come. She couldn't see the airlock door anymore, but she judged that they had come several stories underground down the long, sloped tunnel.

"We might have to find another way," Hjalmar said. Rabia turned back to the roadblock. She couldn't see an opening either.

"Can't we move a few close to the top? They weigh quite a bit less here on the moon than what we're used to."

"But the mass is still the same. They're bulky."

"We could work together."

"If we lose control... getting hit by one of those is still going to hurt."

"Do you honestly think if you find another way, it won't also be blocked? These people knew this place better than you. Plus, tick tick."

"I know. OK, let's try, but slowly."

They climbed up the pile of carts, and Hjalmar chose a cart that was already perched fairly precariously near the ceiling. It looked like one hard tug would pull it free.

"Hopefully this isn't a *deep* pile of carts," Hjalmar said, getting a grip on the side mirror and the back of one seat. Rabia did the same on the other side, choosing carefully where she planted her feet.

"Pull on three," Hjalmar said, and she nodded. "One. Two. Three."

The cart resisted their efforts to move it. Although she couldn't hear through her helmet, she could feel a shuddering under her palms and imagined the shriek of metal against metal. Then it came free all at once. Rabia let go right away, but Hjalmar was half a second slower and went tumbling after it down the side of the roadblock. Rabia wanted to reach out to catch him, but pulling that one cart free had shifted the entire mass and her carefully selected footholds were moving under her. She pinwheeled her arms to stay on her feet, the ceiling now too far away for her to use it to steady herself.

When the pileup finally settled, she was about half a meter lower down. "Hjalmar, you OK?" she asked.

"Nothing broken," his voice answered inside her helmet, but she still couldn't see where he was. Then one of the carts below her shifted a bit, and he crawled out.

"Your suit's intact?" she asked.

"There's a scratch in my helmet, right down the middle," he said, sounding irritated. "But otherwise, I'm five by five."

"Come on back up," she said. "We have enough room up here to crawl across the top now."

Hjalmar bounded up the side of the roadblock and the two of them crawled on their bellies for several meters before emerging on the other side. Hjalmar plunged through first. She heard his soft grunt as he landed on the ground below.

"Yes, it's exactly like a city," he said, and Rabia plunged down after him. It was a little awkward; there wasn't enough room to pull her knees up and get her feet under her and she poured out the other end headfirst. But the slow fall gave her plenty of time to somersault around and land right side up in a low crouch. Only when she stood back up did she notice what Hjalmar was looking at.

There was light all around them, a grayish, diffuse light, but it filled the space in a way their headlamps couldn't. The hallway had ended in a circular atrium, the ceiling several stories overhead. This was where the light was coming from: the slowly dawning sun shining through skylights.

Directly in front of them was a massive stone basin with a tall spindle jutting up from the middle, all enclosed under a glass dome twice as high. Rabia stepped forward, pressing her hands against the glass.

"What is it?"

"That's a fountain, when the water is on," Hjalmar said. "We're in the shopping district."

Rabia followed him around the fountain. The floor under their feet was covered with elaborately patterned tile. The walls were tiled as well, although they were harder to see, covered as they were with dried brown vines and leaves in the process of changing from veined paper to dust.

"A garden?" Rabia said.

"Once," Hjalmar said. "Chandi V was supposed to be a lot like this place was. Most of it was torn out to make room for refugees, and the rest... well, overpopulation runs things down fast."

The atrium opened up onto an even larger space, a long promenade running between two stacks of balconies. These also had once been garden-like, with ivy growing up the walls, flowers on every balcony wall, and trees evenly spaced in a long row down the center of the promenade. Or so Rabia imagined; everything was skeletal and grayish-brown now.

"We could fit all of Barnacle Town in here," she said, barely above a whisper.

"And these are just the shops. The residential areas are off to the right, the hospital and schools off to the left. Engineering is straight ahead and a little deeper down."

"We should hurry," Rabia said, chastising herself for getting distracted by the view. Hjalmar didn't answer, just traversed the promenade in long, loping strides. Rabia followed as well as she could. Hjalmar had clearly been on the moon before.

"This way," Hjalmar said after passing through another fountain atrium. The hallway at this end was also blocked by stacks of carts. This time,

Hjalmar found a space to crawl through close to the floor and Rabia followed.

When she emerged, she found Hjalmar standing over something, or rather someone; she could see bony legs sprawled across the floor. Rabia stood to look over Hjalmar's shoulder and considered changing that *someone* back to *something*. The miner jumpsuit that contained it was still bright yellow, but what was inside was blackened and dense-looking. Not papery like the leaves, but thick and waxy, as if it would take some work to stick a knife in it. Rabia turned away. That was one benefit of her helmet: she didn't have to turn far to block out the sight.

"Remarkably preserved," Hjalmar said, nudging it with his foot.

"Don't," Rabia said.

"I don't see any injuries. I wonder what he died from. Perhaps he was the last, manning this station until he died of old age."

"Manning against what? These blockades— were they expecting an invasion? Who could invade?"

"Let's get to engineering," Hjalmar said. "Once the systems are up and I have access to the logs, I'll know more."

Rabia nodded, anxious to get away from the mummy dressed like a lunar miner. Signs at the end of the hallway pointed out what Hjalmar had already told her about the location of things. The hallway that went straight ahead to engineering was smaller, more to human scale.

"How much farther?" Rabia asked after several long minutes of bounding down the hallway that spiraled down deeper and deeper into the lunar surface.

"Just a bit," Hjalmar said, then pulled up short. Rabia caught onto him to stop her own forward momentum.

The hallway ended in a massive pair of double doors with ENGINEERING written across them. Before the doors was a twisted mass of mummified bodies.

"What happened here?" Rabia wondered aloud. She could see tears in the miners' clothing, dried blood everywhere. There had been a fight here. Had the guy at the top of the hallway been the only survivor? But then who had he been waiting for there?

"They fought here before the doors," Hjalmar said, picking his way through the tangle of desiccated arms and legs. "I hope this doesn't mean the doors are locked from the inside."

"These are miners; there must be explosives somewhere," Rabia said.

"If there were, they would have used them."

Hjalmar pushed at the doors, but they were shut fast. Of course, the panel next to them did nothing, but he tried it anyway.

"What now?" Rabia asked. It was hard to think past the loud ticking of her mental clock. She remembered the dark orange images on Hjalmar's screen. He had said that's where the survivors were. He had also said that they couldn't stay up there forever.

"Let me think," Hjalmar said, slumping down against the wall, mindless of the bodies all around him.

Rabia tried to wait patiently, but the image of bits of Barnacle Town raining down on the lunar surface wouldn't leave her mind. She couldn't fail now at the end because of a locked door. She rushed forward, pounding and prying at where the two doors met. This place was decades old—surely it would give.

"Rabia, stop!" Hjalmar said, getting up from the floor. "I know you think there's no problem that can't be solved by throwing a little anger at it, but I really do have this under control."

"I don't solve problems with anger," Rabia said. She knew she'd be more convincing if she took some of the edge off her voice, softened her tone a little.

"Says the girl who wins arguments with slaps."

"That wasn't about winning the argument," Rabia said, but now it was shame she couldn't keep out of her voice.

"Really?"

"If I had wanted to hurt you, I would have thrown a punch."

"I don't doubt. But a slap is a pretty broadly recognized method of shaming or rebuking. Which apparently you couldn't do with words."

"Hey, I did try to do it with words."

"Not very many."

"I can't believe you're arguing with me about this. You were the one being obstinate at the time. If I shouldn't have slapped you, you shouldn't have been so... dense."

"It's not appropriate to hit people, Rabia."

"Gods, I know that!"

"Do you? Because I know my household security staff pretty well. I know that colorful nose of yours was not an unprovoked shaming gesture."

Rabia blinked back hot tears. "I don't want to talk about me right now. This isn't the time. We need to get inside this door or people are going to die."

Hjalmar nodded and was silent for a minute more, then perked up suddenly. "You wait here. I'll have this door open in a moment."

"Where are you going? I'll go with you," Rabia said.

"No, just wait here."

"In the dark? With all the dead bodies?" Rabia asked.

"Please."

Rabia frowned at him. He was hiding something. He had been hiding something before, back in the shuttle, when he'd found that the debris field was defining itself all around this station, and he was hiding something now.

"Just hurry," Rabia said.

Hjalmar disappeared back up the hallway. There was a secret way into engineering, then. Something these miners hadn't known, but Chandi family members did. It didn't matter. The important thing now was getting inside as quickly as possible, and arguing about being left to wait would only delay things.

Also, Rabia knew a thing or two about finding hidden places. So long as she knew it existed, eventually she would find it.

"Omesh, please be safe," she whispered. "I'm nearly there. Please, just hold on."

Then the lights came on. The doors opened with loud, grinding complaints. Rabia had expected to see Hjalmar there, perhaps making a bit of a *ta-da* gesture with his arms. But then, that wasn't really his style. She stepped inside and found him at the far end of the room, moving from console to console, bringing systems up and monitoring their progress.

"One man remembered the protocols," he said, indicating with a jerk of his helmet the lone figure in a chair, his jumpsuit engineering green rather than miner yellow.

"So you're flipping the switch?" Rabia asked.

"Already done. I'm testing for pathogens in the air now. The initial results are negative, but I'm having the medbots in the infirmary set up some cultures to be sure."

"How long will that take?" Rabia asked.

"For a true negative? Days. Don't worry, I wasn't planning to wait. But if there is still a pathogen here, we'll want to know, right?"

"You mean we might bring everybody down here just to have them die from the plague?"

"If I thought that was likely, I'd never have come myself," he said. "But it is a risk. I thought I should tell you."

"OK, but let's keep it between us until we know for sure."

"I was planning on that," Hjalmar said. Something beeped on the panel he was watching and he hit a few more buttons, then moved on to the next.

"The assembly room will be warm and full of breathable air within the hour. Once the cleaning bots are online, I'll have them haul away the bodies before we let everyone into the station proper."

"Can I help?" she asked as he again moved from panel to panel, fingers flying.

"No. Actually, to your left is the comm. Call the ships in. The harbor pilot system will be on-line by the time they get here."

"OK, but how do we get people not in space suits from their ships into the assembly room?"

Hjalmar stopped working, hands on hips and frowning at the floor.

"It's just one problem after another, isn't it?" Rabia said. She could hear the despair creeping in at the corners of her voice, threatening to crack it like thin ice. Hjalmar reached across the console to squeeze her hand. He didn't say she was forgiven for slapping him, but she felt like he meant it. The touch was comforting but muted through their space suit gloves. If only the atmosphere were up, and she could feel the warmth of his skin on hers, maybe then she wouldn't feel so isolated and powerless.

She took a deep breath to pull herself together, then looked up at him. But whatever she had been about to say died on her lips. The look he was giving her was so intense she nearly staggered back from it, but the warmth spreading through her was tempered by her confusion. Why now? Why suddenly now, this look? Then his gaze dipped down to her mouth, and she was sure if they weren't both wearing helmets, he'd be kissing her.

Rabia pulled her hand away, but the confusion and arousal fighting for dominance in her kept her tongue-tied.

"We'll think of something," Hjalmar said at last, as if nothing had just passed between them, and went back to pushing buttons. "Just tell them to come home and we'll think of something."

Rabia nodded and turned to the communication console. She concentrated on not letting her hands shake as she touched the buttons, on bringing her mind back to the task at hand. She touched the front of her hip where, under her space suit, Omesh's compass was nestled in her pocket. Then she turned on the mic and started making the calls.

CHAPTER TWENTY-SEVEN

TAKASHI

Tak found a tiny little corner to hide away in and be alone for a few minutes. It hadn't been easy to find, and it wasn't particularly comfortable; he was wedged where the roof of one of the school buildings met the ceiling of the cargo hold and there wasn't much space between, but the wedging was nice after all the floating. It was dark in his hidey-hole and the stink of the ship was inescapable, but the din of quiet weeping was a mere susurrus here. Tak put his head on his arms and wished he could sleep.

Hiroku had been right about the bathroom. There was a constant line and too many little children who just couldn't wait. The refugees had taken to wearing strips of cloth tied around their noses and mouths and trying not to think too much about what was floating in the air around them.

The food was already all gone. Worse, they were constantly in direct sunlight and the heat in the cargo hold was building. There had been no need to shed heat in Barnacle Town; the space station had been aligned to keep its solar panels facing the sun while orbiting the moon, and Barnacle Town had been built around the curve in the station hull, in the shade. Just the body heat of all the people packed in here would be miserable enough, but the sun was going to bake them alive if they didn't get into the shadow of the moon soon.

Hiroku had been right about all of it; there were just too many people, and no one was coming to their rescue.

"Oh, there you are," one of the other rikishi said, poking his head into Tak's space and startling him awake. He hadn't realized he'd dropped off. "I've been looking for you everywhere. You're wanted on the bridge."

"OK, thanks," Tak said, not bothering with Japanese. Did they need him to go EVA again? What good would that do? At least it would get him out of this place for a precious hour.

"There you are," Kenko said when Tak moved

aft into the command area. "Your friend came through."

"What?"

"Rabia, the kung fu girl. She just called on the radio and sent us coordinates to an abandoned lunar station. She's got life support for thousands, for as long as we need it."

"And food?"

"She didn't mention food," Kenko said. "One thing at a time, though, right?"

"I guess. When do we land?"

"Soon. Hiroku-sama wanted you to suit up. There are only two of them down there, and they're going to need a hand setting up some sort of emergency airlock that will seal on the side of this ship so we can unload our people."

"Of course."

Kenko helped him back into the suit. "We refilled the air tanks, and Toyonoshima fixed your indicator."

"He's sure?" Tak asked, tapping the display.

"He says he tested it out, and it passed."

Tak glanced toward the cockpit. "Do the two of them even know how to land this thing?" he asked in a low voice. "And please don't tell me they've tested a simulated landing."

"No worries," Kenko said, checking the settings on the radio in Tak's helmet before handing it to him. "The station has a program that lands all incoming craft by remote."

"That will work for us, but what about the other derelicts out there? They don't have working navigation or piloting systems."

"Takashi, they can't even land."

"After we unload the refugees, we're going to have to come back up and get them."

"Hiroku-sama is already working on a plan. He's been talking to the other dons by radio."

"The dons all made it?"

"I don't know about all. Most of them did, though, and they're still in charge."

"We'll see about that," Tak said. He went into the airlock and closed his eyes to nap through the pressurization. He didn't feel any sort of descent, but opened his eyes when he felt the ship slowing. Then a tow hook clanged onto the belly of the ship. The lunar cities loved their harbor pilot programs and tow hooks; they could pack ships in tighter than sardines in a can without the interference of a human pilot worrying about his paint job.

When the shuttle came to a stop Tak cranked the door open and hopped down from the airlock, landing on the hangar deck in a bounce and using the momentum to carry him to where two figures in space suits stood waiting by what looked like a giant plastic tent.

"Tak, is that you?" Rabia's voice buzzed in his ear. Before he even answered, she had tackled him, hugging him tight.

"Yeah, it's me," Tak said. "Thanks for the rescue." She pulled back from the hug and he saw her face for the first time. "What happened to you?"

"It's not important," she said with a dismissive wave. "Where's Omesh? He's with you, right? In the school?"

"No, he went to his aunt. They might have made it to one of the other dons' ships, or maybe they rode down in the sleeper pod with the equipment Teresa gave him," Tak said. Rabia was turned toward the tent so he couldn't see her face. "I'm sure he's OK."

"I just had a thought," Rabia said, looking up at the other figure. Tak saw a few locks of long silvery hair floating around the boy's face and recognized him from the zero G fight. Hjalmar.

"Lots of people lost each other," Hjalmar said as if finishing her thought.

"We should take names. When everyone comes through the airlock—it's the best time. A natural bottleneck. Otherwise, we might never keep track of everybody."

"Barnacle Towners. It would be like herding cats, I suppose?" Hjalmar said.

"Cats who are almost pathologically suspicious of anything like a census, yes," Rabia said.

"There's a working computer terminal at the door to the assembly room," Hjalmar said. "I'm going to be piloting the shuttle to bring the other survivors down, so you'll have to take care of the census on your own."

"Don't worry," Tak said. "The other rikishi have put themselves in charge on our ship. They will bring the refugees on board in small groups and make sure they all give their names. Think of them like your own little security force."

"Or not so little," Rabia said, giving him a playful jab in the arm. "Thanks."

"This is the emergency inflatable airlock equipment," Hjalmar said, lifting up a corner of the tent. "It should be big enough to fit over the cargo doors of your ship. It will form its own seal and inflate. The other end runs to the airlock door; we already have that all set up."

"Let me get inside first," Rabia said. "I have to set up that computer."

"OK," Hjalmar said. "I'll see you when we have everyone down safe." Rabia nodded, then gave Tak a nod of farewell too before bounding across the hangar.

"How are you planning on getting people down?" Tak asked as he and Hjalmar dragged the tent across the floor to the rear of the cargo ship. It wasn't heavy, especially not in lunar gravity, but it was bulky and awkward.

"Tow lines," Hjalmar said. "You want to help? I can do the EVA myself, but it'd be faster if there were two of us."

"Sure," Tak said. "But are you sure that will work? Some of the pieces are quite large. How are you not going to crash?"

"I'm not going to land towing things. I'm going to bring them over to the lunar space elevator. This place was a mining operation designed to bring materials up to orbit to be used in manufacturing space stations, you know. We just had to turn it back on."

"Space stations that would go out to the asteroid belt?" Tak asked.

"Exactly," Hjalmar said.

"Well, isn't that a coincidence?" Tak grumbled under his breath.

"Exactly," Hjalmar said, his voice hard. They had the tent up against the bottom of the cargo doors. Hjalmar tapped at a console built into the fabric and it began to inflate. It pressed up against the surface of the ship, making a seal.

"Neat trick," Tak said, stepping back out of the way.

"It was state-of-the-art just at the moment that civilization collapsed," Hjalmar said. "Shall we?"

"Don't we want to make sure they get through the airlock, OK?"

"Not enough time. Rabia has the station computer systems to help if there's a problem. Let's go."

"OK," Tak agreed, but he switched his helmet radio to the channel the cargo ship's radio was on. "Kenko, you there?"

"Here," Kenko said. "What's going on?"

"Give it a few more minutes, then open the cargo bay doors. There is an airlock sealed there. You and the other rikishi take charge. Rabia is waiting at the other end and she wants to get everyone's name as they pass so we can help families find other survivors later. I'm going back up to bring in the other ships."

"Good luck," Kenko said.

"You too."

Hjalmar was already scaling the side of his shuttle and Tak jogged to catch up, bounding up to land beside Hjalmar just as he had gotten the door open. If he had gotten nothing else from sumo, hours of doing shiko had given him very strong legs.

Hjalmar unfastened his helmet, shaking out his long silver hair before strapping into the pilot seat. Tak took off his own helmet, running his hand over his modest ginger locks. Almost long enough to wear in a chonmage. Not that it mattered.

"My name's Tak O'Reilly, by the way," he said, extending a hand. Hjalmar shook it quickly, then got back to the business of preparing for takeoff. "And you're Hjalmar Chandi."

"I am."

"And how did a Chandi end up heading our rescue effort?"

"Because Rabia asked me to."

"So you're telling me you're crossing your very powerful family, rescuing hundreds—no, thousands—of people, just because a girl asked you to?"

Hjalmar stopped cold and turned his head to give Tak a look of cold contempt.

"Not that it's any of my business," Tak said quickly.

"You're right about that much," Hjalmar said as the tow hook backed the shuttle out of its berth, then dragged it out the hangar door.

"I just find it a little suspicious, is all."

"Is that so?"

"The dons are expecting to take over here.

They plan to build their Barnacle Town all over again—only this time we won't be outside of Chandi Corporation, we'll be inside it. Won't we?"

"I can leave them up in space if you prefer," Hjalmar said.

"No, we'll bring them down," Tak said. Hjalmar fired the engines, and they left the lunar surface, streaking back up into space. "I'm new to Barnacle Town, relatively speaking, but even in the little bit of time I've spent there, I'd say you'd have a better time getting Haven under corporate control than these people."

"I couldn't care less one way or the other," Hjalmar said. "I'm just doing what Rabia asked."

"Fair enough," Tak said. "So, how is this space elevator rescue going to work?"

"I sent up the climbers as soon as the systems were up; they should be far enough up the cable by now that we won't have to tow the ships far. They've stayed clustered together, so that makes it easy. We'll both EVA out, hook one of the tow lines onto something convenient on the derelict, then move on to the next and do the same."

"How are we going to know which are inhabited?"

"Everything else already fell to the surface," Hjalmar said. "Look." He turned on a screen in the console between them. "Do you see the heat signatures? They're all burning something to stay up there. I have no clue what they jury-rigged to do it, but they're staying up there."

"It's twelve ships?"

"Maybe fifteen," Hjalmar said, pointing to some spots where the orange was so dark it was nearly black.

Hjalmar maneuvered the shuttle to a point just outside the cluster of ships, then unstrapped from his seat and put on his helmet. Tak followed suit.

"The tow lines are already attached to the back of this shuttle," Hjalmar said as the airlock cycled. "Just make your way aft, grab six or so, and jump for the nearest derelict."

"OK," Tak said, trying not to sound as nervous as he felt.

"Here's an air gun," Hjalmar said, opening up a tool compartment and handing him the holstered gun. "But you should also be attached to a tow line at all times. Here's a belt for that." He handed Tak what looked like a utility belt with plenty of loops and pouches, all bereft of tools. Next to the buckle was a meter-long cable ending in a closed hook.

"Good," Tak said, strapping the belt and air gun holster around his waist. He doubted he had the skills to aim himself back to the shuttle correctly; he'd probably just propel himself out into the black.

"Don't worry," Hjalmar said as the outer door slid open. "It's just like zero G fighting."

"Dude, I don't do zero G fighting. I was there watching you."

Tak followed Hjalmar back along the exterior of the shuttle. Hjalmar opened another compartment and reached inside, then pushed off from the shuttle, arching his back as he torpedoed through space, six long tethers trailing behind him as they unwound from their neat piles in the bottom of the compartment. Tak hooked a foot into a ladder rung and carefully took out six more hooks. They seemed awfully small for the job. Then he turned and looked around. Hjalmar was off to his left, already jumping to a second ship, so he pushed off toward the closest ship to his right.

It wasn't hard to find a place to attach the hook; all the ships had ladder rungs or loops to latch cargo to. The long jumps between were nerve-wracking. Tak was deathly afraid of getting caught with nothing in reach and no momentum left. Which was silly; he had both a handful of tethers he could follow back to the shuttle and an air gun.

He didn't see the sleeper pod anywhere around, and it gnawed at his gut.

The last ship proved more of a challenge, as it was drifting nearly out of range of the tether line. Tak hooked his feet around a rung, grasping the tether in both hands and using every muscle in his body to try to bring the two together. His muscles burned and the sound of his own groaning echoed around his ears, but it was useless; the ship was just too massive.

"I've finished mine," Hjalmar's voice crackled in his helmet. "I think you're on the last one now."

"Nearly there," Tak said, letting go of the ship and looping the tether over his own ankle twice. Then he undid the belt around his waist that kept him attached to the tether, fastened it around the rung of the ship, and latched it shut. He unwound the tether from his ankle. The end just barely reached the belt.

"I hope that holds," Tak said, taking a moment to just float. That burst of mighty futile effort trying to pull the ship closer had really worn him out.

"Are you coming in?" Hjalmar asked.

"Give me a moment," Tak said.

"You sound out of breath," Hjalmar said.

"I'm OK," Tak said. "This last one was too far out, so I tried to pull it closer."

"All right," Hjalmar said, sounding uncon-vinced. "How's your air?"

Tak looked down at his indicator. "Half full."

"Really. I came back nearly empty."

"I'm coming in," Tak said, pulling himself hand over hand along the tether.

"Any nausea, headaches?"

"I have a headache, but I'm sure it's just dehy-dration," Tak said. "I don't have any water left in this suit and my tongue is big and cottony." Then he cursed as he missed a grab and just caught himself before letting go with the other hand. Too caught up in his rhythm, he guessed. He stopped moving, waiting for the heebie-jeebies in his stomach to settle.

"What is it?" Hjalmar asked.

"Just almost floated off into the black," Tak said, looking around. The ships around him were like dark lurking shadows, but the stars beyond were brighter than he'd ever seen them.

"What?"

"Yeah, I guess I left my air gun back there with my belt."

"You're not attached to the line?"

"No, I had to use that to bring the last ship in. It was too far away."

"I'm coming out to get you," Hjalmar said.

"No, I'm nearly there," Tak said, but when he

looked up, he couldn't pick out which shadow was his destination. The tether would lead him there, if he could just keep moving.

"You're hypoxic. You realize this," Hjalmar said.

"Yeah, I was starting to get that impression," Tak said. Left hand, right hand—that was all he needed to focus on. But slower than before; the next slip could be his last.

"Tak! Tak!"

Tak shook his head, trying to wake himself up. He was still holding the tether, but he'd definitely just fallen asleep there.

Sleep, sleep, the stars were singing. He was so tired.

"I'm here," he managed to say. He wouldn't open his eyes; he could just focus on keeping his hands gripped on the line. "You can tow us all back in; I'll just wait here."

"Like hell," Hjalmar grumbled, and Tak felt something pulling on him. Hjalmar wasn't talking to him from the shuttle; he was right there. "Let go of the line. I've got you."

Tak let go of the line.

When he opened his eyes, he was back in the passenger seat of the shuttle. An oxygen mask was strapped to his face, and he reached up to push it aside.

"Leave it," Hjalmar growled. "I'm sorry you're thirsty, but I want you to keep breathing pure oxygen for a bit longer."

"That's OK, I feel nauseous anyway," Tak said. "Did we get everybody?"

"All the heat signatures are now being pulled along behind us, yes."

"You've been to the curry stand, right? The curry stand Omesh's uncle runs? You've been there. You know what the sleeper pod looks like?" It was irritating, trying to talk with a plastic mask over his face, but he had to know if Omesh was OK.

"No, I was never there."

"It was one of the pods from the days when they built space stations like that, lots of discrete units you could lock together, no gravity of any kind..."

"I didn't see anything like that," Hjalmar said, leaning over to look at something on the control panel. "Just derelict spaceships. One big thing, like a starfish made out of shipping containers. I don't know how anyone survived in that. I even knocked on it first to be sure there was someone in there, and they knocked back, so I guess they did something right. No sleeper pods, though."

"Maybe it's still OK," Tak said. "Teresa gave

him rover parts so he could land on the surface. Maybe he made it down OK."

"You think there's someone who landed and didn't crash?" Hjalmar asked as he took off his helmet.

"Or crash-landed. It's possible."

Hjalmar rubbed at his mouth, thinking. "I'll send some bots out to look. It's full daylight out there. It's hot."

"I'm sure he planned for that," Tak said. "What now up here?"

"Time to get all these people moving to the elevator."

"How are you going to do that without them bumping into each other?"

"Impossible," Hjalmar said. "I'll just go slow and hope they don't bump much."

"Then we go EVA again?"

"No, the climbers have loading bots. They'll catch hold of the tethers, one per climber, so they stay nicely spaced."

"This place has robots for everything, huh?"

"Pretty much," Hjalmar said, firing a short burst to get them moving.

"An army of robots?" Tak asked.

"We're back on this, are we? I swear to you, I'm not luring you into a trap here. Why would I?"

"Cheap labor."

Hjalmar made a show of concentrating on his piloting, and Tak had the disconcerting impression that he was having his own epiphany.

"It's true, isn't it?" Tak said, leaning forward to try to look him in the eye. "It's true, only you didn't know it."

"It can't be. Too Machiavellian, even for my grandfather."

"OK. Who controls the army of robots?"

"They aren't military robots. They clean and mine and load cargo."

"Who controls them?"

"Anyone at a console. Rabia can give the commands to load the elevator climbers from where she is, if it makes you feel better," Hjalmar said.

"I'm sure she can, but I'm betting the chip in your head identifies you as a member of the Chandi family, and as such, you can override any other commands."

"You're awfully paranoid. I'm not the enemy. I'm not even planning to stay. You all can make your New Barnacle Town—I wish you joy. As soon as these people are inside and accounted for, I'm taking this shuttle back to Chandi V. Happy?"

"There is no happy here."

"No, there isn't."

They sat in stony silence as the loader bots with their tentacle-like appendages retrieved the ends of the tow lines from the back of the shuttle, pulling one ship after another down to the lunar surface. The climbers moved slowly and the air in the shuttle was warm, almost stuffy.

Tak woke with a start. "What was that clang?"

"Tow hook," Hjalmar said. "We're back in the hangar."

"Oh," Tak said, rubbing at his face. "Good. Can I take this off?"

"Yes, but I'm taking you to the infirmary first thing. Some of the machines there still work; I want to check your blood oxygen level at the very least."

Tak was just glad to get the mask off his face. Not that wearing a helmet was much of an improvement, but it would only be for a few minutes. When they jumped out of the shuttle, he saw the sumo school ship still parked. The inflatable airlock was gone.

"The elevator is on the far side of the crater," Hjalmar explained without being asked. "There's a maglev that runs from there to here. I imagine Rabia had some bots bring the inflatable down to that end so she can get the people onto the train."

Tak ignored the slight stress he was giving to Rabia commanding the bots. She might be in control now, but he wasn't wrong about the Corporation being able to override her as soon as they wanted to. It was just a matter of when the Corporation found a use for the refugees that were putting themselves in the Chandi family's debt. "This place is huge. There's no way we're getting it for free."

"No, there's not," Hjalmar sighed, and they went through the airlock. Rabia was waiting on the other side, arms crossed but bouncing on her toes.

"Did you find him?" Rabia demanded before Tak even had his helmet off.

"I didn't see the sleeper pod, but that doesn't necessarily mean anything," Tak said. "He could have gone onto one of the dons' ships. Or maybe he landed on the surface like he planned to."

"The ships will be here shortly. If he's there, we'll find him," Hjalmar said. "The rovers on the surface are exploring the wreckage. They haven't found anything that could have survivors in it yet, but it's a big debris field."

"Don't give up, Rabia," Tak said.

She nodded, lips drawn tight. "I sent your other rikishi on the train to get everyone here," she said. "How long until the rest of the station is breathable?"

Hjalmar's eyes moved up and to the left. "Twelve hours."

"Ugh."

Rabia led the way down the hall to the assembly room. The refugees from the sumo school were enjoying the wealth of space.

"The bathrooms in the front of the room are functional," Rabia said. "I had some bots bring in all the extra jumpsuits they could find. They're old, but they're clean. There's plenty of water, but so far, no food."

"Nothing was stored?" Tak asked. "There's no hundred-year-old can of peaches or anything?"

"Things got complicated near the end here," Hjalmar said. "The greenhouses were shut down when they should have been left operating."

"You've seen the logs? What happened?" Rabia asked.

"It's a long story," Hjalmar said. "Here comes the train."

Rabia ran to take her place, helping everyone sign in at one of the workstations.

"I don't mind the lack of peaches so much, but even hundred-year-old freeze-dried coffee sounds pretty good to me right now. What are we going to do about the food situation?" Tak asked.

"Something will work itself out," Hjalmar said.

"What's that mean?"

"You weren't fed by Chandi Corporation when you were on the hull of the space station, were you? You had suppliers. They'll find you here."

Tak felt another catnap coming on. The colors on the jumpsuits everyone was pulling on after cleaning up in the bathrooms were jarringly bright and he just wanted to shut his eyes for a bit, or maybe just half close them to mute the colors a little.

"Come on. Infirmary's this way," Hjalmar said, his gaze as cold as ever, but Tak guessed that his momentary near-lapse of consciousness had not gone unnoticed.

The infirmary was a short walk away, which made sense; the harbor area was probably an accident and injury hot spot. Tak slumped tiredly into the chair Hjalmar pointed out to him and drifted off before the machines were even hooked up to him.

He was vaguely aware of a buzzing conversation happening near him but jerked awake when the whispers became shouts.

"I won't do it. I won't. I knew something didn't feel right about all this. I knew it. Your sister!" Rabia was fuming, hands on hips and jutting her face up into Hjalmar's in a way that almost made her lack of height seem an advantage.

"What's going on?" Tak asked, sitting up from his slump. He was still covered with sensors—on his hand, his arm, all over his chest. It was like being caught in a spiderweb, and his brain was too fuzzy to untangle it all.

"I thought you already knew that," Hjalmar said to Rabia. Tak looked up at him. He was outwardly being calm, if a bit defensive, and who wouldn't be with Rabia raging in your face? But there was something in his eyes, something in his manner when Tak had been needling him about things in the shuttle.

He was angry too. He was keeping it buried, hidden, but Tak suspected that in his own way he was even angrier than Rabia, who was at the moment nearly turning purple.

"You tell them!" Rabia said, jabbing Hjalmar in the chest with one angry finger. "I won't."

"I won't have to," Hjalmar said. "There's a holo-projector in the front of the assembly room. My grandfather and sister will be appearing on it momentarily. They'll do all the telling."

"And you'll do nothing?"

"We saved thousands of lives today. But that doesn't come for free."

Rabia looked like she couldn't believe what she was hearing. Hjalmar let her glare at him for a while longer, then sighed heavily. "Are you going to slap me now?"

"No," Rabia said and punched him in the face. His head rocked back and a spray of blood droplets arced through the air, falling slowly to the floor. By the time Hjalmar was back upright, Rabia was gone.

"Damn. You could have told her it wasn't your fault," Tak said.

"How do you know it wasn't?" Hjalmar asked, touching his nose gently.

"I know. I would guess you just got screwed harder than the rest of us."

"Maybe not harder," Hjalmar said, opening a drawer and taking out a square of gauze to press to his face. "More personally."

"So you get screwed by your own family, and it makes you feel better to let her break your nose? Martyr."

"It's not broken," Hjalmar said, but he rather pointedly didn't address the rest of Tak's remark.

"Did you find Omesh?"

"He wasn't on any of the ships," Hjalmar said. "The bots found something that might be a sleeper pod. I was going to tell her, but my sister got to her first."

"How did your sister—"

"Rabia was logged onto the system," Hjalmar said.

"Implant," Tak guessed. Chandi family standard issue.

"I'm going out on one of the buggies to see for

myself. You're still in your suit—do you want to ride along?"

"Sure," Tak said. "I just had a catnap; I'm good for another day's work, at least."

Which would have sounded more convincing if his stomach hadn't punctuated it with a loud growl.

CHAPTER TWENTY-EIGHT

OMESH

Anjali wasn't singing her happy little song anymore. She was singing something Omesh didn't recognize, something low and mournful. She would stop occasionally, as if drifting off to sleep, but then pick it up again several moments later, not missing a word between.

Omesh sat in front of the only access panel in the sleeper pod. He examined and reexamined all the connections, but it was all useless. The part that had failed was outside the pod and he couldn't get to it. The louvers that were supposed to open to help shed the heat must not have opened. Some connection had broken, or something was blocking their function. There had been some bumping after the detonation of Barnacle

Town—nothing major, but perhaps it had been enough to jar something loose or jam something down.

Omesh closed the panel with a sigh. There was simply nothing he could do about the heat without going outside, and even if he had kept the suit he had worn out of Chandi V, the pod had no airlock.

Anjali lapsed into another silence. She was still wearing all of her bridal clothes, although she looked like a limp flower left too long in a dry vase now. Omesh was wearing just a pair of shorts and still felt too hot. He guessed it was about 110 now. He knew it would get hotter.

Omesh moved things out of his pod until he reached his computer. Then he turned it on and watched as it hunted for a network to connect to. The lunar cities all had their own networks. If one were near enough, he could get a message out.

Not that he even knew who could help him now, but one problem at a time.

There was nothing there. Omesh sat on the floor with the computer on his knees, clicking a button to make it look again. Something flashed, just for a moment, a signal too weak to connect to. Omesh tried again, but again it only flickered before disappearing. He shut off the computer to save the battery. Perhaps he'd try again later.

Anjali's song warbled back to life. Omesh smiled despite himself. His head still throbbed from where he had rammed the ceiling on landing, but the bleeding had stopped. That had been hours ago, when it had been cool and comfortable and Omesh had been so happy. All they had to do now was wait. Anjali had been worried, but Omesh had told her they had air enough for a few days, food enough for more. They would be fine.

"Omesh," Anjali called softly.

"Yes, Auntie-ji?"

"Tell me the story again about the babies in Mexico?"

"We have plenty of air, Auntie," he said. Talking made his headache worse, but he didn't want to tell her that.

"Will you tell me the story?"

"Little Raj is going to be fine," Omesh said in his best storyteller's voice. "He is better equipped to deal with being here than you or I. Newborns are special; they are designed to be tough. Birth is traumatic, and so the little ones are built to deal with trauma at the beginning of life. They have bodies packed with fluids and a metabolism prepared to maximize what they have."

"And you know this because of the babies," Anjali prompted.

"Yes, once when I was researching something

for school, I read a story about these babies in Mexico. There was a terrible earthquake that hit their biggest city, and all of these buildings, including the hospital, were leveled. It was days later, more than a week actually, when workers moving rubble found the babies. They had been in the nursery when the earthquake hit, and they were all still alive. Hungry, thirsty, and barely able to cry, but they were all alive. And they all lived out full lives."

"They sound like little yogis," Anjali said. "Maybe they had been before and hadn't yet forgotten what they had learned in their past life. Where is Mexico? Near the Himalayas?"

"No," Omesh said, trying not to sound surprised. "It's on the other side of the Earth, the part that connects North America to South America."

"Oh, OK," Anjali said, her eyes darting up and to the side as if correcting her mental map. "You are so lucky, being born on Earth and able to go to school. My grandmother taught me how to read a little and how to do enough math to run our little shop, but there was no time and no books to learn more."

Omesh closed his eyes. It was impossible to sleep in the heat; it felt like something was pressing down on his chest and he couldn't breathe properly. His head throbbed.

"Omesh?" Anjali said again.

"Yes, Auntie-ji?"

"Raj isn't moving."

Omesh got up, crawling into the pod with Anjali. She had unwrapped Raj from his blankets and he was lying naked beside her, hair wet from where she had been bathing him to try to keep him cool. Omesh touched his little hands and feet. His skin was hot but clammy, and he didn't respond to being touched at all. Omesh pressed his fingers to Raj's neck and almost burst into tears when he felt the pulse.

"He's going to be OK," Omesh said. "It's just the heat." Of course, babies went into heatstroke far quicker than adults, but Omesh didn't mention it. There was nothing they could do either way, and Omesh sensed that Anjali already knew this, anyway. It was why she had wanted him to repeat his story. It had seemed comforting at the time.

"What can we do?" Anjali asked.

"Are you hungry?" he asked.

"Not really."

"You should probably eat anyway," Omesh said, looking around. There was no way to cook the grain, and the vegetables were starting to blacken in the heat and didn't look appetizing at all.

"There is day-old naan in that basket over

there," Anjali said. Omesh fetched it and sat beside her once more. Anjali sat up, keeping Raj in his sling close to her breast.

"If he wakes at all, try to get him to nurse," Omesh said, although he doubted Raj would wake without medical help. "He needs the fluids."

"Of course," Anjali said. They ate in silence, sharing some uncomfortably hot water, and Omesh went back to his pod to try his computer again. Still nothing, just a little flicker that was too remote to latch onto. Omesh clutched his head in his hands.

What had gone wrong? He had planned so carefully.

His own tears felt scalding hot on his skin.

"Omesh, what is that knocking?" Anjali asked.

Omesh picked up his head, listening. He heard nothing. His aunt must be imagining things. He was about to open his mouth to find a nice way to tell her so when he heard it too; someone was knocking on the door.

Omesh leapt to his feet and bounded over to the door, pounding and yelling nonsense. Anjali was sitting up, Raj in her arms, watching him with big eyes. She was afraid to be happy too soon. Omesh pressed his ear to the door, but the hull was too thick to hear through. The answering knock was loud enough, though.

"Someone is out there," Omesh said. "Someone is definitely out there."

"Your friend?" Anjali asked.

"I hope so."

An eternity later, they felt something pick them up. Or several somethings; it was hard to tell from the inside of a closed box with no windows. Then they were moved and then set down again. Another long moment later they were on the move at a velocity that could only mean some sort of vehicle, bouncing over the lunar landscape, tracing what seemed like an excessively serpentine course.

"It seems less hot," Anjali said. Omesh hadn't noticed. He wasn't sure now if he was just imagining it, from the power of her suggestion or just wishful thinking. Maybe it was cooler; their rescuers might have noticed the problem with the louvers and did what Omesh couldn't: opened them. Or perhaps their route was taking them into the shade of a mountain range.

Then they stopped again, and it was definitely getting cooler. Anjali was still sitting up with Raj in her arms.

"Is he waking up?" Omesh asked.

"No," Anjali said. "He's so still."

There was a sound outside the door, too muffled to make out. Omesh hunted around for his shirt and shoes. It was an effort just to keep moving, as if the heat had sapped every bit of energy out of him.

Someone knocked hard on the door again. Omesh didn't know what to do. There was no way to tell from the knocks whether it was safe to try opening the door or if he should wait. They had stopped moving, but unless they'd been brought through an airlock, and Omesh didn't think they had, opening the door would kill all three of them.

After several long, stupid minutes and more knocking, he remembered his computer. But only because it was chirping at him. He had left it on after that second attempt to catch the signal. Omesh opened it and waited for the screen to come up. There was a message displayed.

"Omesh, open the door. It's safe. Hjalmar."

"She did it," Omesh said, rushing back to the door and throwing it open. Anjali followed him out in a tent and then down the long tunnel that ended in another, smaller tent and then the airlock.

He and Anjali both sighed out loud when the cool air of the lunar station met them. Then it felt too cold, and Omesh wished he'd dressed more warmly. His hands were shaking to the point where buttoning up his shirt was nearly impossible, and he wondered in a detached way whether his head injury or heatstroke were to blame when he was knocked into the wall by a human torpedo.

"Omesh!" Rabia cried. He managed a small urk in response. She pulled back and looked hard at him. "You look terrible."

"I doubt I look as bad as you," he said, reaching up to touch her face but then thinking better of it. "You look like Alain. Was it Alain?"

"No, it was... well, me. I was stupid," Rabia said. Then she looked over at Anjali with Raj held tight against her. "Are you OK?"

"Raj has heatstroke," Omesh said. "I think we all do, but he seems comatose." There was the sound of a door opening behind him and he turned to see two space-suited figures emerging from a second airlock. The larger took his helmet off and gave Omesh a painfully tight hug.

"Good to see you," Tak said as he released him.

"You were out there for a long time," Hjalmar said once his helmet was off. "The infirmary is down this way; we should head there first."

"The baby is in bad shape," Rabia said in a low voice.

Hjalmar looked past Omesh to the still infant in Anjali's arms, and his face hardened. "He needs more than the infirmary," Hjalmar said.

"There was a hospital, you said," Rabia said. She wasn't quite looking at him, not speaking directly to him, and Omesh couldn't help noticing that Hjalmar's nose had a puffy look to it, a fresher injury than Rabia's. A lot had been happening while he was baking in his pod, apparently.

"There isn't enough atmo yet between here and the hospital," Hjalmar said.

"He's small—can you keep him inside your suit?" she asked.

"No," Omesh and Hjalmar said at once. Hjalmar gave Omesh a steady look, as if weighing options before coming to a decision. "Let's go to the infirmary first. I think we should find what Omesh needs there."

"He's not well himself," Rabia said as they left the airlock and started down a massive hallway.

"I can see that," Hjalmar said.

"Raj first," Omesh said. "Then I'll worry about me."

There were people gathered in the hallway, Barnacle Towners, some walking and some just sitting against the wall in dazed shock. Rabia kept a hold on Omesh's arm, guiding him down the hall, and Tak did the same for Anjali, his arm around her shoulders as she held little Raj. Anjali kept the end of her sari over her head, holding the hem with one shaking hand. All the grief she wasn't expressing aloud or even on her face was in that hand.

"Prakash wasn't with you?" Rabia asked.

"I didn't find him. Maybe he's here?"

"I'm sorry," Rabia said. "I've kept a list of the names of everyone as they came into the station. He isn't here."

"Maybe he's still up there?"

"Hjalmar and Tak already brought all the ships down that had survivors in them. You were the only one to crash down onto the surface; we nearly didn't find you at all. But Hjalmar has the station bots still moving through the debris field. Maybe we will find more survivors."

Omesh nodded, but he didn't have any hope. It had gotten so hot out there; he didn't think he and Anjali could have lasted another hour.

They reached the infirmary, which was bigger than Omesh had expected. It had ten beds and more chairs with an assortment of equipment and carts all on wheels for easy movement from station to station.

"Where are we?" Anjali asked.

"I believe it's called Chandi Lunar Station I. I don't think there's a Chandi Lunar Station II; I guess they were just very optimistic. It's a mining site. There is a lunar space elevator that runs from here up to Chandi Lunar Station III up at the La-grange point, Earth-Moon L2."

"This is part of what that speech was about then. Getting out to the asteroid belt to build more space stations," Omesh said.

"Unfortunately, yes. By coming in the door, you were committing yourself as a Chandi Corporation employee. I don't know what it all means yet. I don't think anybody does," Rabia said.

"Rabia, you take care of Anjali at bed one," Hjalmar said. "Cold compresses, and get her to drink something, but not too much. Sips."

"The baby?" Rabia asked.

"We'll be taking him in a minute, but she can hold him for now."

"How will we be taking him?" Omesh asked. Hjalmar reached into a cold storage unit and took out two bottles, handing one to Rabia and the other to Omesh. Omesh put the nipple in his mouth and took a cautious sip. More than water; it was sweet and lemony. Some sort of electrolyte drink.

"We have oxygen tanks here," Hjalmar said, opening another cupboard. "The masks are not baby-sized, but if he's in a contained space, an airtight space, that shouldn't matter. Will one of these totes work?"

Omesh looked over the equipment even as

Hjalmar fetched more and more things from around the infirmary. Omesh looked up at him quizzically.

"I saw your pod. I know what you can do. I just don't know what you need," Hjalmar said almost apologetically.

"How far is the hospital?"

Hjalmar's eyes rolled off to the side, then snapped back. "We could be there inside of ten minutes."

"We? I don't have a suit," Omesh said.

"Tak, give Omesh your suit," Hjalmar called, and Tak, who had been helping Rabia with Anjali, nodded and started to strip it off. "It'll be big on you, clumsy, but it'll hold air."

Omesh selected an airtight container with a handle on the top, then unlatching the seal and emptying out the medical equipment stored inside it.

"Here," Hjalmar said, handing Omesh a small air bottle.

"He's going to bounce around in here," Omesh said worriedly.

"He'll be fine," Hjalmar said after a moment's thought. "I'll tape the bottle to the side of the box. I'll carry him. I'm used to the moon; I can move smoothly and not jostle him too much."

"I wish there were a way to monitor him," Omesh said.

"We'll move as quickly as we can. It's only ten minutes."

"A lot can happen in ten minutes."

But there was nothing else to be done. Anjali wrapped Raj tightly in a blanket before kissing him goodbye, but Hjalmar peeled it back off again after putting him in the box.

"At this point, I'm more worried about him being too warm than too cold," he said to Omesh, and Omesh nodded. He doubled-checked the gauge on the air bottle after opening it, then snapped down the lid.

"Let's go," he said. Tak helped him seal his helmet and the two of them bounded back down the hall to the airlock. Omesh quickly realized how much Rabia had been helping him from the airlock to the infirmary; walking on his own, he could barely control his movements. And he was so tired.

"You doing OK?" Hjalmar asked as they cycled through the airlock to the rest of the station.

"If you need to, leave me behind," Omesh said, trying not to sound as out of breath as he felt.

"There are signs," Hjalmar said. "The hospital is pointed out at every crossing. If you lose me."

"Thanks," Omesh said. The door opened, and

they headed out down a hallway exactly like the one they had just passed through. It sloped downhill and Omesh bit his lip in concentration, afraid he'd pick up too much speed and end up tumbling down the ramp.

"Roadblock ahead," Hjalmar said as they neared the bottom. "Rabia and I made a crawl space above; just follow me."

"K," Omesh said. Hjalmar jumped halfway up the pile of motorized carts, catching a side-view mirror one-handed and pausing before leaping the rest of the way up. Omesh watched carefully, but the crate in Hjalmar's hand was as still as it was possible for it to be, even when Hjalmar's other limbs were scrambling. But then he'd seen how he fought in free fall; his body control was well trained.

Beyond the roadblock was an open mall filled with sunlight and dead plants. Omesh didn't notice much, keeping his head down and focusing on his steps. He was finding a rhythm, and it might have been getting easier if he weren't so exhausted. He looked up only as often as he needed to make sure he was still following Hjalmar.

At the other end of the mall, the hallway sloped downhill again and passed more and more cross corridors. It wasn't far to the hospital area; Omesh supposed that if the mall was the high-population area, it made sense to keep the hospital close to it. Hjalmar opened the door using the keypad, then closed it behind him. He stopped at another cold storage locker for two more bottles like the last one he'd given Omesh, then led the way down more hallways. Different-colored stripes were painted on the wall, some branching off down one hallway, some down another. When they finally took a turn, it was down a pink-striped hallway. Hjalmar opened the door to the neonatal unit and closed it behind him.

"I've prioritized this room for oxygen," Hjalmar said. "We should be able to remove our helmets in about twenty minutes."

"Twenty minutes?"

"Don't worry, we're getting Raj out before then," Hjalmar said. He looked around the room, then carried the crate over to the largest of the incubators, setting it inside and shutting the clear plastic lid. He looked over the controls for the many machines connected to the incubator, then began turning some on.

"Smaller space—it will be livable quicker," he said. "Here, I should have done this before we left the infirmary." He turned Omesh around, fiddled with something on the pack on his back, and turned him back. "There's a drink straw next to your mouth; I've connected the electrolyte replacement drink to it. It's important that you drink that. Your brain is going to need the glucose."

"OK," Omesh said, working his lips to get the straw in his mouth and taking a long pull of lemony sweetness. He wondered if this was what nectar tasted like to butterflies and bees.

"I'm opening Raj's box now," Hjalmar said, awkwardly putting his space suit gloves into the gloves built into the sides of the incubator. He un-latched the lid and gently tipped the box on its side, catching Raj in the palm of his other double-gloved hand. Omesh could see the baby's mouth working, his face red and irritated, although no sound carried.

"He's crying," Omesh said, almost crying him-self in relief.

"That's good," Hjalmar said. "It means there's air in there."

"It means he's awake!" Omesh said.

"Go to the other side of the incubator," Hjalmar directed. "I need you to hand me the sensors that are lined up there one by one."

Omesh did so. The sensors were small squares on the ends of wires, and it took all of Omesh's concentration to close his fingers down on one and pick it up through the two gloves.

"Keep drinking," Hjalmar reminded him as he

placed the first square on Raj's bare chest over his heart. The monitor at the end of the incubator came to life, mostly showing errors because it was getting data from only one of its many sensors, but showing a pulse rate.

"It's in the red. Too high?" Omesh asked.

"He's upset, that's probably part of it," Hjalmar said, taking the next sensor from Omesh and putting it slightly below the first. It was a long process, and when they were finished, Hjalmar gave the nod and they both removed their helmets.

"We're stuck here until the rest of the station is running," Hjalmar said. "Twelve hours." He handed Omesh the second bottle and Omesh dutifully took a drink. Hjalmar took off the rest of his suit while keeping his eyes on the incubator monitors. He touched the display screen, moving quickly through several windows of information.

"Do you understand it all?" Omesh asked.

"He's stabilized," Hjalmar said. "O2 sat, body temp, everything. The cold walk through the station to get here probably helped him as much as anything. Still, tough kid."

"Is he going to be OK?"

"I'm not really sure," Hjalmar said. "I don't actually have medical training. I have the user manuals for all this equipment in my head, accessible at a moment's notice, but my understanding of it all..."

"What's the next step?"

"Do you remember that roadblock we climbed over to get here? Well, before the last men left here died, there was a lot of fighting. Things were damaged. Some, like those carts, because they were used for other things, but others were destroyed just because someone wanted to destroy something."

"Things like the carts are fixable, but anything smashed to bits isn't," Omesh guessed.

"We came into the hospital through the maternity area," Hjalmar said. "It was the quickest route. But large parts of the rest of the hospital, and particularly the ER and lab areas, have been very badly damaged. I have camera feeds," he added, touching his forehead.

"Things you need to assess Raj?"

"Perhaps. But even Raj aside, we're going to need as much of that equipment operational as possible."

"What are you saying to me?" Omesh asked.

"I have lots of data. User manual–type stuff; I know what this is all supposed to do and a little about how it does it. But if it's broken and the parts to repair it aren't available, I'm useless. Which is where you come in. I saw your pod, all the mods you did to get it down to the surface. You are the kind of thinker we need for this job."

"I've never worked with medical equipment before," Omesh said.

"I know. But if you combine what I know with what you can do, I think we can have a working hospital going in short order. And we're going to need one. People like your aunt ought to be kept under observation and on IV to be sure they're OK. Others were hurt just getting here."

"You talk like you're staying," Omesh said.

"I am," Hjalmar said. "I have to. I volunteered." He said that word with just a hint of a sneer.

"Rabia said we were all Chandi Corporation employees now," Omesh said.

"Yes."

"Just for stepping in the door. When the alternative was death."

"Yes. And I am your COO. Chief operations officer."

"Just for stepping in the door?"

To Omesh's surprise, Hjalmar laughed. And it wasn't a sardonic laugh, it was a genuine bout of mirth.

"Seriously, is this some sort of punishment for you? I mean, these people aren't going to like it. Judging by your face, some of them already really don't."

"Punishment? No, I don't think so," Hjalmar said. "Just my dark destiny."

He turned to scroll through more screens on the monitor and Omesh, taking another sip of his drink, didn't push. Clearly, the window between getting back on his feet and having to deal with the next batch of Barnacle Town problems was going to be a very narrow one indeed. And he still hadn't found his uncle.

CHAPTER TWENTY-NINE

RABIA

Rabia stood in the empty store. Her store, or at least her space. It was on the top level of the mall, the last one on the end, apparently not prime retail space, as it had been empty before the plague hit.

It was perfect. She had no weapons, no mirrors, but those were just nice extras, and she could probably scare up the mirrors. The important thing was she had space, more than enough space to have two dozen students at a time, all whirling and kicking. Not that she felt remotely qualified to teach, but she didn't think the students she was likely to get would mind much.

She could screen off one corner to make her

own little sleep space. That's what the other Barnacle Towners were doing. The corporate employees that came to speak, one after another via hologram, when they had all still been in the assembly room, had given everyone a space assignment in the residential area and another in the shopping district for those who identified themselves as business owners. Which was all of Barnacle Town; even the scavengers would identify themselves as business owners if it meant getting more space to call their own. But it took some adjusting, all this space for so few people. Nearly everyone had left their residential apartments empty, preferring to sleep where they worked, even though every store came with a locking shutter and there were security cameras everywhere monitored with smart software and hence there was little need to protect one's goods night and day.

No, the transition to corporate employees was not going smoothly. Many had agreed to attend the video-conferenced training program on how to run the mining equipment—interest in new ways to earn money was always high—but there was already grumbling about how they would expect to be paid. That was a fresh concept for Chandi Corporation; no one had been paid since before the plague. The Corporation gave you food and shelter, kept you clothed and educated just enough to do your job; it even entertained you. But it didn't pay money. The few coins circulating through the noncorporate communities like Haven and Barnacle Town had no value in the corporate world. How could they pay anyone?

They were all stuck here for now; one of Hjalmar's cultures had come back inconclusive. Not positive, just inconclusive. Hjalmar himself had said it was most likely an error made when he'd set up the plates, but the protocols must be followed. It would be very interesting when the six-month quarantine lifted and everyone was free to go. Six months of living here could be habit-forming.

Rabia went back out of her shop space, walking slowly along the balcony with her hands deep in the pockets of her Chandi Corporation jumpsuit. By the time the quarantine was up, she'd be past her eighteenth birthday. She could never go home now, and she hadn't even kissed her parents goodbye. She could talk to them by video link whenever she wanted to, but it wasn't the same.

"You've got a store now?"

Rabia stopped, looking around until she found

him. Alain, sitting on a bench with his back to the balcony.

"A school, actually."

"You're going to teach kung fu?"

"I thought I might try it."

"I guess if you and Si Fu kept up after he stopped teaching the rest of us, you've been at it for, what, eight years?"

"Sounds about right." Rabia sat down next to him on the bench. Something was missing. What was it? "Where's Tom?"

"Tom..." But Alain stopped, touching the back of his hand to his mouth and closing his eyes. He gave a small shake of his head.

"Oh. I'm sorry."

"We were running in and out of the ship, bringing in all the people we could find before the detonations started. Kids mostly. Some of the little ones were so frightened you couldn't even get them to move. We had to pick them up and carry them inside, then go back out for more. I guess he went out one more time than I did. I thought he was there behind me when I shut the door. I could swear I saw him there, just over my shoulder. But he wasn't."

"I'm sorry," Rabia said. "You guys seemed close."

"He was my boyfriend."

"Oh. Oh. I didn't know that."

"Why would you? We haven't really talked in years."

"I guess not," Rabia said. "I'm sorry."

"You don't have to keep saying that," Alain said.

"But this time I mean about your face. I'm really sorry." Alain nodded offhandedly, as if he still wasn't buying it. "Look, before Si Fu died, he was trying to teach me all these things, ways to control my temper. I don't know what's wrong with me, but I'm just not getting it. I mean, I thought I had a handle on it, but it turns out I'm only good at controlling my temper when I'm not being provoked. Which is just useless."

Alain still didn't respond, his eyes fixed on the toes of his shoes. Then he sat back, rubbing his hands on his thighs with the air of someone who's just come to a decision. "Do you remember when you first started class?"

"Yeah," Rabia said slowly.

"You came only because you wanted the si fu to tell you tales of China, as I recall. You'd been reading something, you said. But Si Fu said if you were going to come into his school, you were going to learn."

"I remember."

"Do you remember dropping under crescent kicks?"

"Oh!" Rabia said with an embarrassed grin. "You're bringing that up? Come on, I was never an athletic kid."

"That's for sure. You were so pathetic. First you were hardly even trying—"

"Come on, I had the thighs of a little girl who liked to read a lot!"

"You had the thighs of a little girl who was going to be spending a lot of time getting kicked in the head," Alain said. "But you saw you weren't going low enough, so you decided to show me you could drop just as low as I."

"I remember, I remember," Rabia said. "That was one hell of a muscle pull."

"But you came back," Alain said. "Which frankly I hadn't expected you to do. And you kept at it. I'm betting if I tried a crescent kick on you now, you'd be ducking under and going for the groin jab without even having to think. And I don't just mean you wouldn't have to think through the moves; you wouldn't even think 'I'm dropping now.' It would be instinctive."

"Do you want to try it?" Rabia asked.

"No," Alain said, "but you see my point? Whatever the emotional equivalent is of having the muscle tone of a little girl who spends all her time reading stories, that's where you are. You're going to need a lot more work than, say, me to get to the place where the moves you want to be able to make are instinctive."

"So I'm going to need to do some emotional sparring? Have someone piss me off just for practice?"

"I'd work on the forms first, grasshopper," Alain said. "I don't think you have the fundamentals down well enough yet for sparring."

Rabia nodded; what he said felt very true. Then another thought came to her. "Do you want to help me with my school?"

"Seriously?"

"You were always better at it than I was."

"Were," Alain repeated. "Before I quit. It's been years."

"It'll come back."

"I'll think about it," Alain said, and his mood turned brooding again. "Well, see you around," he said at last, pushing off the bench and sauntering down the walkway.

"Yeah, see you," Rabia said. She closed up her shop, then paused, reluctant. Even her feet didn't want to take the steps in the right direction. But she had been putting this moment off long enough.

She knew what she had to do, but she wasn't

sure how to start. Fences could be mended, but it was hard to unburn a bridge. With an exasperated sigh, she headed to the nearest flight of stairs to bound her way down to the hospital and into the neonatal unit.

Raj was still there, nestled inside a carefully controlled environment. He was awake now, big brown eyes peering all around in that unfocused gaze newborns have. She walked up to the box, slipped her hands into the gloves built into the wall, and stuck out a finger for him to grasp.

"I was wondering if you'd stop by," Hjalmar said, appearing from behind a bank of half-dismantled machines.

"Yeah. Where's Omesh and Anjali?"

"Anjali is still in the recovery ward with the other injured."

"Still? I didn't know she was here at all," Rabia said.

"Heatstroke on top of labor has left her in a delicate state and I've been keeping her on IV fluids. Unlike the rest of us, she's sort of eating. Glucose drip."

"And Omesh?"

"He was here up until about an hour ago when I kicked him out. He would keep working on these machines until he collapsed, I think. I told him to get some rest, but I'm guessing he went to set up the curry shop. He and Anjali are planning to be open as soon as the food shipment comes down the elevator from Chandi III."

"I'll have to see if he needs a hand," Rabia said, but Raj's grasp on her finger just wouldn't let her leave. "How is this one?"

"He'll be fine. I'm planning on letting him go home with Anjali tomorrow morning."

"So you're a doctor now? Like you're a pilot?"

"No," Hjalmar said. "The machines run themselves, the diagnostic computers suggest what tests to run. I've just been doing what I've been told. I have sent all his scans and lab work results to my own physician back on Earth. He looked them over and he doesn't see any sign that Raj will have any lasting damage. His mother kept him as cool as she could; it seems like it was enough."

"That's good news," Rabia said, her eyes on the baby. "It would be tough to lose a husband and a baby one after the other."

"Yes," Hjalmar said, clearing his throat awkwardly.

"You swear this wasn't all some master plan?" she asked at last.

"I swear it wasn't all some master plan that I was in on. That's the most I can swear to."

"But why not just move everyone down here

directly? Why detonate their town and kill half the population?"

"Rabia, honestly, I don't know if they were planning on using this place all along or not. For all I know, Ulrika came up with the plan the very moment she seemed to, when she showed it to us on her reader. In that case, they just turned a bad situation around in their favor."

"Particularly as they still aren't sure if this place is a death trap waiting to happen or not," Rabia said. "We could be infected already."

"I don't think so," Hjalmar said. "But yes, it works out well for them that Barnacle Town is taking the risk and not their own employees."

"And one plate was inconclusive."

"I must have set it up wrong."

"Maybe you set it up right, but the computer was told to read it as inconclusive, anyway."

"If you're going to second-guess everything, you're going to go mad," Hjalmar said, then gave a sharp, humorless laugh. "Trust me on that one."

"But it all smells so fishy," Rabia said. "Maybe the whole thing was planned from the start. Maybe they didn't think they needed all of Barnacle Town as miners. Maybe they only wanted a psychologically traumatized half that would be willing to do just about anything to survive after so very nearly dying."

"I don't know, Rabia. Maybe."

"I don't know either," Rabia admitted. "I don't know who are good guys and who are bad guys. The dons saved a lot of people. But I've been hearing a lot of stories and it seems like there was a lot of choosing going on. They might not have picked who lived and who died, but they did pick who would be saved first, who would be kept safest."

"Don't you think that's just human nature?" Hjalmar asked. "They were looking out for their own families."

"They were looking out for their own tribes, and it's not the same thing. I think it might mean trouble."

"You worry too much," Hjalmar said. "This place won't get crowded for several generations yet. What is there to fight over?"

"I suppose," Rabia said. It would be easier to dismiss her unease as paranoia if she wasn't so sure that Alain felt it, too. She had seen the grief grinding down on him, but she had also seen something else in his eyes. He was very on edge, like the danger wasn't passed yet. Rabia didn't trust what Chandi Corporation told her, but she trusted Alain's instincts. "So, are you mad?"

"About what?" Hjalmar asked.

"About being stuck here with us for six months

until the quarantine lifts. All I'm missing out on is getting kicked off the space station, but you have a whole life out there."

"I know what you're missing out on," Hjalmar said with a pointed look. "And I'm perfectly content to be here. It's as good a place as any."

"Well, if you do get bored, I'm opening up a kung fu school. Not that you need lessons on fighting or anything, but stop by sometime and we'll spar."

"I doubt I'll be bored," Hjalmar said wryly. "I've been appointed the chief operations officer here, and until I find some competent employees, I'll be quite busy indeed."

"Well, all right then," Rabia said. It suddenly felt like a wall had gone up between them. She was still a kid with nothing but free time. While he was doing a job, most forty-year-olds were still aspiring to have one day if they worked very, very hard. "I guess I'll see you around."

Rabia went back to the mall, hands in pockets, feeling strangely bereft. She didn't think she trusted Hjalmar, and it was probably better if she didn't spend a lot of time bonding with someone she couldn't trust. But not being with him was still perceptibly less good-feeling than being with him. She was pathetic.

She had to stop and consult a wall monitor directory to find the curry shop. The corporation was as anal as ever, every shop assignment labeled. She was sure that a lot of moving around had been going on, either voluntary or involuntary, and the labels on the map were already outdated, but she was also certain that no one would move the curry stand. It was too popular of a fixture.

No one knew what had happened to Prakash. Rabia had asked everyone she recognized, people she knew had been his neighbors, but no one had seen him that day. No one knew what had happened to him. He might as well have winked out of existence the moment he left Anjali alone in the sleeper pod to find the midwife. The midwife had survived in one of the dons' ships, but she had never seen Prakash that day. Mama Polly had helped Anjali deliver her baby instead. It felt strange, not knowing what had happened to him.

Omesh had a motorized cart parked in front of his shop. It was loaded with things from the old curry stand.

"You packed all this?" Rabia asked, picking up a pot in one hand, a rolling pin in another.

"No," Omesh said, standing up and stretching his back. Judging from the stack of crates against the back wall, he'd been doing the hauling thing for quite some time. "Anjali did it."

"While she was in labor?"

"She said it was soothing," Omesh said with a soft smile.

"Tough babe," Rabia said. "Do you need some help?"

"If you like," Omesh said. "Our personal things go in the storage room back behind the kitchen. I put the beds from the apartment in there."

"So you're storing things where, then?"

"Right now, against the wall there," Omesh said. "When I've separated what we need on hand from what we can put in the apartment for now, I'll move things again. I just wanted things mostly in place before Anjali comes home tomorrow."

"With Raj," Rabia added.

"What's that?"

"Hjalmar says Raj is doing fine, and when Anjali comes home tomorrow, she can bring Raj with her."

"That's wonderful," Omesh said, his face lighting up. He still looked a wreck, like he'd lived a brutal decade since the moment she had hugged him goodbye in the Chandi V airlock, but at least he was a happy wreck.

"I forgot to give this to you yesterday," Rabia said, digging the compass out of her pocket. "A promise is a promise."

"I never doubted you," Omesh said, smiling

down at the bit of gold she pressed into his palm. "You really came through. Thank you."

"It's going to cost us," Rabia said. "And I don't think we've even seen all the hidden charges yet."

"We'll manage," Omesh said. "It's what we do."

"And this time there's no airlock door between us," Rabia said. They shared a weary smile.

CHAPTER THIRTY

TAKASHI

Tak flew, bounced, flew, bounced, flew, and bounced off the far wall. Kenko's laughter echoed through the open space, the other rikishi joining in, but it was not a mocking laugh. Sumo at one-sixth gravity was an often ridiculous sight, but until the quarantine lifted and they moved on to their new home, they would all have to accept looking ridiculous.

"What were you thinking?" Kenko asked when Tak had made his way back across the expanse of hangar. The school was still in the ship's hold, all the buildings and gardens put back just as they were before they had been trampled by hundreds of refugees, but the open space of the mechanic's hangar was more convenient for training. It was an airlocked elevator ride down from the main hangar. The immensity of this lunar station was still leaving Tak in awe.

"I was trying to get a hold on you," he said. "Holds are better than charges in this gravity. Or so I thought."

"Yes, so you thought," Kenko said, still chuckling.

The group started breaking up, practice time over.

"Do you want to get some curry?" Tak asked.

"You have studying to do," Kenko said. "You've barely made a dent in *The Five Rings*."

"I know; I will get right on it." Not that he was in a hurry. His spoken Japanese had progressed more than he would have thought possible in the last few weeks under Kenko's careful tutelage, but written Japanese was still a painful challenge. "After curry?" he asked hopefully.

"All right," Kenko relented. The two changed out of their fight belts and into their outside clothes, Tak in his usual geta and yukata; Kenko, who wrestled at a higher division, got to wear a coat and tabi socks with setta, a quieter, non-wooden type of sandal. He also spent more time on his hair than Tak, getting his topknot just so before they could go. Tak's hair was just long enough to make a stubby little topknot of his own.

There had been no official ruling on whether he was still a student in good standing or not. Hiroku had not said a word to him. Perhaps in a few weeks, when the quarantine lifted, the school would move on to Mars and leave him behind.

He hoped not. He enjoyed the sport. And his hair was finally long enough.

The ships that were towed down by the lunar space elevator had been brought here, as good a place to store them as any. The bots that roamed the debris field hauled the larger pieces here as well. There were always a few people out among the wreckage of Barnacle Town; even in a station that provided nearly anything they could want, the art of salvage and creative reuse was still prized.

Kenko and Tak strolled through the marketplace, constantly dodging packs of wildly running children. No one loved the surplus of space more than the kids. Barnacle Towners had a taste for family-run businesses, and family-run business to a Barnacle Towner meant the constant close presence of children. The corporate idea of collecting them together in one play space and leaving them under someone else's care all day was repellent to Barnacle Towners, even if you called that play space a school. But with everyone watching out for everyone else's kids, they couldn't get into too much trouble.

Tak bet it rocked, being a kid here.

It was a little too late for lunch and a little too early for dinner, so the curry stand was empty when they reached it, or nearly so. Rabia was there as she nearly always was, working on the computer the corporation had assigned her, plowing through the station archives which were so different from the ones she had grown up with.

"Konnichiwa, rikishi," she said with a little bow. Her hair was green now and cut in a straight but swingy style that just barely extended past her earlobes. She was constantly having to sweep it out of her face, but she seemed to be enjoying it.

"We just added a new item to the menu," Omesh said, pointing up at the display screen behind him. "Number twelve, the rikishi special."

"What's in a rikishi special?" Tak asked.

"A little bit of everything," Anjali said, coming out of the kitchen. "Available in separate bowls or all together to make one big stew. Enough to feed four normal men or one slightly scrawny rikishi."

"Better have two of those, then," Tak said.

"Two for me as well," Kenko said. Anjali laughed.

"Have you worked out the formalities to settle

here, then?" Tak asked. "I mean permanently, after the quarantine lifts?"

"Very nearly," Omesh said, coming around the counter so the three of them could sit at Rabia's table. "The corporation does love its bureaucratic hoop jumping. But this is good for my aunt. She's so much happier here than in space. The corporation would have to make some extremely overzealous demands for her to opt out of employment."

"What sort of employment will she have to do?" Tak asked.

"Just what she's doing right now, running the curry stand in the mall," Omesh said. "Although at some point they'll probably force us to live in our assigned residence and not just use it for storage."

"So, will you be attending school or working or what?"

"That I don't know. Not yet. But the quarantine doesn't lift for another couple of weeks, so I have plenty of time to decide."

"Do you guys know where you'll be going yet?" Rabia asked the two rikishi.

"Not yet, but rumor says Mars," Kenko said. "There is talk that some corporations are working together to erect a new dome, to ease overcrowding. If they do, we might have a space there. In the meantime, we're either staying here or relocating to another space station."

"I think we'd have to be relocating," Tak said. "There is a lot of space here, but the gravity is no good for sumo training. We have to get back on a station with one-G spin."

Kenko nodded his agreement.

"And what are your plans after the quarantine lifts?" Tak asked as Omesh hopped up to help Anjali with trays loaded with food. Tak and Kenko dug in with gusto; it made such a nice change from the endless bowls of chankonabe back at the school.

"I turn eighteen before then, so I won't be able to go home. I suppose I'll stay here. There's lots that needs to be done; I'm sure I'll find something. In the meantime, Kenko hasn't finished telling me all of his grandmother's stories."

"That would take a lifetime," Kenko said.

There was a squawk from behind the counter and the sound of Anjali cooing softly as she picked up her baby.

"How is your nephew doing?" Tak asked.

"He seems normal," Omesh said, but a little line of worry ran through his forehead. "I keep looking in his eyes, as if I could see his brain in there. He seems just as bright and aware as any other baby. Considering he's only a few months old, that's not much, though."

Someone else came into the shop then and Omesh got up to go back behind the counter.

Rabia gave Tak a hard look. "No reprisals for what you did?" she asked.

"It doesn't seem so," Tak said. "Hiroku and Toyonoshima have barely been around since we landed. Don business, I suspect. No one has said anything about what we did or what's happening next. Kenko and the other advanced students are running the school, and we assume we'll still be at the scheduled bouts, but we don't really know."

"The uncertainty must suck," Rabia said.

Tak shrugged. "Feels normal to me; I've never known where my life was going more than a day at a time. I suppose when Hiroku gets back to stable business he could kick me out, but I'm willing to bet he doesn't if I'm good. And I'm good."

"He is," Kenko said, then added, "in practice. Actual matches can be very different things. You've yet to be tested, little rikishi."

"I'm motivated," Tak said.

"Still looking to save up for a ship?" Rabia asked.

"Hell yeah. Still looking to buy into a third of it?"

"I don't know how much money I'll earn running a school, but sure," Rabia said. "That little bit of seeing the universe I did between Chandi V and Chandi Lunar Station I left me hungry to see more."

"What about you, Omesh?" Tak said as Omesh brought a bowl of food to their table and pulled up a chair to enjoy a quick meal before the dinner rush. Omesh chewed thoughtfully.

"It's going to take a few years to earn enough, right?" Omesh said, and Tak nodded. "Then I'm in. When Raj is old enough to help Anjali, then I can think about leaving, but not before."

"You're still finishing Earth school, right?" Rabia asked.

Omesh nodded. "Keeping the options open, even the remote ones."

"Did we settle on a name for the ship?" Tak asked. "You came up with one, one that meant friendship? That sounded cool."

"Yeah, but it was the name of a slave ship," she reminded him.

"How about *Mitwa*?" Omesh asked. "It means friend, no slave connotations."

"*Mitwa*," Rabia said, as if tasting the word.

"I like it," Tak said.

Anjali, still out of sight behind the counter with Raj, began to sing softly.

"First you need the money," Kenko said. "And that means staying on at the school."

"And that means being the best at everything," Tak picked up with a sigh. "And that includes reading Japanese." He looked at the empty bowls wistfully, but in truth, he was stuffed. "Omesh, Anjali, the rikishi special is divine. Be prepared— once we tell the others at school, you could get a lot of business."

"No such thing as too much business," Omesh said, even as the first dinner customers stepped up to the counter. He hastily wiped the last of the sauce from his bowl with a chunk of roti and crammed it in his mouth, giving Tak a wave before getting back to work.

"Good luck with the studying," Rabia said, barely looking up herself. She was already engrossed in something she was reading on her computer.

"Goodbye, boys," Anjali said from the kitchen door, a sleeping Raj curled against her shoulder.

"Goodbye, Auntie," Tak said. The two rikishi fell into step, heading back to the hangar and their school. "Did you see the size of that baby?"

"Healthy baby," Kenko said. "Once he's walking, he'll thin out."

"Yeah, but what if he doesn't? The kid would make one heck of a wrestler. Did you see how low his center of gravity is?"

Kenko laughed. "Let's see how you do in an actual bout first. Then we can worry about rounding up new recruits."

CHAPTER THIRTY-ONE

OMESH

Omesh turned on the lights, bathing the curry stand in warm simulated lantern light. The mall beyond the reach of his lamps wasn't fully dark yet, but it would be soon. The station did a good job of simulating sunset and night during the long lunar days, but sunrise and day were somewhat less convincing during the lunar nights.

He stepped back out to the counter to find the last person he had expected to see waiting for him there.

"I'm guessing you're not here to eat," he said.

"No," Alain said. "You and I need to talk."

"What do we have in common?" Omesh asked.

"Barnacle Town. These next few months, while Chandi Corporation tries to make us all over into employees, tries to seduce us with everything it has to offer... I'm not mocking it, in a lot of ways they are offering these people something they would never have anywhere else, something worth having."

"Like?" Omesh prompted, curious what Alain would say.

"Schools, for one," Alain said. "Access to a fully functioning hospital for two."

"I'm sensing you have an 'on the other hand'."

"The dons. They aren't going to take this lying down."

"Won't they just negotiate with Chandi Corporation for a way to still be in a power position?"

"I would have thought so. That's what they had going on before all this went down. But..."

"Hjalmar is in charge, and he's a Chandi," Omesh guessed.

"Exactly. That's not the move of someone looking to negotiate the power structure. There are rumors that security soldiers are on their way here, will in fact be here before the quarantine lifts to make sure that Hjalmar is the one and only one in charge."

"I haven't heard that," Omesh said. "I work a lot with Hjalmar, getting equipment back up and running, systems back online. He never even hinted—"

"Would he?" Alain interrupted. Omesh said nothing; he honestly didn't know. "Anyway, it doesn't even matter if it's true or not; the dons are behaving as if it were, amassing little armies of their own."

Omesh sighed deeply and rubbed at his forehead. He had known it wasn't all over. He had let himself forget it in the past few weeks, but he had known. The power plays and violence were not over, not remotely.

"So what do we do?"

"I don't know yet," Alain said. "I don't know. I'm just trying to keep my eyes open and see what's happening. Maybe stop the big things before they happen if I can. I guess I'm giving you a heads-up to do the same."

"I will," Omesh said.

He knew what he was really saying. Omesh had access to people Alain didn't, and vice versa. Alain couldn't talk directly with Hjalmar or likely even with Rabia in her nebulous corporate state without raising eyebrows among the dons, but he could go to everyone's favorite curry stand. And Omesh could never see himself moving through Alain's world, although the information gathered there could be crucial to keeping the peace.

"You put a bomb on the space station power supply. For the dons."

"I've been thinking a lot since then. I thought I could help the people who need helping by working within the structure the dons control, but I see now that's a lie. I'm trying to find a new way, but it's still about the people. I'm alone here."

Omesh didn't say anything. Rabia had told him about Tom. Omesh thought it was a good bet that Tom had been the only person Alain had really trusted.

"You're not alone," he said at last. "I'll help you. But no bombs."

"No, no bombs," Alain said. "But we have to do something. We're caught between two power structures, both wanting total control. We're going to be torn to pieces."

"Two powers," Omesh said thoughtfully. "But we're not exactly powerless, either."

"No, I would never say that about Barnacle Town," Alain agreed. "But I would say directionless."

"You know what we need?" Omesh said, leaning over the counter conspiratorially.

"What do we need?"

"Let me tell you about a little thing known as civil disobedience."

A slow smile spread across Alain's face. "Yes, tell me all about it. That sounds absolutely delicious."

NEW SERIES: THE FORGOTTEN PLANET

Coming soon from Ratatoskr Press Books, the new YA sci-fi series THE FORGOTTEN PLANET starts with book 1: Raiding the Forgotten Derelict.

History sleeps beneath them all, but only she sees it.

Lafayette Eloi always knew her parents thought differently from others. They kept their books buried beneath her mother's house. They spoke an old language in the dead of night, whispering behind closed doors and bolted shutters. She grew up in a village where no one was related to her, and she never knew why.

Then, after her mother died, her father came to

fetch her. Now she and her mother's dog assist her father in his work. The work discussed in whispers in the dark. The work that had cost Lafayette so much all her young life.

But now she learns just how much her father's work means to their entire world. Only no one knows anything about it. Only her father. And only Lafayette.

Because the work that consumed her father's entire life and her mother's too now nibbles at the fringe's of Lafayette's own life. And she cannot refuse its call.

Raiding the Forgotten Derelict, first book in the new YA sci-fu series THE FORGOTTEN PLANET, available in September 2024 from Ratatoskr Press Books.

COMPLETE SERIES: THE RITCHIE AND FITZ SCI-FI MURDER MYSTERIES

The Ritchie and Fitz Sci-Fi Murder Mysteries starts with Murder on the Intergalactic Railway.

For Murdina Ritchie, acceptance at the Oymyakon Foreign Service Academy means one last chance at her dream of becoming a diplomat for the Union of Free Worlds. For Shackleton Fitz IV, it represents his last chance not to fail out of military service entirely.

Strange that fate should throw them together now, among the last group of students admitted after the start of the semester. They had once shared the strongest of friendships. But that all ended a long time ago.

But when an insufferable but politically important woman turns up murdered, the two agree to put their differences aside and work together to solve the case.

Because the murderer might strike again. But more importantly, solving a murder would just have to impress the dour colonel who clearly thinks neither of them belong at his academy.

Murder on the Intergalactic Railway, the first book in the Ritchie and Fitz Sci-Fi Murder Mysteries.

COMPLETE SERIES: THE TRAVELS OF SCOUT SHANNON

The complete six-book series THE TRAVELS OF SCOUT SHANNON begin with book one, Under Falling Skies.

Scout Shannon's whole family died the day the Space Farers dropped an asteroid on their domed city. Now she lives alone, out in the wild with only her dogs for company. She prefers it that way.

But Scout finds herself at a crossroads. One road leads back to a quiet life snug under the protective dome of a city. The other road leads to a life in the rebellion, a life of adventure and excitement but also danger. Dare she try to find the rebels hiding in the hills?

Then a chance encounter with a stranger from the other side of the galaxy threatens to derail what remains of Scout's life. The entire galaxy awaits her, if she survives the next four days.

"Under Falling Skies", a young adult science fiction novel, set on a remote planet with a distinctly Old West feel. For fans of gunslinging women and young girl assassins. And dogs.

Under Falling Skies, the first book in THE TRAVELS OF SCOUT SHANNON, available everywhere now.

SCI-FI SERIAL PODCAST!

Check out my new monthly podcast of serialized science fiction: THE TALES OF THE CHAI MAKHANI TRIO!

Elyot loathes the massive Commonwealth ships that hover menacingly over his home world of Adghal. He hates the Commonwealth enforcers who harass the populace even more. But with his mother missing and presumed dead, Elyot keeps his head down and strives to avoid notice. And he succeeds until the day two strangers enter his life...

New episodes of this sci-fi serial drop every 1st of the month.

Now streaming on Apple Podcasts, Google Podcasts, Spotify, Stitcher and more. Also available in eBook and print everywhere books or sold. For a complete episode listing, check out the page on my website.

ALSO FROM KATE MACLEOD

Love heists and capers? Then check out my new series, THE VIC HARPER CAPERS. The action starts with the novella THE THIRD POLE JOB.

Vic Harper and her gang retired wealthy from their life of thievery and heists. Whether in a luxury condo overlooking the river in Minneapolis or in a modernist mansion built into the side of a mountain in Colorado, life comes easy now.

Perhaps too easy.

When an old friend asks for a favor his niece, Vic and her mentor Chase Woodward leap at the chance to relieve a little of the boredom. But a quick bit of B&E in a wealthy suburb of Chicago leads to an even greater challenge.

The prize? Nothing much. Just the opportunity to level a playing field for their friend's niece.

But the heist? May prove to be their toughest ever. Because to get to the prize, they'll have to climb a mountain.

And not just any mountain. Their prize waits on the summit of Mount Everest.

THE THIRD POLE JOB, the first novella in the Vic Harper Caper series. For those who love capers, heists and other impossible missions.

ALSO FROM RATATOSKR PRESS

Also from Ratatoskr Press, The Witches Three Cozy Mystery Series by Cate Martin, a mix of mystery and magic that begins with Book 1: Charm School.

Amanda Clarke thinks of herself as perfectly ordinary in every way. Just a small-town girl who serves breakfast all day in a little diner nestled next to the highway, nothing but dairy farms for miles around. She fits in there.

But then an old woman she never met dies, and Amanda was named in her will. Now Amanda packs a bag and heads to the big city, to Miss Zenobia Weekes' Charm School for Exceptional Young Ladies. And it's not in just any neighborhood. No, she finds herself on Summit

Avenue in St. Paul, a street lined with gorgeous old houses, the former homes of lumber barons, railroad millionaires, even the writer F. Scott Fitzgerald. Why, Amanda can practically hear the jazz music still playing across the decades.

Scratch that. The music really, literally, still plays in the backyard of the charm school. Because the house stretches across time itself. Without a witch to protect this tear in the fabric of the world, anything can spill over. Like music.

Or like murder.

The complete series is out now, and it all starts with Charm School.

FREE EBOOK!

Like exclusive, free content?

To get two prequel short stories to THE RITCHIE AND FITZ SCI-FI MURDER MYSTERIES as well as a bonus prequel novelette to the completed six-book series THE TRAVELS OF SCOUT SHANNON, signup for my monthly newsletter at KateMacLeodWrites.com.

Thank you!

ABOUT THE AUTHOR

Photograph © 2016 Jonathan Conklin

Kate MacLeod has written stories which have appeared in Analog, Strange Horizons and Mythic Delirium, among other places. She is also the author of two young adult science fictions series: The Travels of Scout Shannon, and The Ritchie and Fitz Sci-Fi Murder Mysteries. She also contributes to a serialized science fiction podcast called The Tales of the Chai Makhani Trio. She currently lives in Minneapolis, Minnesota.

Find out more about the author and sign up for her newsletter at KateMacLeodWrites.com.

ALSO BY KATE MACLEOD

Novels

The Slums of the Solar System:

Mitwa

The Mars of Malcontents

The Whole World for Each

Books 1-3 Box Set

The Travels of Scout Shannon:

Under Falling Skies

In Quaking Hills

Among Treacherous Stars

Against Impassable Barriers

Over Freezing Altitudes

At Galactic Central

The Travels of Scout Shannon Books 1-3

The Travels of Scout Shannon Books 4-6

The Travels of Scout Shannon Books 1-6

The Ritchie and Fitz Sci-Fi Murder Mysteries:

Murder on the Intergalactic Railway

Murder in the Skies

Body in the Catacombs

Death on the Summit

An Undiplomatic Murder

A Lethal Betrayal

The Forgotten Planet

<u>Raiding the Forgotten Derelict</u> (Forthcoming September 2024)

Sci-Fi Novellas

The Intergenerational Tree

I Rise into a Daybreak

Caper Novellas

The Third Pole Job

The Twelve Days of Christmas Job

10-Story Collections

Tales of Blood and Ink

Tales of Old Gods and New

5-Story Collections

Tales from Heian-Kyo and Others

Tales from the Edges and Ends

Tales from Forgotten Days

Tales from Ancient and Future Times

Tales from Across Space